ALESSANDRO NARDONE
THE PREDESTINED

Translation by Miriam Mazza

www.thepredestined.com

Title | The Predestined
Author | Alessandro Nardone
ISBN | 978-88-91185-61-7

Alessandro Nardone
Lake Como - Italy
www.nardone.org
alessandro@nardone.org
Facebook: facebook.com/alessandronardone
Twitter: twitter.com/alenardone
Youtube: youtube.com/alenardone

To Irene and Vittoria Amelia

And to Gregorio, my father

Preface

YOU should see my desk: it's literally overrun with books, newspaper clippings, documents, maps and photographs printed with my computer. All in no particular order, *of course*.

Can you imagine the offices of CIA or FBI while they are working on a case? You have certainly seen them in dozens of movies. So, with all due respect to Irene, my room is very reminiscent of them. This is the material I used to create the book you are holding in your hands and that, as soon as you turn this page, will catapult you straight to Los Angeles, California.

Let's get back to us. In the last months you have certainly read and heard about the scandal that the Italian press has dubbed as Datagate, which shows an obvious and disquieting reality: in fact we are all intercepted. Phone conversations, e-mails, social networks, it makes no difference. The National Security Agency has the power to know everything about everyone, including all Heads of State.

How much truth there is in the revelations of Snowden and Assange? Where is the line between right and wrong, when you are dealing with national security? Our privacy, a substantial part of our individual freedom, is expendable on the altar of the concept theoretically higher (but also more abstract) of general freedom? In all this, which is the role of the powerful lobbies that, in the thesis of someone, are pulling the strings of power?

Well, nothing of what I wrote in The Predestined answers these questions because they are nothing more the same questions on which I am keeping on questioning. As I said at the beginning – although it contains some real names – this book is just a fantastic journey and therefore, as written by Stephen King in his postscript 22/11/63, is «only an interesting simulation» blossomed in my mind during a conversation that took place in circumstances totally accidental, on board of a train travelling to Zurich.

The woman I was sitting next to, confided in me and, coincidentally, she stroke up a conversation just as I was reading an article about the revelations of Snowden. Among the many things she told me during those three hours, what struck me most was contained in her last sentence she uttered just before she left.

«Let me say something about Prism project, for which I have been working for many years: much of what is written in newspapers is true. I think that not everything is right, but in this case, the unjust is a necessary evil.».

Put yourselves in my shoes. Wouldn't you have been curious with a shocking revelation like that? Well, I was, and also very much, to the point that I ventured to ask her to give me her name, her email, or her mobile number or if I could have found her in Facebook.

Nothing to do.

When she got off the train I stood for a few seconds near the window to observe her walking away from me, briskly. After few steps she turned around, giving me the impression she was seeking confirmation that I was following her with my eyes.

She had to feel my eyes on her, I thought.

Her refusal left me a bitter taste. Damn, I was so curious, I wanted to know more. I took my backpack, noticing an old notebook on the seat. My eyes widened. It was her notebook, I had no doubt. I dropped my backpack and immediately I began to leaf through it.

On those handwritten sheets it was written about a little girl that escaped an attack and about a young officer trained in secret, in England. Then, many pages torn. At last, in confused, wider and uncertain handwriting

> *I like Switzerland... but not my new name.*
> *I have changed many...*
> *The important thing is THEY would not discover me.*
> *For this reason, henceforth, I will only use a pencil!*

Incipit

THERE are people spending their life pursuing their dreams, and there are people who do everything to chase them away, to escape from them. But let's proceed with order. I love seagulls. I remember that in my childhood I spent hours and hours watching them, down to the pier in San Pedro.

I loved to lose myself in their trajectories, and it seemed to me to grasp the meaning of their cries, to the point of being able to distinguish them, depending on the time of the day. For example, in the evening, when the lights of the sunset tinged the ocean of a sparkling red, they loved to chase and challenge themselves who could do the most daring evolutions, exactly as we children did riding our BMX. We spent whole days running up and down the harbour, we had a great fun, Matt and I. We were always together, from morning to night. However sometimes I also felt the need to sit a bit on my own, and I used to go on a bench of the Fish Market, watching my friends seagulls. Sue, the waiter of the restaurant, always used to find five minutes to bring me some marshmallows and sit there with me, telling me stories of when she was a little girl spending her days in the boat with her father, who was a fisherman. She always told me that she would have liked to find a boy of her same age who would love to hang out there on the pier, enjoying that miracle with her, but all boys she met were all stupid and therefore she preferred to stay alone. I loved so much to spend that time of the day with her, even if my friends teased me telling me that standing there watching the sunset and the seagulls was something for sissies.

Already at that time, I did not care anything about what others said, even if they were my best friends. As a matter of fact, because I loved them, I hoped for them that one day they would have understood how important is to be able to capture the beauty and the importance of some simple moments of our life. Then came that damn day, when my mother told me that we should have left California in a few weeks, because dad had received, directly from President Reagan, an important position in the US consulate in Italy. «Alex, in Europe will be fine, moreover Rome is a great city, you'll love it. I'm sure you'll make lots of new friends».

I was not able to find the strength to cry and not even to answer her, nothing at all. The only thing that instinctively I managed to do was to jump on my bike and go down to the harbour.

I sat crouched on a bench, with my arms around my knees, and I didn't want to know anything about anyone or anything else. As I watched the seagulls I felt an immense sense of nostalgia, as if those places, smells and colours were no more mine, I felt out of place, even if that was still my home. Then I thought about my friends, my school, and all those sunsets spent together with Sue. All over. No, it was not fair. At one point I felt someone touching my shoulder, I hoped to find Sue, but it was little Maggie, the daughter of our neighbours, who was one year younger than me. We had never talked so much, but we used to smile each other every time we met.

It was weird. Even that time she didn't say anything, she just sat next to me and took me by the hand.

We watched the sunset and the seagulls, silently, together.

It was the 10th of October of 1986.

1

September 11

If I should walk through the valley of darkness,
I fear no evil, for you are with me.
PSALM 23

New York, September 11, 2001

"...now listen to the call of the Mayor of New York, Rudolph Giuliani: move away from the business district south of Manhattan, head north..."

DAMN, what time is it? I had the feeling I felt asleep just five minutes ago, how was it possible that the alarm clock was already ringing? Moreover in my room it was pitch dark. I did not even remember what time I came back home, I could only remember that the evening at the Yale Club was really hard, because of that Italian wine I brought to my former classmates. It was so excellent you did not realize how strong it was, while drinking it. So, once I got home, before throwing myself to bed, I took off the phone ringer and I lowered the blinds to all windows.

Actually I was not used to do so, because I always loved to wake up early in the morning, but that day I had no specific commitments, therefore I pointed the alarm rather late, few minutes after eleven. In short, I would have taken it slowly. First of all a quick shower, then newspapers and later I would have walked up to Landmark Coffee Shop, on 158 avenue, where I would have enjoyed the best pancakes of all Manhattan.

After I rubbed my eyes for the umpteenth time, I decided to get out of bed and check what time it was. I was still numb of sleep, and I perceived the words coming out of the radio as a simple background buzz. I dragged myself to the bathroom, and I slipped right under the shower. The warm water flowing on me was a sort of miracle, managing to cuddle me and wake me up at the same time.

I would have stayed there much longer, if it was not for my stomach which had begun to grumble with increasing insistence, craving for the pancakes with butter and syrup that I had not eaten for months. A real caloric bomb, but who cares, I thought, sometimes you can do it. After having dried myself, I went back in my room, turned on the light and, before starting to get myself dressed, I took the phone which was in charge, on the nightstand beside my bed.

Twelve missed calls.

What the hell had happened? Looking at the phone calls, I saw that four were made by my mother, six came from the office of my father, one was Matt and the other one was made by a number I had not in my phone book. At first I thought someone had been sick, and immediately I tried to call back, but the phone told me that the network was absent and it was possible to make only emergency calls. I switched it off and back on, I checked that the sim card was properly in place, but there was nothing to do, that fucking phone did not want to work. My hands began to sweat. I went to the window and, while I was nervously turning up the shutter, instinctively I began to hear the excited voices coming from the radio. At that moment I understood everything.

"... both towers of the World Trade Centre had collapsed, Manhattan is in chaos, and even the Pentagon is under attack. The White House has been evacuated. We repeat again that Mayor Giuliani called on the citizens to get away from..."

I took the television remote control, pressed one, and I was faced with that terrifying sequence of images showing a column of smoke coming from the side of the North Tower, while a moment later a plane crashed into the South Tower, which was immediately engulfed in flames.

The scream of a journalist off camera, the words in large letters "America under attack", human beings throwing themselves into the void in order not to be devoured by the flames. Maybe – I thought in those moments of panic and madness – those people loved seagulls as I love them, and in those moments in which they felt hopelessly hunted by death and destruction, perhaps they must have implored God to transform them into seagulls, saving them from a fate too horrible and too cruel to be true. Then the collapse, first the South Tower and then the North Tower. In slow motion. I have no words, said the journalist on CNN. Well, I was also enable to say a word, I was petrified, stupefied, motionless. Unconsciously, among the myriad of thoughts that ran through my head like a sharp blade of a katana, I hoped to be in the middle of a bad dream or in front of the trailer of the movie Independence Day. In short, I was refusing to accept what was happening.

Suddenly, I came to my senses. I dressed hurriedly wearing the same shirt and trousers I was wearing the night before, I took my wallet, my mobile phone and I left my house. I absolutely wanted to see with my eyes what was going on. My apartment was in Broadway Road, near Lafayette Station, and generally by foot, I had only a little over half an hour to reach the area of Lower Manhattan, where the World Trade Centre was.

Once crossed the threshold of the door, I found myself in a surreal scene. First of all the silence. Yes, because in the middle of what seemed to have all characteristics of the most shocking terrorist attack in modern history, one would expect screams and chaos. Instead it was the opposite. There was a multitude of people intent to move away from the area of the attacks, and everything was wrapped in an unreal, almost deadly, otherworldly silence. They all seemed to come towards me, because I was one of the very few people who walked southward. Some of them tried, so nervously as unnecessarily, to call or even to send a text message, others were completely covered with white powder, others gave up walking and sat on the roadsides, bursting into tears. At one point, a girl fell into my harms, begging me to let her call her boyfriend with my mobile because her phone was not working. She was crying bitterly, and I did not dare to say no, to deny her some hope, even though I knew that only a miracle would have been able to make my phone work.

While she was dialling the number, she told me that her boyfriend was working in one of the two towers, but she was sure he managed to escape before the collapse. Realizing that even from my phone every call was impossible, she thanked me whispering «He's safe, isn't he?», I put my hand on her right shoulder, and doing my best to be credible, I tried to reassure her replying with a yes.

I looked up, I made just two or three steps, and I realized that from that point on, the track was completely covered by a layer of white powder, and that on my blue shirt fell something that at first glance seemed to be confetti, but was nothing more than scraps of burnt paper, just like the air I was breathing.

Suddenly I was bumped violently into my legs with a shopping cart of a black homeless dressed with a green heavy parka, who said looking straight into my eyes: «Hey boy, where are you going? There's hell over there! Jesus Christ is taking revenge, this is the Doomsday, boy, the Doomsday!».

I tried to make one step, managing to take him off my way and, turning around, I saw that guy trying to stop anyone who walked in his opposite direction. The street corners were manned by soldiers, who distributed bottles of water to passersby, inviting them to go north, but I managed to keep going on.

The sky was dark, it seemed it had been swallowed by that white dust, leaving just a glimpse of a so pale sun that was not even able to project our shadows. At each step we were leaving behind our footsteps, the layer of dust settled on the ground had become a couple of inches at least, giving the impression of walking on sand. I had totally lost track of time and space. But something told me that I had to push myself as far as possible, that my eyes had to see what was happening.

In the meanwhile I kept on thinking about my parents, who were certainly experiencing hours of panic, because they could not manage to speak with me, and I hoped that in Los Angeles and Rome, where they were, nothing horrible had happened similar to what was happening in New York, I was terribly worried. On the other hand, it was hours I had not received their news. I tried to concentrate and think, trying to remember if any of my friends were inside the Twin Towers. But I wasn't able.

Looking around myself, I saw groups of people praying, shops and bars were empty, cars were abandoned in the middle of the roads, but a moment later I thought about the night before, when those same streets were lit and full of people. It seemed that ages had passed, but only a few hours had elapsed.

As soon as I reached Wall Street, I was stopped by some military, along with a group of people that was proceeding southward like me: «From this point on it's all blocked, it's war zone». Many of the people nearby began to argue that they had to go to World Trade Centre to rescue their families who were there, they had to look for them, but the soldiers were inflexible: «Sorry but everything is collapsing, you all would put your lives at risk». In those moments I realized for the first time in my short life what face has despair. I could see it, carved into the eyes and faces of those women and men destroyed by grief, who wanted to defy death to keep alive even one glimmer of hope. Husband, wife, son, friend, parents. Each of them had a piece of their lives beyond that block, in the midst of the most enormous pile of debris that the world has ever known, each of them just wanted to go there digging through the rubble still smoking, hoping to hear the voice of their loved ones still alive. I was astonished in front of so much pain. Suddenly, when some of them began to get angry, I heard a phone ringing. It was mine.

Immediately I put my hand into my trousers pocket, and, on the screen, I saw it was the same number from which someone had tried to call me few hours before, it was the same number that it was not in my phone book. Who could it be? I pressed the green button and answered:

«Hallo!»

«Alex, thank God you're alive! It's me, Maggie.»

«Maggie? But... how is it possible? We haven't spoken each other since years,... how did you get this number? Where are you?», I asked her.

«Now it doesn't matter, I just wanted to be sure that nothing has happened to you. Go to a safe place, I'll call you in the next few days.», she said curtly.

«Maggie, wait!», I shouted.

As soon as I realized what had just happened, a middle-aged man began to ask politely but insistently to let him use my phone. At the same moment a woman accidentally bumped into me, making me lose the balance for a moment. I managed not to fall down, but my phone slipped from my hand, falling among the feet of all those people who stood there, hoping to go on.

The man and the woman immediately realized what had happened, apologizing for their impetuosity and bent down with me to help me to look for my phone. Hopeless undertaking. That damn white powder kept entering into my eyes and, I could barely see the feet of the people around me. To make matters worse, the military asked everyone to take a few steps back, bringing us much far than the point where my phone dropped. Shit, just right now! I exclaimed to myself. In the meanwhile, the man and the woman who unwittingly made me lose the only means through which I could hope to get in touch with the rest of the world, kept on begging me to forgive them.

On the other hand, how could I blame them? For a moment, the ringing of my phone had rekindled also their hopes. So I hugged them both, I asked them to stop apologizing, and I tried to comfort them saying that they would find their loved ones.

In despair I knew that I could not reach World Trade Centre, therefore I decided to walk towards home where, at least, I could have tried to connect to internet. As I walked backward that apocalyptic path, for few minutes I did nothing but think about the phone call of little Maggie. It had been many years since we saw each other.

I remember she called me when I was in Rome to wish me happy birthday, then nothing more happened, until today. The last image I could remember was the day when we left Los Angeles and moved to Italy. Fifteen years have passed since then, I did not even know how she was looking like, where she was living or what she was doing, but in some ways, I always felt her presence, much more than most of the people I had to see every day. Weird, really weird, I thought.

After an indefinite lapse of time, I went back on earth realizing that I had lost my phone and also her phone number. How could I find her? I would have plenty of time to think about it. As soon as I reached the door of my apartment I let out a sigh of relief, I was safe, but, at the same time, thinking about the terror snaking through the streets, I felt a strong sense of guilt, I felt privileged. The television, which I had left on, continued to transmit images of that shocking disaster, alternating them with some shots taken in the streets of Manhattan, among that desperate and silent multitude of which, until few minutes before, I was part of. I had a great desire to have a shower, to take off that tremendous mixture of sweat and white powder but first of all I wanted to call my parents. Thus I went to the desk and turned on my computer, which now seemed so slow. As soon as I opened Windows, I switched the modem on and tried to connect, even if television had just said that it was very difficult to access network. Come on, come on, connect! I closed my eyes for a moment, and as soon as I opened them I saw that the computer was connected. Yes! Without hesitating not even a moment, with the fear that connection could abandon me at any time, I opened Outlook and wrote immediately an email to mom and dad, telling them I was fine, unfortunately I lost my phone and I would have called them in the evening. Then I wrote another email to the mailing list which included friends and former college buddies, seventy contacts more or less:

First of all I want to tell you all I'm fine, at least from a physical point of view. As for the rest I feel destroyed. I just got back home, I tried to reach WTC by foot but it was impossible. I will remember what I saw today for the rest of my life: I saw despair in the eyes of all the people who stopped me in the street begging me to help them to find their loved ones. No, such a tragedy can not be explained. There are no words to describe the smell of death I breathed in the streets of New York and that now I feel stuck on me. Hell is here, today. Well, I hope with all my heart that the bastards who did this to our people and our nation, will live every minute of their revolting existence in the awareness of being dead men walking. They must feel themselves hunted down and they must pay dearly for what they did.
Sorry for my outburst, but it is all too strong today.
Answer me right away, I love you all.

After taking a shower, I spent half an hour listening to the first comments on CNN, and then I went out. On television I heard that a place where to donate blood had been set up few meters from my house. I stood in that very long queue formed by people who, like me, wanted to give their little help to the tens of thousands wounded who were in need.

We were all stunned and frightened, but we were still standing.

2

Personally

Where there is freedom, there is my Country.
BENJAMIN FRANKLIN

Yale University
New Heaven
August 15, 2004

«COME ON, Alex, are you really convinced that your generation is better than mine? I am sorry to contradict you, but I only see lot of disinterest and too much disillusion, and very few of real ideals». Who was in front of me was Professor Swenson, with whom I stayed in contact even after I finished my studies. He was one of the few people with whom I liked to talk, not because we shared the same ideas, but for his innate ability to bring out the best in me, always giving me new points of reflection. When I was in New York I often went to meet him in his office, and our exchanges of opinion could last five minutes up to five hours. In the last years I approached active politics, attending the Young Guns of the GOP and organizing some events for Tea Parties, but it was a commitment in its embryonic stage and therefore very superficial.

I did not mean to escape from the burden of what I thought was my passion, but I told myself I would have thrown myself in it with heart and soul as soon as I had found the right conditions to do really something good for the community. I had never done anything just to do it, not even the most trivial things. In this, I looked like Ron, my father. I still remember when, in the evening, he was trying to make me understand maths, and, through it, the principle for which the final result depends mainly on the most basic operations. The problem today is that we tend to take too much things for granted, ignoring more often those elementary operations in favour of things to which we ascribe more importance. Fatal mistake: in the mass, the detail makes the difference. Over the years, the belief that most of the evils of our time were chargeable above all to the carelessness of those who had the responsibility to rule the World, affecting seriously well-being and freedom in the ratio of power and control, was gradually strengthened in me. So, that morning I decided to visit Professor Swenson to understand if, he too, coming from the generation before mine, shared the same feeling of frustration as I was. I wanted to understand. «Ideals must be also transmitted! I think it's too easy to point the finger at the younger generations, while everything is falling apart. Today, however, politicians like Kerry try to make propaganda also using the deaths of September 11. Would these be the "true ideals" to which you are referring, professor?». Swenson fell silent for a moment, just the time to place his glasses, pushing them back on the nose with his forefinger.

«Here it is, Alex, this is precisely the point. Do you really think that in front of certain attitudes it is sufficient just to be indignant? What is it that drives you to be so arrogant as to think that you all are better than others, and therefore you do not have to play the same game together with them?», he asked me.

«Okay, but this is not enough, Peter! Look around yourself, Rome is burning, and we are again splitting, even if slowly. The point here is not only to win a war against an enemy that we know little or nothing of, the stakes are terribly higher…», I replied, getting excited.

«What do you mean?», he asked.

«I mean that, or we are able to constantly keep the faith alive in values such as freedom and attachment to our nation, or they will have won, and the sacrifice of all those guys fighting at the front will be vain, this is what I mean», I explained, staring straight in his eyes.

«You convinced me, Alex. You are right. If I know you well, and I think so, from your words I understand that you have decided to get serious...»

«Lincoln said that who is silent instead of protesting is a coward, right? You taught me this, do you remember? Well, in my life I've been afraid so many times and I'm not ashamed to admit it, but I've never been a coward», I told him.

«I know. My task was simply to show you the path, prodding you...», he admitted, while a slight smile popped up on his face.

«And you succeeded, as usual».

«Always count on me, son, and God bless you».

3

Maggie Jones

It is difficult to notice what you see everyday.
David Foster Wallace

Washington DC
October 10, 2012
11 AM

«Mr. Anderson, I have a call for you, a certain Maggie Jones, I told her you were in a meeting, but she insisted so much, she says it's urgent». The mere sound of that name, was enough to make disappear all the people in front of me, on the other side of my desk.

«Gentlemen, I'm sorry, but we'll have to postpone our meeting this afternoon. I have an urgency, see you later». Their expressions betrayed a not so light veil of impatience, but they immediately understood and left the office. I felt strangely nervous, my hands began to sweat, and I felt the need to loosen my tie.

«Hallo Meg, please put me through Mrs. Jones»

«Maggie, is it you?», I asked, as soon as my ear approached the phone .

«Yes Alex, it's me», she answered.

«Damn, where have you been? In all these years I've been looking for you everywhere: telephone directories, Facebook, internet… absolutely nothing. Why haven't you called me anymore?»

«Because I knew you were fine. Although we did not call each other, I have followed everything you have done, step by step. Since that day when you left, in 1986, I have always been there for you, Alex. You won't believe it, but this is true»

Maggie's voice sounded awfully familiar, but eleven years had passed since the last time I heard her. However, even if I had not heard from her anymore since that bloody September 11, not a day nor a week passed without thinking about her. I had no idea where she was, but I felt her terribly close to me, exactly as she said.

«I believe you, Maggie…»

«I know»

«Listen, where are you now? Why don't we meet? I could take the first flight to Los Angeles, and…»

«Not now, Alex, it's not time, now you have more important things to think about, trust me.»

«But what does this mean? I don't understand. For which strange reason, seeing you should distract my attention from what I am doing? It isn't logical!»

«If I tell you so, it's because it's the truth. We will see each other, Alex, but not now, it's not the right time.»

«And when?»

«In exactly one year, starting from today, I will be waiting for you at San Pedro, on the same bench we used to meet.»

«In one year? You must be joking? I want to see you right now… Maggie, is there something you can not tell me?»

«Don't ask explanations, that's it. Don't forget Alex, if you won't be there we will have no other opportunities to see each other again, so do not miss, no matter what happens. Now I have to say goodbye.», she replied laconically. I tried to talk to her again, but nothing to do, she had already switched off.

I was incredulous, that conversation had left me literally speechless. Without hesitating not even for an instant, I called Meg, my secretary, and asked her to trace the number from which the call had come. At that point, I wanted to go through with it, and figure out who really was Maggie Jones, and why she was behaving so enigmatically. All things considered, I didn't know anything about her and, all along all those years, she could have become anyone. I was not feeling in danger, however that situation was starting to trouble me. I thought for a moment whether to warn the head of the security service of the Capitol, basically it was a duty because of the delicacy of my role as a Representative in Congress, moreover in the midst of my election campaign.

But I decided to postpone, because something was telling me that little Maggie was in good faith, and also because it would have the taste of a sort of betrayal to do something like that. I was hoping not to be wrong.

American Airlines flight to Los Angeles
6 PM

I had a really hard day, but finally I was on the flight back to California. During the election campaign, I was working at a so hectic pace, that the only moments of relax were the ones I could spend on board. That evening, however, aided by the fact that I would have landed quite late, I did not scheduled any meetings. I needed to recharge my batteries for the flurry of meetings that the election committee had organized on my district, the number 33 of California.

My opponent, Democrat Trevor Spencer, was a tough nut to crack but, despite the competition was particularly fierce, I had kept with him a very good personal relationship. He was nearly thirty years older than me, and was a great friend of my father. I have very fond memories of evenings spent with them two talking about politics. Even then, when I was a boy, I had a strong propensity for Republicans, perhaps powered by the fact that I grew up with the myth of a President of the calibre of Ronald Reagan who, better than anyone else, was able to represent a courageous America, the one of *Reaganomics*, able to create prosperity for all by betting on itself, based on a model of efficient State and minimally invasive. Furthermore, despite the divergence between our respective points of view, Spencer admired the verve I used to put in my speeches, and he never missed an opportunity to encourage me to follow my passion for active politics. Among the memories I cherish most closely, there is a note in which he congratulated for my election to Congress, in 2010.

Among all those I received, his note had a particular value, simply because on that occasion he challenged me for the seat in the House of Representatives, ending with his defeat:

Dearest Alex,
you know, a part of me says that perhaps I had better not to encourage you to do politics, when you were a little boy! Joking aside, it may seem strange to you, but the fact that I have been beaten by you, gives a less bitter flavour to my defeat. Of course, nobody likes to lose, but I know your family and your love for your Country, so I'm sure you will serve our people at your best.

If you like, I will always be ready to cooperate.

Ad maiora!

Trevor Spencer

It's useless to say that, thanks to his deep humanity, Trevor managed to maintain an excellent result in the entire district but, despite this, polls were saying I was leading for five points at least. So many points, but not enough to put me in a position to rest on my laurels.

Not at all, I had to fight for every vote, without taking anything for granted, both for the undoubted qualities of my opponent, but also because Democrats could count on the bonus of "Obama factor" who, being the outgoing President, was clearly favourite over Mitt Romney who, furthermore, was also in the mood for gaffes that had put him in serious troubles with public opinion more than once. The plane was about to take off, as usual I took the window seat and, next to me sat a woman and I had the impression of having already seen her somewhere.

But on the spur of the moment, I did not pay much attention, because of the great weariness that was about to overwhelm me and the consequent lack of desire to communicate. Thus, I took advantage on the fact she had not noticed me, to put my headphones into my ears and listen to music, hiding myself behind the Los Angeles Times, that I hadn't had time to read yet that day.

> *I hate the world today*
> *You're so good to me*
> *I know but I can't change*
> *Tried to tell you*
> *But you look at me like maybe*
> *I'm an angel underneath*
> *Innocent and sweet*
> *Yesterday I cried*
> *Must have been relieved to see*
> *The softer side*
> *I can understand how you'd be so confused*
> *I don't envy you*
> *I'm a little bit of everything*
> *All rolled into one*

Suddenly, while I was reading an article of local politics, the radio of the airline sent an old song that I hadn't heard for years, *Bitch* by Meredith Brooks. Right away I averted my attention from the newspaper, and I began to force myself to remember in which year that song appeared. 1999 or 2000? Damn, it was impossible to use Shazam because I was flying. While I was absorbed in that useless dilemma, a hand lowered my newspaper with some force, making me jump with fright.

«Ah, so it's you!».
So the mystery of my neighbour was revealed, it was Veronica Hayes, news correspondent in Washington for Los Angeles Times. I found her in front of me, with a smile on her face which seemed to say, here I caught you!

Actually, looking at her outside of an official context, Mrs. Hayes was a very attractive woman: black hair and blue eyes, that I had never noticed because of her thick-rimmed glasses, that she could afford because of her very good features.

«Damn, Veronica, you scared the life out of me!», I uttered, positively surprised to have found her in front of me.

«Eheh, I had no doubt, but honestly I could not resist. How come in economy class?», she asked, with impertinent air.

«I always travel in economy because usually you journalists travel in business!»

«Actually it's the opposite, however, it's a good joke for a politician amidst the election campaign. By the way, have you got some preview news to give me?»

«Actually I have a question, I am assailed by a doubt to which I must give an answer...»

«If I can, I'll help you willingly. Come on, I'm listening.»

«Before I was risking a heart attack because of you, I was listening to *Bitch*, the song of Meredith Brooks and...»

At the point, Veronica interrupted me with a laugh that made all passengers turned their heads.

«Well, why do you find it so funny?», I whispered to her.

«Cause I knew what you were asking, because I was wondering about the same thing, as we listen to the same radio: In which year appeared that song? Am I right?», she asked.

«Bingo! Therefore you don't even know... in this case I think I will not be able to close my eyes and sleep for the whole time of our flight!», I exclaimed amused.

We spent the rest of the journey chatting, initially about our musical tastes and about some frivolous arguments, and then, within few minutes, we spoke about politics and elections. Argument that I would have postponed with pleasure but at that point it became almost inevitable. Therefore, once landed, Veronica snatched me the promise of a complete interview.

We fixed the appointment on Sunday morning in the headquarters of my election committee in San Pedro, so the article could be published on Monday, the day of the largest circulation for Los Angeles Times.

We said goodbye outside the airport where, waiting for me, there was Matt who, in addition to being my best friend, was also a man of great skills of communication and, therefore, was the responsible for the organization of my election campaign.

«Cute girl, why haven't you introduced me to her?», he started, without even saying hallo.

«Matt, stop it, and moreover she is not the right one for you.», I immediately interrupted him.

«You're a real asshole, let me decide if a woman is right or not for me. Come on, tell me who is she!», he insisted.

«That was Veronica Hayes, does it mean something to you?»

«Do you mean that Veronica Hayes? The Los Angeles Times' journalist?»

«Exactly.»

«Well, actually you are right: I swear I won't make a pass at her… at least until the election campaign is over!»

Matt Payne was my crazy brother. I admit that, in some moments, especially in those where stress reached the highest peaks, I used to see in him what I wanted to be, that is the kind of person who loves life in an easygoing way, like an eternal boy with the Peter Pan syndrome. I'm not saying that Matt was an inexperienced or a superficial person, on the contrary he was a great professional man, as well as a very good creative, qualities that enabled him to found an agency of communication that was one of the most quoted and respected in the market. Furthermore, his professional success allowed him to live exactly as he wanted, that is free from any kind of commitment except surfing in Manhattan Beach at sunset. For him it was an absolutely unavoidable appointment, a true lifestyle. Handsome, one meter and ninety tall, blonde bob, perfect body, constantly tanned: anyone, even far away, would immediately identified him as the archetype of the Californian surfer.

As it was late, that evening I would have slept at his house, so that we would have some time together to update us on the appointments he planned for me from the next day up to the weekend. He lived right on Paseo del Mar, between Almeria and Emily Street but, since I had not eaten anything in the last ten hours, before going back home, we stopped at In-n-Out; actually, as it was late, I could also have resisted until the next day, but the lure of my favourite cheeseburger was really too strong to be able to ignore it.

Furthermore, you can find that chain of fast-food only in California, and it is inevitable that each time I come back home from Washington I am always looking forward to bite one of those sandwiches. In short, I can say that In-n-Out and Fish Market in San Pedro are my culinary points of reference, since I was a boy. I know it may sound banal, but to go to those places every time I came back home and find the same flavours as always, it was a bit like travelling backwards in time. Many things changed, but some other remained always the same.

After that night snack, we finally arrived home. It was nearly two in the morning, but the myriad of commitments that we had to face did not allow us to give too much time to rest. So, after we drank a Red Bull, Matt and I we sat comfortable on the sofa, skimming through event reports, lists of people to contact or meet, and press releases. After about half an hour, Matt went in the back room for few minutes, and then came back with an handmade cigarette in his hands.

«I hope this is not what I think…», I said glaring at him. In fact, Matt knew perfectly well how much I loathed any kind of drugs, including marijuana.

«Come on Alex, this is a natural one, I smoke it to relax my nerves. I think it would do you good also, you know», he answered, before licking the rim of the rolling paper and then close the "cigarette".

«I do not relax at all, you know what I think about it. It's a long time I'm keeping on telling you the same things, is it possible that you don't want to make up your mind and grow up, Matt? Fuck, you are almost forty! Apart from the damage caused to your brain because of that stuff, have you ever thought what newspapers would write if they find out that the head of my election campaign cultivates marijuana plants in the garden of his house?», I asked him. I was totally flipped out.

At that point, Matt slipped the joint on his right ear, and sat down in front of me. He stood in silence for a few moments: evidently my words affected him, he wanted to think, in order to avoid to answer me in a wrong way. The same attitude he had when we were kids, and we ended up arguing.

«Listen Alex, you are like a brother to me, I'm serious. But you and I, we are different, it's high time you realize it. Perhaps it's due to our diversity that we have always got on well, and we're friends since we were born...», he answered, evidently disappointed.

«I know that, but I...», I tried to intervene.

«Don't interrupt, now it's my turn to speak! I understand that you are very nervous for this election campaign, and so am I, but you have to know that in front of you there is someone who is not a crazy person who does not know what he's doing. It's simple, I love to do some things that you don't. This is normal, brother. Therefore, when I am feeling very tired and I want to smoke a joint, I smoke a joint. Also because I don't believe I have created troubles to you until now, am I wrong?».

I must confess that, while I was listening to him, I felt terribly guilty, and my eyes became watery. Who was I to judge him? Moreover, in front of me there was the most precious friend I ever had, who was able to do anything for me, and without asking anything in return. So I listened to my instinct and hugged him.

«I care for you, Matt», surprised at my reaction, he looked into my eyes, gave me a light slap on my head, and stood up.

«This means I can smoke it, am I right?», he told me, making one of his typical jeering smile.

«Just open the windows, I don't want to breathe that shit. Come on, it's late, let's look at these two things and then let's go to sleep».

After about three quarters of an hour, inevitably dazed by the second-hand smoke of the joint of Matt, I took a shower and went to bed. However, even if I was very tired, I could not get to sleep. After having spent a very long time turning around and around, I took my phone and I began to watch Facebook and Twitter, I had several private messages, but at that time of the night I fancied everything except answering them. I had many thoughts in my mind that I wasn't able to stop, I was restless. Anyway, after a quarter of an hour or maybe even half an hour, I felt I was finally about to give up, and that my eyes were about to close.

4

The dream

We live most of our dreams with much more intensity
then our existence when awake.
HERMANN HESSE

Down at the port of San Pedro
on that bench

IT was just a handful of seconds after eleven in the morning, yet it seemed to me an eternity. I felt choked by a sense of insecurity and fear, it made me feel unable to move, even though I was in front of what I considered to be the ultimate expression of freedom and peace, my ocean and my seagulls. One minute past eleven, two minutes past eleven, three minutes past eleven. Nothing. An annoying doubt started to creep in my mind: and what if that situation was wrong? Was I wrong to trust? Suddenly I felt hunted, in danger. It was a very ugly, frightening feeling.

I began to sweat, and to think in a very fast but also confused way about all the things I should have done and that I would not, about my career that I had built so painstakingly and would have nullified, about all the people who believed in me and that I would disappoint, about people I loved and that I would never see again, and about that love, the true love, that I had not lived yet, about the son I had not had yet.

I saw that endless series of images running before my eyes, at an impressive speed. Just a matter of moments, I was thinking, without even knowing why. At a certain point I realized that I was peremptorily refusing the hypothesis that this could be really my end, so I got up from the bench with the intention to go away and turn the page as soon as possible. I was tormented for such a long time about it, but I didn't want to know anymore. I did not have time to turn myself and go away that I found myself in front of her, little Maggie.

«Damn Maggie, you were going to cause me a heart attack!», I exclaimed.
I must have looked so pale, I was sweating, and all that anxiety had even caused me to be out of breath. In short, I was like crap.

«Hey Alex, what's wrong? Calm down. Come on, sit down», she told me, taking my right hand.

«What happened to you, are you not feeling well?», she asked me, staring at the sea.
I tried to calm myself down, to think that everything was okay, but that damn doubt was keeping on devouring my mind telling me that I should not be there.

«I'm just a little bit stressed. What about you, how are you?», I asked her, clumsily trying to break that tension.
Despite the fact I had asked her that question, and that she was still holding my hand, Maggie persisted in not looking into my eyes.

After a moment, I broke that heavy silence.

«Now it's my turn to make you questions. What's wrong, Maggie? Why don't you dare to look me in my eyes? Is there something I don't know that I should know?», I asked her impetuously, raising the tone of my voice.

At that point, some tears began to fall slowly from Maggie's blue eyes, and once they reached her cheekbones they picked up speed and then got lost in the void, just below her chin.

«Please forgive me, Alex...», she said sobbing and turning to me for the first time.

I had not even time to figure out what the hell was going on, when behind me I heard the typical screech of tires biting the asphalt. I turned quickly. A van with darkened windows, came towards us, slammed on the brakes a few meters near the bench on which we were still sitting. Maggie held my hand tightly.

«Forgive me...».

Four guys, dressed in black from head to foot and with faces covered by a balaclava, came out from the van. They were armed with M4. I tried to pray, but not even a prayer came to my mind. Little Maggie left my hand, and she jumped down the bench, rolling on the ground. I looked up and saw that the men were pointing their M4 against me. Matter of moments, I thought to myself, then I heard the shots. Darkness.

«Hey, Alex, are you feeling ok?».

Opening my eyes, with incredulity, I found myself in bed and not on that bench and, in front of me, there weren't four armed terrorists with the intent to shoot me, but there was Matt, who had a look that was a middle way between worried and teased. I sat up and I realized to be completely wet, drenched in sweat.

«I had a very strange dream.», I sighed, still groggy.

«I noticed it, my friend, your screams reached my room. Have you dreamt of having sex with Sarah Palin?», he said, trying to joke about it.

«Give it a rest, stop with your stupid jokes. I'm very worried, Matt… I dreamt I was with little Maggie and at some point some hooded dudes arrived, I mean a real commando, do you understand? They had made an agreement with her, and…».

«Bang?»

«Yes, bang. They mowed me down.»

«I would say it's a pretty obvious dream, especially for a politician ready to be re-elected. What surprises me is that little Maggie is still on your mind: fuck, last time you saw her was 1986, how is it possible you are still thinking about her?»

«She called me, Matt!»

«When?»

«Yesterday, she called me at the Capitol.»

«Really? Why haven't you told me?»

«Because yesterday night I did not fancy to talk about it. Anyway, the strange thing about that phone call is that Maggie gave me an appointment, in a year.»

«In a year?»

«Exactly. Her words have been 'I'll wait for you on that bench, do not ask me explanations, that's it. You'll have to be there, no matter what happens'. Crazy, isn't it?»

«Bloody hell, Alex, this story is disquieting! Dream aside, if I were you I would not ignore it, above all I would inform someone in Washington, it's for your safety.»

Matt was right, that situation had too many grey areas, and my institutional role required to inform the security authorities. But what I wanted to avoid absolutely was the risk that it could become of public domain.

The representative Anderson haunted by a childhood friend, is she maybe his lover?

I could already imagine the newspapers headlines, and the consequent collapse of consents. In fact, just a slightest thing was enough to subvert the outcome of an election, guess a story through which all media would definitely have fun to create alleged links with love or sex. It would be my end. I needed a person of utmost confidence.

The first name that came to my mind was that of Carl Nowitzki, an old friend of my father, who, among other things, was a member of the National Security Branch, an FBI department specialized in intelligence and counter-terrorism, created in 2005 by President George W. Bush. Yes, he was the right person without any doubt.

I would have called him in the afternoon in order to make an appointment on Monday or, at the latest, on Tuesday. I should not allow to let pass too much time, for any reason in the world.

Thinking about it made me feel better, so I got out of bed and went to look out the window, from which I could enjoy a magnificent view, at which you surely gape. Moreover, that day the sky was so blue that you can not distinguish it from the impressive expanse of water of the ocean, which merged into a wonderful whole. After breakfast and having spent at least ten minutes in the shower, I got ready to go, along with Matt, to my appointment with the Committee of the Veterans of the Navy, which would have been held outdoors, right under the monument of South Harbour Boulevard.

While we were in the car, I realized that I had not yet switched on the ringtone of my phone, so I took it from the inside pocket of my jacket, and I saw that I had received a message on my private email on Facebook. It was Veronica Hayes.

Beautiful day. We all needed it. I was thinking that we are not obliged to wait until Sunday to see each other. We can wait but also not.
Ps: '97 is the year of that song, years go by so quickly!

Wow, I thought, have you seen what Hayes has done? That message painted a smug grin on my face, which was soon transformed into a hint of laughter, due to the fact that Matt, to whom I imposed to forget that woman just a few hours before, was just sitting right next to me, driving his pick-up.

«What's the matter, man, why are you laughing?», he asked me in an insolent tone.

«Nothing particular, it's just some crap that people publish on Facebook».

I did not feel to tell him that Veronica wrote me, at least not yet.

Indeed I'm convinced that it would be perfect to have dinner together in such a beautiful evening…

I sent my reply, instinctively, without thinking about it. My goodness, have I made a bullshit? I wondered for a moment after having pressed "send". But Veronica's answer was almost instantaneous.

Is it an invitation?

Yes, I'd say it is.

So I'd say that I accept gladly.

I'm very pleased…
… 8.30PM at Fish Market?

I will have dinner with a journalist, I must have gone mad, or maybe not. Furthermore Veronica had been really cute and nice, so much that the five and half hour flight from Washington to Los Angeles, which usually seemed to me to never end, passed in a flash. Anyway I would have behaved as a good boy, I told myself, also because she was a journalist, moreover one of the most important newspaper for me, especially at that time.

«Knock knock… is there anyone? Hey, we got there, make an effort to be more talkative than this morning with me, I remind you that you're in election campaign!», Matt was right.

«Don't worry, I'm full of energy!», I told him, patting him on the shoulder.

We found Darren Walch to welcome us, one of the most fervent supporters of mine, who ran up to me and hugged me, taking me with him where there was the crowd of people waiting for us. Also Darren was an old friend of my family, one of those who could say with full rights "I held Alex on my knees".

Fisherman since four generations at least, he had been one of the people who contributed most to make me become a true lover of the sea and its legends. I remember as it was yesterday, when I used to beg my parents to let me go out in the boat with him.

«Darren has to work, he doesn't have time to give heed to you», my mother often used to tell me, but, sometimes, when school was closed, she let me go as a reward, also thanks to Darren's reassurance, who used to pick me up at dawn.

«I'm glad to introduce you the future President of the United States of America!», he exclaimed in a proud and amused tone, while his arm was still around my neck.

Obviously, with those people there was absolutely no need for pleasantries, as I knew them all, one by one. As I was also aware of their requests, of which I became the carrier in most circumstances at the Congress. They loved me also for this reason, because I had proven to be really one of them, defending their interests. Through tangible facts, and not only words. Let's say that, more than anything else, those kinds of meetings were needed to cheer up the morale, to distribute our propaganda material, and to take pictures and shoot videos that, in most cases, those same people would have shared in few minutes on social networks through their smart phones. Classic example of 2.0 election campaign, some journalist would have written.

After over an hour, Matt and I we looked each other, agreeing that it was time to say goodbye to our Veteran friends, and get back to the office.

«Thank you very much for everything you are doing. You know, I do really care for you.», I whispered into Darren's ear while he was hugging me before I went away by car.

«You'll see, you will get to the top, boy. We are all on your side, remember it!», he said aloud, eliciting screams of incitement of all the people I had just greeted.

«You behaved better than I thought, well done!», Matt told me, as soon as he put the car in motion.

«Why? Did you have any doubt? Listen, I haven't grown foolish!», I uttered.

«Well, bro', considering the state in which I found you this morning, I had plenty of doubts!», while he was still speaking, he opened with his right hand a sort of refrigerator that he had built under the dashboard, and took a bottle of cold beer and, through a lightning movement, he opened the bottle using a bottle opener that was fixed with a lot of adhesive tape just above the compartment of the car radio, and he drank almost half with just one sip.

«Ah, that's what I needed, my throat was on fire! Hey, do you want one? They're down there.»

«You are a real asshole! Apart from the fact that it's not even noon, do you think is it right to drink beer while driving? Is it so difficult for you to wait until we reach the office?»

«Alex, may I tell you something? When you behave in this way you seem a fucking old man of seventy, not even my mother used to break my balls in this way! For Christ's sake, you're thirty-seven, calm down and try to enjoy your life!»

«Have you finished with your reprimands?»

«Reprimands? I? You are totally mad, you need a headshrinker, that's what I think!»

«Ok, listen, about enjoying life, guess with whom I'm going to dinner tonight...»

«Wow, a dinner date, are you sure you feel good? I was waiting for such news since years, I'm serious! I want to know, who's the lucky girl?»

«Veronica Hayes, she wrote me on Facebook this morning and...»

«You son of a bitch! But wasn't she a compromising woman, to keep at a distance?»

«In this case I have to admit that you're right.»

«Listen, my friend, you know what I think? Although I would have gladly screwed her, now I hope with all my heart that you'll screw her. Also because, let's say, a little bit of healthy sex will benefit you, you'll see!», he exclaimed.

I did not even answer him. After having eaten something quick with Matt and other volunteers of the committee, I withdrew into my office for few minutes, being careful to close the door. I had to call Nowitzki, and I didn't want anyone listening, even if it was trustworthy people. I picked up my phone and entered into the phone book, which I slid downwards until I found his number, that was a mobile.

I called him immediately, without any hesitation.

«Inspector Nowitzki, with whom am I speaking?», he replied promptly, without letting end the first ring.

«Carl, I'm sorry to bother you, I'm Alex Anderson.», I told him immediately, realizing that it was lunch time.

«Hey son, how are you? No bother at all, are you joking? What do I owe the honour of your call?», he asked me.

His voice, besides having a familiar sound, was sincere and reassuring.

«Telling you the truth, it's a question I'd rather talk to you personally. Now I'm in Los Angeles, but on Monday I'll be back in Washington and...», Carl stopped me immediately.

«We don't need to wait until Monday, I'm also in Los Angeles. We could meet in an hour at Redondo Beach's Starbucks, on the Pacific Coast, do you know it?».

5

Digging into the past

The strongest shadows are where the light is stronger.
JOHANN WOLFGANG VON GOETHE

Redondo Beach
2 PM

I was sitting at a table near the bar, being busy in checking email, while I was sipping a Frappuccino Light. Instinctively I raised my head, and I saw Nowitzki coming in, whom I recognized immediately because of his impressive size and his unmistakable light brown coat. I made him a sign with my hand, and he reached me briskly. My intention was to get up.

«Sit, stay sit, Alex. So, how is your electoral campaign going on? According to what I hear and read, you should get it without problems», he said, proving he was well informed.

«Well, let's say I'm in a good state, but I don't want to take anything as granted, it would be an unforgivable mistake, also because Trevor Spencer is an adversary of respect. What about you, how are you? You are in good form!», I asked him.

«Sometimes appearances can be deceiving, boy. I begin to feel the weight of the years, but all things considered I would say I can not complain. So, you mean to talk about which question?», he asked, cutting short.

I took a moment to think about where to start, while Nowitzki took an handkerchief from a pocket of his blue jacket, which he used to mop a thin film of sweat which was moistening his forehead.

«So Inspector, it's a rather disquieting incident that happened yesterday. Well, to tell you the truth, it's something grinding on for several years and concerns Maggie Jones, who was the daughter of our neighbours when we were still in San Pedro, before moving to Rome. The last time I saw her was in those years, in 1986 to be precise, we were two children. Since then she called me three times: the first, a few years later to make me birthday wishes, the second on September 11, 2001, while I was few hundred meters from the World Trade Centre, and the third yesterday, at Capitol», I explained.

In the meanwhile a waitress came and Carl ordered a large coffee.

«Before keeping on, satisfy my curiosity: I understood she called on your mobile on September 11, as you were few meters from WTC when you spoke with her. Was it you who gave her your phone number?», he asked.

«Not at all! I didn't pay attention then, because of what was happening, but I must admit that this particular came to my mind yesterday», I answered.

«I understand. And what has she told you on that occasion?»

«She asked me if I was fine, she told me to go to a safer place and that she would have called me soon. Honestly I don't know if she ever tried to call me back because, just after that phone call, my phone fell and I could not find it, because of the confusion.»

«Okay, clear. Now tell me about the phone call of yesterday.»

«My secretary announced her, and she put me through, although I was in a meeting at that time. At first I was pleased, but then, when I asked her to meet each other, she told me that it would not have been possible before one year. To be precise she gave me an appointment, "in exactly one year from today in San Pedro", on the same bench where we said goodbye when we were children, "you have to be there, no matter what happens", she said before hanging up.», I told, trying not to forget not even a particular.

Nowitzki coughed a couple of times, covering his mouth with the same handkerchief he used a few minutes before. After that, he turned back to take his little agenda from one of the pockets of his raincoat, which was on the backrest of the chair. Looking carefully, I noticed he wrote down Maggie Jones, September 11, 2001, Capitol and, after having had a quick look at his watch, October 10, 2012.

«Another curiosity: during these years have you ever tried to get in touch with her, or even just to have information about her? Maybe through Facebook, or whatever it's called...», he asked.

«Of course, but there is no trace of that Maggie Jones on internet, not at all. It's weird, considering she's a girl of our age. The only thing I knew was that she and her family were no longer in San Pedro.», I noted.

«In short, apparently you don't know anything about her, while she knows everything, or almost, about you. Have you talked to anyone else about this story, boy?»

«Only to Matt Payne, my best friend, this morning, because of that bad dream.»

«What kind of dream?»

«I made it last night, and basically it's the reason that pushed me to call you: I dreamt that meeting in San Pedro. Maggie made an agreement with a group of armed men who, after arriving on a black van, they drew their guns and shot me down.»

Realizing the discomfort that the story had caused me, Carl tried to reassure me however, without giving up warning me.

«Listen son, if I were you I would not give weight to that dream, sometimes stress and subconscious play nasty tricks on us, trust me. On the other hand, as for the real story, you've done well to inform me, because in effect there are so many questions and you, besides being one of the greatest representatives of our Institution, you are also very exposed to media as a person, and therefore you are potentially subject to mental masturbations of some madman. Today I will get to work to find out who is this Maggie Jones. Having said this, I want you to be calm and don't talk to anyone. Understood?», he said, patting me on the back.

As soon as we went out from Starbucks, just while we were saying goodbye, I noticed that, behind Nowitzki, on the other side of the street, there was a guy who was standing motionless staring at us. It was a man in his fifties, quite distinct looking. Alex, don't be paranoid now! I thought to myself. So, I looked the other way, and I climbed in my car that I had parked next the bar. As I walked away, something told me that I had still the man's eyes focused on me. Needless to say, I was hoping to be wrong. I gave a glance in the rear-view mirror, and I saw he was still there, and was following the trajectory of my car with his head.

Instinctively I stepped on the gas, trying to get away as soon as possible from that figure so disquieting. Another glance in the rear-view mirror. The street was empty, there was no one. But I was still very anxious.

Who the hell was that man?

Why was he staring at me that way?

That kind of question began to torment me.

Then, to reassure me, I thought it might be someone that had recognized me. After all am I a public man, or not? Here everyone knows me, it's normal to attract someone's attention.

A sudden noise made me literally jumped on the seat. It was my phone ringing. Fuck, Alex, calm down! I forced myself, before answering.

«Hey friend, where the hell are you? Do you remember we have an appointment with your committee in half an hour?», it was Matt.

«Of course I remember, I'm in Redondo now, go there, we'll meet each other there», I answered him, realizing that my voice was betraying a slight anxiety.

«What the fuck are you doing in Redondo? Alex, are you sure everything is okay? Come on, get a move on, I wait for you, see you in a while».

I arrived on time. In the doorway of our election headquarters, I found Matt waiting for me, dedicating himself to entertain the twenty ladies who were waiting for me with his usual philanderer jokes. Although my mood was not serene, I managed to hide my emotions and, in this way, the meeting went well. Smiles, handshakes, hugs, some pictures; in short, everything as expected.

After everyone had left, in the office remained just me and Matt, who sat in my chair, putting his feet upon my desk. I hated that.

«Come on Matt, take immediately away your stinking shoes from my desk!», strangely he didn't object, and obeyed to my request.

«Listen Alex, are you sure everything is okay? You were so weird on the phone».

He was right, but I didn't want to tell him about what I had done in the afternoon, at least until I would have received news from Nowitzki. So I told him I was just a little bit tired and, perhaps still troubled by the bad dream I had the night before. Matt and I, we knew each other very well, and in all likelihood he understood that I was hiding something, but he played along and changed the subject.

«So tonight you'll go out with Hayes… make sure to take a break and just try to enjoy, you need it, bro'!»

«You're right, brother. I'm sure it will be a nice evening, Veronica seemed to be a very interesting woman, I think we'll have a very pleasant conversation!»

«And perhaps also something else!»

«You're obsessed about sex! I have already told you that I go out with her just for pleasure, that's it! A man and a woman are not obliged to fuck on their fist date, what the heck!»

«Okay okay, I understand, there's no need to get pissed! Listen, tomorrow, considering that we don't have commitments, I thought to take you to do parasailing at Manhattan Beach. If you like, you may also bring Veronica: parasailing at sunset is very stunning, I'm sure she'll like it.»

«Why not? It might be a good idea, but I will consider whether to invite her or not depending on how the evening will be.», I answered him.

It was nearly six when Matt and I we said goodbye; I had enough time to go home and get ready. In the trunk of my car there was still my trolley that I had brought with me from

Washington, the night before. It was almost ten days since last time I set foot in my home. Before putting the key into the keyhole of the door, I opened the mailbox that, as usual, was full of brochures, among which the first was the one of Trevor Spencer, to which I looked it with great sympathy. I will read it when I come back, I thought.

I put that bundle of papers and the keys on the table at the entrance, I turned on the television, iMac and, after having raised the rolling shutters, I opened the windows to let in a little bit of fresh air. Despite my absence, I found my house in perfect order, thanks to the woman who used to come twice a week to clean: not a speck of dust, beds made, clothes washed and ironed. In short, I would not have to lift a finger. Good, I thought, so I have time to do everything calmly.

First of all I went to my bedroom to take off my clothes, then, when in my underwear, I headed to the fridge looking for a snack not too caloric, just to stop up my appetite until dinner. Low-fat yogurt. Excellent. It was some years that I had started to cure my diet, loosing almost thirty kilos in a few months. To many it seemed incredible to witness such a sudden change in the appearance, and were incredulous when I told them that I had just changed my eating habits, eliminating all craps I was eating before.

I was sure that many of them were convinced that I had followed some particular diet or even done liposuction. But it was all a matter of willpower. Of course I also liked chocolate or Big Mac, but I decided to give me that kind of things only once in a while, as a reward to my resistance.

When in the shower, I remembered the story of Maggie Jones and that guy out of Starbucks. Even forcing myself, I could not say I was completely relaxed, even though I was sure that Nowitzki would have clarified the matter. He will tell me that everything is fine, that little Maggie is just a childhood friend and that, perhaps, in the meantime has got married and started a family, I thought. However that may be, it would be useless to keep on thinking about it, I might as well expect to have something certain in my hands than rather venturing into conjectures powered by a stupid dream.

Thinking well about it, the dinner with Veronica could not have come at a better time, I really needed something or someone that would help me to take a break.

6

Veronica Hayes

Fish Market
Half past eight on the dot

«HI Alex, you're exactly on time, welcome!».

In fact I was really on time. By nature, I hated being late to appointments, I found it a very bad habit, denoting great rudeness. With the exception of hitches, of course. Veronica was really beautiful, even in casual clothes. Unlike the day before, she was not wearing a suit, but a pair of light jeans, a blue shirt and a V-neck white cotton sweater. I appreciated so much when women were wearing that kind of clothing. I found it very attractive. I also got dressed down: blue shirt, beige pants and sneakers.

«Jeez, do you know that dressed like that you seem to be younger? You seem to be another person!», she said amused.

«Everybody says so, and I must admit that this bothered me a few years ago, now I don't mind at all to look younger than my real age!».

After sitting at one of the coloured tables on the large terrace, we got into the restaurant to choose the fish that they were going to cook for us. Just like that, Fish Market was not a restaurant like others, but a store where people could buy fish, take it to the cooks, and then eat it on-the-spot.

I adored it, and also Veronica, who had never stopped there, was pleasantly surprised. First of all we went to the counter of the lobsters, and we chose the two biggest.

«Alex look, they are still alive, I feel so sorry for them...», after having agreed that, irrespective of us, the destiny of those poor lobsters were determined, we went to the counter of the shrimps, where you could choose among a large number of quality and different sizes. I ordered half a kilo of the big ones, I paid, and I took them to the counter of the cooks where, in the meanwhile, our lobsters had already been taken.

«Here they cook exceptionally well, you'll lick your fingers, you'll see!», then we went to the bar and took two margaritas.

«A toast to our dinner!»

«A toast to our dinner!», we drank.

At that time, in Los Angeles, the temperature was really nice, not too hot in the daytime and cool at night, it was a perfect weather.

«You know, Veronica, I was very surprised by your message yesterday...», I told her when we sat down.

«Well, it seems perfectly normal to me, I have always been a very instinctive person, and if I fancy to do something I do it, although sometimes it may seem, how to say... deontologically inappropriate, that's it».

Before answering, I looked into her eyes for few moments.

«To be honest, I found your message very opportune!», I told her in a whisper, because of a sip of margarita went down the wrong pipe.

«Ah, good! I know that what I am about to say may seem a banality, but nowadays it's so terribly difficult to find interesting people with whom exchange opinions in freedom. And so last night, after our lovely talk, do you know what I told to myself? "Hey Veronica, why the hell shouldn't you?", thus I sent you that message on Facebook and... here we are, in spite of all hypocritical stereotypes that I hate so much!», she exclaimed, raising her glass again.

«Who can blame you? Moreover, because of what I do, I'm inclined to meet two types of women: those who want to sleep with me for go-getting, and those who would come to bed with me because they want money. In short, a complete disaster.», I confided her, half serious half facetious.

«Yep, a complete disaster! Tell me Alex, when did you have your last relationship? A serious relationship, I mean.», she asked me out of the blue.

«I see we moved quickly to one million dollar question!», I tried to divert.

«Come on, do not reply as the politician you are, this is not an interview.», she insisted.

«You're right, you're right, I beg your pardon. I might say that lately I have not experienced true stories and, in contrast to what some might think, even the so-called "adventures" were sporadic events. My last true relationship dates back about eight years ago: that's it, I can say I have loved her truly, but unfortunately we had to break up due to force majeure.», I admitted, with a veil of melancholy.

«Seriously? I might know these causes? Well, I mean, usually true love knows no reasons...», Veronica rightly objected.

«I was here, and I had just undertaken the role of District Attorney of Los Angeles, while she had the chance to make come true the dream of her life...»

«Which was?»

«To drive airplanes. She desired it since her childhood. So, after few years spent as an hostess for the American, she won a place to attend Swissair pilots course, in Geneva. At first she wanted to refuse in order not to mess up our relationship, but I didn't agree. I didn't want to become the cause that, one day, she could have regretted, so I told her that dreams are made to be pursued, just as I was doing, and I convinced her to go...»

«Heavens, Alex, although you can not see because I'm wearing a shirt, but you gave me gooseflesh! After that, have you ever seen each other again?»

«In the beginning we tried. She came to Los Angeles, I went to Geneva. But this meant only to hurt us because, once aboard that plane, pain and nostalgia prevailed, it was inevitable. Moreover, at that point, it was right that we could live our lives fully. It was a spontaneous decision for both, and since then we have not seen or heard each other, that's it.», I told her.

The silence caused by my words was interrupted by the waitress who served us two huge trays, one crammed full of prawns, cooked in their typical sauce with tomatoes and peppers, and the other one with the two lobsters, accompanied by two wooden hammers, which were used to crack the claws, containing the best part of the pulp.

«How wonderful, will we be able to eat all this food?», she exclaimed. We also ordered two pints of beer.

«Now it's your turn! If I have well understood, you are single too...», I immediately replied.

«You have understood very well. My last relationship, unlike yours, is much less romantic: when I was working at San Francisco Chronicles I fell in love with my editor who, besides having twenty years more than me, he also had a wife and two children. Moral of the story: I spent two terrible years believing his continuous promises "Soon I will file for divorce...", he was telling me. All bullshit! And so one day, I looked at myself in the mirror, and I told myself that I could not let me go for an asshole like that. And out of the blue, I moved to Los Angeles. That's my story.», she confided.

I kept my eyes on her, for all the time she was speaking. I liked to listen to her more and more. When she ended, I realized that a piece of pepper had stuck just below the right side of her lip, thus, without saying a word, I stretched out my hand and grabbed it. She stared at me, astonished, for a moment, and then she smiled at me.

«Thanks', I must be so funny with that thing stuck on my face!».

We kept on talking for another half an hour, and in the meantime we ordered other two margaritas. The evening with her was very pleasant.

Suddenly I felt my phone vibrating. What does Matt want now? I thought. I stretched out my leg to take the phone out of my pocket, and watching the display I saw that it was not Matt, but Nowitzki.

At first it scared the life out of me, I immediately changed expression.

«Is it all right, Alex?», Veronica asked me, visibly worried.

«Yes, everything's okay. I have to answer, just give me two minutes.», and I got up from the table, I sat in the most isolated corner of the terrace, leaning on the railing that overlooked the ocean, just in front of the white ship. I felt some thrills down my back, but it wasn't cold. «Hallo, Inspector!», I said.

«Ah, here you are, thank God. Hi boy, I was afraid you would not answer me. Listen, I have news for you about that person…»

«Oh really, and what kind of news?»

«The kind of news that I can not tell on the phone. We have to speak face to face, Alex. Is it fine for you to meet tomorrow in the early morning, because I have the flight to Washington at eleven?»

«Of course it's fine, but at least tell me something, don't leave me thinking all night!»

«Listen boy, I've just said that I can not. Anyway sleep well tonight, I will tell you everything tomorrow morning. I'll be waiting for you at the same bar as today at seven thirty. Good night.»

Damn! What the hell has Nowitzki discovered, that was so serious that he could not tell me on the phone? That night I wouldn't be able to sleep, I was sure. I went back to the table, where I found Veronica who, in order not to look at me while I was on the phone, was lazily watching her iPhone, which she turned off as soon as I sat down. «It seems that a train has been passed on you, Alex, are you really sure that everything is ok?», she asked me, taking off her glasses. A gesture that seemed a metaphor of another removed barrier, between her eyes and mine. A sort of «Alex, you can trust me», I thought to myself.

It's true, Nowitzki told me not to tell anyone about this story but, all things considered, aside Matt, with whom could I confide in? With no one. During my career, one of the first rules I learnt, was to mistrust. You'll have to be like St. Thomas if you want to build a career, my father used to tell me. Certainly, that attitude had partly contributed to make me become what I was but, considering all things, I have reached the age of thirty without anyone to whom I could tell freely what I was thinking, condemning myself to keep all inside myself.

In my heart I knew that the person in front of me, though nice, was practically a stranger or almost and that moreover was a journalist, thus the last category to which I should let know about that intricate and strange story. In short, I was in a shitty situation. However, inside me, something was telling me that it could be a good occasion to learn to trust someone. Of course it was a risk, and also big, but only those who have the courage to move away from the shore can, in the end, find a wave that can change their lives.

«Listen Veronica, if I tell you a story, do you swear it will remain between us?», I asked her.

«Definitely, don't doubt, Alex», she immediately answered.

Yes, I decided that I could trust in Veronica.

«Okay, but not here, do you mind if we talk about it while we take a ride by car?», Veronica nodded and, after having insisted, I paid the bill, we left the restaurant and we got in my car. As I hadn't a particular direction, I decided to go to Paseo del Mar, towards Palos Verdes.

It was a true outburst, a kind of liberation. I told her about the story of Maggie, from beginning to end, about her phone calls, that there was no trace of her anywhere, I told her about the appointment in a year and also the bad dream I had the night before, and I ended with the call of Nowitzki and that disquieting guy that was staring at me in Redondo Beach. I was a flood of words. Veronica listened without batting an eyelid, and as soon as I finished, she tried to reassure me.

«Now I understand why you were so anxious, you're right, it's really a disquieting story! Honestly, what I can tell you, without saying set phrases and clichés, it can be summarized in two points. On one hand, you're right to watch out, because of your position and considered that unluckily this world is full of crazy people. However, on the other hand I also say not to worry because the highest authority in such circumstances is working on this case, and has surely taken all necessary precautions: people working at National Security Branch are very serious, you know it!».

While I was listening to her, I kept both hands firmly on the steering wheel. I loved driving on that road, it was one of the things that could give me a sense of freedom, and driving with Veronica next to me, made me feel free, gave me also a feeling of peace and security. I was no longer alone.

«Well, you're right Veronica, ultimately I believed in what you said, and then, perhaps, tomorrow Nowitzki will simply tell me that Maggie is an activist of Green Peace. Who knows? Of course it's useless to count chickens before they hatch, although I must confess it's really hard not to think about it...», I answered. When I finished speaking, Veronica took the phone and gave a quick glance at the display.

«It's already midnight, Alex, and tomorrow morning you'll have to wake up at dawn. Are you sure you want to be alone tonight?», she asked me, without any malice in her proposal.

«Actually I don't feel to be alone tonight. Are you sure you don't mind to stay with me?»

«Not at all», she answered, «I just have to pick up my laptop in my car».

After a stop at the Fish Market parking, we drove towards my house, which was on the thirty-sixth, not far from Matt's. We were almost there when, at the corner of Mayler street, I thought to see with the corner of my eye the same guy of Starbucks walking on the sidewalk, in the opposite direction to ours.

Damn, that guy is coming from my house! I immediately thought.

I was petrified. Instinctively I stopped the car in the middle of the road, and I made a U-turn.

«Hey Alex, what's up?», Veronica asked me worried.

«Have you seen him? It's the same guy of this afternoon, the one who was staring at me. He was coming from my house, now I want to discover who the hell he is and what the fuck he wants from me!», I told her in excited tone.

The tension was so high that I could even seen it, in front of my eyes.

«Are you crazy? Let it go, Alex, he may be dangerous!», she shouted.

«I have to. Wait here», I saw him from behind.

I pulled the emergency brake and stepped from the car. Evidently he understood and quickened his pace. I started to run in order to catch him.

«Hey, I'm talking to you! Stop!», he turned for a moment, removing all my doubts, it was really him.

My heart was exploding in my chest. I was really afraid, both for me and for Veronica, but I wanted to know. No matter what. I was reaching him, more or less ten meters were between us, but he suddenly stopped, he turned to me and stared at me with the same disquieting look of few hours before.

7

National interest

The fate shuffles cards and we play.
Arthur Schopenhauer

«WHO the hell are you, huh? What the hell do you want from me?», I shouted in his face, trying to intimidate him.

He didn't move a muscles. All of him was frightening me: his expression, which showed no emotion; his blue eyes, like two marbles; and his indifference with which he looked like a robot, more than a man of flesh and blood. In the meanwhile, Veronica got out of the car, which was parked in the middle of the road. In the background we heard the rattle of the engine, while the headlights, even those lit, were enlightening our legs.

«Tell your lady not to move from there», were the first words he uttered, in a monotonous tone.

«Veronica, don't approach!», I screamed, keeping on looking at that guy.

«So tell me what do you want from me!», in response, he took a handkerchief out from the pocket of his jacket, he took off his drop-rimmed glasses, and began to clean its lenses.

«Well Mr. Anderson, as a member of the United States Congress, you should know, and I have no doubts you know it, that there is something which is above my safety, or yours or that of the President himself. I'm talking about *national interest*. Now, what I might advise is to focus your attention on your political activities, which I know you are carrying on with some success, leaving aside issues that could, in some way, compromising that something I mentioned a moment ago.».

I admit that, for a moment, the multitude of words that I wanted to say, choked in my throat. I was speechless. In those interminable moments I tried to understand what he meant, which was the connection, but although I was striving with all my whole being, I could not find it. At the end it finally came to my mind, Maggie.

«What do you mean?», I asked him in a whisper.

«Exactly what I have just said, Mr. Anderson. I have nothing to add.», he replied with his usual phlegm.

At that very moment, I heard the roar of an engine and I turned round. It was a van with black windows, just like the one of my dream. Damn! I thought. It ran at full speed very close to my car, and stopped right next to us. Now it's really over, I thought half-closing my eyes. I imagined myself lying on the roadside, killed like a dog by that commando of hooded men. But I was more afraid for Veronica than for me.

«Veronica, run!», I shouted at her, using all the breath I had in my body, but she stayed there, motionless. The noise of the sliding door that suddenly opened, made me jump. I could not breathe. Inside the van was dark, and nobody came out.

«Well, Mr. Anderson, I'm sure you'll forgive me, but it's very late and the time at our disposal has expired.», he said, going towards the van. After that, he grabbed the handle, got in the running board and turned his back to me.

«I hope that we will no longer need to meet each other in the future. My regards to you and your lady, Mr. Anderson».
The hatchback closed suddenly behind him, and the van left at full speed, leaving the tire marks on the asphalt.

«My God, Alex, do you feel ok?», Veronica asked, hurrying towards me.

«Well, I think so…»

«Okay, come on, let's go home.».

I could hardly believe what was happening to me. We got in the car, I made a U-turn, and we drove the few meters remaining to reach my house. As soon as we were at home, I turned the entrance light on and began to look around. That guy could have been here, I was thinking. So I began to pass nervously my hand over the doorframes and under the tables, in order to check if there were some bugs, minicam, or some other damn things. I was feeling observed, as if I had still that man's eyes focused on me.

«Now calm down, Alex, otherwise you go crazy. In such cases it's a good idea to try to think over.».

Veronica was right. I stopped, literally falling on the couch.

«Were you able to hear what he said?»

«Every single word.»

«What do you think about it?»

«Whatever it is, in this story there must be something much bigger than you and I can image.»

«Do you think so?»

«Absolutely…»

«I try to call Nowitzki…»

«Don't. You may have your phone under control and, whatever Nowitzki has to tell you, it's not worth to risk it, also because you'll meet him in a few hours. At this point, what is certain is that Maggie Jones is not an activist of Green Peace!», she exclaimed.

«You are also humorous, really not bad for a journalist!», I answered her, doing nothing to hide my annoyance.

«Forgive my British humour, but I could not resist. Listen Alex, Maggie Jones aside, does some other plausible link come to your mind about this whole story?», she asked, trying to reason with me.

«Absolutely not! You've also followed my activity, in these years it never happened to expose myself to matters that could have transcended into something else, never! Of course, being a DA I should have some enemies, but I can't connect none of them to this whole mess.», I thought aloud.

«Well, at this point it seems obvious to me that everything revolves around this Maggie Jones, and that we just have to wait until tomorrow morning to learn more…», she ascertained.

In fact, at that point, the only thing to do was just to wait. Sure as hell, it was easier said than done, given the tension that lingered. Neither I nor Veronica fancied to sleep, so while I went to the kitchen to make a coffee, she opened her bag and pulled out her laptop, placing it on the dining room table.

«Can you give me your wi-fi password?», she asked me.

«John Kennedy, written as one word», I replied.

«Hum, very original for a Republican», she whispered.

As soon as coffee was ready, I poured it into two cups of the White House, which I arranged on a tray with sugar and sweetener. I went into the dining room, I saw that Veronica was on Google, concentrated to search something about Maggie.

«See? Most of the results of my research are about the restaurant in London that bears the name of that lady. But also going forward, there is no trace of Maggie Jones whom we are looking for. Trust me, I've checked lot of times.», I told her, while I was serving coffee.

«Sugar or sweetener?», I asked her.

«Nothing, I drink it bitter, thanks», she replied without taking her eyes from the monitor.

While I was sipping my coffee, I stopped to watch Veronica, and I thought about how I was feeling close to her, being surprised for how she managed to stay calm in a similar situation. If she had not been there, I thought, I would be in total panic. We were both absorbed, she on computer, and I in those thoughts.

However, that silence somehow pleasant was suddenly interrupted by the sound of a message coming from my Mac, on the other side of the room.

We looked at each other for a moment in the eyes.

«I go and see who it is», I told her.

She nodded. As soon as I took the mouse, I saw I had received a private message on Twitter. At the beginning, as I didn't know the sender, I thought it was one of the hundred spam email.

Then, reading the first words, I decided to open it.

I know you are in front of your computer.
At this point we can not wait any longer,
we have to meet as soon as possible.

I was petrified.

«Alex, who is it?», Veronica asked me.

«Come here to see», I replied in a trembling voice.

She stood up from the chair and joined me at the computer.

«Maggie Jones», she exclaimed.

«So it seems. How does she know I'm in front of the computer?», I asked instinctively.

«It seems she knows much more, you have to answer her, now.»

Are you Maggie, aren't you?

Yes, I am.

Can you explain me what the hell is going on?

Sure, but not here, we have to see each other.

I don't think it's a good idea.

There's something you have to know, Alex.

How can I trust?

Sorry, but you have no choice.

«Now what do I tell her?», I asked Veronica.

I felt as if someone had thrown me in a completely unreal situation.

«First you have to listen to what Nowitzki has to tell you, you can't trust, Alex. Try to gain time, tell her you'll meet in the next days».

Ok, but not before Saturday.

I hope with all my heart that it won't be too late.

Too late for what?
Only two days are missing...

I'll keep in touch.
Veronica, please, stay close to him.

That last message left us both dumbstruck. How did she know that Veronica was there with me? For a while we didn't dare to say anything, not even a word. Again gripped by worry, I immediately turned my computer off. So at least for a while she will leave us in peace, I thought. But, as soon as my eyes looked instinctively at the phone, that weak attempt of reassurance crumbled in a flash.

«This time I'm literally speechless, Alex…», Veronica managed to say.

That message had shaken her too. In that moment I felt I had to get the situation under control. «We are not safe here, take your bag and let's go!», I said without thinking twice.

«Where do you want to go? It's three o'clock in the night!», she replied on the spur of the moment.

«Don't worry, trust me.», I answered her.

She did not object and followed me. We took the car and, in less than five minutes, we were at the door of Matt's house.

I rang the bell once, twice, three times, but nothing happened. Is it possible that he doesn't hear? I was wondering.

«There's nobody», Veronica ascertained.

I began to worry. Maybe that guy has gone to his house? Maybe he had kidnapped him? Maybe he has wounded him? While those questions were bouncing in my head like a pinball, the door opened and he came out, wearing a silk robe and half-closed eyes.

«Matt, my friend, you're alive!», I exclaimed, hugging him.

«Hey hey, but what is happening now? Maybe you came here to tell me that you're waiting for a baby, aren't you?»

In normal conditions I would have just glared at him but, on that occasion, his joke helped to diffuse the tension, even if only momentarily, of that night that never seemed to end.

As soon as we set foot in his house, we realized that Matt was not alone, but with one of his girlfriends, who joined us wearing a half open nightgown, from which came abundantly out one of her remade breasts.

«Guys, I introduce you to Rhonda, she's my… well, she's a friend of mine.».

Platinum blonde hair, blue eyes, some adjustment here and there, deeply tanned, in other words, Matt's friend seemed to have just come out from the set of Baywatch. After having shaken hands, Veronica smiled at me for a moment, evidently she must have read in my eyes that we were thinking exactly the same thing.

«Matt, you don't mind if Veronica and I spend the night here?», I asked, interrupting those very boring pleasantries.

«Of course I don't, bro'. But, tell me, did something happen? You two are not even close to having a pretty face.», he asked me, visible worried.

On the other hand, I was deceiving myself in believing to hide something to Matt, who knew me better than anyone else.

Moreover, he was aware about the call of Maggie and the bad dream I had the night before, he perfectly knew how those episodes had troubled me.

But I didn't fancy to tell him everything at that time of the night and, moreover, not in front of the bad copy of Pamela Anderson. I had no intention at all. I would have told him everything in the morning, on my way back from the meeting with Nowitzki.

«Tomorrow I'll tell you, Matt, now we all are tired», needless to say he seized on the opportunity, in fact he didn't insist.

«All right, here you are at home, Rhonda and I go back to bed… please, don't make too much noise you two!», he said going back to his bedroom.

«Nice person, your friend», Veronica said, amused, «he is the one who came to pick you up at the airport, isn't he?», she asked me.

«Yes, precisely him. He's a little bit crazy, but I do really care for him, and I can trust him blindly.», I told her.

As soon as we reached the guest bedroom, that is the one where I used to sleep usually, I showed the bathroom to Veronica and I opened the wardrobe, in order to take a pillow and a blanket, which I arranged on the ground at the foot of the bed.

«What the heck are you doing?» she asked me.

«Well, don't you see? I'm arranging the bed for tonight. I would never want you to think badly…» I answered her, while I was undoing the buttons of my shirt which I felt to have worn for more than a century.

«Are you crazy? Collect your stuff and come straight to bed! I don't think bad at all, and moreover I'm able to defend myself, don't worry.».

As I was so tired, I accepted her invitation and I slipped under the sheets, being very careful not to invade her side of the bed. We kept talking for a while, but after few minutes, we both fell asleep.

In the meanwhile, the moonlight was penetrating through the half closed shutters, illuminating our room .

We were both exhausted, but we were together.

8

The Tomb

Who fights against monsters should be careful not to become himself a monster. And if you look into an abyss for long time, the abyss will also look within yourself.
FRIEDRICH NIETZSCHE

Yale University
Wednesday April 11, 1998
Two o'clock in the morning

«HEY Anderson, open that damn door!».

I opened my eyes wide, it was pitch dark. Who the fuck is it now? I wondered, stunned with sleep.

«Who is it?», I asked aloud.

«Anderson, damn it, open the door!»

The voice seemed that of Mark Donovan, a senior student whom I knew quite well, but not enough to imagine him visiting me in the middle of the night.

My first thought was that something had happened, so I opened the door and I found myself in front of him and Paul Underwood, his classmate and leading man of the university rowing team.

«Hey guys, what do I owe this visit?», I asked them, rubbing my eyes.

«Put some clothes on and let's go, we have no time to waste, tonight it's your turn.», Mark told me.

«What the hell…», I did not have time to finish my sentence, that Paul gave me a hard push on my chest.

«Are you deaf Anderson? Have you heard what Mark said? Hurry up, fuck!».

Although I didn't have the slightest idea of what they wanted, I thought that the best thing to do was not to provoke them, therefore I obeyed. I quickly put on a pair of jeans, a t-shirt, my Nike shoes that were beside the bed and, without saying a word, I followed them.

Outside there must have been twelve degrees more or less, I had gooseflesh. We walked across the High Street, a long straight road that splits almost all the old campus that, at that time, was completely deserted. As soon as we arrived near the Yale Art Gallery, we passed under the Whitman Gate and suddenly we stopped.

«We have arrived», Donovan said in a low voice, holding out an arm to block me.

For a split second I did not realize, but, when I turned to the left, I understood everything.

Damn, we were right in front of the Tomb, the headquarters of Skull and Bones, the secret society founded in the midst of 1800 by Alphonso Taft, father of US President, and by General Russell.

Unconsciously, during my time at Yale, I always avoided passing in front of that building, whose gloomy appearance had the strange power to make me feel anxious. From the outside, it was a real cement cube, with a front door permanently barred by several padlocks and four vertical little windows that had to be walled up or, at least, bolted from the inside.

Nobody knew exactly what there was inside. Of course, I was aware of the existence of Skull and Bones as everyone but, maybe because of my scepticism, I never became fond of its history, and for that reason I did not give heed to rumours circulating at the university. For example, according to one rumour, the relics of Geronimo, the last Apache, were stolen and brought into the Tomb.

All bullshit, only stupid urban legends, I used to think. Actually, to be completely honest, I considered that society a snobbish and elitist lobby made for preppies, therefore light years away from tickling the slightest interest in me.

«It's your turn, Anderson, try not to fail.», Underwood told me grabbing my shoulder in a rude way and then pushed me, almost bumping my face against the door

«Hey, what is this, eh? Many thanks, but I'm not interested in these craps!», I shouted in his face, looking at both with a provocative defiance.

The reaction of that bastard Underwood was to dash me in the pit of my stomach. The pain sent me down on my knees, I could not breathe.

Donovan caught my hair, and sharply made me look up, cracking my neck bones.

«Craps, eh? Listen to me, ugly piece of shit, if it was not for your father you would have never had the privilege of being here, is that clear? So now raise your bad ass and execute the orders without a murmur, if you don't want to come to a bitter end!».

My father? What the hell had he to do with Skull and Bones? He had never even mentioned that secret society! Damn, I was in total blackout.

Suddenly I heard a disquieting squeak, it came from the door which was opening behind me, and that, through another hard push of Underwood, swallowed me.

Unbalanced by that unexpected push, I lost my balance and I fell with my ass on the ground.

At once I looked around myself.

In the middle of the ceiling, an old wrought iron chandelier was hanging, in which dozens of candles were burning, many of them being hidden by wax casting that seemed to be there since more than hundred years.

Other chandeliers, just like those you can see in churches, were placed in each corner of the room, with the exception of the frontal corner, where there was a recess which, at first sight, seemed to be a crypt.

In front of it, side by side, there were fifteen people, who wore a purple-red cloak with a white hem. They all were standing with their arms folded and stared at me. In silence.

When I was able to bring them into focus, I realized that I knew them all, one by one. All Yale's senior students. Here they are, the ill-famed bonesmen, I thought to myself, while I was wondering what was going to happen to me that night.

«Alex, Alex!», someone was calling my name in a whisper.

I turned myself to the right and I saw another person, dressed in the same way, but with his head covered by a hood made of a very rough material, it seemed jute or something like that. After having made a nod with his head towards other bonesmen, he walked towards me.

He walked terribly slowly, and every step was marked by a chorus of «Uh», uttered by the people who were in that room.

«Uh uh uh uh», the more I saw him approaching, and the more my heart was beating like crazy, with such speed that I could feel its pulses in every part of my body.

When he arrived in front of me, I swallowed, sending down the little saliva left in my mouth. We peered at each other for a few seconds, until, when moving my head a few centimetres towards the chandelier light, I finally managed to look through the two holes on the hood.

In a split second I recognized that look.

I was petrified.

«Alex, Alex!».

I opened my eyes, thank God Veronica was there!

«Damn Alex, you scared the life out of me, you should have heard you, you breathed heavily and kept on moving... you had a bad dream, haven't you?», she asked me, while she was wearing her glasses, that she took from the nightstand.

«Right, I think I had a bad dream, but I don't remember anything. Better!»

«Yes, better not to remember...», she replied, getting out from bed.

I gave a glance at the clock and saw that it was a quarter to six .

«It's high time I get ready, in more than an hour I'll have to be in Redondo», I told her.

«Listen Alex, irrespective of whether Nowitzki will tell you, I want you to go on with your activities for your election campaign in full swing, first of all because you can not fail, and then because no one should suspect that something has happened to you. Especially my colleagues. In this regard, I was thinking we might anticipate the interview we fixed on Sunday and make it today, what about it?».

Once again in few hours, I totally agreed with what Veronica was saying. I should start to worry, I thought, succeeding in cracking a shy smile. But at least it was a smile.

«Well, do you find it so funny?», she asked me, almost irritated.

«Absolutely not, the fact is that I rarely get on well with someone so often. Indeed, to be honest it had never happened before!», I answered her, succeeding in making her smile.

After getting dressed, we gathered our things and left the house, being very careful not to make any noise that could wake Matt and his friend Rhonda. That morning the sky was quite cloudy.

«It's too early, you'll see that the sun will come out around ten», I told Veronica, while we got into the car.

«I don't think it's a good idea to show up together, at the meeting with Nowitzki...» she said, reading again in my mind.

«Indeed. Moreover you're also a journalist... how about that! Listen, thinking about it, just after Starbucks there's a McDonalds, you may wait there, what do you think about it?», I suggested.

«I think it's perfect, so I will also have time to check emails and begin to baste your interview. But let's get a move on, we have to be there before him, we can not risk being seen together.».

Saying so she was forcing an open door, I knew that road like my pockets and, moreover, I loved to drive through it at full speed, when I was at the wheel of my Buick Skylark of fifty-four.

I considered that car as a veritable oracle, because it was a model objectively beautiful and sought but, above all, because it was given to me by Philip Anderson, my grandfather, to whom I was very attached and who was a fundamental point of reference to me, perhaps just like my father and mother.

In fact, from him I inherited much of my passion for politics, considering that he was Senator of the United States of America for more than twenty years handing down, moreover, to both my father and me, the family tradition to attend Yale University, where we had reached the fourth generation, through my degree. To be exact, five, considering also my mother. It was there where they met, she and my father, who was two years older than her: both were activists of the Yale Political Union, and editors of the Daily News, the famous university newspaper.

In other words, I can say that a great part of my family's destinies intertwined thanks to the instructions of my grandfather Philip, considering Yale as their main hub.

«How silent you are…», suddenly Veronica said.

«You're right, I'm sorry, I was thinking about Philip, my grandfather.» I told her.

«The former Senator, right? Good, you gave me another idea for your interview!», she promptly replied.

> *Lady writer on the TV*
> *She knew all about a history*
> *You couldn't hardly write your name*
> *I think I want it just the same as the ...*
> *Lady writer on the TV*
> *Talking about the Virgin Mary*
> *You know I'm talking about you and me*
> *And the lady writer on the TV*
> *Talking about the Virgin Mary*
> *Yeah you know I'm talking about you and me*
> *And the lady writer on the TV*

«Do you remember this song?», I asked her, after having started the song.

«Sure, I love Dire Straits! And this one… you have good taste in music, do you know?», she exclaimed, acquiring for a moment the same relaxed and enjoyed tone of few hours before, when we were pleasantly seated at the Fish Market.

In the meanwhile we reached Redondo, it was a quarter to seven. Although we arrived well in advance, we decided not to risk, thus we separated immediately. So, I passed the intersection and left Veronica in front of McDonalds.

«Listen Alex, for whatever you may need, you can find me here or on the phone.», she told me, before closing the car door.

Gosh, is it possible I am already missing her? I thought for a while, as I walked back the few meters that separated me from the place of the appointment.

At Starbucks there was no one, except for the three girls working there. One of them was busy arranging donuts and cookies into the glass exhibitor that was on the counter, the other one was counting the money that were in the cash register and the third one was busy cleaning the windows of the restaurant, with spray and newsprint.

I went to the counter, ordered a large coffee and a chocolate cookie, and I sat down at the same table of the day before. Needless to say, waiting in loneliness contributed to raise dramatically my anxiety.

I was not even hungry, strange thing, because in normal conditions, on mornings I would devour anything within arm's reach.

Anyway I tried to eat that huge hyper caloric cookie, accompanying each bite with a generous sip of coffee. In the meantime, I took my phone and I began to look lazily at the news of the day.

I checked my emails, Facebook and Twitter notifications. I read lot of times Maggie's messages, and then I looked nervously at the clock. It was a quarter past seven.

It was nearly time.

In the meanwhile, the clouds began to thin out, letting some bursts of light come in, thanks to which that day seemed to be less surly.

9
The truth

THE nervous incessant drumming of my fingers on the wooden table seemed to punctuate the time of the movements of the three girls while they were working, probably still sleepy. Finally, at seven-thirty, I heard the so long awaited sound of the front door.

It was him, Nowitzki. Getting up abruptly, I bumped my legs rather violently against the table, because I was so happy to see that man materializing in front of me. It was incredible, after all that had happened.

«Hey boy, you look bad, are you sure to feel good?» he told me, bypassing all sorts of pleasantries.

«Let's say I have lived better nights than the one just passed...», I answered, betraying the tiredness due to the fact that I've slept only a couple of hours more or less.

He immediately made a sign to the nearest waitress, to whom he ordered one big coffee and two chocolate donuts.

«Sooner or later it will be good to stop, or this junk food will be my ruin!», he said conscious to lie to himself, before devouring half in one bite. After having quickly cleaned fingers and mouth with one of the paper towels that were on the table, he picked up his leather bag, opened it, and pulled out a file, leaning it closed on the table.

«Carl don't keep me on my toes, what can you say about this Maggie Jones? I want to know what all this story is about!», I said in a firm tone, staring into his eyes. And so, after having looked around to make sure no one was watching, he opened the file with a movement of his right hand, from which he took an old photo of a little girl with blond hair.

It was little Maggie, portrayed in an image that, more or less, seemed to go back to the time when I was still in San Pedro.

«Do you recognize her, Alex?», he asked abruptly.

«Of course I recognize her, it's her, Maggie… don't you have a more recent photo?», I replied, without hesitation.

«Impossible, boy, Maggie Jones died with her parents on August 8, in 1989. Here it is, read.».

His tone was sterile and detached, as the perfect FBI official usually has. After I was made aware of that news, he pulled an old newspaper clipping from the file, and handed it to me.

Los Angeles Times – August 9, 1989

Hawaii, Californian family dies at sea, the research for a body of a girl of only nine years have been suspended

by Debra Chang – A whole family wiped out, aboard their sailboat, by the unexpected blind fury of the sea. The tragedy happened yesterday, off the island of Oahu, the Hawaiian archipelago, where all the three components of the Jones family have lost their lives. Coming from California, living in San Pedro, Frank and Linda Jones used to spend their summer holidays in Hawaii, along with Maggie, their daughter of nine years. However, yesterday something must have gone wrong. Maybe because of a freak wave caused by a bigger boat, their sailing boat capsized violently, leaving no escape to the unfortunate family. Rescue operations were useless - warned by some tourists on board on another boat - they discovered the lifeless bodies of the couple, but not that one of little Maggie. And as time passes, the chance to find it becomes thin, said the head of the Coast Guard in Honolulu: «Until now there is no trace of the child's body on the surface of the sea». Mayor Tom Bradley has personally met the families of the victims to express them «the deep feeling and closeness of the entire city of Los Angeles».

I turned pale. I had to read those lines again as to realize what was happening. On one hand I was shocked by the news, I was unaware of the death of Maggie and her parents, and on the other I was bewildered by the tangle of questions that began to jump like grasshoppers across my mind.

I was hoping that, at any moment, someone would tell me that it was a bad joke.

My phone rang.

I gave it a look, and I saw it was a message from Veronica, of which I read quick only the preview:

How is it going? You are on Huffing...

I glanced up, and looked at Nowitzki, who in the meantime had taken off his hazelnut overcoat.

«What happens, Carl?», I asked him.

«This news has shocked you, hasn't it? It's an understandable reaction. I suppose now you're probably making yourself more than one question.», he answered, understanding the state in which I was.

«Absolutely I've a lot of questions! If Maggie Jones has died, who phoned me on September 11? Who was looking for me at the Capitol? And who wrote me last night, after the meeting with that guy?», I exclaimed loudly, attracting the looks of the waitresses.

«Alt, alt, stop everything, boy! Are you telling me that Maggie has called you again? And who is the guy you are referring to?», he asked, beating his fists on the table.

I told him what happened last night, about that guy with glasses who stared at us the day before, and that I saw him again few hours later on my way home, telling him what he said to me, word by word. And then I told him about Maggie's messages, when I was at home.

I was completely befuddled. At first I thought to omit the fact that I was with Veronica but, at that point, I thought I had no choice. So I let the cat out of the bag.

Nowitzki listened in silence. As soon as I finished, he showed me another sheet he held in his file.

«Look, we were able to find the places from which the phone calls have been made by… Maggie, or whoever she is. The first one, made on September 11, was made from a public phone in London; the second one, that you received the other day in Washington, came from a phone booth located few dozen meters from the Capitol, that is near you.», he explained, pointing his index finger on the exact spot from which the phone call had been made.

«I do not know what to think, I'm serious. Do you have some idea who these people might be?», I asked him, in despair.

«Assumptions, but I prefer to keep them for me. You have to help me to understand a few things about you. Women, possible enemies, strange episodes: you will not have secrets with me. In cases like this, the most insignificant details make the difference, remember it.»

«Right, details, my father used to say so…»

«And he was right. Listen, I don't want to scare you, but through the elements we have in our hands, I would exclude the possibility of a simple mythomaniac who wants to torment you. What is certain is that someone is watching you very closely. What about the reasons? We don't know them, but prevention is better than a cure. Therefore I arranged a person who has to protect you. I postponed my return to Washington, I'll wait for you at three PM in my office, on Wilshire Boulevard, in the meanwhile try to behave as if nothing has happened, and get your thoughts about every episode of your life in order. The answer to all our questions lies hidden in some corner of your past.»

«Behave as if nothing has happened, easy to say…»

«But you have to! Listen, now go to McDonalds and pick her up, and tell your friend Veronica that she's also invited… see you later, my son, take care of yourself.»

The fact that Nowitzki knew about Veronica surprised me, but not so much. Indeed, it will seem paradoxical, but in some way it reassured me. Moreover he was one of the bigwig of our intelligence and, although there was no need, it was the proof that he knew his stuff. In short, I was in good hands.

While we were saying goodbye, Nowitzki placed his leather bag on the table and slipped in the file on Maggie Jones. Instinctively, the corner of my eye fell right there, and I saw another folder, on which was written a name that I knew very well: Philip Anderson, my grandfather.

I hoped that the meeting would help to clear my head, to untie all knots, but it did nothing but entangled the knot further.

Damn it!

I gathered my things quickly, got into my car and went to McDonalds. As soon as I arrived there, I looked through the window and saw Veronica, who was sitting in front of her computer while she was sipping a coffee. I liked the way she was holding the cup with both hands. I did not understand why, but I thought it was a movement even sensual in some ways.

I stood there a few moments watching her, probably she was writing my interview and, occasionally turned her eyes away from her laptop to look at the phone.

She was impatient, she was waiting for me. I turned off the car and entered. What a coincidence, at that precise moment she looked up and saw me, greeting me with an intense smile. «Come on tell me, I'm dying of curiosity!», she exclaimed immediately.

«Eh, it's not easy. I can begin telling you that it's really a mess, and that in the afternoon Nowitzki wants to meet us at FBI. He knew you were here.», I told her, with a rather soft tone.

«Well, after all it's his job, such thing was even predictable... what about the rest? Has he discovered something about this Maggie Jones?», she asked me.

Before answering, I took her coffee and made a sip.

«How disgusting, it's without sugar!», I said while a shudder ran through my back.

«Ah ah, you should see your face! You should know I drink it without sugar... Come on tell me!» she said, pulling my hand. She was looking forward wanting to know everything.

«As a start, they succeeded in tracing the two calls I received: the one made on September 11 was made from a phone booth in London, while the one of the other day, at the Capitol, was made from a public phone that is just few meters near my office…», while I was talking, Veronica nodded and drew circles on the table, passing her index finger on the drops of coffee that I had spilled a moment before.

«Has he discovered something about Maggie?», she asked me.

«This is the best part, brace yourself… Maggie Jones died in 1989, Veronica! He showed me the newspaper clipping containing the news, it was an accident on a sailboat, at Hawaii, that killed also her parents. However, Maggie's body has never been found».

That news was so shocking to turn pale even Veronica, who up to that moment had shown great coolness. She kept silent for few moments.

While she was reflecting on what I had just said, she took some napkins and cleaned the table. Maybe those gestures helped to calm her nerves.

«Damn it Alex, if I did not know you well, I would think you are kidding me. In short, I can say this story is really crazy, and as time passes it becomes even more incredible. And I'm a journalist… tell me, in addition to this, are there other twists? Just to know…», she asked with a hint of sarcasm.

«Yours is a rhetorical question…», I answered her.

She understood at once.

«What do you mean? What else could have happened?» she asked.

«I trust Nowitzki, but when he opened his bag to put away the file on Maggie, with the corner of my eye I saw there was another folder, on which was written the name of my grandfather, Philip».

As soon as I said the name of my grandfather, Veronica took her laptop and turned it to me.

«Read this, this morning the Huffington Post opens with an editorial on you, in which Arianna Huffington defines you as the rising star of the Republicans».
She did not even have time to finish her sentence, that I dragged the laptop towards me.

«Are you kidding me?», I asked her.

«Not at all! But that's not all, because in her article she also talks about your father and grandfather, and about the great influence of your family in the party, also because of your membership in Skull and Bones. Why haven't you told me you were part of that secret society?», she asked me, raising her voice.

«Wait, let me read!»

With Rooney in trouble, the Republicans are already looking to 2016 in the name of Alex Anderson

by Arianna Huffington – From Texas to California, step can be short, indeed, very short. It seems that in the destiny of Republicans there is written that their fortune coincide with some families. Two, to be precise. The first one, obviously, is the Bush family, who managed to "place" two presidents (George and George W.) and one governor (Jeb). The second one is unknown to most people, but we bet it will be not for much longer. We are speaking about Anderson family, whose forefather is the grandfather Philip, Senator for over twenty years, and includes also dad Ron, influential official and former US consul in Italy and, finally, the child prodigy Alex, who has been elected to Congress being only thirty-five and has his re-election already in his pocket, of course. This young man – who in only two years in Washington has become appreciated for his sparkling opposition to the Obama administration – besides having potential, he also manages to be a trendsetter on social networks, conquering every day a very mixed public, which goes from the middle-aged man who likes to stay informed, up to the cheeky teenager who shares her photos because she is literally in love with him. After all, it`s useless to be hypocrites, the image is a fundamental component, and the descendant of Anderson family has it in abundance. Obama docet. As for his communication skills, it`s emblematic the nice spot of his first election campaign, which was able to score over one million hits on YouTube. Therefore, in summary, there are political qualities, even those communicative, and physical appearance as well. It`s a lot, of course, but it`s not enough to aspire to the office of President of the United States. One element is still missing but, even in this case, young Anderson seems to have what it takes. What do I mean? Wishing to be unclear we could talk about simple cursus honorum but, as the Huffington Post loves to be precise, we say Skull and Bones. Does it mean something to you? But of course, who does not know the most famous and influential secret society in the Globe? Good. So it happens that both Bush senior and Bush son are so proudly part of it, just like Anderson, starting from his grandfather up to "little" Alex. Life is strange, isn`t it? The fact is that, taken for granted the defeat of Romney (which is also an expedient), the year 2016 is closer to Republicans more than you might think. In the same way Texas and California are also close, whose destinies have crossed in a "Tomb" near Yale. Maybe also the destiny of the United States of America should pass (again) through it, it is true Mr. Anderson?

I opened my eyes wide. It's obvious that in some ways I was pleased, damn, the Huffington Post was the most influential blog of all the United States, in short, it was a real Bible in its field. An editorial like that was tantamount to an investiture, it was a stroke of luck. However on the other hand, the fact that my name was compared to that of Skull and Bones left me a bitter taste, and also caused another storm of questions in my mind in just few hours.

«So Alex, tell me something about this», Veronica said, clearly annoyed at my silence. Just when I was about to speak , my phone rang.

«Just one minute, it's Matt, I have to answer him», Veronica nodded.

«Hallo Matt, how are…»

He immediately interrupted me

«Alex Anderson, you are the most tough motherfucker I've ever known! Arianna Huffington presents you as a candidate for the White House, and don't you tell me? Five hundred people have called me this morning, and I didn't know anything about this story. I swear on my surfboard I'll get back at you, my friend!», he exclaimed in a both serious and funny way, as always it was impossible to understand if he was joking or not.

«Hey hey, calm down, I have just read it now, Veronica has just shown it to me...», also in this case, he did not give me time to end my sentence.

«Ah, now I understand, you're still with Hayes... listen bro', I would like to remind you that you are, rather, we are in election campaign, and you have to move your ass and bring it immediately here, to San Pedro. If it's not too much trouble, of course. And since we're on the subject, remember that when you become the President of the United States, I'll be for Sorensen!», he said, bursting into one of his typical laughter.

«You can bet on it, brother! In one hour I'll be at the committee, okay?», I told him, trying to cut him short.

«I'm waiting for you, and you will also tell me what the fuck happened tonight...», he exclaimed.

«Okay, see you in a while.», I told him but, just as I was about to hang up...

«Hey Alex, wait a moment!»

«What else, Matt...»

«If you want me to organize some ritual with skulls or something like that, you only have to ask!»

«Fuck you, Matt!»

After that idiot joke, I hung up on him. It was the least I could do.

«Forgive me, but if I had not answered him, he would have continued to bother me. What we were saying?», I asked Veronica, intentionally skating over Skull and Bones, in the hope she'd overlook it.

«Anderson listen, it's useless with me... however I reiterate the point: I asked you why you've never told me about your Skull and Bones membership, I would appreciate if you answer me .».

I did not want to talk about Skull and Bones, I could not talk about Skull and Bones. For no reason in the world. However, I had to give her an answer, considering what we were living together.

«Veronica, I want to be honest with you all the way. Please believe me when I say it's a subject that I prefer not to talk about...», I was abruptly interrupted also by her.

«Damn Alex, it's high time you trust someone! It almost seems that you don't want to realize that what has happened to you tonight could be related to this particular. No, it's not my intention to add fuel to the fire, but don't you think it's a strange coincidence this article has been published just today? Well, I think so! Thus, since I'm here because I want to help you, so please put an end to it and stop being mysterious. Is that clear enough, Mr. Anderson?».

Damn, what a personality! I thought to myself, while she was speaking. Needless to say that her determination struck me, Veronica was proving to be a woman with all qualities, who, step by step, was succeeding in the Titanic challenge to shake something inside me. Behaving like that, she was eroding the armour I was wearing to protect myself from the rest of the world. I did not know yet if it was an entirely positive thing, but, in that situation, I had to take some risks.

«Veronica, all I can tell you is that it was not my choice, and it's important you know it. Concerning the rest, you do not even imagine how much I would like to talk about it openly, but I can not, because if I do it I would put you in danger. It's dealing with people who don't care about anything, I've already said too much. You do understand it, don't you?», I asked her staring at her beautiful blue eyes.

«No, I don't understand. But I realize you should live certain situations on your skin, in order to understand them. For me it's fine if you tell me this is the way things are, what matters the most is that you can get out from this damned surreal situation as soon as possible. Anyway, I'll be by your side. If you like it or not!».

10

Skull and Bones

A child can inherit from his father, nose, eyes and even intelligence, but not the soul. The soul is new to every man.
HERMANN HESSE

The Tomb
Wednesday April 11, 1998
2.32 AM

«ONE day you'll thank me for this, Alex.», he whispered.

It was him, my father.

I even had no time to realize it, that Donovan and Underwood lifted me up by my arms.

«Stand up, Anderson!», Paul the yokel screamed in my ear.

I obeyed.

After giving me a knowing glance, my father stood at the centre of the room, he opened his arms, and began to articulate aloud what seemed to be the opening ceremony of Skull and Bones "meeting".

Each sentence was uttered by him and repeated by all the others, in chorus.

The tone seemed to be an old chant of asylum.

As soon as he started, Donovan and Underwood, who were still next to me, turned to me and said almost simultaneously «You repeat also».

Even then, I preferred not to object.

If we are here, it's because
God our Lord so willed

Brothers for life, together through our blood,
we will be advocates of others' fate

We have a close fist,
with which we'll punish the children of betrayal

Wind blows strong, time runs fast,
but we and Skull and Bones will always govern

I solemnly promise
And I swear on my honour

That Skull and Bones
I will keep under wraps
And if someone speaks about it
Be certainly sure

That Skull and Bones don't forgive
And his life will be a hell for sure

Eternal life to Skull and Bones!

Those sentences sounded to me simply horrifying. However, after having declared them, I felt as if something had actually changed in me.

It was a real strange feeling, as if that absurd nursery rhyme had created a sort of spell, of which I began to feel the effects. Of course, I was in that situation against my will, and I had always considered that kind of things in the same way as grotesque and pointless liturgies but, damn it, from that moment on I began to feel myself as part of something. Of that something.

No, I could never betray that oath. I thought, closing my eyes for a while.

«Welcome among Bonesmen, Anderson!», Mark told me, using a tone totally opposed to that of a few minutes before.

«Now undress yourself and lie down there.», he whispered, showing me a rectangular basement in rough stone, which was in the centre of the room, next to the crypt where, it was said, Geronimo's relics were contained.

While I was taking off my shirt and trousers, all other Bonesmen arranged themselves around that rectangle of stone, forming a circle.

My father, who in the meanwhile nodded to me with a movement of his head, opened an old wooden chest, and took out a purple robe, the same as those worn by the others.

With his left hand, he invited me to lie down.

One, two, three, four, five steps, and I reached that piece of stone that seemed to be there just waiting for me. I looked around myself, everyone was watching me in silence. I laid down. That stone was so cold, that I felt like being on a sheet of ice.

In no time at all, every inch of my body was shaken by shivers that soon turned into a strange tingling. I stared at that old wrought iron chandelier, which was perfectly perpendicular to me.

At that very moment, I saw something falling on me, I turned myself instinctively in order to avoid it. I closed my eyes, and I felt a burning sensation on my right cheekbone.

It was a drop of wax, fallen from one of the dozens of the candles stuck in the chandelier.

I opened my eyes, and I saw the circle tightening around me, and my father holding a purple cloak with both hands.

Orietur in tenebris lux tua!

After having shouted that sentence at the top of his voice, he opened his hands tumbling the cloak over me, and went to sit on a sort of throne made into the wall, right behind my head.

Although I knew he was my father, on that occasion he was so different from the man who had grown me up, and in some ways I felt him more than a stranger.

Paradoxical, as everything that was happening around me. Another handful of endless seconds, and he broke again that agonizing silence.

My brothers, Brothers of Skull and Bones,
for us, tied through an unbreakable covenant, what is happening
tonight is a key event,
it's the appointment with life.
History and tradition are intertwined, for us belonging to
Skull and Bones,
granting eternal life to ideals that bind us together
and in the name of which we fight, every day.

In one word, my Brothers, one of the fundamental principles on
which Skull and Bones is based is:

CON – TI – NUI - TY

Right, continuity.

In a world where everything is thrown on the corners of the
streets, and one gets rid of thoughts and beliefs more easily than
with a pair of old shoes,
It is imperative, for us Brothers of Skull and Bones,
to act in continuity with whom have preceded us,
in the heavy work of maintaining the thin thread on which lies
the destinies of the United States of America and, consequently,
of the rest of the Planet.

Starting from William Huntington Russell and Alphonso Taft,
the Brothers who founded Skull and Bones,
up to Presidents William Howard Taft,
George Bush and George W. Bush,
up to John Kerry,
and up to the dozens of Senators, Members of Congress, and
servants of the Nation within the Institutions,
we say thank you, on behalf of Skull and Bones and
the United States of America!

Together we win challenges with destiny, my Brothers.

Together we can direct the breath of the wind changing the course of history.

Together we make history, my Brothers.

Under the sign of unity and continuity, tonight Alex Anderson, grandson of Philip and son of mine, joins us.
The blood tie that binds him and me, will merge, in a while, into the one that keeps all of us united.

I'm so proud of you, my son.

Before I named some of our basic principles, we all know them well, which are enclosed and symbolized by the cloak that we wear.

Purple-red, that is ardour and sacrifice in the name of common Cause.

And white, that is the oath of absolute loyalty to it and to its Brothers.

Tonight, after passing the last test that awaits you, also you Alex, you'll have the privilege of wearing the vestiges of Skull and Bones.

Starting from tonight, you also will be asked to write through your hands the destiny of the United States of America .

What Skull and Bones asks you in return, is to demonstrate your absolute devotion telling your Brothers about a secret that you jealously guard in the depths of your memory, and about which you have never spoken a word to anyone.

You'll have to do it now. This is your last test.

I swallowed so hard that the muscles of my face twitched for a moment, giving me the impression of dying suffocated because of that stupid drop of saliva. Maybe it was due because of the cold, that had penetrated into my bones. But not only.

I felt, deep into my bowels, something strange taking possession of me. A real tangle of thoughts gathered in my head, that, cell by cell, decomposed my certainties and then reassembled them to its liking.

My ego was about to be rewritten, there, that night.

At first, that state prevented me from accessing my memory, it seemed that someone had changed its password.

I kept my eyes closed, hoping it would help me not to feel observed, and to make sure to regain, even for just a moment, a little bit of intimacy. I felt the weight of their looks crushing me like a boulder.

I opened my eyes, I had goose bumps all over my body. I was numbed by that damn cold and, to make matters worse, from time to time some drops of incandescent wax fell on me from the chandelier.

A real torture.

Suddenly, I felt a sharp pain in my head, as if someone was squeezing my temples with full force.

Then a red light, similar to a blaze, behind which appeared the entrance to the room of my memories.

I entered in it, and in a dark corner I seemed to see something. Covered with dust and eroded by time that had passed since then, there was that memory that years before I placed there, with the illusion that it would never emerge again.

«I remember it was late October, in 1986, and a few days later we would have left California to move to Rome because of the new assignment of my father. In any way I did not want to accept that new reality, which would force me to leave the places where I grew up, my dearest friends, and especially little Maggie. I came to hate my father for that. With all my might. Sometimes I even prayed that something would happen to him at work, like to be fired, so that we would no longer had to leave. I tried to hide the strong pain I felt inside, but I was not always able to so, I became rather taciturn. I had the strange feeling to stay on my own, rarely meet friends and people I loved, because I was hoping that by doing so the pain would be more controlled, when I would have to abandon them. At night, when mom or dad used to put me to bed, I pretended to fall asleep, and then I let myself go. I cried, I cried for hours, smothering my moans in the pillow in order not to be heard. I thought of Matt, Sue, Maggie, my seagulls friends, and I saw them drifting away further and further. I tried to reach them, but it was like walking backwards on the tape of an escalator. I walked, I walked, but I was still standing in the same place, while they became smaller, and looked at me with tears in their eyes, as if to say «Sorry, goodbye, Alex». All this was excruciating, and it happened every night. One day, Maggie gave me an appointment at sunset at the usual bench, down to the pier. She said she had to talk to me about something important, that perhaps could be the solution of our problem. When she arrived, she told me that the night before she had hidden herself behind the door of the living room, and she heard what people were saying in a movie that her parents were watching. «There were two lovers forced to separate, then the man took a knife, he made a cut on his arm and began to bleed. Then he took her arm, and made another cut. At first she was screaming, she didn't want to, but he said that by joining the blood of both, they would have stayed together forever, for all the days of their lives and even beyond. We could do the same, so we will never part, what do you think?». Of course I accepted immediately. We collected the few dollars we had in our pockets, jumped on our bikes and went to the hardware store of Bob to buy a knife, telling him it was for my mother. Then we went to the bottom of the harbour, because at that time there was nobody, all people had stopped working, we hid behind one of those huge container, and we took ourselves by our hands. I must confess I felt a little bit of fear, but I mustered up courage. I pulled the knife from my school backpack and, after having chosen the point where to do it, I plunged the knife edge in the middle of my left forearm more or less. I gritted my teeth, and since I had not seen the blood coming out yet, I closed my eyes and pressed the knife with more power. Then I looked Maggie into her eyes, she nodded and offered her arm. «Close your eyes!», I told her. «No, I want to watch.», she objected without thinking twice. Instinctively, at the beginning, I tried to do it with a certain delicacy in order to make her feel less pain as possible but, at some point, I realized I also had to use force with her. So I did, and blood came out. I looked at my arm, realizing that the blood had flowed down, reaching my wrist and dripping on the floor, into the middle of the mixture of dust and sand that was there. Our eyes were lost in each other, and the only sounds we heard in the distance were the cries of seagulls and the sirens of ships. Our sounds. «Together forever». We declared those words together, whispering. Just enough so that they could echo in eternity. For us, at least, it was so. Facing towards the sunset, we lifted our arms up to the sky and we joined them, creating a sort of X. My blood mingled with hers, and through this, our destinies became a common destiny. We held our arms together for a while, we wanted to give that rite all time to get into our bloodstream. We watched them, while they seemed to merge among the sun's rays. We stood there for a while, then we threw the knife into the sea and we went back home. I told my parents I got myself that cut because of a bad fall by bike. Here it is, this is the story of the scar I still have on my body, and the secret I have never told anyone».

As soon as I finished to speak, a long applause began. I raised my head to look around myself, and I saw that, while clapping their hands, some of them smiled, and others said some jokes softly. It must be positive comments about me, I thought with a hint of relief. Suddenly I felt better, lighter. My father came up to me, with his hands he interrupted the applause, and invited me to stand up.

Alex Anderson, Philip's grandson and son of mine,
from this moment your oath of eternal fidelity to Skull and Bones
can be considered valid for all purposes.

The Codes of conduct of Skull and Bones, whose unique existing
copy is carved on the two bas-reliefs behind my shoulder,
are your doctrine.

Eternal life to Skull and Bones!

«Hey, I'm talking to you, could you listen to me? May I know what's wrong with you?» I was behind the wheel of my car and, sitting next to me, there was Veronica.

It had to be at least the third time she was trying to draw my attention, saying something.

I was lost in thought, completely absorbed by that memory.

«You're right, I'm sorry, I was still thinking about Maggie's death. That news has shocked me. What were we saying?», I said, turning myself towards her for a moment.

«We were saying it's a good idea to go back home for a moment. Look at yourself, you look like coming out from a scene of the Warriors of the night, you have to shave and take a shower, if you want to be presentable at least. Remember you are in election campaign, Mr. Anderson!», she was right, but I began to be annoyed by the fact she was keeping on calling me Mr. Anderson using that tone.

«Listen, why do you keep calling me Mr. Anderson?», I asked her, evidently overheated.

«Why, is it bothering you? You should be used to it, everyone calls you in this way...» she replied, with a sly smile.

«You mean all strangers, but certainly not the people I lov...», I stopped myself, when I realized exactly what I had just said.

«Wow, be careful... I've heard well, by chance have you just said that you love me?», her words were framed by a smile that had became even bigger.

I felt terribly embarrassed, I was not used to reveal my feelings to others. I was in trouble, I didn't know how to answer but, just as I was about to open my mouth, I was saved by the ringing of my phone, amplified by the speakerphone of my car.

PRIVATE NUMBER

«Come on, answer…», Veronica said.

«On principle, I never answer to anonymous calls…», I told her, while the phone's ringing persisted.

«Come on answer, it might be important, maybe it's Nowitzki with some news for you!».

I agreed and immediately I answered the phone, pressing the green button on the speakerphone's screen.

We both could hear.

An annoying noise came out from my car's speakers, it looked like someone was hitting iron with a hammer or something like that, then a rustle caused by the wind, but aside those background noises, there was no word yet. Veronica and I, we looked at each other.

«Hallo, who's speaking?», I said aloud.

Nothing.

I tried again.

«Hallo! If you don't speak, I hang up!», I intimidated.

Nothing.

Whoever it was, I was annoyed, so I pressed the red button, hanging up.

In one second the phone began to ring again, always a private number.

Veronica looked at me, and pressed the green button. Again those noises.

«Who the hell are you?» I said.

Suddenly, a voice.

It was disturbed by that background noise, it seemed like a whisper, he said a word, but it was incomprehensible. Then, a sentence.

«They hear everything…», it was someone speaking in a low voice, but we both heard those words clearly.

Then, they hung up.

«They hear everything… what the hell does it mean?», I asked Veronica.

«Whatever it means, this is not a reassuring conversation, you know what I mean… I think you should immediately call Nowitzki, maybe FBI can trace straight away the number from which you received the phone call…»

Veronica was visibly shocked.

«I prefer not, not on the phone, I do not trust. We'll tell him today, face to face. What is certain is that if they want to intimidate me, they choose the wrong person. Whatever they want from me, they will not have it, be sure about it!».

11

Still him

The known world goes on regularly in the sunlight.
The unknown world peeks at us from the shadows.
FERNANDO PESSOA

WHEN we got home it was nearly half past nine, and the sky had brightened up. I left the bigger bathroom to Veronica and I, before going into the one next to my room, turned on my Mac and switched on a little bit of music, at full blast.

... I wanna' be high
so high
I wanna' be free to know the things I do are right
I wanna' be free
just me
Oh baby...
that's why I'm easy
I'm easy like Sunday morning
that's why I'm easy
I'm easy like Sunday morning...

Yes, music. I could not live without it, my best ideas were born and grown being inspired by it. Even the concentration, which for me was important, I could find it only replacing the silence surrounding me in moments of solitude with the notes of my favourite music.

This was one of those moments.

I was very exhausted, both mentally and physically, but I wasn't sleepy. I stood in front of the mirror, looking at myself. After taking off shirt and trousers, I balled them up and threw them into the clothes hamper.

Score, on the first shot.

Since I had lost lots of kilos, I rediscovered the pleasure of looking at me in the mirror, and I did it quite often. Of course I admit that it was an attitude a little bit cocky, but I was not ashamed of it for the simple fact that, to me, that physical change was so radical, it was a real achievement, with efforts and sacrifices.

In short, I was proud of it.

After I brushed my teeth, I took two steps and stretched my arm to open the shower water. Unconsciously, my eyes fell on the scar I did with Maggie. It was pretty thick, about four centimetres long, and it used to become more evident when sunbathing. Looking at it, it did not always remind me the way I got it.

Time passing, you get used to it, as you get used to a tattoo: during the first months you look at it on every occasion, then more and more rarely, until you just ignore it.

The signs on our bodies become part of us, it's inevitable. That morning, however, that memory came back strongly to my mind, resurrecting parts of my memory that I believed dead and buried.

Moreover, questions were multiplying constantly, instigated by the incredible sequence of the events of the last hours. As Maggie was dead, who was on the phone? Who was the guy with glasses? Why Nowitzki was keeping a file on my grandfather in his bag? Who was on the phone, half an hour ago?

But, above all, as Veronica pointed out rightly, was it really a coincidence the fact that Arianna Huffington's article appeared today, compatible with all this mess?

That article, moreover, aimed to emphasize my membership and that of my family to Skull and Bones, drawing a parallel with Bush. In short, politics and power, that is the perfect mix for a story able to fill pages of newspapers and excite readers for months, even years.

From now on, Skull and Bones would be an indelible mark for me, for the rest of my days.

It's part of the game, Alex. I thought to myself

Of course, when you decide to become a public personality, one must take the fact in account, that his privacy can be sieved, and this is right.

I was unnerved by what was revolving around that story, which, minute by minute, was enriched with new pieces. The problem was that they all seemed to come from different boxes and that, therefore, they did not wedge one in another.

Those thoughts moved so fast in front of my eyes, that I didn't realize that, in the meantime, the steam from the shadow had fogged up mirror and windows, a sign meaning that I was there stock-still since several minutes.

I opened the window to let some air in, I took off my pants and went under the stream of hot water. Ah, how wonderful! I thought with relief, while water was flowing on my shoulders and the rest of my back, that, when I'm stressed, it's literally devastated by contractures. During those few minutes I tried not to think, but I was unable to.

Once I finished, I rolled up the towel around my waist and began to comb my hair in front of the mirror that, in the meantime, had returned to reflect my image. Suddenly, the door opened, and Veronica came in, giving me the phone.

«Sorry, I thought you were ready!», she exclaimed showing a little bit of embarrassment.

«Your phone kept on ringing, how come it took you so long?», she asked.

«I was away thinking, it often happens when I'm in the shower», I told her.

She half smiled to me and she leaned on the cabinet that was beside the washbasin. For some moments, I was bewildered by the delicious aroma coming from her long hair just washed.

«Do you often dream?», she asked me, out of the blue.

«I've always dreamt a lot, since I was a child. Even with open eyes. Why this question?»

«Well, because I also dream a lot, and I believe that in certain circumstances all the answers we seek are hidden just in what we dream…»

«I'm also convinced about that, you know? And I'd love to be able to fall asleep to make a dream that can help me to figure out what the hell is going on. But in this case I can not really find the heart of this matter.»

«Neither do I, but we'll find it soon, you'll see.»

There was a special atmosphere, we could not stop looking at each other. No, it was not a simple physical attraction, what I felt when I was with her, it was a sort of positive vibrations, as if there was an affinity between us going beyond, able to dilate the few hours spent together since we met, it seemed to be years or even centuries.

I was perfectly at my ease, with her.

Moments, split seconds.

I could not move away her blue eyes on me, and so she with mine.

Suddenly I felt the overwhelming need, I would say visceral, to hug her and kiss her. In such a situation, for the first time I had no doubts, I just wanted it.

Strong and strange feeling, that I had never experienced before in my life.

One step, one step was the exact distance between us.

I did it, I seized her hips and she seized mine.

We were eyes to eyes.

That was the moment.

But at that moment, the ringing of my phone woke us from that lucid dream making us come back abruptly into reality.

We watched the screen, it was Nowitzki.

«Reply, why do you wait? He phoned you also some minutes ago, it must be something important!», she said, hanging it to me.

I agreed and replied immediately.

«Hallo Carl, here I am!», I exclaimed.

«Damn, boy, it's more than half an hour I'm trying to talk to you, what happened to you? Listen, I have important news, but we can't wait until three o'clock before meeting. Come here in an hour.», he said, whereupon he hung up immediately, without giving me time to say «Okay».

«So what?», Veronica asked me.

«He said he has important news, and that he's waiting for us in an hour, at FBI. Of course he did not reveal anything in advance...», I told her.

«As expected. Come on, dress yourself, we have to hurry up!», she said, going out from the bathroom in a rush. Evidently, also Veronica could not wait, as me: what are the so important news to push a FBI bigwig as Nowitzki to ask us to rush to him? I had not the faintest idea about it, but in my heart, I was hoping it was something positive, able to put an end to this story, or to clarify it at least. I went into my room, opened the wardrobe and, without even looking, I took out the first shirt and trousers within my arm's reach.

I was ready in less than a minute. I went into the bathroom to take my phone, and I reached Veronica, who was looking nervously at the clock, in front of the entrance door.

We had to hurry, considered that ten minutes had already passed since the phone call and to reach the FBI headquarters, on Wilshire Boulevard, at that time it would take us forty minutes at least.

In the best case. Once outside we got in my car, we crossed San Pedro and took the lane on Harbour, the long straight road that would have taken us to destination, in the heart of Los Angeles, Beverly Hill. Thank God, the traffic was pretty fluent, without hitches we would be on time.

For some moments we were both silent, a lapse of time in which I thought about what Nowitzki would have told us little later, but also I thought about our "near-kiss" and the extraordinary intensity of that moment.

Maybe she's thinking the same thing, I wondered.

I looked at her for a moment, and I saw she was watching outside the window.

«Hey Veronica...», I whispered her.

«Yes, sorry, I was lost in my thoughts. I was trying to line up all the events and give a logical sense, in order to understand. It's something we do often, we journalists...», she said, leaning her head on her hand.

«I've also tried before, when I was in the shower, but at this point I think only Nowitzki can provide us the missing elements, now it's a matter of minutes, and we'll know everything, I hope so... also because I have had enough of this entire situation!», I said.

We were at the height of Huntington Park, we would arrive in a quarter of an hour. In the rush I forgot to wear my watch and, just when I took the phone to see what time it was, it began to ring, it was Matt.

I replied immediately.

«Hallo Matt! I had a hitc...», he stopped me right away.

He must be bothered by my behaviour and he was right, since he was unaware of what was happening.

«Hitch my arse! Where the hell are you? Here there are more than fifty people waiting for you. Voters, do you remember? No, you don't, because according to your behaviour it seems that you've forgotten you are in the middle of the election campaign, what the fuck!», He was really beside himself, in more than thirty years it happened only once or twice he was so angry.

Once, when I forced him to give up a surf contest to take me to a convention of Republicans which, at the end, was absolutely useless; and then in 2008, when Lakers lost NBA championship, which was missing for the last six years, against the hated rival Celtics.

«Listen, you're right, but in the last hours some things have happened with regard to the story of Maggie. I can not tell you anything more by phone, this afternoon I will explain you. In the meanwhile offer my excuses to those people, and tell them I'll wait for them all at the closing dinner of the election campaign. I care for you, brother!», I told him, trying to calm him down.

«Okay, don't worry, I'll take care of everything here. Hey Veronica, are you there with him?», he asked, having understood we were using the speakerphone. «Hi Matt, yes I'm here...», she promptly answered.

«Whatever it may be, stay with him... Alex is a dickhead, but I care for him, pretty please!», he said, trying to diffuse the tension, which had become quite heavy.

«Don't worry Matt, I'll do my best!», Veronica said.

«Now I have say goodbye, we're almost there, see you later!», I said, hanging up.

We had just entered into La Ciniega, which meant that after a few meters we would have to turn right and take Wilshire. After a while, on the right we saw the squared big building in which were FBI offices.

«Here it is, that's it», Veronica said.

Since I never had the opportunity to go there, I had no idea where to park and where the entrance was, and so, after about fifty meters, I slowed down and took the right lane, receiving also some horn blares from the cars behind me.

After passing the intersection for Sacramento, we saw from the opposite direction to ours, the guy with glasses of the other night walking along.

We were shocked.

Veronica stuck her head out the window, and I looked in the rear-view mirror.

«It was him, I'm sure! And I bet he was coming from FBI...», Veronica exclaimed nervously.

Seeing that man coming from there, where we were about to go, plunged myself into a deep feeling of discomfort. I was sweating cold, and I had a very bad presentiment.

No, it could not be a coincidence! I thought to myself.

«It's baffling, what was he doing there?», I asked her.

In the meanwhile I passed the traffic light and turned right, alongside the building.

«God willing, we'll know it soon. Hey, what the hell...», once near the entrance, we were both speechless.

Again.

Under FBI headquarters, there were four police cars with flashing lights and an ambulance came at great speed with sirens wailing, from which came out doctors and nurses who, with stretch and their equipment, ran towards to the front door.

In the meanwhile, some policemen were delimiting the area with yellow and black tape, while others had formed a crowd and were speaking in an agitated manner with two men looking quite classy, both in dark suits.

In the air there was a great tension, something serious must have happened.

Veronica and I, we looked at each other, stunned.

As soon as I reached the parking barrier, I lowered the window and told the agent we had an appointment with Inspector Nowitzki and gave him our documents. After having taken a look at our personal details, he brought the transceiver to his mouth and turned his back to us. It was obvious he didn't want us to listen.

After a while, and after having given us back our car licenses, he raised the barrier and let us go.

«Park there, Agent Ortega is waiting for you at the entrance, he will take care of you and will take you to the Inspector.» he said, pointing with his hand the colonnade near the main entrance.

«Alex, I'm sorry to tell you that I have a bad feeling…», Veronica whispered to me while I raised the window and stepped on the gas.

«Wouldn't you know, I was thinking exactly the same thing. I hope with all my heart that Nowitzki has some good news…», I said, while I was manoeuvring in order to park.

Once out of the car, we walked towards the entrance where there was a Hispanic man in his forties, waiting for us.

«Mr. Anderson?», he asked.

I nodded with my head.

«I'm pleased to meet you, I'm Agent Ortega. Please, follow me, I'll show you the way.», he said using a very friendly tone.

We bent to pass under the tape that had just been placed by policemen, and followed him. In the lobby, we could not help to notice that there were moments of great confusion. The echo of all those people talking nervously to each other and of mobile phones ringing, resounded from one side to another of that room.

«Agent, what happened?», Veronica asked Ortega.

«Nothing that I am authorized to tell you, Mrs. Hayes», he replied coldly.

We got into an elevator, and Ortega pressed the button of the twenty-third floor. As soon as the door closed in front of us, we looked each other in the eyes. That silence was heavy but, luckily, the elevator ride lasted only the time to give us some other glances, and the sound of the bell indicating the arrival at destination, was providential.

Finally we would have met Nowitzki, I thought with relief. Beforehand, I had never wanted to meet someone so much. We walked down a long corridor, at the end of which there was a large meeting room.

«Take a seat. Inspector will join you shortly. Would you like to have something? Maybe water or coffee?», Ortega said in his gentle but detached manner.

«No, thank you.», we both replied.

Once alone, Veronica put her hand into her bag and took out her phone.

«I want to see if internet says what happened», she said.

«I have some doubts, however, try…», I replied.

After a couple of minutes, she had to agree with me, there was nothing on the most important websites. Pretty strange, since, whatever it was, it was happening in the headquarters of FBI, which is not exactly the most remote corner of the city.

Suddenly, we heard that someone was about to open the door. Nowitzki, I thought.

But it was Ortega and two other men.

The first one could be more or less the same age as Ortega, while the second one, whom I thought was a familiar face, must have been about sixty-five years.

«Sirs, I introduce you to Agent Richardson and Frank Da Silva, head of the counter-terrorism division of the National Security Branch», Ortega said.

«Please Sirs, sit down», Da Silva added, he was the oldest among the three.

That's why it seemed to me to know him, certainly I must have seen him in Washington.

«The pleasure is mine. I don't want to be rude, but given the circumstances, I'm sure you will understand the apprehension on my side and that of Mrs. Hayes. Honestly, I want to know about your presence, since our appointment was with Inspector Nowitzki...», I said, ignoring the customary pleasantries.

After a quick glance at each other, Da Silva stopped Ortega with a wave of his hand, and began to speak

«Inspector Nowitzki died forty minutes ago in his office. Apparently it's a suicide, Mr. Anderson. And, according to our information, you are the last person with whom he talked on the phone, that's the reason for our presence. As you can easily imagine, we would have done without».

12

Nothing happens by chance

Everything seems chaotic, except our mess.
NICÓLAS GÓMEZ DÁVILA

I watched Da Silva's lips articulating those words, that kept on echoing in my mind as if they were repeated in slow motion.

«Inspector Nowitzki died».

Then, in my ears, a drone.

I looked down, I looked at my hands, and I realized they were so soaking wet as to have left my footprints surrounded by a white halo on the glass surface of the table.

Again I looked at Da Silva, then Ortega, Richardson and, finally, Veronica.

«Mr. Anderson, are you sure you're feeling good?», the latter asked me.

«If I say yes, I'd lie to you, Inspector Da Silva…», I replied, with just a whisper, after swallowing with difficulty.

«I understand this news has shocked you, as it has all of us, after all. I worked with Nowitzki for over thirty years, it's a life. As I know him, I find hard to believe he has killed himself, and believe me, I'll find out who's underneath this story, even if it's the last thing I do! Now, according to the information we have collected, it's clear that also you and Mrs. Hayes are risking very seriously, therefore from now on you will be under our close protection: Mr. Anderson, you're the key to solve this case, we must not waste even a moment; there is much more at stake than we can imagine.», Da Silva said, with excited tone.

I was in the middle of something bigger than me, and I had no idea on how to get out of it.

«Listen, since I've been elected to Congress, I have always carried my political activity acting openly, never giving in to logics of interest that were not linked with our Nation...», I tried to argue.

«Maybe that's the problem, Mr. Anderson, maybe in these two years you have antagonized too much enemies, have you ever thought about it?», Ortega said.

«I don't believe so, Inspector Ortega, and anyway I have always acted in good faith», I replied bitterly.

«What we have to do now is to dig, to dig in your past and present relations in order to find the elements that can bring us to close this case. There is already a dead, Mr. Anderson and, even if you don't want to accept it, you are in the sights of these people; you are not only an ordinary citizen, but also one of the politicians of larger perspective in our country, at least according to what has been written this morning on an influential blog as Huffington Post. It can't be a coincidence what is happening to you, do you understand it, don't you?», Da Silva asked me.

He was right, it could not be a coincidence, of course.

But, anyway, I could not find the connection between me and these people.

Calm down, Alex, and think, trying to analyze every detail, I thought to myself.

«I'm aware this is all illogical, but I just don't understand why all this is happening to me, nor who these people are. At this point you have to help me, maybe telling me what Nowitzki had discovered before... yes, well, before he committed suicide.», I said, pausing on the look of Da Silva, who did not hesitate, not even a moment, to answer me back.

«Until proven otherwise, here I'm the only one who can decide what to tell or not, Mr. Anderson, is it clear? Therefore, first of all, you and Mrs. Hayes, have to tell us everything. And when I say everything, I mean every detail, including the most insignificant one. Come on, we're all ears».

And so it was that Veronica and I, we told word for word the odyssey we had experienced in the last twenty-four hours, starting with the phone calls I received from Maggie Jones, or whoever she was, my meetings with Nowitzki, and ending with the guy with glasses, that we saw just before arriving at FBI headquarters.

I told them what Nowitzki discovered about Maggie Jones who, in reality, had died several years ago, and I showed them the messages I received the night before on my Twitter account, in which the real or imaginary Maggie told me we would have to meet "before it's too late".

Yes, but for what? And above all, if I had accepted it, who would come to that meeting? I kept on wondering.

Veronica added some details about the physical aspect of that man «white, could be sixty-five, one meter and eighty-five tall, and a slender body. Very smart, you could see he was wearing brand clothes, and wore very thick-rimmed glasses, as used in the eighties».

Then the van.

«Were you able to read the number plate?», Richardson asked, speaking for the first time.

«Honestly, at that moment I was so agitated that I have not even thought about it…», I answered.

«However I was able, well, not all, but I was impressed by the three final numbers, because they are the same as the final sequence of my old phone number: 424. They were preceded by three letters, I think one was a B, but I'm not sure. That van arrived and left at full speed.», Veronica added.

«Good, it's little, but that's something. Ortega, make a search of all number plates ending with that numerical sequence and containing the letter B. If we are lucky, knowing it's a black van, we should be able to trace its owners. You, Richardson, go immediately down to Landis's office and tell him to make instantly an identikit of that guy. If he should kick up a fuss, tell him on my behalf that it's the right time he gets a report. Mr. Anderson, I need your passwords to access to your Twitter account, so that we can verify the source of those messages and check them with the source of the phone calls. In the meantime, I will assign you two men, so that they can come with you to your electoral meetings and then take you back here, let's say, in three hours. One last thing: Mrs. Hayes, needless to say this story must remain among us, have I explained that clearly?», Veronica and I, we could only nod in silence, in front of the resoluteness of Da

Silva, who was demonstrating how he came to have such a delicate role.

When we crossed the threshold of the office door, Veronica held my arm hugging me.

That gesture surprised me but, at the same time, it helped to loosen my tension.

Da Silva took briskly the corridor leading to the office and told Ortega and Richardson to take us to their colleagues who should have to protect us. On our way back on the elevator, there was less tension than before, certainly due to the fact that now we had some more elements to work on.

Once we left the elevator, we noticed that everything in the entrance hall was back to normal. There was no ambulance, no police cars with flashing lights, no people in agitation. In front of such calm scenery, no one could have imagined that, just two hours ago, in that same place has reigned chaos.

Needless to say we are at FBI, I thought, exchanging a meaningful look with Veronica who, for sure, was thinking the same thing.

We followed Ortega and Richardson, who took us outside the building, up to my car, where we immediately met a man and a woman. They had to be our guardian angels.

«Without any pleasantries, I introduce you to Agents Scott and Rice, who were chosen by Inspector Da Silva for your personal safety. For every transfer, you are obliged to refer to them, they will have the power to give you directives that you must follow, no ifs, ands or buts. See you later.», Ortega said.

Veronica and I, we introduced ourselves immediately.

Agent Tina Scott was a woman in her forties, good looking but seemingly glacial. Tall, brown hair, dressed in a pinstripe suite, very formal. Rice, on the other hand, was an Afro-American with a much more human look than that of his colleague, to the point that, while shaking our hands, he let go a hint of a shy smile.

He wore a grey suit and, at a guess, must be our age.

«Mr. Anderson, we will follow you with our unmarked car, which is the grey Chrysler parked over there. Here is a secure mobile, on which we'll call you whenever we needed it.

Once you reach your destination, try to behave as if nothing has happened. It may occur that you don't see us, but be sure that we shall see you and anyone approaching you. Is everything clear?», Scott said, without showing the slightest emotion.

«Okay, everything's clear, then let's go, we have to go to San Pedro, the headquarters of my election committee, where we will find some people waiting for us. What if I don't see you any more in the rear-mirror?», I asked.

«Start to worry, Mr. Anderson.», Rice said promptly, not allowing us to understand if it was a macabre joke or not.

«Do you think they are listening to what we say?», Veronica asked me, as soon as we closed the car door.

«I think it's very likely, but the point is another: listening on us are the good guys or the bad guys?», I asked her.

«Right now we can expect everything, what about lowering the roof?», she replied.

«Good idea, today is a wonderful day!», I said, winking at her.

After lowering the roof, I also turned on the radio, and I pumped up the volume so that, if someone wanted to listen to us, at least should have a hard time. I shifted into reverse and drove towards the exit, where we found the same agent of some hours ago who, as soon as he saw us coming, promptly raised the barrier, making a sign with his hand to pass.

We drove around the block and I kept on staring at the rear-view mirror in order to be sure that the grey Chrysler with Scott and Rice was behind us, until we took the Harbour.

«Now try to relax, Alex, it's their job, do you think they have difficulty to follow you through the traffic? Rather tell me, what do you think what happened to Nowitzki? According to what Da Silva told us, he must have died more or less twenty minutes after he phoned you. On my side I would not even bet a dollar on the hypothesis of suicide. As I think none of us in that room, even more so after having told them we saw the guy with glasses going away just when we were arriving. It can not be a coincidence!», Veronica stated, while she was busy looking for a radio station from which we could hear the latest news.

«Coincidence? How about that. Da Silva is right, Nowitzki was definitely not the kind of person to kill himself, moreover, on the phone he had plenty of energy, evidently he must have discovered something important about Maggie and that guy with glasses about whom he wanted to warn us, otherwise such a tragedy can not be explained, moreover in the headquarters of FBI, one of the safest places in the world. No, Veronica, what most worries me is that, whoever he is and whatever he wants, certainly he's not a common criminal, in fact Washington has assigned the case to Da Silva, who is the head of counter-terrorism unit. I would pay gold to know what Nowitzki had discovered and why this morning he had a folder on my grandfather in his bag...», I told her.

«Well, Alex, don't play dumb, it's clear that the first thing that catches the eye is that you all belong to that sect... hum, secret society, Skull and Bones, that is also, not coincidentally, the detail on which Huffington focused her article on you. As it is said, three clues make one proof, don't you believe so?», Veronica asked me. Pointless to deny that her question so allusive, if not rhetoric, annoyed me, and also a lot.

«What do you mean by saying so?», I asked her, at first blush.

«Damn, Alex, why are you keeping on pretending not to understand? I mean that Skull and Bones is not exactly the Sunday club, but it's a secret society from which came out some of the most powerful men in America and among them, strangely enough, none of them wants to talk. Including you. It's normal that the public opinion is making some questions, don't you think so? Today a person has died, and still you insist on not wanting to speak about this argument, it's incredible!», Veronica said, raising her voice and pointing the finger of her right hand toward me.

Of course, I understood that the argument could tickle the interest of journalists and public opinion, it was a succulent morsel for them. But I never wanted to break the oath which I made before my father, never ever.

Furthermore, I could not see the slightest utility, considering that there was no connection between Skull and Bones and what was happening.

I took my right hand from the steering wheel and I grabbed Veronica's hand. My gesture was meant to be conciliatory, in order to calm her down and to reason with her.

«Listen, Veronica, I understand that the aura of mystery around it contributes to the proliferation of urban legends, but I guarantee you, and please do believe me, if I were touched only by the slightest suspicion that Skull and Bones have something to do with it, well, I would not hesitate to talk about it. Think about it, Veronica, the facts say that neither Maggie nor that guy, have nothing to do with the secret society I attended when I was a student at Yale. That's it. Everything else are suggestions, nothing more!», I said with decision.

«Suggestions, eh? I really hope you're right, Mr. Anderson.», she cut short, turning towards the window.

Say what you say but give me that bomb beat from Dre
Let me serenade the streets of LA
From Oakland to Sac-town, the Bay Area and back down
Cali is where they put they mack down, give me love

California knows how to party
California knows how to party
In the city of LA
In the city of good ol' Watts
In the city, the city of Compton
We keep it rocking, we keep it rocking

«Wow, what a musical piece...», after ten minutes, Veronica broke her silence, and turned the volume up further. She was right. Years were passing, but that song by 2Pac seemed to have been released the day before, it was an absolute masterpiece, which had a very special flavour for us Californians.

«I also love it, it seems to me yesterday when I heard it on the radio for the first time, but eighteen years have already passed, it's incredible!», I told her.

«Yeah, sometimes I think songs are made to travel through time, you know? Just take one, get on board, close your eyes for some moments and... poof! You find yourself back in time of ten or twenty years...», Veronica said, with a hint of melancholy.

«However, then they finish, and you find yourself thrown into the present, which is not a bad thing, in my opinion.», I replied, trying to say, between the lines, that despite everything, I liked my present, because I was there with her.

«It's not bad for those who are having good time, but for whose who have the misfortune to live on memories and have stopped dreaming.», she said.

«Well, I have so many dreams, and I keep them in a closet crammed full of desires!», I said, cracking a smile.

«This is nice. I don't know why, but it's not absolutely hard to image the desire that occupies the first place in your list, Alex.», she replied.

«Ah yes? And what would it be?», I asked her.

«Well, to solve this damn situation, it's obvious.», she said, with a tone of determination.

I could not say she was wrong, indeed, but let's say that, in addition to that, my desire was also to know her more and more.

I liked Veronica, and, in all probability, the fact that I was living that adventure with her, was amplifying the bond that was gradually forming between us.

In any case, it was not certain the right moment to broach such conversation with her, also because the priorities we had to face were very different.

After ten minutes we should have reached San Pedro, where, along with Matt, I would find dozens and dozens of people whom I should pay heed to, which it wasn't easy, given my mood.

Life goes on, Alex, and this is one of the crucial moments for your career, try not to be influenced by what is happening and do your best to win the election! I thought.

For sure it was not easy, but I had to succeed in it absolutely, also because not doing so it would have meant throwing away a whole life spent in pursue of that goal. Moreover right now, when even the national media were becoming aware of me. It would have been a real prank!

Suddenly, my thoughts were rudely interrupted by the sound coming from my phone.

I had received a notification.

During a whole day, I used to receive dozens of notifications, it happened when I received a new mail or when someone was interacting with one of my profiles on social networks.

«Veronica, please, look who is it?», I asked, passing her my phone.

«Yes, give it to me, I read it, you drive.», she said, while unlocking the display.

«It's a Twitter notification, wait, I open and read it.», she said, after a while.

Then, twenty, thirty seconds.

Not a single word.

Veronica's eyes were glued to my phone, without saying anything.

«So, are you going to tell me what it is?», I asked nervously.

I was restless.

She turned to me, staring at me with a look on her face that meant nothing good.

«It's still her, Maggie…», she said laconically.

Her words had the same effect on me as a punch in the face from Mike Tyson.

I was stunned.

I grabbed the phone with my right hand, and I looked down to read that message.

Alex, you're in danger.

«What the hell do I reply?», I asked Veronica.

«Let's phone Da Silva and ask him. Come on, give me the phone that Scott gave you!», she exclaimed.

I stretched out my left hand, and I began to open the glove compartment of the car door.

Here it is!

I gave it immediately to Veronica, who searched the number and immediately pressed the green button to start the phone call.

«Hallo, Inspector Da Silva, it's me, Veronica Hayes, do you hear me?», by sheer coincidence, just at that moment, something told me that I had to look in the rear-view mirror.

I had just the time to look up, and I saw the black van and… boom!

It banged my car at full speed, trying to push us out of the road. Still I did not realize fully what was happening, but I managed to keep control of my car.

«Hey, are you fine?», I asked Veronica, who was busy looking for the phone, which had slipped out of her hand because of the impact of a moment before.

«Yes, yes, I'm fine, don't think about me, keep your eyes on the road!», she exclaimed. I gave another look in the mirror, that damn van was still behind us, in spite of the grey Chrysler with Rice and Scott. Vanished.

At that time, traffic on the Harbour was beginning to be pretty intense: thousands of cars were clogging that long straight road being very careful not to exceed the limit of fifty-five miles per hour.

All, except us and the van chasing us. While driving, I tried to isolate myself from everything else in order to stay focused.

The honking cars I passed going zigzag and, above all, the black van glued to my bumper: I had to pretend they didn't exist. No, I would not give it even a centimetre. Suddenly, after a few meters, we found no cars.

I looked at the mirror and realized that the van was gone.

«Here it is!», Veronica screamed.

I turned immediately to my window, and I saw it right next to us but, because of the darkened windows, we could not even see who was driving.

Damn, this is the end! I thought, closing my eyes for a split second.

I opened them and I saw that the van, instead of shooting at us or throwing us off the road, had accelerated, overtaking us at full speed and getting lost in the horizon in a matter of seconds.

Veronica and I, we turned and looked at each other, without being able to utter a single word.

We were incredulous, to say the least.

«What the fuc...», that curse of mine was immediately interrupted by the FBI phone, which began to ring.

«Hallo, Inspector!», I replied immediately.

«Thank goodness! Alex, it's me, Da Silva, are you okay?», he asked me, implying that he was aware of what had just happened.

«Yes, we're safe and sound, but we lost Scott and Rice.», I told him.

«I know, they were blocked about three miles before you, those damn guys shot their tires. Take the first exit and go back at the intersection with the Pacific, you'll find two police cars waiting for you, they will escort you up to here. See you in a while».

13

Under control

Who controls the past controls the future.
Who controls the present controls the past.
GEORGE ORWELL

FBI headquarters
about half an hour later

«THUS sirs, I think it's clear to everyone that we are in front of a proper warning. I say warning because, if they only wanted to, they would have taken less than a second to shoot you all down. Therefore, from this moment on, we change tactic. I have several reasons to think that the time at our disposal is very little, so we will have to find them, whoever they are. About forty-five minutes ago, Alex Anderson received another message in which the alleged Maggie Jones, besides asking him to meet immediately, said explicitly that the people close to him, that is Veronica Hayes and Matt Payne, are in danger. Mr. Payne is already on board on one of our cars, and will join us in a few minutes. Now, what we have to do, is to organize a meeting between Alex Anderson and this mysterious Maggie Jones, hoping that on that occasion we will be able to find out who is behind this whole story. Alex, are you sure to do it? Of course you will not be alone.», Da Silva asked me.

«Of course... of course I agree, I'm willing to do anything as to put an end to it.», I replied with a confidential tone, without hesitation.

In that office, besides him and me, there were also Veronica, Ortega, Richardson, Rice and Scott, who listened impassively to the words of their chief.

«Good, this is just what my ears wanted to hear. Take your phone and reply that message, asking time and place for the meeting».

I took my iPhone out from my pocket, I went on Twitter, and I saw that in the meanwhile Maggie had sent me another message, which contained only three ellipsis that, in the slang of the Web, meant that she was waiting for my reply.

> *Here I am Maggie, sorry.*
> *Where and at what time?*

After I pressed the send button, I raised my head and saw that all eyes were focused on my phone. We did not hear a pin drop, waiting for Maggie's answer raised the tension second by second.

Good riddance, where have you been?

> *Let's say I had some problems with traffic…*

Two hours from now,
at the end of San Pedro harbour.

> *Okay Maggie, I'll be there.*

Ah, one thing.

> *Yes, I'm here.*

Tell your FBI friends
there with you, not to make bullshit,
because they would worsen the situation.
I want to help you, the bad guys are the others.

> *Ok. Listen Maggie,*
> *who would be the bad guys?*

One hour and fifty-seven
minutes, Alex. See you later.

> *See you later.*

I had not even time to count to three, that Da Silva immediately got back to the argument.

«Good, because we have an appointment. Bad, because in all probability among us there is a mole. Whoever he is, we are going to flush him out, and I'll have the personal satisfaction to make him spend a couple of hours in hell. That damn traitor will have to beg me to send him to prison, I swear by God! Ortega and Richardson, take the men of your unit and run to guard the south side of the harbour. You, Scott and Rice, will accompany me and Mrs. Hayes, in the meanwhile go to retrieve another car. Alex and Veronica, follow me».

We got up immediately and followed Da Silva out of the office, along the corridor. Although his size was quite impressive, we had difficulty to keep up with his brisk pace.

We passed the atrium of the elevators, and arrived in front of a security door, which Da Silva opened passing his badge in the card reader which was placed on the wall, at the height of the handle.

«This way, let's go!», he said, turning to us for a moment. We went down by foot six flights of a fire escape, and we found ourselves in front of another door, which the Inspector opened again with his magnetic card.

We came out to another corridor.

That place, apparently, reminded very closely to a hospital: white walls, polished floor and, in the air, a strong smell of detergent. Without any particular reason, I always felt uncomfortable in hospitals. We turned once to the right, then to the left, and we entered into another long corridor, at the end of which there was a large door to push.

Da Silva opened and held it with one arm, made us a signal to enter and followed us. We were on a freight elevator. As soon as the door closed completely, Da Silva pushed the -2 button.

«Ready to see the belly of FBI?», he said, cracking a smile, trying evidently to calm the tension.

«What is it, Inspector?», I asked him, while walls and doors were alternating in front of us.

«Wait and you'll see.», he replied.

After a moment, the light panel on which all floors were reported, brightened the inscription of -2, we had arrived.

Da Silva leaned his shoulder to the metal door to open it, and we found ourselves in a huge open space fully painted in green where, moreover, it was very cold.

«Cold, isn't it? Down here, there will be 15 degrees, more or less!», Da Silva exclaimed. The echo of his words bounced from wall to wall of that huge rectangle of concrete, which we crossed completely, until we reached another alarmed door.

«This is the last one», Inspector said, while the white light and the metal beeping testified that his badge was authorized to open it.

We were in a sort of antechamber where, on the right, there was a desk, and behind it there was an entire wall full of safety deposit boxes, similar to those that are in the banks. To welcome us, we found a small man, in his sixties, who immediately hugged Da Silva.

«Frank, I've heard about Nowitzki...», both had tears in their eyes, and it was clear they were in great confidence.

«We're here for this reason, Bill.», he told him.

«I thought so. Whoever those sons of a bitch are, get back at them, Frank!», Bill exclaimed, with emotion in his voice.

«You can bet my friend, you can bet...», Da Silva comforted him with affectionate tone, giving him a few pats on his shoulder.

«Come on, now let us in, we don't have a minute to lose!», Inspector said. From his white shirt, Bill took out his badge, kept in a sling, he inserted it into the card reader near the door, then put his right index finger on a small liquid crystal panel and...beep. The door opened.

«Sirs, welcome into the "Sheriff of America"!», Da Silva exclaimed, showing off some pride.

As soon as we entered, both Veronica and I, we remained literally stunned, speechless.

We had not even time to look each other into our eyes, that the door through which we had entered closed behind us. Da

Silva was right, the place where we had arrived, was the FBI belly, indeed, at a closer look, it was the real FBI.

In fact, our descent into the hell of the Californian headquarters, had takes us in what, at first glance, seemed to be a headquarters into the headquarters.

«What you have in front of your eyes, is the true operation headquarters: over six hundred people work here, round the clock, three hundred sixty-five days a year. In these offices we sift out, in real time, all kind of information that could even remotely be linked to the interest and safety of our Nation. Phone calls, e-mails, social networks, credit cards, images coming from our satellite camera... everything goes through in what we call filters, which are nothing more than a series of very strict procedures that allow us to know who is doing what, where, why and with whom...», Da Silva explained, who was abruptly interrupted by Veronica.

«Inspector, if I have well understood, you are saying that we are all radiographed to x-rays, aren't we?»

«Broadly speaking, things are in this way, Mrs. Hayes...»

«Don't you think all this is pretty disquieting? And what about you, Alex? Don't tell me that at the Congress you all don't know anything about this whole story! Yes, well, I mean... you all know what we buy when we go to do shopping, the confidences we do on the phone with our best friend, or with whom we go to bed. Is this the great democracy in the world?»

«Mrs. Hayes, if you want to keep a great democracy such as ours, it must have the necessary tools to defend itself from any threat. In my opinion, if this is the price to be paid in order to safe millions of lives, well, it's worthwhile to take it upon our shoulders...»

«Well, I would like to be sure about it as you are, Inspector...»

At that point I decided to intervene, and I took Veronica's forearm.

«Listen Veronica, as a matter of principle I might agree with you, but Inspector is right: a great Nation like ours must do everything to defend itself. It's very easy to judge without knowing all the facts, as you journalists do so often, as well as you forgot easily about September 11. Veronica, that day I was in New York, and I saw with my own eyes what it means to be killed without mercy, like sewer rats. Well, it's good that you know it's thanks to this defence program, from the year two thousand and one up to today, we were able to prevent other catastrophes like that, or maybe even worse, only Gods knows...»

The looks of Veronica and Da Silva locked for some long and silent moments.

«Thank you, Sir.», Inspector told me, mimicking a bow with a small movement of his head.

«What's the reason of your calling me "Sir"?», I asked him, surprised by his sudden deference.

«Because the words you have just spoken, are the words of a true statesman. You deserve all the good that people say about you, Sir.», at first I felt a sense of emotion. Of course, over the years I got used to compliments, especially during the election campaign, or when I had the spotlights on me for some political action of mine. People were in race to shake my hand and tell me that, sooner or later, I would be the best President in the history of the United States of America.

Bullshit.

People have repeated the same empty phrases to who knows how many other politicians.

The sign of respect that I had just received, however, it had a very special taste, because it came from a person as Da Silva who, not surprisingly, was the head of the counter-terrorism unit. In short, a true servant of the Nation.

His blue eyes pointed toward me, made me realize immediately that also Veronica understood the meaning of our exchange of opinions, so that she hadn't nothing more to complain.

«Come on, we have an important appointment, in less than one hour and a half. We've to hurry up!», Da Silva exclaimed, retrieving the grit of few moments before.

We walked along the main corridor that looked like a real labyrinth of desks, computers and LCD screens. The background was a sort of noise that reminded very closely the noises that you can hear in Wall Street, during negotiations.

Phones ringing, people standing up to call the colleague sitting twenty desks away, others who seem to be somewhere else as they are so immersed in what they are reading on the screen of their computers.

We ended our walk entering into a room, where we found a woman waiting for us, she was wearing a white coat, having the appearance of a doctor, or something like that.

«Helen, these are Alex Anderson and Veronica Hayes, you already know everything, right?», Da Silva asked.

«For sure Frank, I prepare them immediately.», she said. «You have twenty minutes, not more, hurry up.», Da Silva said going out from the room.

What the hell are they going to do now? I wondered looking around myself.

In front of us there was a huge LCD monitor, on which, at intervals of about ten seconds, different images were alternating: a busy intersection, a man entering into a phone booth, a Police Officer biting into a hot dog, and so on.

«Mr. Anderson, empty your pockets and take off shirt and trousers, please.», suddenly Helen said, pointing the bed next to her desk.

«What is this, a medical examination? I'm very well…», I told her.

«No medical exams, Sir. As you have heard right now, my job is to prepare yourself for the mission of today, therefore, if you are so kind to do strictly what I'm going to say in the next few minutes, you will avoid unpleasant inconveniences to yourself.», she replied coldly.

Wow, this must be Scott's sister! I thought as I began to unbutton my shirt, and then my trousers.

«Good, put everything on the chair and sit down on the bed.», Helen said while, with one key in the bunch of keys on her desk, opened one of the cupboards that were around the entire perimeter of the room, and took out a long metal box.

After having placed it on the desk, she pressed a code on the alphanumeric keypad that was on the right side, and so that mysterious black box opened, illuminating her face with a pale blue light.

«Don't move, please.», she ordered me, then, with a tweezers, she picked something microscopic from the box. With the other hand she fumbled in the pocket of her lab coat and took out a very small flashlight, that she used to illuminate my right ear.

«Good, don't move...», she whispered, and introduced the tweezers in it.

Whatever it was, that thing was cold, and I felt the exact point where she had placed it. Anyway I managed to stay still.

«Here it is, this is ready. The microphone in your ear will allow you to listen to Da Silva's instructions and be located within two hundred kilometres range.», Helen said, going back to the black box, from which she took out a strange silver bib, and she handed me a tube containing an ointment or something like that.

«Take it, spread it on all your torso», she told me.

«What is it?», I asked, while I was trying to read the microscopic legends printed on the package.

«It's a connective paste, it will help your skin to adhere to perfection with the fibre of the bulletproof vest, as not to interfere with your movements.», she explained, showing me the bib.

«Is that a bulletproof vest? It's thirty millimetres thick more or less!», Veronica exclaimed, she was curious about it.

«Thank God, our research is far more ahead than what you see in Hollywood movies, Mrs. Hayes», Helen answered.

Because of its importance, I tried to spread that slimy paste as evenly as possible, then I took the vest and wore it.

The sensation was very strange, similar to that of a clay mask drying on the skin. I felt stiff.

«Okay, now you can dress yourself, you are ready for your appointment, Mr. Anderson.», Helen said, inviting me to get down of the bed, to give way to Veronica to whom she only installed the microphone in her ear.

«So, are they ready?», Da Silva said, catapulting himself hastily into the room, without even knocking.

«They're both ready, Frank...», Helen answered.

«Damn, it's very late, what are you still doing there? Hurry up, holy smoke!», he screamed, not giving even a look to Helen.

The appointment with Maggie was approaching quickly, and, minute by minute, the tension was devouring our time, becoming increasingly heavier and menacing. We followed Da Silva, who took us to another office.

«Hey Frank, where have you been? I was waiting for you!», said the man who welcomed us wearing a long pair of black gloves, which covered completely both his forearms.

«Alex, Veronica, this crazy man is Josh Spengler, his job is to help us not to make mistakes.», Da Silva stated.

«Well, it's an important task. Josh, don't you fancy to come and work in my staff?», I asked him with a smile.

«I don't think it's the appropriate moment for jokes...», Veronica objected, pinching my arm.

«I'm pleased to meet you, I'm sure you'll forgive me for my speed, but time is a really tyrant...», Josh said, while pressing one of the buttons on the back of his left glove. Darkness.

Lights went out and, simultaneously, the images of the harbour of San Pedro appeared on the walls of the room. Crazy! I thought to myself, opening my eyes widely: it was just like being there, we could even hear background noises.

«Sirs, this is what we have called "Place Machine", a program based on the development of the technology of the so-called augmented reality, that certainly you all know...», Josh said, who, while speaking, controlled the direction of the frame of what we were watching, through the movement of his hands.

«The interesting thing about "Place Machine" is that we can go back in time to see what really happened at a certain time and in a particular place, through images with a definition closer to infinity and, therefore, not fallible.», Da Silva added.

«Amazing. I imagine that this "Place Machine" is part of "Prism"...», I said.

«You imagine well, Alex. Moreover, as your role requires it, you should also know very well that this and other aspects of

"Prism" are covered by the State Secret, for obvious reasons. Ergo, Mrs. Hayes, think that what you are seeing is just a figment of your imagination… got it?», Da Silva told Veronica.

«Received, Inspector.», she said, doing nothing to hide her annoyance.

«Good. Go on Josh, now it's your turn, explain us what we are going to do.», Da Silva exclaimed, pointing to the spot where the meeting would take place. With a slight movement of his hands, Spengler moved the frame, projecting us among the steel containers at the harbour.

«As you can see, this is a rather difficult zone to manage, because without preventive controls, it's virtually impossible to know what all those containers actually contain. For this reason, the greatest danger is ambushes. Another critical problem is the possibility of being attacked by the sea, considering that people with whom we have to do, seem to be professionals. Now, according to what you can see too, the situation is quiet and, in the last two hours, we did not record any suspicious movement. But I say again to be careful, because danger really could be behind the corner.», Josh explained. Veronica and I, we looked at each other, we were afraid.

«Thank you Josh, your job will be very precious. Before you switch off, I want to add another detail, which helps to reassure Alex and Veronica. You see, on the roof of the harbour's offices, there are ten of our sharpshooters: four on the right side, four on the left, and two at the ends. In short, as I told you, you will have your back covered, Alex.», Da Silva said, however failing to reassure me completely.

Lights came on suddenly and, from the harbour of San Pedro, we found ourselves back in an apparently normal office.

The effect was that of teleportation, or something like that.

«I hope I will not need them, and that everything will be resolved quickly. I have had enough of this whole story…», I said.

«Be calm son, tonight you will dedicate yourself again to your electoral campaign, I guarantee it. Now let's go, your Maggie is expecting us!».

14

Adam Jameson

Great feats, usually,
are accomplished through great dangers.
HERODOTUS

ACCORDING to my phone clock, more or less fourteen minutes were missing to my appointment with Maggie. At a rough guess, unless unforeseen events, we would arrive on time. We were driving along the Harbour aboard a gigantic dark blue Lincoln Navigator, not just the kind of car with which you would pass unnoticed; Da Silva was driving, I sat next to him, and Veronica on one of the big rear seats. We were silent for most of the trip, the classic calm before the storm.

Moreover, those moments of apparent calm were useful to do some order among facts and thoughts crowding our minds. Although he was trying not to show any emotion, Inspector Da Silva had to be understandably very shocked by Nowitzki's death who, as I understood, was not just a colleague, but also the friend of a lifetime and the companion of thousand adventures.

In my opinion, as I've heard him on the phone, I did not even take into consideration the possibility of suicide, and I firmly believed that the presence of that guy with glasses was much, much more than just a coincidence.

And then, there was Maggie. Was it really her who I would meet? No, she wasn't, according to the article that Nowitzki made me read. Okay, the body had not been found, but the idea that she was still alive, maybe for some kind of machination, was really hard to believe. Instead, if she was dead, who ever could have the interest to use her name to approach me? In short, even forcing myself, I could not find elements that could reassure me.

In all cases, it was a situation with disquieting details, of which yet I knew little or nothing. I was scared by that dense air of mystery. On the other side, however, I also knew that I could not absolutely let fear overwhelm me, because I would have risked to collapse because of it. Rather, I had to control it, the fear.

It was like when you decide to ride a wave with a surfboard: you have to keep it at bay, take confidence with it, and be sure to «feel it» under your feet, to become one with it, being aware that the slightest distraction would mean to lose balance and be swallowed by the wall of water.

In short, I had to be strong and take head of the situation, because it was not only me to be in danger, but also the people dearest to me and, in all likelihood, a part of our national security. Indeed, whatever was the identity of the people chasing me, they had targeted me as a representative of the Congress of the United States of America and, whatever their goal was, they did not have the slightest hesitation to kill a FBI Inspector to achieve it, moreover circumventing the security measures of one the safest places that should be on the face of the earth.

Deer Island, November 6, 2010

Brothers of mine, brothers of Skull and Bones,
it's an honour for me, in this our festive evening,
to inform you that our Alex Anderson,
Ron's son and Philip's grandson, has been elected
to the House of Representatives of the United States of America,
gaining the District 33 with a clear victory
in the State of California.
To him, who of course is here with us tonight,
I ask you all to give a big applause:

welcome back, Brother Alex Anderson!

«Alex Anderson, now you're a real authority!», Bill Aames told me laughing, and raised his glass of wine, inviting me to toast with him.

We were sitting at the table in the centre of the ballroom, in the chalet where Skull and Bones used to organize, at least twice a year, a big party with all Bonesmen and their families.

It was a convivial meeting, useful to strengthen important relationships, of course, but also and above all it was the occasion to organize meetings about subjects that, for obvious reasons, had to be discussed only personally. Bill was my classmate at Yale, bur our relationship intensified when I also joined Skull and Bones.

Unlike me, perhaps inspired by my grandfather since a kid, I was straight away attracted to politics, Bill has always preferred to stay behind the scenes, attitude that led him to work at CIA.

«Tell me, Bill, which case are you dealing with?», I asked him.

«If I tell you, I would be a very bad CIA agent, don't you think so?», he replied.

As the kind of work he had chosen had always fascinated me very much, every time we met, I always tried to make him tell me something.

«Come on, Bill, I am a representative of the Congress...», I insisted.

«Now let's go and have dinner, maybe later we'll have occasion to talk about it.», he said, looking around, making me understand that he would rather talk about it when we were alone.

At some point, someone touched my shoulder, I turned and saw it was Adam Jameson, notoriously one of the most influential men in the United States: collaborator of Bush Senior and Dick Cheney, he was at the head of CIA for over seven years, since 2001.

«Alex, may I have the honour to greet you?», he asked
me with a smile. Immediately I stood up and, to my
astonishment, Adam hugged me strongly.

«Mr. Jameson, the honour is mine, are you cheating?», I
exclaimed.

«You gentlemen don't be disappointed if a steal the guest
of honour for a few moments...», Adam said, addressing the
people at my table, then took my harm and led me outside, under
the entrance porch.

We were practically on the river bank, and that damp cold
had immediately penetrated into my bones.

«Do you know for what I'm sorry, Alex? That your
grandfather Philip is not here with us tonight. He would be proud
of you.», he said.

«I'm also sorry for this, Mr. Jameson, and very much. I
have thought about him so often during these days, but I like to
believe that somehow he sees and knows.»

«Oh, no doubt about it. Good old Philip not only sees and
knows, but also provides, as he has always done, after all. With
your election, you will have the opportunity to follow in his
steps, carrying on the family tradition and, more importantly,
making the interests of your country. This is the greatest, but at
the same time the most burdensome responsibility that a man can
bear. You see Alex, your grandfather and I, we were classmates
at Yale, we decided together to marry the noble cause of Skull
and Bones and then, although with different roles, we have both
contributed to the maintenance of peace and well-being of the
American people.»

«I know it, Sir, that's why I admire you both, and you
have been and will always be my example. I will do everything
as I possibly can, in order to be worthy of such a difficult task.»

«And you will be worthy. What I mean to tell you tonight
is that, this is only the first stage of the path we all have
imagined for you, Alex.»

«Path? What do you mean?»

«I mean that your grandfather Philip, your father Ron and
I, along with all the other Brothers of Skull and Bones, we have
always worked at trying to put before our eyes a more distant

horizon, than ours. This is the kind of approach that allows to lay solid foundations for the future, in the name of the ideal continuity. A sort of life insurance. People wonder why from Skull and Bones come out presidents, statesmen, and high-level businessmen. This is one of the reason, I mean the principle of continuity, of foresight. Think about it, Alex, in a world like today, a country like ours would literally be in disarray, with no reference points, and so we are!»

«I'm also convinced about it, Sir, but one particular still escapes me, that is what you would have organized for myself.»

«The fortunes of a great nation like ours depend on the quality of its ruling class, and a respectable ruling class doesn't come from nothing, fortuitous events aside. To make sure that the system can last, it's absolutely necessary to make a selection among the best minds, but not only. Family traditions, schooling, events seemingly banal but useful to have a framework on the personality and the political orientation, of course. In short, we take into consideration each kind of element at our disposal in order to choose people to whom entrust positions of command. You have done very well until now, if you'll keep on following the path we have mapped out for you, well, sooner than you imagine, you could aspire to be the next Bonesman President of the United States, dear Alex.».

Jameson's words paralyzed me. Suddenly, I was not feeling cold anymore, and every muscle in my body twitched, preventing any movement, I even found it hard to swallow.

«Well, Sir, I'm flattered, but now my only goal is to do well at the Congress, then we'll see...»

«Good answer. I'm sure you'll do your best in Washington. Listen Alex, before going inside to celebrate, I have another thing to tell you, and it's about your personal safety, as well as your political career. In the future, someone could try to put you out misleading you, with the sole intent to subvert some very delicate balances on which rest the foundations of our Nation. You have to know that if a similar circumstance should ever happen, you wouldn't be the only one to be in danger.»

«Hey Alex, are you here or what?», it was Veronica who, in order to draw my attention, besides calling me, was also pulling at my shoulder. We were still on the Harbour, we would reach our destination in few minutes.

«Yes, I'm here, I was lost in my thoughts...», I answered her.

«Take this, read here.», she told me, handing me her iPhone on which the CNN application was open.

Los Angeles, FBI Inspector died by heart attack in his office

From our correspondent – The tragic event has occurred today in the late morning at FBI headquarters in California, in the heart of Los Angeles. Inspector Carl Nowitzki was in his office when he was suddenly struck by cardiac arrest. Unfortunately, the rescue team has been useless, alerted almost immediately by a co-worker who went to his office to give him some documents. In a very brief note, FBI top brass expressed «sorrow and dismay for the loss of one of our best men». Nowitzki, aged sixty-two, worked twenty-five years in the counter-terrorism division and, since 2005, was part of the National Security Branch. His family announced that the funeral will be held in private form.

«Inspector, what about this?», I asked Da Silva, turning to me to take a look at my phone display.

«You should know that the national interest comes before everything.», he replied icily.

Through the mirror, I saw that Veronica was about to answer, but I stopped her immediately, grabbing her calf with my hand.

For sure, that was not the right moment to start another polemical discussion about the greatest systems, perhaps it could also not be shared, but it was at least understandable that, in the midst of an investigation of that scale, FBI tended to nip any voice in the bud.

130

Suddenly Da Silva's phone rang, and after just one ring the auto answer put immediately into operation the speakerphone of the car.

«Inspector Da Silva, I'm Ortega, can you hear me?»

«Loud and clear, tell me how is it going on there?»

«For the moment, not even a fly is flying, Inspector. There is still no trace of the friend of Mr. Anderson, we are waiting. Are you coming?»

«Yes, we'll be there with you in five minutes. Please, be careful!»

At that moment Da Silva turned right, taking the exit to San Pedro. By now we had arrived, and the tension was rocketed to the point of being bounced back. I would have never said so, but I felt strangely calm. Veronica put her head between the two seats and took my hand.

«Everything will be fine...», she told me.

«Is it true Inspector?», she asked Da Silva, who just nodded and stopped the car next to a black van, from which Ortega and Richardson came out immediately.

«Here we are, we arrived, this is our mobile base. Alex, try to behave as natural as possible, and execute to the letter all instructions I will give you through the earphone. Don't do it your own way, in no case and for no reason in the world!», Da Silva advised.

«Do I go with him?», Veronica asked.

«No, you'll follow the operation here with us, Mrs. Hayes.», he replied. I opened the door and stepped out from that huge car.

I was at my place.

I breathed deeply, slipped my hands into my pockets and I walked, just as I had done millions of times, when I used to walk in those parts.

«For the moment, we don't see Maggie, boy.», he scared the life out of me.

It was the voice of Da Silva, that through the earphone came in my eardrum at a crazy volume.

Is it possible that she has insisted so much and then she would stand me up? I wondered.

No, it would make no sense.

Suddenly, as I was approaching the area of the containers, I had a revelation. If my instinct was right, Maggie was not waiting for me there but in the port area where we made our oath.

So I walked to the right and I speeded my pace.

«Boy! Where the hell are you going?», Da Silva shouted, making me jump again in fright.

«Don't worry Inspector, I know what I do!», I told him. In front of me there was an old red container with the inscription California Logistics, I passed it and saw the silhouette of a blond woman sitting on the wall, by the sea.

Bingo, it must be her, then she is alive! I thought.

A cold shiver ran down my whole back, in a moment, before my eyes, I saw all the images of her and me, when we were children. Less than thirty meters were separating us. Just a few more steps and I would know everything.

«Hey Maggie, it's me, Alex!», I shouted, while I was reaching her, but she did not turn, she stood still.

Her lack of reaction to my words made me fall in a vacuum triggered by a bad presentiment.

I felt there was something wrong, and that I would have risked losing everything. At the same time, however, I was aware I would no longer have the opportunity to hang back, I felt trapped.

I was just a couple of steps away from her, who showed no signs of the slightest movement. I saw her long blond hair, coming down on a purple checked shirt .

«Maggie…», I whispered, standing.

Nothing at all, she was still motionless.

Is it really her? And what if she is a madwoman or a terrorist? I wondered.

I breathed slowly, I gave a glance toward the two seagulls that, just at that moment, flew in front of us, I took up courage and I bent down to sit next to her.

At that point, I really wanted to know who was hiding behind that long blond hair.

15

Highway to hell

Men do not care neither truth, nor freedom, nor justice.
These are uncomfortable things and men are comfortable with lie
and slavery and injustice.
They roll in like pigs.
ORIANA FALLACI

«DON'T make risky moves, Alex! Before approaching, wait till she turns!», Da Silva said in the microphone.

By then I had already decided what to do. Just a matter of seconds. I put my hands on the wall, I sat up and, having turned my head toward her, I was literally petrified.

The one next to me was not Maggie Jones, but a dummy, just like those standing in shop windows.

I stood for a few moments to look at it, pausing on its lifeless and sad eyes, which seemed to really look at the sea.

«Damn Alex, answer me, that's an order!», Da Silva screamed. Even if I wanted to, I was not able, I was completely speechless, words choked in my throat.

I looked down and saw that, leaning on its hands, there was a letter.

Without thinking, I grabbed it.

The envelope was white, I turned it realizing that there was nothing written on it.

I narrowed my eyes for a moment, thinking about the attacks with anthrax or with explosive that had happened since September 11.

«Inspector, can you hear me?», I asked Da Silva in a whisper.

«Loud and clear, boy, it was about time you answered me! What's going on over there?», he asked me.

«Maggie Jones is actually a dummy, Inspector.», I told him.

«Listen to me Alex, don't move for any reason, now we come to pick you up.», he said.

«Inspector, there's a letter, do you authorize me to open it?», I asked him. Da Silva temporized for a few moments.

«Okay boy, open it, it may contain instructions, but be careful, avoid sudden movements, that damn dummy could be a trap!», he warned.

By weight and thickness, that envelope seemed to contain no more than two or three sheets.

I rose it in the direction of the sun, trying to look at the content backlit, and I saw there were sheets that seemed to have been written with the computer, but it was absolutely impossible to decipher the content. Therefore, using my short nails, I tried to grab a corner of its closure. I wanted to open it, but without breaking it.

After a few tries I succeeded in it, I pulled out the sheets, and immediately began to read what was written in it.

Alex,
I told you I didn't want your FBI friends in the way, didn't I? Did you really think I'd be so stupid to be there in person? I don't know, what you would expect from me, maybe that I would make a bow to your friend Da Silva and that I would have stretched my wrists saying «please, welcome, feel free to arrest me, Inspector!»?

I have to think that you underestimate my intelligence, it will be good that you and your FBI friends understand that I and only I am the one who's dictating the rules of the game. Do you want a demonstration? In a moment I will give it to you, but first I have a few things to tell you. In these days you have made yourself thousand questions, haven't you? I understand it, it's perfectly understandable. Among all questions, the most important is: why? It's a very simple concept, even trivial, that is every action creates an effect. Cause and effect, precisely.

Concerning you, the cause lies in having chosen to represent a sick nation, which for decades worked to subvert reality, bend and reshape it according to its interests. Indeed, to say it all, we're not even talking about the interests of a whole nation, and therefore of its People – which would make the pill less bitter – but we are talking about the interests of a very small number of people, real predestined who, since they were born, act and operate in the name of power and profit. That's it.

Well-being? Rights? Equality? Democracy? Freedom? Homeland? These are the real chemical weapons, used to dope the minds of people and manipulate their consciences, in order to reduce each individual to the state of a headless body, and you all use them as the gear of your filthy system, making them do all the saints days a job they hate to let them pay the debts that you have created.

Work, work, work! Spend, spend, spend!

Yes, that's right dear Alex, you are the slave traders of the new millennium, because you have reduced People to be like slaves, deceiving them to be free but locking them, in fact, in a web from which they will never get out. Just like hamsters in their cages run vainly chasing the small piece of cheese, so Americans get up at five in the morning and live a life of hell chasing absolutely useless things, which they could easily do without.

Run into debt for a car, spend thousand dollars to buy a bag that's worth two, or a sweatshirt printed with a name of a guy who they don't even know. Then, for good measure, go to stuff themselves in a fast-food and sink on the sofa in front of television, daily session of brainwashing.

And so on, day after day, week after week, month after month, year after year, life after life.

In front of all this, you'd think that the good old Orwell was too optimistic, in his stories!

And then there are the imperialist wars. Yes, because when the blood of just one People is not enough, then it is necessary to go elsewhere, to look for victims in which sink your jaws and suck, greedily suck.

On the other hand, history teaches, or not, Alex? The masons and their corporations locate the prey, while you politicians, with the lame excuse of "exporting democracy", draw your gun and shoot at them, without even thinking about it. You just execute. The choice between security and freedom is false, it's an excuse invented by the industrial complex that lies behind the security establishment.

Wherever you choose to go, you expand, you drain it out of every resource, and then you abandon it, arid and devastated because of your transit. Just like a virus.

Do you think that millions and millions of deaths every day is a fair price for the profit of your lobbies? Evidently it is.

Thank God, however, the bell jar under which you stay safe has began to crack and, crack after crack, the whole rotten of which you all are guilty has began to leak.

Today, especially with the advent of the Net, lot of people begin to open their eyes, even those who have chosen to be an integral part of the system, they are no more hesitating because they are fed up with being accomplices of this permanent massacre of yours.

You are one of the predestined I mentioned it at the beginning, when you were still a child, someone had already decided everything for you: from the studies you would have done, through the people who would attend, up to your political career. That someone has decided that, in a future closer more than you imagine, you will be called to pick up the legacy of the Bush at the White House.

It's all written, Alex. But don't deceive yourself, because you may be just a stupid pawn in their hands, a sort of remote-controlled robot that will have to set a limit to itself to occupy that place taking responsibility for the choices made by others.

With his dull and servile attitude towards the system, President Obama has played his last card, and he played it poorly.

Rather than promote the change, he obeyed orders obstructing true patriots like Chuck Dillinger, who had the courage to make public all documents, which the whole humanity has the sacred right to know. Obama should have recognized him as a hero, but he portrayed him as a computer terrorist; instead it's a paradox because the real terrorist is him, your President, a fierce wolf disguised as a docile lamb.

The events of the last hours are nothing but the first effects of the realignment of forces currently ongoing within the system I have so far described briefly. It's a process at which we have worked for years, the largest "truth operation" of recent and past history, which would open the door to a new model of society based on equality, in the wake of that great Revolution thanks to which, the cancers of capitalism and consumerism have been extirpated from millions of people in the world.
One worth's one. Stop with the money and the slavery coming from it. Wealth has to be divided into equal parts. We have to ban the dishonest and lethal concept of ownership and possession.

This is true freedom, my dear. And at this same concept of freedom are working, for the moment still in the shadows, many pieces of this puppet state, more than you or your friends can even remotely imagine.

What will be put in place, is the mother of all battles, that is the clash between the part of the state that wants to preserve the regime, and that one that struggles to assert a 2.0 Revolution.

You and your friends of the sect you belong to, Skull and Bones, you are the emblem of the rot we fight. Your father Ron and your grandfather Philip, along with Prescott and George Bush, have written your destiny believing this would be also the one of the whole nation.

However, they have not dealt with us, the partisans of the new millennium, cyberpunk militants.

Now it's up to you, Alex. In or out. Choose to marry the partisan struggle, or you will have to deal with us, even before facing your history.

But now you should start running...

I had not fully realized those words, or rather, the last sentence had managed to overshadow everything else.

I began to sweat, and suddenly I was panting.

«Damn, Alex! What the hell are you doing?», Da Silva shouted in my ear, through that powerful microphone. I jumped.

Matter of moments, I had to get up and start running.

So I tried to bend that letter, but I lost precious seconds because of the hustle and my sweaty hands. I felt perfectly the beat of my heart, as if its sound seemed to come from the microphone.

> *I'm on the highway to hell*
> *highway to hell*
> *on the highway to hell*
> *I'm on the highway to hell*

Just when I managed to put that damn letter into my pocket, I jumped again.

In a deafening volume, Highway to Hell by AC/DC came out from the dummy. I had just time to turn around, and along with the song, a strange laugh came out, and then, the same metallic voice began to scan numbers.

Twenty, nineteen, eighteen...

Fuck, it's a countdown, run! I thought.

I jumped up, even injuring my finger, cutting it with the corner of the concrete wall on which I was sitting, and I began to run with all the strength I had in my body, without looking behind.

> *I'm on the highway to hell*
> *highway to hell*
> *on the highway to hell*
> *I'm on the highway to hell*
> *don't stop me*

In front of me there was only a huge expanse of concrete, no cranes, no cars: in short, no obstacle. I heard only the notes of the song on which that voice overlapped, keeping on marking the countdown, it seemed to come out from a B-movie of science fiction of the eighties.

Whatever would happen, I only knew that I wanted to reach the end staying as far away from that damn dummy.

> *Ten, nine, eight, seven...*

So I closed my eyes, just as I was used to do as a child to find the concentration during the final sprint of races with Matt.

In my mind I thought about the strides of Usain Bolt or Carl Lewis, and I tried to tell my legs to do the same.

> *Six, five, four...*

«Run, run boy, put yourself out to do it, run and don't look behind!», Da Silva urged me, making me come to mind for a moment the old Mickey, Rocky's trainer.

> *I'm on the highway to hell*
> *I'm on the highway to hell*
> *I'm on the highway to hell*

and I'm goin' down
all the way, way down
I'm on the highway to hell

Three, two, one...

Boom.

The roar was devastating.

I was literally overwhelmed by the blast, which caused me to fly a few meters away, throwing myself on the ground with violence.

I hit my chin on the asphalt, and immediately I felt a strong smell of burning.

I opened my eyes for a moment, but I could not find the strength to turn around and see what had happened. I looked at my saliva drip to the floor, mixing itself with the sand dust and smog that covered the entire area of the harbour.

«Alex, Alex!», I could hear the voices repeating my name getting mingled with the sound of sirens, but I felt them far away, even more far away.

«My God, Alex, answer me, please!», I saw the face of Veronica next to mine, I wanted to answer, but I could not.

I tried to smile, then, darkness.

Darkness.

16

The Power

It is the power, not the truth that creates laws.
THOMAS HOBBES

Yale University
New Heaven
November 7, 2010

«TELL me Alex, how do you feel to be on the other side of the barricade?», since I was elected, that was the first time I was able to meet Professor Swenson who, although living on the other side of the country, greatly helped me during the election campaign, especially as related to the drafting of the program and of my public interventions.

Weigh words is crucial, especially in politics and he could be really formidable in this.

«More or less like David versus Goliath...», I said, in response to his provocation.

«Well, let's say that soon you will understand that it would be better to have Goliath as your friend. Of course I don't want to discourage you, also because you know how much I trust you, but I want to be sure that you don't lose yourself in Pindaric flights. You're young, I could also say "greenhorn", and if you really want to change the system, you must know how to be able to gamble your chances only doing it from the inside, otherwise, you and all your good intentions will be defeated. A real waste, in short.», he said, with his usual tone, which was the perfect synthesis between an attentive and inflexible father, and an older brother with whom you can confide.

«This is true, Peter, and it's a concept I accepted when I decided to run for Congress, but this doesn't mean, however, to become a passive gear of the system. Well, I know I would be presumptuous and even a little bit not responsible if I thought to go to Washington and make the revolution in just one day, but I am also aware of the fact that today more than ever we need people capable of sustaining uncomfortable or even unpopular positions, if necessary.»

«As a matter of principle I can only agree with you, indeed, I also say that there would be something wrong if a guy elected in his thirties, in one of the most influential assembly in the Planet, was not animated by your verve. To be clear, I have absolutely no desire to discourage you, but I just want to warn you, because soon you will find yourself to deal with opposing forces, whose interests lay since years on established balances but, at the same time, infinitely fragile more than you can even remotely imagine; and you know very well that balances are important for the survival of a Nation like ours.»

«Right, however you will agree with me that great men of our history have become great when they found the courage to break up some equilibrium which were consolidated since a long time...»

«Theoretically it's right, but there are many examples demonstrating the contrary. Take Kennedy: we remember him for all the good he was able to do, for example in the field of civil rights or the landing of man on the moon, it is true, but everyone also remembers the deep scar of the Bay of Pigs. A big mistake, which led us to the brink of catastrophe. Here it is, I believe that a man called to serve the interests of his People, along with his legitimate ambitions, should always bear in mind the national interest which, however, doesn't always correspond to the right thing to do. I know this is a difficult concept to accept, but things are exactly in this way, Alex.»

«Are you trying to tell me that, if necessary, I should sacrifice what would be right to do on the altar of an undefined national interest?»

«That's it, and you will need time and experience to fully understand this principle. The national interest is something that is above everything and everyone, that must be defended at all costs, as from it derives the stability that allows the United States to be the great Nation to which each of us is proud to belong. This is particularly true what regards our internal security, that is the defence for the safety of every single American citizen. Take September eleven: who would have expected that the greatest military power could ever suffer such an attack on its territory? I tell you, no one. Exactly as no one would have expected our defeat in Vietnam, against an apparently shabby army. In both cases we were beaten with the weapon of unpredictability, because our enemies, knowing there would be no game facing us with conventional methods, had the cunning to take us by surprise. With guerrillas on trees, or with suicide bombers, little changes, the concept is absolutely identical. Having established the sacred right of a Nation to defend itself and its borders, we must accept the fact that this involves a price to be paid, most often a very high price, I'm aware of it, but you'd agree with me it's an indispensable compromise for anyone having the courage to assume the burden of governing.»

«I don't disagree, but let's say I hope never to be called upon to take decisions that are contrary to the principles of democracy and freedom...»

«Oh, you will be for sure! Do not fool ourselves, Alex, although I never faced this issue intentionally in order not to embarrass you, don't you believe that maybe I know that you and your family are the direct expression of a secret society of the weight of Skull and Bones? Come on, you're talking with your friend Steven Swenson, not with a CNN journalist! Do you really believe that the immense occult power behind yourself which, incidentally, will get you much higher than you are now, won't it force you, one day, to take uncomfortable or disapproving decisions?»

«To be honest I had no doubt you knew about it, but I always appreciated your discretion on this subject. I'm serious. Although I'm still young, I'm not missing the obvious, I'm aware that the power entails to come to terms with our conscience, but let's say that, once achieved it, I hope to have the necessary ability and courage to use the power, and use it to do good.»

«I hope it with all my heart, Alex, but you'd be an exception, because, whether you like it or not, you won't be able to use it, because it will be the power using you.»

«He's opening his eyes, come here!», I could see very confused images, as if I wore a pair of glasses with fogged lenses.

On my right a window, from which came the bright daylight, in front of me a television and, on the left, the blurred silhouette of a woman, who seemed to be at the door calling to someone.

I felt numb, my mouth was completely dry, I made a big effort to open it. I raised my arms, I put hands on my face and I began to move my fingers and to rotate my wrists.

In the meanwhile, images were becoming sharper.

Where the hell am I? I thought.

"... in a statement released a few seconds ago, Charles Murphy, Chief of Los Angeles Police, said that the powerful explosion that occurred about two hours ago at the harbour, was caused by a short circuit of the electrical system of a crane, confirming also there are neither dead nor injured. But now let's talk about Red Sox, connecting us with Boston..."

A short circuit? Incredulous, I stared at the TV while a CNN reporter was giving the news. Sure, on one hand it was much better this way, because if people knew the truth, probably my re-election would be compromised.

However on the other hand, the fact that reality was manipulated with such ease, in both cases of the explosion and the death of Nowitzki, confirmed that I was mixed up in something big. Suddenly I saw Matt coming in.

«Hey Alex, my friend, how are you?», he asked me, looking at me with tears in his eyes.

«I'm happy to see you, you know?», I replied in a whisper. After a moment, also Veronica arrived, she approached the bed and gently stroked my hair.

«I was sure you could do it. How do you feel?», she also asked.

«Well, apart from a few blows here and there. Have you heard CNN?», I asked both.

«Yes, we have heard it too. Better that way, since you're involved in election campaign. Doctors say that you got away with nothing more than a few bruises, you were lucky.», Veronica said.

«Then can I go?»

«Not yet, Alex, they want to keep you under observation until tomorrow morning.»

«Until tomorrow morning? No way, I'm fine, I want to get out of this place and immediately go on with my election campaign. I've already wasted enough time, I begin to be tired of this whole story!»

What a coincidence, at that moment came the head of the department holding in his hands what, in all probability, should be my medical records.

«Good day Mr. Anderson, my name is Miguel Colón, pleased to meet you.», he said, sounding extremely friendly.

«It's my pleasure Doctor, thank you for what you've done for me...», I replied, holding out my hand.

«Do not thank me, we are here for this. If I have well understood, I've heard you want to interrupt your recovery...», he stated.

«That's right, Doctor, I feel very good, and in the next few hours I have a lot of important commitments.», I said.

«Listen, you have not suffered any trauma, despite that, as a doctor, I suggest you to stay here for the night, only for scruple. Having said this, if you sign the form of responsibility assumption, I can not keep you here against your will.», I quickly consulted Veronica and Matt looking at them in the eyes and, a moment later, I did not hesitate to answer him.

«Tell me where I have to sign.»

17

Cryptographic message

Every dawn has its doubts.
ALDA MERINI

FBI headquarters
A few minutes later

«WHAT do you mean saying he has left? I had ordered to inform me as soon as he regained consciousness, you idiots!».

Sitting behind his massive desk, Frank Da Silva was furious. After hanging up the phone with violence, he grabbed a Kleenex and wiped his forehead; despite the air conditioner in his office was constantly on eighteen degrees, he began to sweat.

Evidently, he felt that the solution of that damn case was beginning to slip away from his hands. He hated that kind of frustration which, in almost forty years of career, he had felt only a couple of times. No, he was not used to it, to be put upon.

A moment later his eyes felt on the file folder he had taken a few hours before from the desk of Nowitzki, and without hesitating further, he opened it and began to read.

The file folder on Maggie Jones contained some newspaper clippings dating back to August 1989, reporting the news of her parents death, confirming that, despite the research had gone on for several days, her body was never found.

As he was about to put away those papers, he found there was a post-it hidden inside the file folder. No doubt, it's Nowitzki's handwriting. He thought to himself.

Maggie Jones' body has never been found...
Is it a coincidence? It may also be,

After reading and rereading it, Da Silva stuck that yellow ticket on a corner of his computer monitor, he stood up, and began to go around in circles in his office several times. This was his way to concentrate.

London, London, London… he was just thinking about the possible links between Maggie Jones and the British capital.

Suddenly, he remembered a sentence in the letter that Alex found on the dummy; he opened it nervously, and began to read it again.

The index of his right hand flowed on each line, and stopped at the name he was looking for: Chuck Dillinger.

Yes, he, the author of Datagate scandal, the man who dared to betray the oath made to the Nation, divulging top secret data about the espionage activity of NSA, the Agency for National Security.

Although relations among FBI, CIA and NSA had never been idyllic, Da Silva did not have the slightest hesitation in putting himself and his best men at the service of the "cause", that was to capture Dillinger, prosecute him and throw him into the prisons of the nation, so that his exemplary punishment would serve as a warning to all his followers, to discourage them in following his footsteps.

But the problem was that the former CIA specialist, after a daring escape to Russia, succeeded in vanishing without a trace.

Vanished, disappeared.

On the table there were lots of hypotheses, taking into consideration the different friendships he could boast with some so-called "scoundrel" governments. The fact was that no one knew where he was or with whom.

Of course, there were many odds, it was pure coincidence, but something told Da Silva he should trust the instinct of Nowitzki.

Those minutes of concentration were interrupted by the ringing of the phone, it was Ortega.

«Tell me you have good news.», Da Silva said.

«Yes, I've just spoken with them on the phone, they are going back to San Pedro, tonight Anderson will take part in a television debate with Trevor Spencer, the appointment is at 8 PM on CBS.», Ortega answered.

«What do you mean at 8 PM? You and Richardson have to lift your butt and immediately join them, you have to stay with them all the time, have you understood ?», Da Silva ordered.

«Perfectly, we will immediately go, talk to you later.», Ortega said, with a submissive tone. After hanging up, Da Silva kept on checking carefully the documentation assembled by Nowitzki, looking for some elements that could help him to unravel that very complicated knot.

The names of Maggie Jones and Chuck Dillinger kept on swirling around in his head, but as soon as he had the file folder about Philip Anderson, the grandfather of Alex, he did not hesitate even a moment and opened it.

The first thing he found was an old black and white photo portraying fifteen people, of which twelve were standing, two were sitting and the one at the centre, was leaning his hands on a small round table on which stood out the black standard of Skull and Bones, a skull and a parchment.

All strictly in suit and tie.

They had young faces and their expression were not like those thoughtless, that ninety-nine time out of one hundred you see in the photos made during university days.

Da Silva paused on the look of each of them, noting that in those eyes a strange light was hidden, in some ways disquieting, as if through their gazes they were trying to communicate something to anyone who had bumped into that portrait of them.

A sort of threat, a warning.

Then he looked, one by one, at the faces of those boys, among them he immediately recognized Bush Senior, who was the young man sitting on the right and, immediately after, Philip Anderson, the guy at the centre of the image.

As if seized by a sort of hypnosis, Da Silva could not take his eyes off that face.

Suddenly, the picture began to move.

Shit, the earthquake! He thought first.

But it was just enough to look down a few centimetres to realize that to be shaken, was not the earth under his feet, but his hands.

Frightened, he put that yellowed picture face down, and he began to rummage in his desk drawer.

«Here they are!», he exclaimed, as soon as he found the cigar box he left there about three years ago, when he smoked the last one before quitting.

He opened it, and saw there were still three left.

It was Toscano cigars, by far his favourite ones.

With his hands still trembling, he took one out, brought it to his nose and sniffed it, obtaining from that intense scent of tobacco a feeling of pleasure, which he had deliberately removed, convinced by his relatives and colleagues that little waiver could have helped immensely his health.

Right, health.

He looked at it, lingering for a few interminable seconds.

To hell! He thought while, stretching himself with the other hand he grabbed the big crystal lighter on the edge of the desk.

He lit the cigar, took a breath and inhaled deeply, narrowing his eyes and slipping forward in his chair.
A little later, the trembling of his hands calmed down.

San Pedro
Headquarters of Alex's election committee

«I can not believe it. Shit, I can not believe this fucking story is happening to you, it's not right! Any idea who might be behind it? Yes, well, I mean… you are not believing the story of

Maggie who reappears out of nowhere to save your ass!», Matt exclaimed nervously, when, while going back to San Pedro, Veronica and I, we told him everything, word for word.

«Listen Matt, telling you the truth, I also do not believe this is the real Maggie, however, after all that has happened to us in the last forty-eight hours, I would not be surprised of the contrary. Indeed, can I tell you that for me it makes little difference? Maggie or not, what is sure is that Dillinger and his followers wanted to send me a sort of warning, no doubt about it.», I told him.

«Okay, Chuck Dillinger wanted to warn you. But the point is another: of what?», Veronica asked, confronting us with the question as big as a house behind which, in all probability, was hiding the solution of that story.

«In the letter, in addition to the usual cheap propagandistic rhetorical, there is an explicit reference to me saying that, according to them, I would soon be designated to be at the White House, thanks to the kind courtesy of Skull and Bones, my grandfather and my father who, all together, had made this decision when Matt and I were still spending our days running around San Pedro riding our BMX. This is pure madness, in short.», I said.

«Well, coming to think about it, is it a coincidence that just yesterday Huffington wrote the same thing in her article?», Matt remarked.

«Right! Think about it, Alex, the most influential journalist in the country has dedicated an article to the same argument they talk about in the letter. The same. At this point, one of the two things: either Chuck Dillinger reduced himself to take inspiration from Huffington Post, a hypothesis I would tend to exclude, or the Director has received a "tip-off" from Dillinger and wrote the article.», Veronica stated, beating her fists on the table.

For a moment we stood watching us in silence. I dragged her Mac Book towards me, went on Google, searching the article by Huffington and read it again.

Actually so many things had happened, that I had not even had time to dwell on what they had written about me.

Indeed, Veronica and Matt were right, the thesis was the same, difficult even impossible that this could be a mere coincidence, also and especially considering the timing. Then I went on my Facebook and Twitter profiles, realizing that, within twenty-four hours, I had received thousands of messages and tweets, thanks to that article.

Of course, among them there were the usual crazy men threatening and insulting me because of my belonging to Skull and Bones, but it was a small minority. On the contrary, for the most part, it was messages in which people made me compliments for my «candidacy», or even encouraging me.

«Hey Alex, please stop playing with that shitty computer!», Matt said with his usual indolent tone.

«Shut up and rather look here! In one day, my Facebook page has gained over ten thousand Like, and on Twitter I have twenty thousand new followers. Incredible!», I said, showing them my profiles.

«Well, paradoxically, it seems that Dillinger is helping you instead of penalizing you...», Veronica remarked.

«This is a macabre statement, considering there is a dead man, but it is so. At this point we should decide what kind of behaviour we have to take in public with respect to this thing, starting with my debate tonight. I imagine that your journalist colleagues are looking forward to criticizing me about this story of Skull and Bones. We can not make mistakes with our strategy, otherwise we're fucked.», I warned.

«That's for sure, actually I believe that many have already begun to embellish the news. One option might be that you adopt the same conduct which have held Bush and Kerry, about their belonging to Skull and Bones, that is you should say just a laconic no comment.», Veronica said.

«I agree with her, Alex. Also because, as far as I know, I don't believe that your friends of the "cult" would be too happy if you start to speak about them in public...or am I wrong?», Matt said.

Of course what they were asserting was more than reasonable as well as understandable, given that their goal was to protect me from further dangers, also and above all because I had already enough tough nuts to crack. In their position, however, there was something that was not convincing me. Suddenly, in my mind peeked out a chat I had with Adam Jameson at Deer Island.

One moment… that night, the former Head of CIA warned me about everything! I thought.

In my ears began to buzz every single word of that conversation, in which Jameson warned me telling me that, if I got sidetracked, I would not be the only one to run a risk.

As often happened to me, while I pondered, I began to doodle something on one of the scratchpad on my desk.

With the corner of my eye, I saw Veronica and Matt exchanging a worried glance, a clear sign that they were waiting with impatience for my answer.

«Guys, the truth is that I'm very torn. Right now I can not tell you which line we have to take, there are too many variables swirling around in my head, and I would need more time to reason on it…», I said, breaking the silence.

«The problem is that we don't have time, and you know it.», Veronica answered back.

«Indisputable remark. We don't have time, you're right. Therefore, I would say that for the moment I will follow your advice, and I will refuse to talk about Skull and Bones. It is understood, however, that if some other "signal" arrives, I might even change strategy. Currently, we can no more think day by day, but hour by hour.», I said, looking them both in the eyes. At that moment, the glass door of the office opened, and Ortega and Richardson came in, seeming not to be happy to see me.

As soon as they crossed the threshold, I stood up and went to welcome them.

«Agent Ortega, Agent Richardson, welcome. May I offer you something? Maybe a coffee, or a Coke…», I told them with an extremely friendly tone.

From their unconvinced handshakes, I felt there was something wrong.

Evidently, leaving the hospital without telling them, I must have put them in trouble with their boss. I thought.

«No, thank you Mr. Anderson, we're fine. Take your mobile, you forgot to ask us for it because of your hurry…», Richardson said, with a polemic tone not even too veiled.

«Oh yeah, thanks. Listen, I know that, going away on my own, I've caused you a headache, but I didn't mean to put you in trouble. I apologize, okay? I hope the matter can be considered closed.», I said, without waiting them to rebuke me, maybe with useless talking-to seasoned of codes and laws.

«No matter, Mr. Anderson, our only problem was the fact you're in danger, and we must think about protecting you, that's all. Having said this, don't worry, my colleague and I, we don't have any problem.», Ortega said promptly, taking a noticeably more accommodate attitude.

«Well sirs, giving the time, I would say it's high time to organize ourselves: Alex, you have about ten minutes to go and shave yourself and smarten up, as soon as you've finished we'll run to CBS. Unless Veronica doesn't want to look at you while you undress, we will do the briefing on the debate in the car on the way.», Matt said, rubbing his hands together, managing to snatch a shy laugh at Veronica and attracting upon himself the severe glances of the two FBI agents who, considering the way they stared at him, gave the impression of having put him a label.

Without being persuading, I reached briskly my office that, in those frantic weeks, had become a sort of a studio, a second home.

Of course, given the pace I was required to keep, there was a great mess that, however, followed a precise logic. Mine. In fact, in the midst of that mess I was always able to find anything immediately, on the contrary, if anyone dared to set it right, I would loose minutes and minutes in tiresome searching.

I took my shirt off, I took my case where razor and shaving cream were kept, and I went into the bathroom, which was connected to the room. I shaved being very careful not to cut myself, I gave myself a quick rinse trying to wash away the unpleasant smell of the hospital I felt stuck on me, I combed my hair, and I walked up to the hanger from which I caught a light blue shirt and a blue suit.

Once dressed, I looked around in search of a convincing tie. With the corner of my eye, I saw an electric blue one on the desk, crumpled next to a can of Diet Coke that probably had been there since some weeks. I put it around my neck, quickly made the knot, and went back to look at me in the mirror.

Tone on tone, perfect! I thought.

«Hey Alex, are you making the permanent to your hair? Get a move, fuck!», Matt yelled from the other room.

«Here I am, I'm ready!», I said aloud, while lacing my shoes.

Despite everything I was with plenty of energy, evidently going to that debate had made me come back into my reality, that is my election campaign and all things I had to do in order to win, and not the movie reality in which Dillinger or whoever had thrown me in the last two days.

We left the office in a hurry, and as we were about to get into the pick up of Matt, Ortega and Richardson stopped us.

«Just a moment, before you get in we want to give a look to check if everything is okay.», said the first, rummaging in every corner.

«Mr. Payne, can you come here a moment?», Richardson said.

Matt and I looked at each other in the eyes, he gulped and reached him.

«I guess this stuff is yours, do your best to make it disappear immediately!», the Agent ordered, waving a joint in front of him.

Matt took it, broke it into two pieces, and threw it right away in a trash next to us a few meters.

«Done, I'm sorry Agent… can we go now?», he said to Richardson.

«Now you can, get in, we will follow you.», Richardson replied icily who, with his strong jaw and his body builder physique, had all the appearance to come out from a police B-movie of the nineties.

«You know what? Serves you right. You're always the same dick-head, is it possible you can never learn?», I told Matt, once we left.

«Now don't start to piss me off, I had forgotten I had it, it must have been there for days…», he replied.

«Yes, well, always the same excuses…», I tried to reply back, but I was immediately interrupted by Veronica.

«Guys, stop it! Rather than discuss about this bullshit, let's talk about the debate of tonight. Alex, knowing the relationship between you and Trevor Spencer, I imagine that the tactics you have in your mind will be full of fair play, which is fine, but for Heaven's sake, you should have some dig at him…», she said.

«The good Trevor is the last of my thoughts, I know him very well. Everything depends if there will be questions about Skull and Bones, for the rest I'm feeling basically peaceful…», I replied.

Suddenly I felt my phone vibrating, it was a call coming from an anonymous number.

I hesitated for a few moments.

«Answer, Alex, what are you waiting for?», Veronica exclaimed.

I paid heed to her and answered immediately.

«Yes, hallo, with whom am I speaking?», I said right away.

«Good evening Alex, I'm Adam. Do you understand which Adam?», he immediately replied.

It was Jameson, the former Head of CIA, to whom I talked two years before at Skull and Bones party, in Deer Island. It was obvious that he knew that in all probability my phone was under control.

«Of course I do! You will not believe it, but I was thinking about you no more than half an hour ago…», I told him.

I did not know exactly why, but the sound of his voice had the power to calm me.

«So we've thought about each other. Listen Alex, I urgently need to talk to you, and you can easily guess about what, but we'll have to meet each other in a safe place, away from prying eyes and ears.», he said.

«It's fine, just tell me when and where and I'll be there.», I answered promptly.

«Not on the phone. I've just sent you a link by sms, open it and follow all instructions word for word. Now I must go.» he said, and hung up the phone, without even giving me the time to say goodbye.

In the meanwhile, I received the sms. I immediately went on the link, which opened in a browser window: it was a pdf file.

With my thumb and index finger I enlarged the image and I started reading what was written in it.

IMPORTANT: *don't read this document aloud, and don't save it on your mobile phone. Send it on an anonymous email account, print a copy and then delete the file.*
Da Silva does not have to know anything about it.

Meeting date: Monday, October 15 - Time: 16.00
Place: Aruba (the exact place will be notified as soon as you reach the airport). We have already provided for your air ticket, here below you'll find a boarding pass with the corresponding times.

OUTBOUND

Departure: *00:35 Monday, October 15*
Terminal: 1 **Los Angeles Intl Airport** *(LAX), Los Angeles, CA*
United States of America

Arrival: *08:11 Monday, October 15*
Terminal: **Charlotte/Douglas Intl Airport** *(CLT), Charlotte, NC*
United States of America

US Airways (US 840) – Seat: 36G - Class: Business

Change of the craft
08:11 Monday, October 15 - 09:35 Monday, October 15
Stopover length: 1 hour 24 minutes

Departure: *09:35 Monday, October 15*
Terminal: **Charlotte/Douglas Intl Airport** *(CLT), Charlotte, NC*
United States of America

Arrival: 14:35 Monday, October 15
Terminal: **Reina Beatrix** *(AUA), Aruba - Aruba*

US Airways (US 874) – Seat: 12F - Class: Business

<u>**RETURN**</u>

Departure: *07:40 Tuesday, October 16*
Terminal: Terminal: **Reina Beatrix** *(AUA), Aruba - Aruba*

Arrival: *10:53 Tuesday, October 16*
Terminal: **Charlotte/Douglas Intl Airport** *(CLT), Charlotte, NC*
United States of America

US Airways (US 877) – Seat: 8A - Class: Business

Change of the craft
10:53 Tuesday, October 16 - 12:10 Tuesday, October 16
Stopover length: 1 hour 17 minutes

Departure: *12:10 Tuesday, October 16*
Terminal: **Charlotte/Douglas Intl Airport** *(CLT), Charlotte, NC*
United States of America

Arrival: 14:31 Tuesday, October 16
Terminal: 1 **Los Angeles Intl Airport** *(LAX), Los Angeles, CA*
United States of America
US Airways (US 1751) – Seat: 3C - Class: Business

«So what? Are you going to tell us who was on the phone?», Veronica asked, while I was realizing that, in less than five hours, I would have to leave for a Caribbean island.

«No one, just an old friend who wants to organize an electoral cocktail with his friends...», I said with a wink, to which both of them replied with a nod, confirming they had understood I could not speak about it, considering that someone was listening to us.

To move around, I opened the note application, I wrote and I gave my mobile to them, so that they could read.

It was the former Head of CIA, he wants to see me.
At twelve and thirty-five AM I have a flight to the island of Aruba, I'll be away for one day, we have to think about how what to do.

18

Real Time

I hate television. I hate it like I hate peanuts.
But I can not stop eating peanuts.
ORSON WELLES

CBS Television City
Beverly Blvd
about twenty minutes later

WE arrived at CBS studios a few minutes before going live. To welcome us, we found Bill Maher, a brilliant journalist who since some years was conducting Real Time successfully, the program that would host the debate between Trevor and me.

It was a political talk, very followed because of its David Letterman slant, therefore it was able to face uncomfortable topics with an irreverent air, even and especially with the presence of those directly involved.

This is why the most coward politicians did their best to avoid it, but, on the other hand, it had also become a so important stage with a lot of followers, to be almost indispensable for the prominent celebrities.

Actors, journalists, singers, writers, politicians, athletes: in America there was no star, from George Clooney to Larry King, who had not passed under the impertinent Caudine Forks of Maher and his Real Time.

«Hi Bill, sorry to be late!», I told him straight away. «Don't worry, we still have a few minutes before going on air. So Alex, how are you doing? I read about you yesterday morning...», he replied, with his usual cryptic smile, reminding very closely that of John Belushi.

While we were talking, a sound engineer reached us and began to fix microphones on me.

«Well, apparently lot of people have read it… if you want to know what I think about it, political fiction aside, I did not mind at all at having such an important space in the middle of my election campaign!», I said, showing off my smug expression that Matt liked to call "of politician".

«Four minutes, everybody in their places!», the director yelled from the recording studio.

«Come on Alex, let's go to our workspace!», Bill said, giving me a pat on my shoulder. I turned around, I beckoned Veronica and Matt, and I reached briskly my position, on the left of Bill, at the big triangular table, which, as always, was the most important part of the scenery of the program. On my left there was my opponent, Trevor Spencer who, as soon as he saw me, came up to hug me.

«Hi son!», he told me, giving me an affectionate pat on my cheek.

«Hi Trevor, you always look great!», I replied, shaking his hand. «Two minutes!», the director warned loudly. I sat down.

«Trevor, Alex, we will start with national and international politics, while we will devote the last five or six minutes to local news, okay?», Bill told us, finishing the sentence raising his right thumb. At that moment I remembered that I still had my iPhone switched on, so I took it out of my pocket and I motioned Veronica to reach me.

«Sixty seconds!»

In the meanwhile, she did not loose time and reached me running through the studio.

«Keep it, in the meantime read the document, but be careful that Ortega and Big Jim won't see you!», I whispered her.

«Thirty seconds, go out immediately who has nothing to do with it!», the director said pissed off, referring to Veronica, who, in the meanwhile, had already gained the exit.

«Ten, nine, eight, seven…», during the countdown I narrowed my eyes in order to focus the subjects I should have talked about.

I always did it when I had to speak in public or before an important meeting.

«Five, four...», just a couple of seconds was enough for me to find the required concentration to make order in my head and give my best in front of all people. Questions, answers, ways of escape.

«Three, two, one... theme song!», during the opening clip I saw Matt pointing the two FBI Agents with a slight movement of his head, and then he started to laugh out loud.

Evidently their regimented attitude, and therefore diametrically opposed to his, had to amuse him so much. He loved to make fun of them. But he had to be careful not to take things too far with those two, because he was risking to be hurt, and also a lot.

«Ladies and gentlemen, good evening, and welcome to Real Time from your Bill Maher! Thus, thus, thus... many people, including myself, are fatalists, and believe there are episodes in people's lives, which are dictated by fate, by destiny. Then, there is another category, less copious than the former, but certainly more exclusive, in fact we could say it is a real club for a few elected: the predestined. Think about true icons capable of making history like John Kennedy and Pope Wojtyla or Maradona, with regard to sport. Yes sir, I mean those people who seem to have a doomed destiny since their birth. In a positive sense, of course. Well, as it is a very rare kind of people, tonight I can say I did a scoop. Yes, because it seems that one of those predestined is here with us: please, look carefully at this man and memorize his face because he will be our next President... here with us there is Alex Anderson! Good evening and welcome to Real Time, President... hem, Mr. Anderson!», Bill started, while behind him as a background, stood out title and first lines of the article in which Arianna Huffington spoke about me.

With Rooney in trouble, the Republicans are already looking to 2016 in the name of Alex Anderson

by Arianna Huffington - From Texas to California, step can be short, indeed, very short. It seems that

in the destiny of Republicans there is written that
their fortune coincides ...

«Good evening Bill! Listen, since you're in the mood of predictions, could you tell me when the Lakers will win the next championship?»

The audience in the studio welcomed my joke with an applause and several laughs, and even Maher had to accept my joke making the best of a bad situation.

«Eh Alex, I'm sorry to disappoint you, but if you go on like this, Godot will come sooner than you... let's go back to us. At a certain point of her article, Arianna Huffington wrote and I quote textually: *"Therefore, in summary, there are political qualities, even those communicative, and physical appearance as well. It's a lot, of course, but it's not enough to aspire to the office of President of the United States"*. And then again: *"One element is still missing but, even in this case, young Anderson seems to have what it takes. What do I mean? Wishing to be unclear we could talk about simple cursus honorum but, as the Huffington Post loves to be precise, we say Skull and Bones. Does it mean something to you?"* that's it, Alex, does it mean anything to you?»

Ready go, straight away a cheap shot.

I had agreed with Veronica and Matt that the line would be that of no comment, at least until new elements would appear to convince us otherwise. However I had to be able to take me off from the corner, and in a brilliant way if possible.

«Well, it means a lot to me, very much indeed. I remember with great enthusiasm the period of the university, also because not so many years have passed since then. Most of the friendships I made at Yale are, up to this day, among those dearest to me, but not only, because I was lucky to have met extraordinary men and women, from whom I learned a lot. Like Prof. Swenson – who I greet – for example. Here it is, in this sense it's true: the people I met in those years have certainly contributed to my human and intellectual growth and, therefore, also to build a good future. This I hope I will be able to do not only for myself, but also and above all for the highest possible number of Americans. Having said that, Bill, Skull and Bones is just a university society just like thousand others. Sure, several students who later made a career have been members of it, but could we say the same about all other university societies, or not? As for the rest, well, I hope Huffington will be right!».

**FBI Headquarters
at that very moment**

«That Anderson is smarter than I thought, are you hearing him at CBS? It seems that the guy has really a genius as people say.», Da Silva said, inhaling another puff of his cigar.

«If he hadn't been a genius at his age, he would not have been already District Attorney and Member of Congress, that's for sure. Listen Frank, it's useless I tell you that we have all eyes on this matter, therefore don't make jokes. I'll call you in the next hours, in the meanwhile try to sleep a little bit, people say you terribly need it.»

**Real Time Studio
Direct broadcast**

The applause of the audience and the glances of Veronica and Matt were the confirmation that, through my answer, I managed to hit the mark without giving the impression of wanting to avoid the subject.

From then on, Bill was milder, also because he had already played his most dangerous card.

The result was a very civilized debate but by no means boring, in which Trevor and I talked with Bill about that very intense electoral campaign and its twists and turns happening day by day, with a particular focus to the gaffes of Romney who, with the "stolen" video in which he said not to care about the lower classes, objectively hit rock bottom.

«Well Alex, after your opponent Trevor Spencer, now it's your turn: give us some good reason why we Californians should vote you.»

«It would be too easy if I do the usual list of promises that are made during the electoral campaign. It would be pointless if, instead, I tried to convince you all merely through my smiles and a few funny jokes. You see Bill, my parents and my grandparents taught me that the highest value to be defended among all is that of truth. That's it, truth comes before everything else. For example, I might also do something good, but if I would hide you the truth on matters of collective interest, well, I would be worth nothing. This is a concept I have completely assimilated during my experience as District Attorney, a job whose aim is the affirmation of justice through the discovery of truth. Think well about it, it's an immense responsibility. My ambition is to win this election in order to keep on defending the rights of all those who did not hit the jackpot in their life. Here it is, I would hurl them a call to hope, so they can get up and start again in order not to destroy what they have done before, but to build something new. Los Angeles needs to keep on taking care of its less fortunate children by giving them a second chance, if it wants to be again competitive on all fronts, and then provide again the opportunity to produce wealth to those who want to do so, supporting young and dynamic realities. As you understand, these are apparently different things, but they go at the same pace. Just as you all and I, all together, we will go at the same pace, with no one left behind.»

The intensity of the applause, which began without the need to be started by the attendant of the studio, was the immediate confirmation of the fact that I had a rather good way with it. Even Ortega and Richardson applauded me, and this meant everything.

«Gentlemen, it seems that our Mr. Anderson is getting serious… good luck! A sincere 'good luck' to you too, Mr. Spencer, it was a real pleasure to have you here with us tonight. I wish you both a good electoral campaign. We will see next week, thank you all very much, good night!»

As the theme song started, we got up all three, and Bill came to me straight away, putting himself between Trevor and me.

«You know me well, boy, you know I would never say something I do not believe it, especially if it's a compliment. But this time you deserve it, you were really good.», Maher said, astonishing me a lot.

«Thank you Bill, I do my best...», I replied, trying to keep a low profile.

«Your best? Shit, you have eaten them all away! At this time Obama would be scared shitless, if there was you instead of Romney!», Matt said, clearly euphoric, intruding into the conversation without even introducing himself.

«Forgive him, he is always behaving in this way, he doesn't do it on purpose. He is Matt Payne, my friend and deus ex machina of my whole electoral campaign.», I said, putting a hand on his shoulder.

Both Bill and Trevor found the incursion of Matt funny and immediately shook his hand.

«The truth is that Alex would have always wanted to be like me, since we were kids. He will never admit it, but I'm his mentor.», Matt added, while Bill and Trevor kept on looking at him amused.

«Come on mentor, I have to take you away, otherwise you'll end up to ruin my reputation. Bill, thanks for everything. Trevor, come here, let me hug you.» I said, jostling Matt and going toward Spencer.

«You will get to the top, boy. But be careful, from now it will be tricky... trust no one, no one!», Trevor whispered to me, before letting me go.

We exchanged one last look, then Matt carted me away by an arm.

«Congratulations Mr. Anderson, excellent performance.», Ortega told me, coming toward me.

«It's true, it was very... effective», Richardson added.

«Well, thank you both, you are very kind. Basically if I am here tonight it's also thanks to you.», I replied, shaking hands with both.

Out of the corner of my eye, I saw Veronica standing a few meters away, watching me silently.

«Pardon me.», I told them, and I went to reach her. «So, what do you think?», I asked her point-black.

I had received a lot of compliments, but I was dying to know her opinion.

«No need to ask! You were extraordinary. And you know I'm telling it as a journalist, not as a friend. Have you noticed the expression of Maher when you answered about the Huffington article? You laid him out right away! Tonight you've earned a lot of points!», Veronica confirmed, as we went out from CBS studios.

«Hey Alex, it's almost half past ten, how about hurrying up? Tomorrow morning you have to wake up very early, do you remember?», Matt said, winking.

Thus I played along with him: I gave a look at my watch and I feigned a yawn

«You're right, and I'm awfully tired! What are you going to do?», I asked the two Agents, not having the slightest idea of how I would be able to take that plane without letting them know.

My hope was that, during the broadcast, Veronica and Matt had invented something.

«A while ago the Central has called telling us to go to rest a few hours, but first we have to accompany you home. Of course.», Ortega said, surprising us three.

«Good!», Matt yelled, drawing upon himself, for the umpteenth time, the attention of the two Agents, whose eyes spoke for themselves. During that silent space of time in which everyone stared at him, Matt realized he would have batten down the hatches.

«I mean that finally tonight we'll all go to bed early, I have not slept two nights, because of this bigwig!», he added, messing my hair with his hand.

That's a thing I have always hated.

«Get over with it, Matt! Please be patient, he is a hopeless case...», I told Ortega and Richardson.

«Don't worry. See you tomorrow morning at your home, if you need something call us immediately on the phone. Good night.», Richardson coldly replied.

«Thanks for everything, have a good sleep.», I told them before getting into the car. As soon as I closed the car door, Veronica gave me a piece of paper.

Well, it seems strange that Da Silva has let them go home, don't you think? There's something fishy about it. Anyway, it's better that way! ;-)

Of course we all stayed silent.

After Matt read the note too, I took the pen in my jacket and I replied her, writing on the other side.

This whole story is strange. I really hope that tomorrow it will be resolved.

Once we reached the walkway of my home, we parked on the road and, after seeing the car of Ortega and Richardson had turned the corner, we stopped to talk on the sidewalk.

On the other hand, if we were intercepted in the car, most likely we were also in the house, I thought. Matt lit a cigarette.

«Let me take a drag.», I told him.

He thought it was unreal.

«Are you sure you are feeling good?», he asked me, handing me his Marlboro Lights. I took a drag, swallowed the smoke and handed it back to him.

«Alex, it's very late, you barely have time to put some clothes in your suitcase, we have to go immediately to the airport.», Veronica said.

I gave a look at the display of my phone and saw it was eleven and four minutes.

«Okay, I'll be ready in a minute!», I said, heading towards the front door.

I ran into my room and took my trolley, in which I put my toothbrush, the iPhone charger, a pair of underpants, one of socks, one shirt, one t-shirt and a pair of bermuda short.

166

Obviously everything in a mess.

Just before leaving, I remembered that Aruba was not in the United States and that, therefore, I would need my passport.

Luckily, unlike other times, I found it at the first attempt, in the drawer of the closet at the entrance.

> *When love comes to town I'm gonna jump that train*
> *When love comes to town I'm gonna catch that plane*
> *Maybe I was wrong to ever let you down*
> *But I did what I did before love came to town*

> *I was there when they crucified my Lord*
> *I held the scabbard when the soldier drew his sword*
> *I threw the dice when they pierced his side*
> *But I've seen love conquer the great divide*

As soon as we got in his pickup, Matt turned on the stereo. Immediately we heard the version of "When love comes to town" sung by U2 and BB King. I thought that, turning up the volume, probably they wouldn't be able to listen to us, exactly as the day before with Veronica.

«Alex, are you sure you want to leave?», she asked me.

«Do you think that perhaps I have any other choice? I'm willing to do anything to put an end to this damned story.», I replied her.

«What if it's a trap? Yes, well, I mean, you barely know that guy, how can you be so sure he is on the good side and not on the bad side?», Matt interfered.

«I don't know, my friend. I don't know. But I have to take this risk, because he's the only one who could help me to get out of this mess.», I replied him.

Indeed, thinking well about it, their doubts were more than reasonable, considering that I was about to board a plane that would have taken me thousands of miles away from my home, without even knowing why.

But, on the other hand, there were also a lot of elements that convinced me to trust Jameson. To begin with he was still the former Head of CIA and, secondly, I had known him in Deer

Island, during a gala evening of Skull and Bones: like me and all other people who where there, he made an oath.

In short, he was one of our people.

19

Aruba

You'll damage your shoes, but you'll grow up along the way.
PABLO NERUDA

Headquarters FBI
Eight o'clock in the morning
Los Angeles time

STRANGE but true, that morning Da Silva got out of the right side of his bed. It was the demonstration that, after the very intense stress suffered in the last forty-eight hours, both his body and his mind had absolute need of a few hours of rest.

The night before he decided to do so, and turned off his bedside lamp a few minutes after ten o'clock, as soon as he had finished watching Real Time, the television program which welcomed Alex Anderson, that is the man at the centre of what was turning out to be the most complicated case of his entire career. It was very hard to relax, rather than spend the whole night racking the brains and tossing and turning in the sheets.

Thankfully, his tiredness got the better of everything else. After waking up, he got ready and went to his office. The first thing he did once he arrived, was to call Ortega to take over from him and Richardson, who must have spent all night monitoring Anderson, down in San Pedro.

Those two poor souls will be dead tired, he thought to himself. He picked up the phone and made the call.

One, two, three, four, five rings.

No reply.

Da Silva began to get nervous but, just as he was about to hang up, here came the voice of Ortega.

«Hallo Boss, here I am. Sorry, I was in the bathroom shaving...»

«Ah ok, wouldn't you know. Listen, I guess you and Richardson you are dead tired, give me an hour and I will send Rice and Scott to take over from you.», Da Silva said.

«Boss, there must be an error: Richardson and I, we went back home yesterday night...», Ortega admitted, immediately interrupted by Da Silva, who just needed a few seconds to lose his good humour.

«Went back home? But, damn, are you out of your mind?», he shouted, straight in the ear of his subordinate.

«Not at all, we came back because Tina called us from the Central saying that you had given orders to...», Ortega tried to answer timidly but, as soon as he realized he was cheated by his colleague, kept silent for a moment.

«Boss, you never told Scott to call us to go home, am I right?», he kept on.

«That's right, my dear third-rate Sherlock Holmes, are you sure it was Scott on the phone?», Da Silva asked him.

«Very sure. It was her, one hundred percent.», Ortega guaranteed.

«Okay. Now I begin to understand a lot of things. Listen, pick up your colleague and run like rockets to San Pedro, perhaps behind this thing there is a trap. Bring me Anderson and his friends, in the meanwhile I will mind Scott...», Da Silva ordered.

On board the aircraft
two and twenty-five P.M.
Aruba time

"Dear passengers, please be advised that we have started the descent and in a few minutes we will be in Aruba. On the ground the weather is clear, with a very pleasant temperature, around thirty-three degrees Celsius. Wishing you a wonderful stay, we would like to thank you for choosing to fly with US Airways. See you soon!"

I was so tired that the journey flew off in a snap. Stopover aside, of which I took advantage to have breakfast and get newspapers, I slept all the time.

I was woken up by the voice of the Captain of the plane.

I opened my eyes and looked at the LCD display in front of me, on which there were a geographic map and a small airplane that had traced the route, from the point of departure to that of arrival.

At first that image reminded me of Indiana Jones trips.

It's many years I don't watch one! I thought.

But, soon after, I realized I was really far away from my home. I'm not saying that I was not used to travel, but that time it was different. I really felt like a dot in the middle of an infinitely greater drawing, and this state of mind made me feel terribly alone.

But at that moment, the only thing that mattered to me was to go to the bottom of that story, a little bit because I felt I was feeling in danger, but also and above all because I really wanted to find out who was behind it and which was his aim.

With the corner of my eye, I saw a hostess passing, being busy in checking that all had the seat belt fastened. She was a very tall woman, with delicate features framing an expression of everlasting girl.

I asked her to bring me coffee. She came back after less than a minute, handing me the tray with a cup of steaming coffee and a chocolate muffin.

«I saw you last night on television, you know? I root for you!», she said softly, showing a beaming smile.

«You're very kind, thank you!», I replied, smiling back.

I awfully needed caffeine. I took the cup and sent down a first big gulp. Then I stopped for a moment staring at the muffin. I was hungry, of course, but I also knew that, if I had swallowed that caloric bomb, I would be regretting it for the rest of the day. I decided to give up and kept on drinking my coffee. I became so since I lost all those kilos.

Before getting off the plane, I took out my jacket and rolled up my shirt sleeves.

On board the air conditioning was very strong, and I had no intention of becoming ill because of the temperature range.

That's all, I don't need now to get sick, I thought.

Going down the steps of the ladder, I immediately realized how fantastic the weather was. Warm but breezy at the right point. I took the corridor leading to the area used for recovering luggage that I passed because I only had my trolley.

I stood in the queue for passport control a few minutes, and after that, I found myself at the exit. Now what shall I do? I wondered, as I looked around. In the instructions Jameson sent me, he had written that someone would tell me the exact place of the meeting once arrived at the airport.

Suddenly, I felt someone touching my back, I turned around quickly.

In front of me there was a black man about a pair of meters tall and rather full-bodied, with salt-and-pepper hair and a very sympathetic face.

«Good morning Mr. Anderson, and welcome to Aruba! My name is Mario, and I have to take you to your friends.», he said, insisting on carrying my luggage.

«It's a pleasure, I'm Alex. Out of curiosity, how did you manage to recognize me?», I asked him, while we were going out.

«Because last night I saw you in Real Time, that Bill Maher is my favourite anchor-man!», he replied, making me sit on the back seat of a black minivan.

«Is it your first time in Aruba, Mr. Anderson?», he asked, looking at me through the rear-view mirror.

«Yes Mario and I hope to come back soon, since I've already fallen in love with your climate.», I replied him.

He smiled.

«Our island has this effect on everyone, you know? Even on us living here. Let's say that living in a place like this helps to enjoy life, to think less of work and a lot to feel good. Do you know what we say in our country, Mr. Anderson? I could die of old age or illness, but never of hunger!», he said, bursting into an Eddie Murphy contagious laugh.

This Mario is very nice! I thought to myself.

«There are days in which I also would like to think in this way, I'm serious. Tell me Mario, where are we going exactly?», I asked him.

In the meanwhile I switched on my phone and inserted the pin code.

«We're going to the most beautiful place of the island, Eagle Beach. Your friends are waiting there, in a very luxurious hotel. You will love it, Mr. Anderson.», he answered.

I nodded and, after selecting a phone company, I stared at the screen waiting to see who had looked for me while I was travelling. Definitely Da Silva, who was supposed to be hitting the roof.

But there was a message, it was Veronica, who had written me on Facebook.

Hi Alex, everything okay? How was your journey?
Matt and I, we have just come out of FBI Headquarters: saying that Da Silva was angry would be simplistic... anyway... Matt told him you had to reach your father in New York. It seems that for the moment they believed it, but I'm sure they're already checking airline tickets... in a while they'll discover where you are.

I told my editorial office I'm sick, they thought I got lost!
Now I get started... answer me, as soon as you arrive!
A special kiss :-D

Good morning, Veronica! :-D
I was just thinking about Da Silva...
The trip went well, and finally, after days, I managed to sleep! Now I'm in the car with a very nice guy who is taking me to the meeting place, a resort in Eagle Beach. I must confess I begin to be a little bit nervous, I hope everything will turn out fine.
Update me, in case of news. Talk to you later.
A big kiss to you too!

In all likelihood, Da Silva had already discovered where I was. However, being the Head of the counter-terrorism division of the National Security Branch, it was easy predictable for him. At that point, though, the thing that I most wanted was to meet Jameson and listen to what he had to tell me, hoping that all the miles I had to do to achieve him would be worthwhile.

«Mr. Anderson, we arrived!», Mario said, stopping the car in front of the entrance of Bucuti & Tara Beach Resort.

«Well Mr. Anderson, we will see each other tomorrow morning. I will come to pick you up at six to bring you back to the airport. I wish you a nice stay and I recommend to move your watch forward three hours!», he said, as he left my luggage to a clerk who had come to welcome us.

«Okay, Mario, thank you for everything, you were really kind. See you tomorrow.», I replied, giving him a twenty dollar bill.

«Thank you, thank you very much Mr. Anderson!», he thanked me. At the reception there was a very friendly clerk to welcome me, who, after asking me an ID card, gave me the badge and immediately took me to my room.

«Here we are Mr. Anderson, your room is number two hundred and two. Mr. Jameson asked me to tell you he will be at the beach bar at four o'clock waiting for you. For any requirement, our staff will be at your total disposal. Enjoy your stay.», after having thanked her, I passed the badge into the card reader, and the door opened.

The room was wide and beautiful, made with great attention to the smallest details and provided with all comforts. Fist of all I put my iPhone on charge, then I felt the irrepressible need to take off my cloths and have a shower.

Bare-ass, I went into the bathroom, and I immediately noticed that, in the middle of the mirror, the was a TV. So cool! I thought.

Without hesitating a single moment, I grabbed the TV remote and turned it on, straight looking for CNN, which was broadcasting the spectacular images of Felix Baumgartner's challenge performed the day before, by jumping from an height of nearly forty thousand meters.

I went under warm water and, while I soaped myself, I listened to the enthusiastic comments of journalists in the studio.

"... Felix Baumgartner did it, he has broken the sound barrier, 1173 mph free body, throwing himself from a capsule 39 kilometres far away from the ground, in the stratosphere ..."

After I dried myself, I brushed my teeth and went into my room to get dressed. I put on shirt and shorts, realizing immediately I had forgotten the slippers. Fortunately, I had left wearing a pair of summer Timberland.

I wore it again and that's that.

More than half an hour was missing to the appointment, but I had no intention to stay in my room. As I was already there, I wanted at least to enjoy the scenery for a few minutes. I picked up my phone and wallet, I left the room, and walked down to the beach, which was located about twenty meters farther.

I crossed the garden around which there were all the rooms, and, as soon as I reached the beach, I was literally speechless. The sand was really white, not beige or grey as in our country, and the beach, full to the brim with light, stood out on a blue sea like a diamond, whose stretch of water was overflow by seagulls and pelicans challenging each other who would have found the next fish.

Being grown there, I loved the seascapes, their scent of salt and the sound of waves. Every time I saw one, I was touched. I picked up my phone, I snapped a photo and, through Facebook, I sent it to Veronica and Matt. Even if only for a few moments, that authentic sight of nature succeeded in not make me think about the reason I was there.

«Wonderful, isn't it?», I straight away recognized the voice, it was that of Adam Jameson.

I turned around and I found himself in front of me.

He was wearing shirt and trousers in white linen, a pair of dark Rayban and his head was protected with a Panama.

«Yeah, a true spectacle. It's a pleasure to see you, Mr. Jameson.», I replied, holding out my hand.

He shook it and hugged me.

«It's my pleasure, boy. I'm sorry I had to make you come up here, but I could not meet you in the United States, it would be too risky for both.», he said.

«I understand. But I'm here now, and the only thing I want to know is… why me?», I asked, staring at him straight in his eyes.

«Alt, alt. We will speak about it Alex, but before I have to explain you the matter in its entirety. Do you like walking on sand?», he asked me, changing his expression out of the blue.

«It's something I love.», I replied.

«Good, then leave your shoes in a corner and follow me. As you see, the beach is very long, we will have all the time we need.», he said, leading the way.

I took off my shoes and left them next the three wooden steps leading to the bar. So it was that we went north, caressing our feet by the water that, from time to time, lapped the shore.

There were very few people, and this was undoubtedly another point in favour of that magnificent place.

«Come on Mr. Jameson, I'm all ears!», I said, after having waited a couple of minutes.

«Alex, before starting it's necessary I make a premise: everything I'm about to tell you, in this case places, events and people, is absolutely top secret, and therefore it's neither demonstrable nor usable in official and unofficial ways. It's my duty to tell it to you, given the delicate nature of your role and considering the relationship that binds me to you and your family. Ergo, our talk today will help you to have the whole picture of the situation, from which you can draw the necessary conclusions in order to understand how you have to behave and, above all, to find a way to come out unscathed from this story. Is that clear?», he asked me.

Basically, he wanted me to understand that the things he was going to tell me would not have been found in any way, only through the facts because covered by State secret.

So, in a few words, he was saying that it would be up to me to demonstrate those theories in a tangible way.

«As always, Mr. Jameson.», I replied, while I enjoyed watching two funny little birds chasing each other in front of us.

«Well, I take it as a compliment. So Alex, as I was telling you before, this story started long time ago. Therefore, we will have to take a rather long step back, let's say of about eleven years, and go back to the frantic days immediately after September eleven. As you may remember, the atmosphere of terror was so dense that we could even breathe it, in every corner of the Nation and, probably, in the whole World. That same World that, a moment after the collapse of the Towers, began to wonder constantly how it was possible that the greatest political and military power of the Earth, could be so vulnerable to the point of being literally put on its knees by a small band of terrorists. We all wondered about it. And so did I, as you know, at that moment, I was expecting everything except to be appointed to direct CIA. But we will talk about this later. Let's start by saying that, in my role as vice Director of CIA, on four occasions I wrote President Clinton in order to externalize my great doubts about the system of national security. The first of these letters is dated ninety-seven, that is four years before September eleven, but four years after the first attack on the World Trade Centre, which, in my opinion, we had forgotten too quickly, denoting a certain superficiality. Now it would be useless to go into details but, as a matter of fact, what I wanted to make the President understand was essentially one, that is the intelligence of the United States of America was not objectively able to predict similar events. The reason is obvious, and you may even find it banal: our main failure was the absolute lack of willingness to start a process of internal renewal, to move with the times and, when possible, even to anticipate them. Self-references, defence of consolidated interests since years, politics and presumption. All elements which have played a key role in taking this paralyzed attitude and consequently in the crystallization of the system. Unfortunately, as it's sadly presumable, those remarks of mine were never accepted. At least not in time. However, after the disaster of September eleven, I was summoned to the White House by Bush and Colin Powell who showed me the 'spontaneous' letter of resignation by the then CIA Director, telling me their decision to give me that position so that I could realize those innovations I have invoked for more than five years ...»

«I would have a bet on it. Honestly I never believed that Murphy had left the direction of CIA out of the blue to devote himself to his children.»

«Well, otherwise I would have to reconsider the good impressions I have of you. The truth is that Murphy was forced to leave because, at the Pentagon, rumours of his incrimination for high treason began to take consistency. A sort of a not too much veiled threat, for those who grew up in that environment. In short, he had no choice. So it happened that, at six thirty on a Wednesday morning, they called to inform me that, after half an hour, I was supposed to board a military plane that would take me to Washington because the President and the Secretary of State "were eager to meet me".»

White House
September 25, 2001

«Dear Adam, I apologize for having summoned you in such a short time, but I was the one to insist with the President in order that this meeting could take place as soon as possible. Without the usual pleasantries, the reason why you're here is that President Bush has carefully read again your reports through which, over the years, you have tried to light a warning bell about the current problems that nowadays are occurring throughout their tragic evidence. I also told the President that our friendship goes back since the war in Vietnam, where we together supervised the investigations on My Lai massacre.», Colin Powell started, as soon as I set foot in the meeting room.

He and Bush were sitting next to each other, and they invited me to sit down on a brown leather armchair placed right next to them. In the past I had been several times at the White House, but you don't get ever used to the solemnity of that place.

Moreover, going there only two weeks after September eleven, gave to that place an even higher meaning. You have shot down our economic centre, hit the Pentagon, but the seat of our institutions is still standing. I thought.

At that time it was a symbol more than ever, just as the stars and stripes flag.

«Thank for your time, Mr. Jameson, it's very important that you are here.», Bush said, standing up to shake my hand.

«Would you like to have a coffee?», he asked me, as soon as we sat down.

«No thank you Mr. President, I'm fine. So tell me, how can I be useful to the cause?», I asked point blank.

Powell took a sheet from the small wooden table standing between the two armchairs, and handed it to me.

«This is the letter through which tomorrow Murphy will leave his office, the President believes that there is no alternative for that office except you, James.», Powell stated.

«That's true, Adam. By the way, can I call you Adam even though we are in the presence of Secretary Powell?», he interrupted us.

«Of course you can, George.», I replied him.

«Good. As you see, I have here all your reports, and I'm not embarrassed in saying that, if they had been taken into due consideration, in all probability now we would not be in this damn situation. Sure, sure, I can perfectly imagine what is passing through your mind in this moment, and I tell you that you're absolutely right. Those who did wrong should take their responsibility, and pay bitterly, especially because they have involved the lives of thousands of Americans!», Bush overheated and, in anger, gave a kick of such violence to the wooden table, making it literally fly a few meters away.

Afterwards, without blinking, he stood up and rearranged it in its right place.

«I'm sorry, I'm just... well, yes, you have understood me...», he said with a faint voice.

I saw him really exhausted, therefore I tried to comfort him laying a hand on his shoulder.

It was an instinctive gesture.

«I must assume that you have already known each other.», Powell said, who watched the scene trying to dissimulate his nervousness by repositioning his glasses.

«Exactly, Colin. Adam and I, we have known each other since university and, more precisely, since our common membership to Skull and Bones. A situation in which I could appreciate his human and intellectual qualities, of which, moreover, his commendable work is giving me confirmation. In short, he is a brother. But this is a detail that has to remain among us, of course», the President pointed out, looking straight into our eyes.

«What detail?», Powell replied jokingly, infecting both of us with a laugh that had the great merit to defuse the tension.

«Joking aside, President I want to thank you from my heart for your nice words, but also for the enormous trust you are placing in me, bestowing me such an important and delicate assignment. I swear I will do my best.», I told them.

«Adam, nowadays the best, mine, yours or anyone else, is no longer enough. I ask you to do the impossible, and I know it's within your reach.», Bush warned me, pointing his index against me.

«Much will depend on the conditions in which I have to operate. Will you give me carte blanche on the choice of men?», I asked them.

«Absolutely.», Bush replied.

«And what about strategies? Will I have a direct line with you, or will I have to lose my time to convince the usual slew of politicians and bureaucrats?», I pressed.

«No intermediate steps, no loss of time. Also because I think we have already lost enough.», the President reassured me again.

«One last request. George, Colin, is your administration ready to support strong initiatives? You have to know that the media of the whole world will demonize any act which, according to their opinion, prevails over the so-called 'fundamental rights', I tell you this because, in order to win, we'll have to get our hands dirty…», I told both, with great determination, to avoid any misunderstanding.

«No doubt about it.», Powell stated.

«Adam, as for me, after what they did to us, I'm willing to buy a one way ticket to hell, if that's the place where I can go and ferret out those miserable killers. And I'll tell you more. The whole world should know that we will do justice, and we will not make prisoners.», Bush replied, striking me positively for his determination.

«Good. So I would say that we all are looking in the same direction and that, therefore, the conditions are favourable in order to get the results that we have set ourselves as a goal.», I stated.

The President, at that point, stood up and, after a few seconds, began to speak.

«I'm glad to have you aboard with us, Adam. Listen, as you're here, let's begin now to discuss about strategies. As you also stated in some passages of your reports, we would like to develop our action mainly on two levels. On one hand, on a political and military level, that will help us to physically eradicate the terrorist cells and regimes foraging them, as well as to demonstrate to the public opinion what we're made of. Napoleon said that 'who hits first strikes twice', isn't it? He was right, and this will be exactly what we will do. But on the other hand, it's my firm intention to promote the biggest campaign of espionage in the entire history of the United States of America. We have the best technology? Well, let's take advantage of it! We can count on the most experienced men? It's time to throw them out of the offices and send them around the world to do counter-espionage! You see, my friends, what I learned from September eleven is that the security of our borders is really priceless. And that the safety of every single American is sacred, and it is worth any sacrifice. At the same time, something that is more than just a simple impression has matured inside me, that is they are many, even among our allies, supporting in order that we, the United States, weaken and that, perhaps, in the meanwhile they become stronger, obviously behind us. As parasites. Do you want some names? I'm referring to several European countries, led by German and France, that would like to share out, respectively, monetary power and leadership among the Mediterranean countries. Non to mention the communist China and Russia, which would do anything so that Islamic terrorism gets the leg up on us. In the end, then, there are those I consider directly colluded with Bin Laden and his followers, that is Iraq, Afghanistan, Iran and, perhaps, North Korea. Well, given that, albeit in different forms, being our enemies or, at least, not our friends, what I want is to make sure we know what they say and what they do, I mean everything, every single word. This is what I call justifiable defence.», Bush stated vehemently.

«Of course I'm completely in accord with the President, I only add that it's our intention supporting you in every way, Adam. As you can imagine, this is a top secret operation, and as such it will allow us to have more freedom of manoeuvres.», Powell added.

20

Security has a price

I know it's a secret because I hear it whispering everywhere.
WILLIAM CONGREVE

On Aruba beach

WALKING on that sand was really nice. Colour aside, it has the distinction of not being sticky like that of all the other beaches where I have been.

No, that sand slid over you, giving you the feeling of walking on something very similar to rice grains, or something like that.

«If I understand correctly, they asked you to spy on all the heads of state of the planet, am I right?», I asked Jameson, after listening to his story with great interest.

«Exactly, Alex. From then on, under my command, a very substantial part of CIA was used in a huge spy operation in all the world. At first we started intercepting the heads of state, then we moved on to intermediate levels, and then, within a short period of time, we started to listen to almost every citizen of planet Earth, when necessary. Telephones, internet, credit cards, satellites. All doors wide open, through which we just entered.», Jameson explained.

«Bu without knocking or asking permission.», I objected.

«Well, this is obvious.», he replied, confident in himself.

«Oh, this is certainly your point of view, a little less from the point of view of citizens who are bugged, don't you think?», I replied immediately.

«Alex, heck, you must not give in to the narrowness of a simple common vision! You are representing your Nation, and you'll be called upon to do so with more and more responsibility, therefore you should strive to have a different outlook, wider and deeper. Security has a price, that's for sure. Sure, some conformists would not accept it, so what? There's so much hypocrisy in this World. After the September eleven, everybody got for the jugular of our intelligence system, and today that we got inverting the course doing what we should have always done, everybody demands for privacy, even if they feed the network with every detail of their private life through social networks. Don't you find it absurd at least?», Jameson provoked.

«Of course it is. Actually, explained in this way, it's flawless ...», I replied.

«But of course! I repeat, with regard to civilians, we are just doing our job, I guarantee you. Moreover, if a person has nothing to hide, what's the problem? It's a different matter concerning other intelligences and other heads of State, but also in this case, I can guarantee that through this job we discovered true conspiracies against us. In those of the United States, I mean. George Bush had been farsighted...», Jameson said, adjusting the panama on his head.

At that moment I stopped walking and turned toward the sea, instinctively.

What wonderful colours, I thought.

Then I watched a pelican that changed direction and went right over my head, and then it accelerated suddenly and nosedived a few centimetres from a man who was taking a bath.

One, two, three seconds, and here it is re-emerging on the surface, to get seated comfortably to eat its prey.

As I watched that scene, my mind went black for a moment, and then immediately after it filled up again.

A strange feeling, which led me to think about how deep was the rift that man was digging between himself and nature.

That's right, that concept came to my mind looking at that bird and perceiving its serenity, usually it happened to me each time I used to run into some seagull.

They had an almost hypnotic effect on me.

I could not help stopping and watching them.

Since childhood, I always thought that, if one day I had to reincarnate into something else, well, I would like to be a seagull.

I loved them, for the simple fact that they had the power to transmit me their serenity singing against the wind with their cries, and their light heartedness painting the sky with their trajectories.

I absorbed them by watching them.

«All this helps to save lot of lives, is it true Adam?», I asked him point blank, interrupting that delightful moment of silence.

«More than you can ever imagine, Alex. During these years, we have blocked attacks and carried out counter-espionage activities, having been decisive to nip any outbreak of war in the bud.», he argued with conviction.

In the meanwhile we started again to walk along the beach.

«According to your answer, I suppose that you are firmly convinced of the fact that it's worth all the hassle. But, if everything was so perfect, what has not worked out?», I urged.

«A very good question. Listen Alex, one of the several points of convergence between me and your father Ron, has always been the belief that, to achieve the best results, it was necessary to take care of every detail, even the most seemingly insignificant one. I, in my own small way, I have always acted like this. Or, at least, I've always tried to. In everything, in my work and in my private life. Unfortunately, however, as far as we can engage in the selection, sooner or later we come across people who can break a very thin balance, precisely because of that detail. For example, as you well know because it's an experience you lived on your skin, Skull and Bones could not boast of his very prestigious history, if the choice of Bonesmen had not gone through a strict and meticulous selection. By the way, tell me, do you know what agoge is?», he asked me, giving for a moment the impression of wanting to interrogate me.

«Of course, it was a series of tests to which underwent the Spartans; those who have not exceeded were not entitled to be citizens of Sparta.», I replied, displaying a certain security.

«Exactly! And in fact, the literal meaning of the term agoge is conduct. Conduct and selection, Alex. The principle is very simple, if not elementary, but that's the real commandment I have always followed in order to choose my collaborators and, more generally, to select each individual employee at CIA. Not surprisingly, it was one of the topics on which I most insisted in all four famous reports that convinced Bush to entrust me that position, because I thought that Murphy was not sufficiently firm on this concept. On the contrary.», he stated.

«Apparently, however, something must have not worked properly in the case of Dillinger.», I said.

«It's obvious. As I said before, even if you do your best to build an almost perfect mechanism, it could happen to you, sooner or later, to bump into the classical crazy variable or, worse yet, into something or someone who has an interest in subverting a certain balance, Alex.», Adam said, staring straight into my eyes .

His statement disquieted me. I froze for a moment, as if I felt the need to catch my breath.

«Are you trying to tell me that it was not a personal initiative of Dillinger, Mr. Jameson? If things were in this way, it would mean that we are dealing with a conspiracy of state, or something like that.», I replied, betraying my concern.

«It would not certain be the first time, and I'm not reinventing the wheel by saying that it will not even be the last. After all, if anyone who has studied history can be perfectly aware of it, guess someone who has the ambition to make history. Alex, I understand it will be hard for you to believe many of the things I'm about to tell you, but knowing the reality is the only way you have to rescue your life and, God willing, to have some chance to avoid the realization of the conspiracy against the State. As you may have figured out, the battle you are fighting is not only for yourself: the destiny of the United States of America, or most of it, is in your hands.».

**FBI Headquarters
at the same moment**

Tina Scott was highly furious.

«But what is this, huh? And don't touch me!», she shouted at Ortega face, who had the ungrateful task of telling her that he had just received orders to bring her to the interrogation room.

«Tina, I'm sure this is a misunderstanding, but you know well that behaving like this you will just worsen your situation. Come on, let's go.», her colleague replied, trying to calm her down.

If it had been asked to her colleagues to define her with an adjective, "cold" would have won unanimously without any doubt. In fact, the characteristic that has always distinguished Scott was her iciness in managing relationships which, however kept pace with great professionalism.

Most likely, these aspects, together with her undoubted physical attractiveness, had caused her to be perceived in the workplace with a certain detachment, especially by male colleagues, who saw her as the classical beautiful woman but impossible.

Furious, Tina decided to follow Ortega, not because of the order he had just given her, but for her desire to face Da Silva and clarify the issue with him as soon as possible.

Entering into the antechamber, Ortega opened the door and invited her to get into that same room in which, they together interrogated dozens and dozens of people.

Scott stared at the chairs for a moment.

This time I have to sit on the side of bad guys, she thought to herself.

After a few moments, also Da Silva came in, who sat next to Ortega and, with a wave of his hand, invited Tina to sit in front of them.

Until a few hours before no one of them would never have imagined to be compelled to face such a situation, regardless of the side of the desk behind which they were sitting at that time.

Goes without saying that, in that room, the air was imbued with tension and embarrassment to say the least.

It did not matter any more they were colleagues and they had fought together years of battles, at that point everyone had his own game to play.

They all were well aware of this: as Tina was aware of the methods used to make anyone feel like a rat during an interrogation, so Da Silva knew that the imperturbability of Scott would be a very difficult stumbling block to overcome.

«Tina, stop looking at me with that face, we're just doing our duty!», Ortega said, breaking the silence.

From her corner, she did not even bat an eyelid.

Flaunting great calm and confidence, she put her right elbow on the table and began to touch her chin with her hand, never stopping to gaze into the eyes of her interlocutors.

«Tina...», Da Silva said, but however he was immediately interrupted by his colleague.

«Tina a holy shit, Frank! I want you to know that as soon as this tomfoolery is over, I will ask to be transferred. I don't want to work with you any longer, you disrespectful people.», she said, in a firm and contemptuous tone.

«You're free to do as you want, anyway this is neither the time nor the place to talk about it. The arguments we have to discuss about now, are other.», Da Silva too replied firmly.

«Come on, speak, I'm all ears...», she said, with a hint of sarcasm.

Da Silva opened a file folder, he frowned and began to browse its content.

«You know Tina, I haven't given a look at your file since some years. So, this morning I decided to refresh my memory, and I found out some very interesting things... Well, let's give a look, Tina Angela Scott, born in Austin, Texas, on June 10 of seventy-one, graduated with highest marks at Yale in ninety-four. Throughout your academic career, you stand out for two main qualities: the first is your extreme propensity to privacy, and the second concerns your state of mind, distinctly analytical. And so far, I would say we are facing the perfect prototype of FBI Agent. A marvel. But, dear Tina, along with your impeccable curriculum, there's also the darkest side of your life, not only you did your best to hide it to anyone who became part of your life, but you've even tried to remove it from your own memory. For a whole life you have experienced it as a disgrace, you have refused it, denied it, and locked it up somewhere deceiving yourself it would never again show up. Am I right?», through that question, Da Silva tried blatantly to demolish the armour behind which Tina had always been able to hide herself, by remaining impassive in front of any kind of attacks and insinuations.

The two colleagues looked at her waiting for a sign of weakness.

Ten, twenty, thirty seconds.

Nothing to do.

Scott stood motionless, without showing any emotion and, above all, without looking down not even for a moment. Realizing that a simple insinuation was not enough, Da Silva, after having had a quick look at the file folder he was holding in his hands, laid it on thicker.

«You know what I mean, Tina, do you? Of course, I mean your dear daddy, who has betrayed the United States of America for years, becoming a KGB whistleblower. He was a traitor, and he bartered his honour with four cheap pennies. Who knows, maybe he has paid your studies in a prestigious and expensive university such as Yale with that money, the money of infamy and betrayal. I knew your father, you know? Of course, for several reasons we never had the possibility to work together, but in the environment there were rumours saying he was a man who liked to enjoy life. That's it, Tina. Maybe now I will reveal you an aspect of your father that not even you knew, and it concerns his inclination to betray. The psychological profile traced by the medical committee that has taken in charge his case after being arrested, clearly shows how this man could not control his instincts, which drove him to betray, to betray all the time: his Nation, as well as his wife, that is your mother. Although it's not considered as an illness, your father seemed to have a real disease. Information of our knowledge says that your dear daddy had betrayed your mom since always and that, moreover, he wasn't satisfied in doing it, so to speak… in a normal way. No, his perversion led him to live sex as a real drug. Once tried, that particular thing was no longer enough to him, and he felt the need to try an even stronger experience than the previous one, and so on. Orgies, prostitutes, places for swingers, transsexuals, and even sadomasochistic parties. Yes, that's right, your father ended up adoring being whipped, beaten and sodomized, with even more "masters" simultaneously. All this explains the several burn wounds we found on most part of his body, and also his acumed condyloma, pathology due to rubbing, which affects people who make passive anal sex with great assiduity. In short, Tina, besides being a bastard betrayer, your father was also a disgusting pervert who liked to have his ass busted, …», Da Silva charged up, never stopping to look up at Tina who, however, was still not showing the slightest emotion.

Shit, she is not human, she's a robot! Ortega thought, watching her with a hint of admiration.

«Listen Frank, I'm still waiting to know the reason why I'm here.», Scott said, in that icy and aloof tone that, over the years, had become her trademark.

Da Silva and Ortega looked quickly at each other. Basically they knew perfectly well that the person in front of them was trained to control not only her own state of mind, but even sweating and heart beats.

Essential techniques, that are integral part of the training program of any FBI agent, who have to learn them to pass the test of lie detector, if they should fall into wrong hands.

The goal is simple, that is to ensure that the intelligence agents, if caught, do not provide any information to the enemy.

Not even under torture.

That's right, because, in many cases, the line between the psychological and the purely physical torture is very thin, even non-existent. Goes without saying that Da Silva, being completely sure that Scott was a mole, had not even thought of crossing that line with her, being convinced that it was enough to bring up the right subject in order to make her nerves collapse thus making a breach in which he could insert himself and convince her to speak.

However, his first attempt failed miserably. So, just to dilate the wait, he took out a box of cigars from his jacket, and lit one.

«You've started smoking again, Anna will never forgive you, do you know it?», Tina glared at him.

«Thank for your thoughtfulness, but it's none of your business what my wife will say about it.», Da Silva replied bitterly.

«Uh, what an authoritative tone. You're probably nervous, aren't you Frank? Seeing your attitude I should assume so, even your forehead is also sweating. A FBI bigwig like you being put in difficulty by a simple agent like me, a real humiliation…», Scott said with determination, proving in that way that she was holding the situation, and not her boss.

«How the fuck you dare, Tina?», Ortega reacted, trying clumsily to take up the defence of his boss who, however, did not allow him to go on.

«I'm beginning to be fed up with this story and with your insolent attitude. Now I want you to tell me why last night you phoned Ortega and Richardson telling them to go home and rest, leaving Anderson and his friends without protection. I hope you have a very plausible explanation!», Da Silva said, raising his voice and beating his fists on the table.

On her side, Scott replied without hesitation.

«Because it was you who ordered it, Frank, you phoned me from home just before you fell asleep. Do you remember? Here, give a look, your call is registered on my mobile, you phoned me at ten twenty-eight.».

Ortega was stunned, and stared at his boss and at that point awaited an answer.

21

Who's Chuck Dillinger?

You must not fight too often with an enemy,
otherwise you will teach him your whole art of war.
NAPOLEON

Eagle Beach, Aruba
in that moment

THE words of Jameson weighed as boulders. I felt as if someone had thrown me in the middle of the final picture of a video game, putting my back against the wall and forcing me to face with my bare hands a monster infinitely bigger and stronger than me.

The university, my career as prosecutor, five years in Washington, the electoral campaign, everything seemed to me so microscopic faced with the enormity of a state conspiracy! Given the fact that the situation was really like Jameson described it, I could not see how I could subvert it.

I, alone.

In the meanwhile, thanks to the sunset, the sky above Aruba began to dress, from the horizon line upward, with a light composed of all shades of orange.

The sun stood out in front of us in his whole clear shape, slipping with the sinuosity of a billiard ball towards the stretch of water.

At that moment, a ship carrying thirty cheerful tourists passed in front of us.

I followed it with my eyes, until it came close to that magnificent blazing ball which, blurring its contours, seemed to wrap it in order to swallow it, and maybe, I thought, to spit it in some other sea, on some other planet.

Both Adam and I, we stopped to enjoy the scene, in silence.

After finishing its run below the horizon, the sun left the stage to a veritable anthology of really sensational colours.

I was literally amazed, I had never seen anything like that in my life.

For a moment I thought of my stupid belief that, having seen the sunset in Ibiza, any other would have seemed less beautiful.

I smiled, thinking that what I had in front of my eyes, more than a simple sunset, it looked like a giant painting by Monet.

Next to us, a boy and a girl, after placing their reflex on the stand, began posing and made several photos with the self-timer. They spoke Italian and, at a guess, they could be the same age as me. They were a nice couple, able to kidnap my eyes, making me feel their great energy. For a moment I thought about Veronica.

I'd like to share this moment with her, I thought.

After the photos, the two took off their t-shirts and headed toward water, holding their hands .

Instinctively, I turned to Jameson.

«Can I?», I asked, while I took off my shirt.

«Go and enjoy this wonder of nature!», he said, adjusting again his hat.

I did not think twice about it, I made a jerk and started running towards the sea.

Not even ten steps, and the water had already reached my neck. I swam a few strokes, and I found myself floating in the midst of an explosion of colours.

I raised my head, I looked around, and I relaxed. I thought that, after all, the wonder I was watching was of such a magnificence that, in its sight, the problems awaiting me began to seem smaller and smaller.

«Hey Alex, have you finished playing the dead afloat?», Adam shouted from the shore. Although grudgingly, I swam towards the shore and I joined him.

«Beautiful, isn't it?», Jameson asked.

«It's rather reductive saying beautiful. Thinking about it, also magnificent is reductive. I'm speechless, even though I was born and grew up in Los Angeles.», I replied, unable to take my eyes away from the 'painting by Monet'.

«It's very understandable. Not by chance, it's thirty years I come here to Aruba whenever I can.», he said, with an expression on his face showing pride and nostalgia for days gone by.

His long sigh and his blankly look confirmed my impression, so I decided to distract him.

«Well, even if the circumstances are not properly the best, I thank you for having made me know this lovely place, Adam. I hope to come back and enjoy it seriously, sooner or later.», I said, laying gently my hand on his shoulder.

«For sure, if you follow my instructions it's more than likely.», he replied, regaining his convinced and convincing tone that shortly before he seemed to have lost.

«Exactly. If I'm not mistaken we were speaking about the fact that Dillinger was part of a much wider plan...», I told him.

In the meanwhile, we started walking in reverse direction towards the resort.

«That's it. The genesis of Dillinger case took place in Afghanistan, in two thousand and two, about a year after the beginning of the Operation that we all know as Enduring Freedom. It was the weeks immediately following the Battle of Tora Bora and the installation of the provisional government headed by Hamid Karzai. The Bush administration, seeing the Taliban enemy staggering, rather than lowering its guard, thought well to further increase the number of US troops, up to ten thousand units. They were determined to launch their coup of grace, in short.»

Command of the US Army
Base area of Bagram, north of Kabul
Four in the morning on the twenty-eighth of February of two thousand and two

«Bloody hell! I begin to hate this fucking place!», Jeff Conlon said in a whisper, as he prepared to take place without pleasure.

«Mr. Conlon, can I do something to cheer your stay with us?», glared Gary Bradshaw, the head of CIA's Special Activities Division, who had summoned a meeting without any notice in the middle of the night, throwing everyone out of bed.

«I'm sorry, Sir.», Jeff replied softly, while his colleagues were sneering.

In just a moment, the cold made them forget the sleepiness of the bed. Behind him, Bradshaw had a cloth on which was projected a freeze-image of a photo taken from above, it seemed to be the entrance to a cave. The Afghans mountains were full of them, and in many cases they were the only places were Talebans and Al Qaeda followers could take refuge.

«Thus Sir, the reason for this urgency is that, according to the information we came into possession, we have very good reasons to believe that Talebans and Al Qaeda men are reorganizing themselves, and they're doing it in the mountains of Shahi-Kot, in Paktia province, at about eighty-five miles south of Kabul. What you see behind me is not a shot at random, but it's a photograph of the last cave in which that son of a bitch answering to the name of Bin Laden took refuge.», Bradshaw asserted.

«Let's go and catch him immediately, that damned!», someone said aloud.

«Keep quiet, keep quiet…we'll seize that bastard, how true is God! Most likely, at this time he is among those mountains to train his troops of Bedouins, inculcating in their heads all that crap about the virgins awaiting them after having blown themselves up and so on. Well, now our Chuck Dillinger will explain you the details of the information he came into possession .», Bradshaw said, beckoning him with his hand in order to be joined. Dillinger stood up and walked over to his boss, who welcomed him laying a hand on his shoulder.

«We have discovered the plan of those bastards thanks to him, listen very carefully what he has to say. Very good Chuck, go on like that.», Bradshaw congratulated, and then he sat in the place left vacant by Dillinger, next to Conlon, who greeted him with a very embarrassed smile.

Although he was not troubled the slightest, Chuck deliberately tried to give the impression of being clumsy. He did not want to seem too much self confident in front of his colleagues.

I've received too many compliments from Bradshaw, if I start to be full of myself, I would be toast. He thought.

Better to play the role of the loser and ingratiate himself with the rest of the group, rather than to be considered the favourite of the boss. Little more than one meter and eighty tall, light brown hair tending to blond, and rather fine lineaments, made him appear handsome but, because of his uncared way of dressing and the horrendous frame of his eyeglasses, he seemed to be the classic shabby geek lacking in taste, one of those who generally prefer t-shirts of two sizes bigger to slim fit shirts, perhaps with their favourite Japanese cartoon character printed on them.

As he reached the location where Bradshaw was before, Chuck put a hand into his pocket, took a USB key, and inserted it in the Mac Book that was connected to the projector.

After opening the folder containing the file he was looking for, he took the laser pointer on the desk, and asked the colleague closer to the switch to turn off the lights.

Click.

The darkness wrapped the meeting room, which was illuminated by the light coming from the screen behind Dillinger and, occasionally, by the light of the control tower that was about ten meters further away.

No one dared to speak, they all waited impatiently that their colleague would start to talk.

«So, as Mr. Bradshaw anticipated a moment ago, what we have seen before is the photo of the last refuge of the great chief of Al Qaeda. He's our number one target. The image was taken two weeks ago by one of our infiltrator who, taking advantage of the assignment to go back to Kabul and find medicines and basic necessities, at ten-thirty last night gave me the information I'm about to show you.», Dillinger said and, pressing a button on the remote control in his hand, he opened the first slide, at whose centre stood the face of whom, obviously, seemed to be one of the leaders of the Talebans.

He wore a white turban and had a very long black beard in the centre and curiously reddish on both sides; judging by the look and the half-open mouth, it seemed that the photo had been taken while he was talking with someone.

«His name is Namir Zemar, according to everyone he's the most famous mujahedin commander still faithful to the Taliban cause. According to our informer, he's the military wing of Bin Laden and Mullah Omar, who have chosen him to train the two hundred men they managed to gather among those mountains. Their goal is clear: to attract our air forces and try to seize them by surprise and attack them using mortars and old Stinger missiles dating back to the times of the Soviet invasion. In the plan of Bin Laden, the shooting down of American airplanes and helicopters would obtain great publicity, through which, essentially, he wants to prove to the whole World the beginning of the revenge of the rebel forces against the American invader.», Dillinger explained, while he was showing some images depicting places and people looking all alike.

Men with their faces covered and mountain sceneries, dry to the point to be considered hostile even by the meagre bushes growing there, which then die at the very first signs of the arrival of the infamous General Winter.

While his colleagues began to exchange some impression in a low voice, Bradshwa turned on the light and reached Dillinger.

«Well done Chuck, really well done. Now go back to your seat, thanks.», his boss dismissed him. and thumped his right hand three times on the desk to call the attention of his men.

«Hey, hey, perhaps the break bell has rang?», he screamed. Magically, they all became silent. Immediately.

«Have you heard with your ears. The pederast with the discoloured beard in the photo is the prosthesis of Bin Laden and Mullah Omar, who, being of course well aware that it's a real suicide, have well thought of directing operations by sitting their ass in a safe place and sending out their gay crony. Now, since these assholes are equipped with rusty mortars and missiles hoping to shoot down one of our warplanes, what shall we do? To begin with we will tell our bombers to fly at high altitude, and therefore out of the reach of their flak. Then we will finish the job with a ground attack, with a thousand of our men and as many units of the Afghan forces, we will grind them. Operation Anaconda will begin on March the second at two o'clock in the night. Come on, let's go to work!», Bradshaw ordered.

«Damn it, I have a great pain in my back! Chuck, I go out to smoke a cigarette.», Conlon said, standing up from his chair. Dillinger was left alone. After looking around, he put a stick into his computer which immediately launched a program to open a secure connection.

A few seconds later, a dialog box appeared on the monitor.

So, how did it go?

Everything as expected.
I told them you're two hundred.

Very good. When?

March 2nd at 2 A.M..
Bombing from a great height
and then ground attack.

How many men?

Two thousand.

They will get what their deserve.

Someone's coming. I close..

Chuck had heard the door opening, it had to be Jeff. In a moment, he closed the program, took the key from the USB port and put it into his pocket.

«Already finished smoking? You were faster than the speed of light...», he said, pretending on working on his computer.

«Friend, there's a terrible cold outside. I swear to God that as soon as I go back home I'll move to Hawaii, would be the last thing I do!», Conlon replied, still trembling.

I hope so, my friend. Dillinger thought, staring at a random corner of the screen of his computer.

Beach of Aruba
at nightfall

«How Operation Anaconda went, is well known history: two helicopters shot down, fifteen deaths and hundreds injured. It was a defeat. Of course the rebels among those mountains were not two hundred, as Dillinger told his colleagues, but estimates were about five thousand.», Jameson concluded.

«In short, Dillinger is a spy of Al Qaeda, he's a traitor!», I exclaimed loudly, realizing immediately that someone might have heard me.

Adam just gave me a glance, glaring at me.

«Sorry to have loosen control, but it's really hard to accept something like that. I can't believe that someone was so willing, it's crazy!», I told Jameson, trying to speak in a low voice.

«Alex, your feeling of anger is totally understandable. We lost many lives, too many, because of him. And we gave a valuable advantage to the enemy. Yes, because that whole operation was nothing but a diversion to allow Bin Laden and Mullah Omar to run away unhindered, while our men were engaged in that tragic battle.», Adam argued.

«Goddamn, why nobody tells the Americans the truth about Chuck Dillinger? An episode like that would be enough to open eyes of the public opinion who keep on considering him as a hero, rather than a criminal!», I asked Jameson.

«Officially because, talking about it after ten years would allow someone to consider the news as a hoax, able to delegitimize him, and about this issue, I'm ready to bet that some newspapers would dabble in it, portraying his as a victim, much more than he's now.», Jameson asserted.

Of course, in theory I could also share his supposition, but this did not change the fact that the attitude of conspiracy of that news was a colossal injustice. While I was thinking about his words, I realized that, in the meantime, we had reached the bar of our resort.

«Hmm, I understand, but however I don't agree. What about the unofficially?», I asked him point-blank.

He stopped and looked around to make sure there was no one.

«Because as I told you before, Dillinger is just the tip of an iceberg, Alex. And, in this case, the recklessness would be our worst counsellor, it would have brought us to end up as the Titanic.», he said, with a lot of apprehension in his eyes.

The fact that he kept things vague, made me overheated further.

«Ok, but may I know who's behind this whole story?», I asked bitterly.

I was impatient, I wanted to know.

«Sure, but first go to your room and take a shower, we will continue our conversation at dinner. Our rendezvous is in front of the restaurant, in one hour.», he replied, showing an unusual calm.

At first his attitude floored me, but I preferred not to object.

«Okay Adam, see you later.», I just answered him, then I turned around and took the way to my room. «Hey Alex, do you like fish, do you?», he asked me.

«Of course I do, I'm from San Pedro, do you remember?», I replied, trying to smile at him.

«Good, see you in a while».

$$22$$

Good ones and bad ones

What lies in the effect was already in its cause.
BERGSON

**FBI Headquarters
interrogation room**

«I have to arrest you, Tina. You leave me no choice.», Da Silva said, putting out his cigar nervously in the ashtray on the table in front of him.

Incredulous, Scott opened her eyes wide, expecting an intervention in her defence by Ortega who, despite having printed on his face an expression of great affliction, was very careful not to contradict his boss. The atmosphere had become from cold to glacial.

«Oh really? Do you want to arrest me? And for what? For having carried out your order?», Tina beat her fists on the table.

On his side, Da Silva answered to the anger of his colleague by just standing up and putting all the sheets he had scattered on the desk into the folder.

«I have nothing more to add.», he said, going towards the door. At that point, also Scott got up from her chair.

«You have nothing else to add, Frank? Well, instead I have something to add, and I demand that what I am about to say is put on paper in the interrogation report: where were you between ten and eleven o'clock the other morning, while Nowitzki was dying in his office, huh? And how come that yesterday night at ten and twenty-eight you called me from home entrusting me the task to tell Ortega and Richardson that they could go back to their homes, knowing that Alex Anderson,

Veronica Hayes and Matt Payne would have remained without any protection? Now I understand why you have not made that phone call yourself directly.», Tina pressed, pointing her finger at Da Silva, who went on a rampage.
«How you dare to address the undersigned in this way, huh? You're a traitor, just like your father!», he inveighed, going back. The two were few centimetres away from each other.

«You know Frank, I think it's evident for everybody that if there's a traitor here, well, that's not me, but you!», she accused him, openly defying her boss.

«Ugly bitch, you'll rot in prison, like that pervert of your father!», only then Ortega, having remained literally petrified for all the time, got cracking and slipped between the two.

«Stop! It's enough! Tina, calm down…», the colleague grabbed Tina's arm, but she wiggled away quickly.

«I swear if you ever touch me again, I'll rip your balls and use them to resole my boots», she threatened him, leaving him speechless.

Suddenly, the door of the interrogation room opened.

«Here nobody arrests nobody. Frank, from this moment the case is mine.».

Aruba
a few minutes after six and thirty in the evening

Hey brother, everything okay?
Here everything's quiet,
reply me as soon as you read my message, ok?
I care for you.

The minutes missing to the appointment with Jameson seemed to be the longest of all my life. After taking another shower, I took my iPhone and started checking emails and social networks.

I had received several messages, but I was too impatient to read them, let alone to answer. I would have done it any other time. The only exception was for Matt, who had sent me a message about two hours before. He will surely be worried, I thought.

I could no longer stay in that room, so, even though there were fifteen minutes left, I decided to go out.

Adrenaline was steadily rising.

I was damn restless, I was dying to know who and what was hidden behind Dillinger, the truth about Maggie Jones and, more than anything else, which was the plan for which they had decided to involve me in this whole story. To understand everything, I still had lots of dots to join, and Jameson was the only one able to help me to draw those lines.

After putting my phone in my pocket, I turned off the lights and went out through the sliding door overlooking onto the garden.

Shit, the badge! I thought, realizing to have left it on the desk, and that I was locked out of my room.

Anyway I decided to go walking towards the restaurant, also because after dinner I would have plenty of time to go to the reception and ask for a duplicate.

Passing through the meadow, I crossed some guests of the resort, which seemed to be frequented only by couples looking for a few days of peace and relax. The classical place to be put up as a desktop wallpaper, with which everyone would change for sure his cold Monday morning back to the office.

At the entrance of the restaurant, I found to welcome me a middle-aged man, extremely polite, who, after asking me the name, quickly consulted the list he was keeping on a lectern.

«His friends are already here, Mr. Anderson. Please, follow me.», he said.

«I think there's a mistake, for all I know the friend waiting for me should be alone. Could you check again, please?», I said.

«No mistake, Sir, Mr. Jameson is waiting you at the table together with someone else. Come on with me.», he replied, inviting me to follow him with a wave of his hand.

At that point I followed him without batting an eyelid. But why is Jameson not alone? Yet we have very confidential things to talk about, and I only trust him! I thought, as we passed a blue satin tent, delimiting the rest of the restaurant, behind which there was only our table. As soon as he saw me coming, Adam stood up.

«Hey Alex, welcome!», he said, making me a sign to sit down next to him. Of the other person, who was sitting in front of him, I could only see his back and his grizzled head.

Who might he be? That surprise made feel more nervous, I felt my heart pulsating into my ears.

One, two, three steps and I reached the table.

Finally also Jameson's guest got up.

Instinctively I stepped back a pace and, at that very moment, he turned.

I was petrified, and the greeting I was about to say stopped in my throat, causing a pile-up of all the words I wanted to say.

It was him, the guy with glasses who followed me right up to my house door, making me that speech about the national interest.

«I can quite easily imagine which are your thoughts in this moment, Mr. Anderson. You'll be surely wondering who I am, the reason of my presence and, above all, what kind of role I play in this whole affair. They are absolutely legitimate questions, to which both I and our mutual friend Adam Jameson will give answer. Obviously only after you take seat between us.», he said, showing no emotion.

His presence floored me, but the strange thing was his voice, cold and monotonous like a robot, there was something familiar. I'm not saying I was glad to hear it again, but near miss, and the full knowledge of a so absurd feeling distressed me even more.

They both looked at me in silence for a long moment, until I stopped the delay, taking a seat next to Adam.

«Can I break the ice at once?», I asked immediately.

«You have to!», Jameson replied instantly.

Self-confident, I looked at the guy in front of me straight into his blue eyes.

«Who the hell are you?», I asked, before opening the napkin and lean it on my legs.

«If you have no objection, I would like to be the one doing the honours.», Adam anticipated him.

He nodded.

«Thus Alex, in the civil registry, the man in front of you answers to the name of Albert Moreau and officially he has never played any role in the American intelligence. Not only, I would also say that technically he does not exist. In jargon we call him a ghost, that is one of those people invisible to society because they are used to perform extremely delicate functions, not to say with a very high risk. Saying that, I mean that these operations are not only dangerous for the safety of those executing them, that would be the lesser of two evils, but also and above all for our national security. I will try to be even more explicit. If Albert is discovered and captured during a mission, the enemy would never discover he's working for us, but would also receive from Albert a series of false information aimed to mislead and sabotage any attempt of attack against us.», Adam said.

«That is, is he doing misinformation?», I asked.

«If necessary he is, but not only. Moreau is the very core of our counter-espionage, Alex. Basically, his main job is to identify infiltrators or traitors, and to keep contacts with any foreign deserters in order to make them cooperate by providing information and, of course, checking its veracity. Most of them betray for money, a small part for ideological reasons, and others for matters generated by a personal discontent.», Jameson explained.

«Hmm, so I guess it was you to flush Dillinger out.», I asked straight to Moreau, who took off his glasses and began to clean the lenses with a care and a calm such as to make that gesture seem as a kind of ritual through which drawing strength and concentration.

After watching them carefully backlit, he wore them again and, putting his elbows on the table, approached me by bending slightly his back.

«You see, Mr. Anderson, the answer to your question is yes, but the fact itself is just a pure detail. Indeed, as Adam has explained you this afternoon, Chuck Dillinger is nothing but the product of a system, a pawn. Ergo, the real problem is not him, but the system itself.», he stated.

Immediately I took advantage of his break and interrupted him, because I had the impression he was keeping on ringing around the problem. I wanted him to tell me how things were exactly.

«I've well understood this story about the system, but when do you decide to be more clear? Give me first and last names!», I said, in a deliberately provocative tone.

He, on his side, did not hesitate a moment to answer me.

«It's my duty to warn you that the more things we will tell you, the more your life will be in danger, Mr. Anderson. Do you really want to put yourself on the line up to this point?», he asked me, looking into my eyes.

«What do I have to lose?», I replied.

«All.», Jameson pontificated.

«Well, at this point, I see no alternatives. Moreover it was you who made me take a plane in a hurry and come up to here. Well, as now I'm here, I want to see it through, whatever it takes!».

They looked at each other.

«As you wish, Mr. Anderson, but you have to know that what I'm about to tell you is covered by state secret, and that never and ever, in no case, you will have or can use this information, or worse yet divulge it. Doing so, you would tarnish the crime of high treason. Now, I imagine that you have certainly read and studied the historical facts more or less reliable about internecine clashes among different parts of the State. In some cases, these are cheap conspiracy theories without any foundation, while in other cases, they are very close to reality. As, for example, in the case of the investigations about the murder of John Kennedy, which was not committed by Oswald but, as the investigations carried out by Jim Garrison demonstrated widely, by the heads of our intelligence with the collaboration of several segments of the State, to be more precise those who had to respond to the powerful lobby of ship-owners, evidently contrary to an eventual withdrawal of American troops from Vietnam.», at that point, Moreau paused and drank some water to clear his throat.

«I see you are changing your expression, and I understand it, given your age, but you must put in your mind that, after our conversation tonight, many of the beliefs you have built over the years, will crumble. On the other hand, the institutions are composed of people, and the human being is by definition fallible, unreliable and, therefore, corruptible. The resulting consequences are the amalgam of power and great economic interests, in the name of which decisions and strategies are oriented. In general, just as among the different animal species, the different power blocks tend to divide the territory, in order to avoid field invasions and in this way they maintain the status quo. In a such framework, the protagonists of the respective blocks, composing the mosaic of the State, are acting. Army, CIA, FBI, Parliament, White House: each of these elements is an organism on its own, and in its turn is composed by different microorganisms behind which lurks a power lobby. Let's take your case. At not even forty years you can boast a career as a District Attorney, a mandate as Representative in Congress, and an almost unanimous recognition as the possible next Republican candidate for the most important seat of the planet, that of the President of the United States of America. According to you, could all this be casual?», he asked me with a clear insolence in his voice.

«Are you maybe insinuating something, eh? If I achieved some positions it was because, unlike many of my peers, instead of thinking about girls and surfing, I have worked my ass off both at university and at work. What do you think? As for politics, then, I won the election by going everywhere around my district and conquering vote on vote. Therefore my answer is no, the results I obtained are not absolutely casual!», I said proudly.

I could remember one by one all the sacrifices and privations I had to face, in order to pursue and achieve my dreams, and I would not have allowed anyone to cast doubt on my good faith.

Not even the head of our counter-terrorism who, fresh as a cucumber, started again to speak.

«Save this kind of claims for your voters, you know very well that the reality is different. Try to imagine how many other top students willing to do, as much as you, if not more, exist in every corner of the United States. Millions. So, why you, eh? Because of your diligence? I don't believe it. Because of your small sacrifices? It's a nonsense. Matter of luck? Not on your life. The truth is that you too are a cog in that system of power. Along with your grandfather Philip and your father Ron, you are part of Skull and Bone, which is one of the most influential lobby on Earth, up to the point to express most of the men composing the American establishment. Therefore, stop lying to yourself, and put in your mind once and for all that you have not reached the power by no means, but it's power that took possession of you. Mr. Anderson, whether you accept it or not, you are a predestined. Just like Dillinger. Of course, you fight on opposite sides, but you are two sides of the same coin.», Moreau declared.

Although I considered a real affront being treated just like a traitor such as Dillinger, I could not answer him on the spur of the moment. For a few moments, I fell prey to a sort of black out, during which I saw passing before my eyes some images of my existence, in rapid sequence, with no particular order.

These images alternated with more or less familiar voices pronouncing words I had heard years and years before.

My grandfather explaining me "Politics is a disease from which you never heal", when we used to read the newspaper together, every Sunday morning.

My mother trying to comfort me because of our move to Rome.

The instant when I realized my father was the man hiding behind that jute hood, celebrating my rite of initiation to Skull and Bones, "One day you'll thank me for this, Alex".

The unforgettable sense of emptiness I felt on September eleven, wandering around the streets of New York.

Matt's embrace. Veronica's eyes. Nowitzki's death.

The explosion down at the Harbour.

The sunsets with Sue.

The oath with Maggie.

The voice of Da Silva.

«Hey Alex, sure to feel good?», Jameson asked me, catapulting me again into reality.

I made a little click, as if someone had suddenly woken me up.

«Yes, thank you Adam, I was just lost in my thoughts, I'm sorry.», I replied with a sigh.

«Don't apologize, an intricate situation like this would destabilize anyone.», Moreau added, strangely with a more human tone.

By far it was the first time I heard him talking like that.

In the meanwhile two waiters arrived, and began to serve us dinner.

«Since you both love seafood, I have taken the liberty to order for all.», Adam said, confirming to the maitre, with whom he seemed to have a certain confidence, that he could also serve the wine.

«Very well, Mr. Jameson, I'll immediately bring you the Italian Arneis as usual.», the maitre replied.

«If I understood correctly, what you are trying to telling me is that Dillinger has betrayed the institutions on precise orders of some piece of our institutions themselves, is it right?», I asked both my interlocutors.

«Perfectly right, Mr. Anderson.», Moreau replied immediately.

«Okay, but for what kind of purpose? Well, I mean, why should the State make war against itself?», I answered back.

«It's a matter of balance, Alex. Balance between partisan and collective interests, between political beliefs antithetical to each other and, above all, balance in the public opinion, the control of which appears to be a determining factor when maintaining the so-called social peace, without which, you teach me, our society would be almost ungovernable.», Jameson argued.

«I understand, Adam, but there's a big difference between your words and putting to death our men on the battlefield or risking to overload the entire intelligence system by making public all information on interceptions. Without even considering that the leakage of these documents has created tensions among us and other countries, endangering the relations with some of our best allies. Although forcing myself, I can not find the connection between all this and the principle of social peace to which you refer.», I replied.

Putting his hand on Jameson's shoulder, who was about to speak again, Moreau interrupted him, stepping in.

«The links are essentially two. The first concerns the internal clash inside our intelligence, with the heads of FBI antagonizing those of CIA. A real hidden operation, whose aim is to conquer the command bridge of the whole intelligence system. With all the benefits achieved from it. The second link, on the other hand, leads straight to that famous control on public opinion that, since always, is the top priority of anyone governing the country. To be governed, public opinion needs relatable characters, just like reading a book or watching a movie. The good ones and the bad ones. So happens that those who have been involved in the casting, have chosen Dillinger to be the bad guy.», Albert stated.

«If Dillinger is the bad guy, who would be the good one?», I asked.

«The one chosen to act the role of the good one who will challenge all bad guys is you, Alex. Thus it is written.», Adam replied, before tasting the white wine that, moments before, the maitre had served.

23

I have no choice

Betrayal never triumphs: which is the reason?
Because if it triumphs, no one dares to call it betrayal.
SIR JOHN HARINGTON

**FBI Headquarters
at the same time**

«And what the hell are you doing here? How dare you come to my place and give orders?», Da Silva yelled, who was in obvious difficulty.

The person standing in front of him against whom I had just inveighed, was John Bennett, the Director of FBI.

Ortega was stunned, while Scott looked undoubtedly relieved. The coming of the great boss was providential, she thought.

Frost dropped also beyond the mirrored glasses, where the whole staff of Da Silva was witnessing what, until a few moments before, was the questioning to their colleague but, unexpectedly, was taking the turn of what appeared to be a real indictment of the Director of FBI against the Head of the counter-terrorism division of the National Security Branch.

«First of all it will be better for you to calm down, Frank. Secondly, until proven otherwise, it happens that I am the boss, and not you. I give orders. Now I ask you to sit up and answer the questions just made by Agent Scott.», Bennett shouted.

Swallowing the bitter pill, Da Silva accepted the invitation of his superior and, without a word, went back to his place.

«So, Frank. I want answers. I want to know where and with whom you were when Nowitzki died, and why yesterday night you phoned Agent Scott giving her that order.», the Director insisted.

Da Silva didn't even give him a second look and kept on looking at the desk, on which he drew some lines by passing his fingers wet with sweat.

«Are you telling me I'm suspected of being a traitor? Is it so John?», he asked, ending his silence.

«This is not a court, but a colleague is dead, and there are too many elements that don't square, Frank. Too many. This story of Dillinger and Datagate is becoming every day more explosive, and it's likely to explode into our hands, at any moment. Logically, the President wants to keep our private business to ourselves, that's why he gave me the mandate to handle the matter personally, giving me carte blanche. This is the way things are, whether you like it or not.», Bennett replied coldly.

«This means that you have doubts about me. Well, well. This must be the gratitude for forty years of honourable service, during which I have never been accused of stealing even a pinhead!»

«Precisely because of your experience, you know that in our world there is no gratitude. Do you remember what old Hoover used to say?»

«Answer to no one, look over your shoulder...»

«Right, Frank. This is the rule in our job, our task is to apply it, even at the cost of calling a colleague with a pristine career like yours into question. But the stakes are too high, and you know it. So, if you can, prove your non-involvement in this story, otherwise cooperate and spill the beans of your own volition. I don't want to get tougher with you.»

By now, Da Silva's hands were dripping sweat to the point of leaving their contour drawn by the white halo of condensation on the lacquered surface of the desk.

For some moments he became estranged from what was around him, focusing on the signs of his hands. Just like he happened to do sometimes on his desk school as a kid, to isolate himself from the rest of the class, hoping thus to disappear.

Poof!

To become invisible to the eyes of all, transparent. And therefore not to be chosen by the professor to have an oral exam.

Island of Aruba
at the dinner table

«This Blangé is simply stunning. Fragrant and fruity, it comes from the north of Italy, from Piedmont to be precise. Think that here at Bucuti they began to order it only for me, but recommending it to a few more guests, it made it one of the most requested white wines in the resort. Come on, don't wait, taste it!», Jameson told with a touch of pride.

Although I was not in the right mood, I drank a toast with them and took a sip of that wine that, actually, was a real pleasure.

Yes, maybe it helps to ease the tension, I thought.

«So, precisely, who's behind Dillinger?», I asked them point blank.

«Great part of FBI, whose aim, as I explained before, is to give us of CIA a bad name. By giving us a budge they would take our place on the top step of the podium, having thus more resources and funding. Which, to be very clear, means more power.», Moreau explained and soon after he drank the last drop of wine left in his glass.

The mere thought that a part of our intelligence services conspired against each other, jeopardizing the safety of the entire country, nauseated me and made me shake the veins in my wrists.

«Albert, you're telling me that FBI has manipulated Dillinger, using him to implement a conspiracy against the state, is that right?», I asked Moreau.

«Not the whole FBI, but a very substantial part of it, that is the one that has always thought its bureau was regarded as a child of a lesser good compared with its CIA cousins whose key roles, however, have almost always been the prerogative of high environments very close to Skull and Bones. This is to clarify you further the positioning of the pawns on the chessboard.», Moreau said.

«And think that now it's precisely FBI that is taking care of the safety of myself and of my friends …», I replied.

«In fact, if we've made you come here to Aruba, was also because you were in the wrong hands, Alex.», Jameson intervened.

His statement disquieted me, making me think immediately of Veronica and Matt.

«What do you mean, Adam, that Da Silva is not protecting me?», I asked worried.

«That's it, Alex. Da Silva is one of those Albert was referring to before, being on the side of Dillinger. The poor Nowitzki, who was unaware of it, sensed there was something wrong, but he was not able to understand that it was Da Silva being two-faced trying to cover Dillinger. So, early in the morning, he went to his boss to explain him what he was discovering.»

two days before at nine forty-four
FBI Headquarters
Carl Nowitzki's office

«Listen, I have important news, but we can not wait until two o'clock to see each other. I wait for you here in an hour.», Nowitzki told Alex Anderson, before hanging up the phone. In the meanwhile, Da Silva came into the office.

«Here I am Carl, I'm all yours. Tell me, which are these important news?», he asked, sitting down in a chair in front of the desk of his colleague.

«A cup of coffee, Frank?», Nowitzki asked, and soon after bit voraciously in a chocolate donut.

«I thought you got it over with this junk food.», Da Silva replied who, that morning, betrayed a strange expression.

They were colleagues since over thirty years and, although neither of them was the kind of person who liked to express their feelings, between them there had always been a friendship going far beyond the simple professional collaboration.

They knew each other like the back of their hands, in short. In fact, a simple look was enough for Nowitzki to perceive that, this morning, his colleague looked at least ambiguous.

«I'll have to die of something, or not?», Carl exclaimed, after having swallowed the last bite of donut with the aid of a sip of coffee.

Da Silva looked at him, but did not answer.

«Frank, tonight I kept on thinking about it. I racked my brain putting together all the elements of this story trying to figure out who had an interest in involving Alex Anderson and why. I have analyzed his whole life as a model boy, the life of his parents and of his grandfather Philip. It seems we are faced with the prototype of perfection: very good family, brilliant school education, his career as district attorney, and now, a fulminating political rise. His grandfather was senator, his father consul, his mother journalist... in short, the Andersons are so perfect that we could make a nice picture of them to hang on the fireplace, don't you think? They are the model that every good father chases every day for himself and his children. They embody the American dream. But I became suspicious just because of all this perfection. And so I realized it was enough to just give a scratch on the surface, to bring out some aspects, so to speak... fishy. One above all, that is their strong bond with Skull and Bones.», Nowitzki explained.

«Well, it's one of the most powerful lobby in the country, but it's not a crime being part of it.», Da Silva interrupted him, taking advantage of a short break of his interlocutor.

«No, it's not, but we know very well to which environments it's related that sect: CIA, Frank. In particular, I discovered that the grandfather of Alex and Adam Jameson were very close friends. It was thanks to Philip Anderson, in fact, that Jameson succeeded in getting into the good books of Bushes who, incidentally, are universally considered to be the true founders of Skull and Bones. So, to sum up, Bush plus Skull and Bones equals Adam Jameson, CIA Director. Therefore, since I still have a good relationship with him, last night I called him on the phone.», Nowitzki said, who was abruptly interrupted by Da Silva, whose expression darkened further.

«Are you telling me you phoned Jameson and blabbed about our case? Is it true, Carl?», He asked, beating his fists on the table.

«Damn it, Frank, what the hell's up with you? Of course I phoned him, and do you want to know what he told me? That behind this whole story there would be a certain Chuck Dillinger.», Carl explained, unable, however, to appease the rage of his boss.

«All bullshits!», Da Silva shouted, managing to make his colleague lose his good temper, who, notoriously, had always been a very quiet and reflective person, so that no one had ever seen him hit the roof.

«Shit Frank, have you lost your mind this morning? According to Jameson, CIA would have the proof that fanatic Dillinger is nothing but a cover up of a consistent part of FBI. Frank, here there is someone who is plotting against the State, and it's our duty to flush him out, without caring for anyone!», Nowitzki exclaimed vehemently, standing from his chair and pointing his finger against Da Silva, who frowned and broke the pen he was holding in his hand, so strong was the tension running through him, pervading every centimetre of his body.

Five, ten, twenty seconds of total silence.

«So, have you nothing to tell me, Frank? At a minimum you should be disgusted as I am!», Carl said, trying to lower the tone of his voice.

On his side, Da Silva struggled to look up, his eyes seemed to be glued on his knees, and gave a quick look of defiance to his colleague.

«If you think to dig the dirt on the good name of FBI playing into the hands of those assholes of CIA, know that you're completely off the track, my friend.», he said in a monotonous tone, before getting up and leaving the room, slamming the door.

In a few seconds Da Silva rushed into his office, telling his secretary not to pass him phone calls.

He closed the door, sat at the computer and, after looking around, turned it on.

Username: dasilvf
Password: ●●●●●●●●

ACCESS DONE

<u>Internal circuit of video surveillance</u>

Cameras south side: ACTIVE
Cameras north side: DEACTIVATE

DEACTIVATION IN PROGRESS

DEACTIVATION MADE WITH SUCCESS

I have no choice, he thought.

He looked intently at an old photo of his family which he kept on his desk, and then closed his eyes for a few seconds.

Darkness.

God, please, have mercy upon me! He implored in a whisper.

He inhaled deeply, as if seeking within himself the strength to get up from his chair, into which he seemed to sink.

It's time to act, hurry up! He thought.

He went back the corridor, turned right and walked again through the threshold of Nowitzki's office.

«Hey Frank, I hope you've calmed. Anderson will be here in a few moments, sit down.», Carl said, trying to give a hint of a smile.

But Da Silva didn't answer.

They looked at each other, Nowitzki immediately sensed that something was wrong, his boss had a very strange light in his eyes that morning.

Matter of moments.

Carl felt a horrible sensation, of that kind that grips the heart when you are touched lightly by a bad feeling.

However, he would not believe it.

No, it can't be, he and I, we have been friends since thirty years, I just have to relax. Nowitzki thought, trying to reassure himself.

A drop of sweat ran down his forehead, and fell on one of the several sheets on his desk. The beating in his chest soon became a veritable flurry.

Matter of moments.

He looked down to take his handkerchief from the right pocket of his hazel overcoat that, as usual, was leaning over the back of his chair.

He looked up, and faced the gun barrel of Da Silva.

Neither of them had the strength to speak, they just gave each other a glance and understood each other immediately, as always.

Nowitzki closed his eyes, as if to say «come on, what are you waiting for, press that fucking trigger!».

A dull noise, choked into the throat of the silencer of that gun, that Da Silva stole from the leather bag of his colleague just a few minutes before.

Tricks of the trade.

The blood came gushing from Carl's steamy skull, and began to trickle down on the ground.

Da Silva breathed and closed his eyes again.

A sudden noise made him jump.

It was Nowitzki, who began to move jerkily.

Once, twice, three times.

At first Da Silva fell prey to a paralysis, then he tried to reason.

Shit, these are only stupid post-mortem spasms! He thought.

Then he placed the weapon carefully in the right hand of his colleague of a lifetime whom he had just killed like a dog, took off the latex gloves and, after having had a quick look to make sure not to have blood splatters on his clothes, opened the office door and began to scream at the top of his voice

«Run, Nowitzki has committed suicide!»

His voice trembled and, in all likelihood, even his soul was faltering.

Ortega was the first to arrive, and looked shocked at the shattered skull of his colleague and at the impressive pool of blood near his feet.

«Why did he do it? Why?», he asked his boss with tears in his eyes, standing still near the door.

«I haven't the faintest idea, but I'll found out, even if it's the last thing I do!», he replied, shaking his head.

24

Against the State

Truth is daughter of time.
FRANCIS BACON

**FBI Headquarters
interrogation room, now**

«That's how things went. Carl's death grieves me, but I had no choice. None of us has the choice, since you decide to take the badge and to do our profession, nobody!», Da Silva confessed, under the astonished gazes of his staff.

If aliens had landed, the atmosphere in that room would have been less surreal than it was at that moment.

Everyone, also Scott, struggled enormously to believe what their ears had just heard. Frank Da Silva, the faultless boss who had taught something to each of them, considered as the FBI emblem. A career and a credibility built daily, brick by brick, in over thirty years of honourable service, completely destroyed in a matter of a few minutes. From hero to zero.

From an undisputed reference point to the worst kind of criminal, branded for ever with the infamous sign of betrayal.

To kill Carl Nowitzki, colleague and friend for over thirty years, in cold blood. How can someone be capable of such brutality? But, above all, what would be the reason which pushed him to do something like that? Ortega, Richardson, Scott, Rice: the mind of everyone of them was crossed by the same question marks. Bennett, who had not taken his eyes off him, seemed unperturbed.

«According to your explanation of what happened, it's clear you have full awareness of the crime you committed.», he said, without showing any emotion.

«If I was not aware of it, I would be a fool, don't you think so? And even if someone might be tempted to assume the contrary, I'm anything but crazy, John. This is clear.», Da Silva said, with his proverbial firmness.

Despite his confession, the two did not seem very willing to give it a rest. Rather, everyone there had the impression, through the cross talk they were witnessing, that the psychological battle between Bennett and Da Silva was just at the beginning.

Moreover, to be seated one-on-one, were by far two of the best men of all the American intelligence. People who were used to put up with hours and hours of exhausting interrogations, scientifically prepared to the systematic lie aimed at throwing off track the enemy, very skilled masters in not let out a single comma of what they don't want to reveal, able to disassemble a whole story and reassemble it as they needed, in a few seconds.

«What do you think will happen now?», Ortega whispered to Scott in a faint voice.

«The III World War is going to break out. At the least.», she said, without taking off her eyes from her phone.

Aruba
at the same moment

Da Silva has just confessed.
Bennett is still interrogating him.
I'll write you as soon as there is any news.

Okay, thanks.

Jameson looked up from the phone and looked at me and Moreau with a certain satisfaction.

«Guess what? It was a message with which I was told that Da Silva has just confessed he was the one to have killed Nowitzki.», he said, showing us the display of his iPhone.

On the moment I felt the world collapsing on me.

Not because I was sorry for Da Silva, but for the simple fact that in this case, Dillinger and his followers knew every detail about myself. My story, each of my movement, my friends.

Even, Veronica and Matt.

I thought of their safety rather than mine.

Nevertheless, I had to take courage and swallowed the knot that was blocking my throat.

«Did you know it, Albert? Veronica and I, we saw you close to FBI that morning.», I asked Moreau right away.

«Of course I knew it. In a way, it was as if I knew it since the night before, when Adam told me he had been contacted by Nowitzki. Therefore we decided to put their phones under control. Needless to say, when I heard your conversation in which Carl asked you to join him immediately in his office, I realized instantly that the situation could have precipitated at any moment, and I ran to the central with the intention to ask Nowitzki to leave with a diversion. But, as we all know, unfortunately I arrived too late.», he explained.

«I understand. Anyway there is something that doesn't square.», I objected.

«That is?», Jameson asked with a hint of astonishment.

«You see, what I just can not understand is why you left me in the hands of Da Silva, knowing from the beginning he was on Dillinger's side. Well, I mean, if he came to kill Nowitzki, he could do the same with me or with my friends, and the simple thought that something might happen to them freaks me out!», I replied dryly.

«I understand your state of mind, but now calm down, Mr. Anderson. As Jameson told you before, we made you come here on purpose, and about your friends, we arranged a precise plan for the preservation of their safety. Nothing will happen to them, please believe me. The reason why we did not intervene immediately is that we needed to flush Da Silva out. Of course, in all fairness, I must confess we had not taken into account that he would be able to push himself up so much, murdering one of his closest and trusted collaborators.», Moreau replied, whose outspokenness floored me in a certain way.

«Alex, reflect: to confirm what Albert says, there is the incontrovertible fact that he and his men have constantly followed you, from the beginning. In fact your meeting last night just a few steps from your house, was not fortuitous.», Jameson added.

It's true that since that rapid succession of events, to me it was difficult to be able to trust someone. But had I options? Objectively no, I reasoned out.

«Okay, you convinced me, I believe you. But now I expect you to tell me how you plan to solve this situation. You should have a plan, I hope. Also because in a few hours I shall go back to Los Angeles, and I would like to understand what I have to do to put an end to this whole story.», I told them.

«The plan is to push out Dillinger and his men and bring them to justice. The White House has given us full mandate in this regard, as it considers a priority to dismantle the spy network to which he makes reference and eradicate every single infiltrated men from the intelligence system of the country. Da Silva was just the first one to be caught. From now on several others will be caught.», Moreau stated.

«I understand. Have you any idea where Dillinger might be hidden?», I asked them.

«We have very good reasons to believe that, through the info received from someone under cover, he came back to United States some months ago. Now it's up to us to be ready when he will try to make his next move.», Jameson replied.

«And in your opinion, which could be his next move? Yes, well, I mean, have you any idea what he might have in mind to do with myself?», I asked both. Adam and Moreau looked for a moment, then Jameson pressed my forearm and spoke again.

«Listen Alex, if you want to know what I think about it, I will tell you bluntly also because, at this point, burying our head in the sand would make no sense.», Jameson said.

«Go on, I'm all ears», I answered him, urging him to continue.

«Let's assume that Dillinger and those manipulating him have moved from a first phase in which they acted in the dark, to a second one, certainly more marked to give forth and emphasize

the "Dillinger character". Let me explain. By disclosing that huge amount of top secret documents to the media, and telling them about the issue of NSA and interceptions, they are clearly trying to transform Chuck Dillinger into a sort of hero, the champion of personal privacy and of freedom of information. Think about it, Alex, nowadays who does not feel involved in this story? Practically no one. In fact, it's enough to have a computer or a mobile phone to empathize with the accusations made by Dillinger. Hence, everyone feels bugged. What's more, many of the most influential newspapers have began to support the thesis that Dillinger, by spreading that information, besides having shown courage, would have made a contribution of historic significance in the defence of democratic principles on which the foundations of our Nation rest. So, if it is true we are facing an escalation, and we are, then each of the events that have taken place so far leads me to suppose that Dillinger is studying the classic coup de théâtre, the sensational action through which destabilize the system in order to demolish it.», Jameson explained, doing nothing to hide his concern.
«If I understand correctly, you're saying Dillinger might even think to kill me .», I interrupted him.

«I say this could be one of the options he is taking into consideration. After all he went close to kill you with the bomb down at the harbour. It's clear this was a demonstrative action, but if something went wrong you would have been killed, no doubt about it. In a certain sense we can say that, up to now, he had fun to play with you like cat and mouse and that, considering you as a kind of emblem of the system he says to fight, by eliminating you he would delete in the bud any possibility that the system may seize again the power.», Adam said, while he was waving his glass with the index and the middle fingers of his right hand.

He watched the movement of his white wine with such care, to make me think for a moment that he was looking for the answers to our questions in it.

«Yes, okay, but this is my first mandate in the parliament, and not as President! I don't understand why he chose me as an emblem!», I said.

«Damn it, Alex, because people begin to identify you and your family as the new Bush. You should start to get used to this idea, no matter how the story with Dillinger will turn out! Moreover the combination is so logical: you're a Republican, you studied at Yale and, as your father and your grandfather, you belong to Skull and Bones. What is taking place is the clash between your power system on one hand and those wishing to remove it on the other, opposing each other. Whether you like it or not, this is the way things are.», Adam replied, raising a little bit the tone of his voice.

Being so obvious, he had me over a barrel, there was little to do.

I had to resign myself to the fact that, in some way, the article by Huffington was a kind of watershed for me. On one hand, great, very great notoriety, and on the other the label, almost indelibly, of Skull and Bones. While I thought about the words of Jameson, a consideration made by Veronica came to my mind.

«Adam, I think you're right. Yes, it's as you say, now people will see me as the designated heir of George Bush, because media have stitched me this character. All right, I accept it, it's part of the game. But what I was thinking about is why the story of my family and Skull and Bones came out right now. Think about it: three days ago Dillinger began to harass me and, oddly enough, just the day before yesterday appeared the article in which one of the most influential journalists of the United States depicts me as the perfect enemy of Chuck Dillinger. In short, is it just an impression of mine, or the concurrence of the events is something more than a simple coincidence?», I asked both.

«Very good remark, Mr. Anderson. It seems quite clear that it's not a coincidence but, on the contrary, it's a clear plan to turn you into the number one enemy to be defeated. This does not mean that Arianna Huffington is part of those who are conspiring against you, indeed, I have good reason to believe that she has done nothing more than take the clue provided by some of her FBI contacts, who gave her that information on a precise mandate of Dillinger.», Moreau supposed.

«And what about Maggie Jones? During our last meeting, Nowitzki showed me an article describing the death of her family by boat, off Hawaii. But there was also written that the body of Maggie was never found. To your knowledge, is she still alive or Dillinger used her name as a bait to attract my attention? And assuming this is the way things are, who was on the other side of the phone on September eleven of two thousand and one?», I asked.

Moreover, that incredible story began precisely with the appearance, on the phone, of little Maggie.

Anyway, I thought, the key to everything could really be hidden behind that name. While I was absorbed in my thoughts, an unconditioned reflex made my gaze drop on the scar that was the eternal oath between her and me.

**FBI interrogation room
at that exact moment**

«I'm aware you're not crazy, Frank. Precisely for this reason, I would like you to help me to understand why a man with a such history as yours, has decided to embrace the cause of those who plot against the State.», Bennett replied, keeping his apparently cold and detached attitude.

Da Silva reacted by showing his disappointment, shaking his head repeatedly.

«You're thick as a brick, John.», he objected.

«Come on, go ahead, what is it I do not understand?», Bennett replied.

«That who is plotting against the State in not Dillinger, but the group of power that has Alex Anderson as a new leader. We're not doing anything but defending the United States of America against those who betrayed it by organizing the attack of September eleven in order to draw the necessary consensus to start their wars, useful only to further enrich their oil tycoons and ship-owners friends. This is the way things are, and even you know it!», Da Silva accused, succeeding in making his interlocutor hit the roof, who jumped on the chair.

«Fuck, Frank, are you completely nuts? Conspiracy theories are enormous hoaxes, even children know it! Moreover you and I, we have spent our best years to develop an intelligence system able to counteract terrorist attacks such as that one. How many attacks have we foiled thanks to interceptions carried out by NSA, eh? How many lives have we saved? Come on, tell me! Have you forgotten all that we have done, and how was the genesis of the Patriot Act? I can not believe that you have freely chosen to move on the side of a traitor such as Dillinger. Nevertheless you know very well which was his role in the defeat of Operation Anaconda. Because of him, we lost tens of men. Holy Christ, Frank, Chuck Dillinger is a fucking spy! How can you play into his hands?», Bennett shouted, with the clear aim to stress Da Silva out in front of his men.

Through his indictment, the Director of CIA made a beeline for the pride of his interlocutor.

If I goad him I could even succeed in making him understand his mistakes and, at that point, convince him that if he cooperates he could redeem himself, even if only partially. Bennett reasoned.

That exchange of accusations between the two men heated further up the already red-hot climate of the room. In the meanwhile also Richardson and Rice came, leaving their posts in the control room to join Ortega and Scott.

«I can see you insist on not wanting to understand, what a pity. But know neither you nor anyone else will be able to stop us!», Da Silva said, in a firm and threatening tone.

«I'm sorry for you, Frank, but maybe you have not realized I've already stopped you, and soon we'll do the same thing with your accomplices, Dillinger first of all.», Bennett replied back.

«Are you so sure, John?», Da Silva replied immediately.

«Of course I am, what are you insinuating?», Bennett said abruptly.

A strange sneer appeared on Da Silva's face.

With great calm he took the packet of Toscano cigars in front of him, and lit one.

«Do you allow me, don't you?», he asked Bennett with irreverent tone, who nodded without however making the slightest effort to hide his irritation.

«About Hoover, do you remember the sentence he used to tell us about our work? It's impossible to divide what we are by what we do. A blacksmith, an employee or a manager can do it, but a FBI Agent can not. We live of our work, which is always and everywhere: in the air we breathe, in what we eat, even in the moments we spend with our children. Physically we are with them, but a part of us is always there on the desk. That part of us that works incessantly, even when we sleep. Well then, in recent years many, too many had the illusion that you could take advantage of the power system, and that, after all, would be worth shaking off the good part, giving way to that of compromise and code of silence. You have sold your soul, and with it you have sold out even that of every American citizen on the planet!», Da Silva pontificated, in a crescendo, at the end of which he stood up, suddenly, surprising Bennett who also stood up in turn.

They were facing each other, only the desk was left to divide them.

«You're babbling, Frank! What are you going to do, huh? Think well and rather collaborate. You still have time to save your face!», Bennett said, holding out his hand for the umpteenth time.

He made a great effort to hold himself back and not to fly into a rage.

Da Silva burst into laughter.

«That's a good one! Save face, huh?», he replied.

«Exactly. I remind you that you've just confessed the murder of your colleague, Frank. And that you've betrayed your Country, collaborating and providing top secret information to a dangerous terrorist network. If you help us to bring those criminals to justice, you may have some hope to avoid the capital punishment.», Bennett said categorically.

The two scrutinized each other silently for a long moment.

«You know what, John? That I'm fed up, this tomfoolery has lasted too long. Ortega, Richardson, Rice, catch them!», Da Silva ordered.

The three obeyed and, at lightning speed, pointed their weapons against Bennett and Scott, pushing her violently toward the centre of the room, a few steps from the desk. Richardson walked toward them.

«Give me your phones, come on!», he ordered, keeping them at gunpoint. Albeit reluctantly, the two could just obey and give their phones to the beefy agent.

«Why do you do this, huh? You're obeying to a man who has just confessed to have killed Nowitzki!», Tina shouted in his face.

In response, Richardson did not hesitate to pack a violent bitch slap in her face, throwing her on the ground.

«Shut up!», told her cruelly.

«What will you do, Frank? Now it's over for you, and you know it. By acting in this way, you would only worsen your situation, and even if you gonna kill me, someone else will catch you, you can bet on it!», Bennett said, pointing his finger menacingly against him.

«You're just fooling yourself, can't you see.», Da Silva replied laconically, and before leaving, he ordered his men to handcuff Bennett and Scott at the desk and locked them into the room.

«You bastards!», Tina whispered disdainfully to Ortega, while he was clutching the handcuffs on her wrists.

The two men exchanged a quick glance, then, after being sure of having well immobilized them, Ortega joined his boss and the others.

Before leaving the room, Da Silva turned one last time toward Bennett and Scott.

«Which was that quote? Answer to no one, look behind yourself... Oh, I forgot to tell you that our guys are keeping an eye on you from the control room, so don't try to fuck up otherwise they'll have to shoot you down. Bye bye!», he told them.

A moment later he went out, closing the door behind himself.

25

An old house

The future torments us,
the past holds us, the present eludes us.
GUSTAVE FLAUBERT

In the meanwhile, in Aruba

«OFFICIALLY Maggie Jones has died on August the seventh in nineteen eighty-nine, but this does not mean that things are necessarily in this way. According to information in our hands, her only first-degree relative is her mother's sister, a certain Christine Williams, whose last known address was in London. Happens that the phone records prove that the famous phone call you were referring to before, came right from the British capital. So, I put two and two together, and I've ordered our agents based in England to gather as much information as possible about that woman, and guess what? Her real name is Marion Ross, and she's a FBI Agent who since the late eighties works undercover right in London. In eighty-five she got married with her colleague Aaron Beck, who was also in service in the UK, and she is mother of Clarissa, born in eighty, however is missing since June two thousand and three, shortly after graduating at UCLA in Los Angeles.», Jameson explained.

«Maggie was born in eighty and died in eighty-nine, a few months before Ross was transferred to London...», I remarked.

«That's right, but there's more. Marion Ross is currently suspended from service because of a disciplinary action accusing her to be the directly responsible for most of the top secret documents related to our intelligence activity in England, then divulged by Dillinger, just the ones from which began the scandal of Datagate. It's a very strange coincidence, isn't it?».

Obviously, the question Adam made me was purely rhetorical.

Fragment by fragment, the sequence of the story began to take shape and to assume a sense. In my mind I tried to put them all together, and imagine every possible option.

Clarissa is actually Maggie?

Is she really dead or is she alive under false pretences?

In this latter case, any clue would suggest she's part of the team of Dillinger.

That being the case, little Maggie would be clearly on the side of the enemy. I reasoned with myself.

«In cases like this it is said that three clues make a proof, is it right?», I replied.

«Yes, it is said so, and moreover it's a principle that you too know well, view and given your experience as District Attorney.», Jameson confirmed.

«Indeed. One of my professors at Yale used to say that, if someone burglarizes your house and at the same time the household vanishes, there are good chances he's the thief. Now however, the point is another: what will happen in a few hours when I go back to Los Angeles?», I asked them.

«I imagine that after the departure of Da Silva, your case has gone into the hands of John Bennett, the current director of FBI, and he will give you someone trustworthy, presumably Agent Tina Scott, that you already know. Anyway, even if unofficially, my working group and I will look after you. Having said this to calm you, I have to tell you in advance that I need your utmost cooperation, Mr. Anderson.», Moreau explained.

«Sure but, specifically, what kind of collaboration?», after my question, Albert opened his briefcase from which he took a strange key, and handed it to me.

I took it and I saw it was attached to a black label on which there were the numbers three hundred sixty-three.

«Alex, this is the key of a safe deposit box located at the luggage storage in the Airport of Los Angeles. Tomorrow, once you get off the plane, the first thing you'll have to do is to open it.», Jameson said.

«Okay, but what does it contain?», I asked intrigued.

«Everything you need to look after yourself.», he replied.

The following day on the plane
midnight and thirty-four Los Angeles time

In a couple of hours I would landed in Los Angeles.

Unlike usual, during the trip I did not sleep much, just a half an hour between a movie and another, however intermittently. I had the feeling that my brain was asking a supplement of energy, as if it meant not to rest even for a second, until I would have discovered the solution of everything.

I felt stalked.

Having nothing to read, I looked out the window for a while. Something I loved to do. That intense blue as ever, and the bed of clouds below us.

Who knows above who or what we are flying, right now. I thought.

Suddenly I felt my eyelids getting heavier and heavier, and I did not resist letting them close.

Suddenly I opened my eyes and I found myself inside an old house.

What the hell am I doing here? I wondered.

Furniture, paintings, electrical appliances, even the smell: looking around I had the distinct feeling of being in a house of the eighties. Somehow, however, that environment had something familiar, as if I had already been there.

From the windows, whose shutters were not completely lowered, filtered some slender but extremely bright sunbeams, able to bring out a real universe consisting of a sparkle of dust particles meandering in the air.

Looking at them carefully, it seemed they were not twirling at random, but following a definite direction. Almost as if each of them was aware of being the pixel of an infinitely more vast and varied plan, a plan in a continuous evolution as it is, after all, the life of each of us.

The sudden sound of a key into the lock of the front door, made me get back immediately. Coming in was a blonde woman, accompanied by the blinding light coming from the outside and to which, obviously, my sleepy eyes were not yet accustomed. I opened them widely and I was able to focus her face.

«Hello Alex, how are you? Maggie is coming, come with me, in the meanwhile I'll make you a snack!», she exclaimed, being happy to see me.

No, I could not believe it.

It was Linda Jones, Maggie's mother.

Instinctively I gave a look outside the door, finding the confirmation I was looking for. Across the street there was my old house in San Pedro, in which I grew up with my parents, before we moved to Rome.

That's it, I was in the house of little Maggie.

«Hey, tell me, has a mouse probably stole your tongue?», Linda asked me, while she was taking off her jacket and hanged it at the coat rack at the entrance.

«No, no mouse, my tongue is in its place...», I replied, not knowing what else to say.

«Ah, I'm glad to hear that, then if your tongue is in its place, it'll be the same for your stomach! Let's go into the kitchen, this morning I've baked chocolate cookies.», she said, bringing me back thirty years with my mind.

Even if I found that situation unreal, instinctively I followed her and sat down on one of the chairs at the big table in the middle of the room.

Linda gave me a cup with milk and Nesquik, approaching the tray of cookies, which had a tempting scent to say the least. For a moment I lingered on the cup: purple background and the logo of Lakers. It was exactly mine, the one that I used whenever I went to see Maggie. I ate those delicious cookies and drank all the milk, almost gulping it down. After that I got up and went to the entrance, where there was a mirror.

«Alex, is everything fine?», Linda asked me, worried to see me go out of the kitchen without a word.

«Fine Linda, I just want to see if Maggie is coming!», I replied her.

In the meanwhile I got in front of the mirror and, as I imagined, I saw the Alex of thirty-seven, and not that of seven.

But she treats me as if she was in front of a child. I thought.

«A few more minutes and she'll be here!», she exclaimed from the kitchen.

What a coincidence, at that exact moment the door opened and she, Maggie, walked in, out of breath and school bag still on her shoulders.

«Hi Alex! Hey mom, it's me!», she said looking at me, as if it were the most normal thing in the world.

I followed her into the kitchen and sat down beside her, intent on observing in silence every single movement of hers.

How beautiful was little Maggie!

«What's up, the cat stole your tongue?», she asked, making me and her mother burst into laughing.

«Well, what have I said so funny?», she said, blushing.

«Nothing my love, it's that a little moment ago I asked Alex if it had been a mouse to steal his tongue!», Linda said, putting a strand of hair, with one hand, behind her ear, that was dangling comically in front of her eyes.

On her side, Maggie smiled and began to dip the chocolate cookies into her milk. As soon as she finished, she took my hand and dragged me off the stool.

«Come with me, I want to show you something!», she said, enthusiastic.

We went up the stairs and got into her bedroom, on the bed there were several clothes, including some swimsuits.

«Look here, mom bought these for me yesterday, do you like them?», she asked me, waving them proudly.

«Very beautiful!», I replied, trying to identify myself as much as possible with myself.

At one point, her blue eyes became unexpectedly sad.

«Alex, do promise me that you will convince your father not to take you to Rome? If you don't promise it, tomorrow I won't leave for holidays!», she threatened, bearing a grudge.

Watching her, I realized how perfectly I knew every single expression of her face, even the most unnoticeable.

«I forgot you leave tomorrow…», I answered her, yet distracted.

«Today you're so weird, you know? It's a month I'm keeping on telling you that on the sixth of August we leave to Hawaii!», she said, opening her eyes wide.

August the sixth, Hawaii.

I chilled to the bone.

Impulsively, my eyes fell on the digital watch on her wrist.

TUE – AUG, 5 1989

August the fifth in nineteen eighty-nine, that is three days before the incident at sea when her parents would lose their lives and she would have disappeared.

I began to sweat cold.

I have to do something! I thought.

Intrigued by my attitude, Maggie stared at me and put her hand on my forehead.

«Are you feeling fine?», she asked me.

«Yes yes, Maggie, I'm feeling fine for sure!», I said lying.

I was still shocked.

So she took again my hand and dragged me out of her room, inviting me to follow her along the corridor.

«Come, I want to show you another thing!», she exclaimed.

My head went out of whack, I had no idea how to behave.

Should I talk to her mother, maybe inventing an excuse in order not to make them leave? I wondered.

One, two, three steps and, in the meanwhile, we came in front of a door.

«Here we are, it's here!», Maggie said, turning the doorknob.

The door opened and I, instinctively, entered.

Slam!

The door shut with a bang, and I found myself literally squeezed between the concrete wall at my back and the wooden wall in front of me.

I felt closed in, very closed in, I could not even move my arms.

I was suffocating.

«Hey Maggie, open this door!», I shouted repeatedly, at the top of my lungs

Once, twice, three times, nothing to do. No reply.

The door was always there, closed, in front of my face. Damn, I'm trapped! I thought, desperate.

I began to sweat cold and, as minutes went by, my breath became more and more laboured.

«Maggie, open this door, please!», yelling and shouting, panic stricken.

«Mr. Anderson, Mr. Anderson...», I opened my eyes, finding two very blue eyes in front of me.

«Maggie!», I cried waking up.

«No sir, I'm not Maggie, my name is Sheila, and I'm disturbing you because you should fasten your seat belts. We're starting the landing phase.», the hostess told me, with extreme kindness.

I stretched all my body, and I had the last sip from the bottle of water I had left on the table.

What a nightmare! I thought still out of whack.

Of course, I was perfectly aware that it had been caused by the revelations that Jameson and Moreau had made me some hours before but, however, what gave me a shock, was the absolute clarity of details besides, obviously, the scene in which I got stuck between two walls.

Crazy.

I had woken up, I was conscious, and yet I was still feeling that awful sensation of darkness, lack of space and impotence. Locked and crushed in a narrow space from which I could never get out.

Prisoner of my fears, most likely.

Moreover, to think about it, that dream was nothing but the transposition of the reality made by my subconscious. It stores our past, processes it and, if necessary, it breaks it up and then reassembles it at its will, just as a director does when running the editing of a movie.

Then, subconscious loves metaphors.

Indeed, we could say it communicates with us almost exclusively through them.

The strong recoil caused by the impact of the wheels of the plane on the ground of the airstrip, stopped abruptly my reflective phase. First of all I turned on the phone and I found the messages from Matt and Veronica, both saying the same thing, that is they were out of there waiting for me.

Finally at home, I thought.

Just being aware to be back in my place and among my friends, was enough to make me feel a little bit more light hearted.

Having only my trolley, as soon as I got off the plane I went straight to the luggage storage, until I found myself in front of the safe-deposit boxes.

In front of me there was the number one thousand two hundred, I went to the left. Eight hundred, six hundred, five hundred, four hundred… three hundred sixty-three.

Here it is, that's it! I thought as soon as I found my box.

I rummaged into my jacket pocket and I took out the riddled key that Moreau gave me in Aruba. I slipped it into the keyhole, just one turn of the key and it opened. Inside there was a black rectangular black bag which, touching it, seemed to contain a metal box. Although I was so curious, the idea to open it in front of all those people didn't even touch me. Thus I put it on my trolley, and walked towards the exit.

After a few minutes spent walking avoiding the rushed men coming from the opposite direction to mine, I glimpsed Matt and Veronica and made them a sign with my hand.

I haven't seen them for a day and a half, but I was dying to hug them again. As I approached, I noticed that Matt was wearing a dark blue t-shirt with the FBI sign printed on it, in large yellow letters.

He's a good friend but he's really stupid, I thought at once.

They both ran towards me. The first to reach me was Matt, hugging me very tight and giving me a kiss on my cheek.

«Hey, bro', welcome back!», he exclaimed.

«Give it to me, I'll carry it», he added, taking my bag.

«Thank you, but be careful, the black bag contains very thorny material.», I told him, already looking at Veronica, who was waiting for me while I was trying to free myself of the grip of Matt.

I hugged her, and she threw her arms around my neck, stroking my nape.

«I'm happy to see you, Mr Anderson.», she whispered in my ear.

«So am I, Mrs Hayes!», I told her.

Once divided, we stood looking at each other into our eyes for a split second, holding our hands and smiling.

«Let's go, let's go, you hopeless romantics! If you keep on being so saccharine, you'll cause me diabetes!», Matt screamed, attracting the attention of all the people around us.

In response, I hit him on his shoulder.

«Shit, Matt, you never change!», I told him annoyed, motioning with my hands to lower the tone of his voice.

«Come on Alex, you've just landed, don't break my balls right away.», he said, with his usual indolent attitude.

«Speaking of breaking the balls, do you think it's the case to go around with a FBI t-shirt?», I asked him.

Veronica, who was next to me, burst into laughter.

«Nice, isn't it? In my car I have one for you too, read carefully what's written below the FBI initials!», he said, stretching it proudly with his hands.

FBI
FEMALE BODY INSPECTOR

As soon as I read what was written on it, I thought immediately of the face of Da Silva, and I also burst out laughing. Evidently it was a good way to play down, if only for a few minutes.

«And from where does this come out?», I asked Matt who, once reached the car park, invited me to get into a white Toyota Prius.

«My uncle has a garage next to the Coliseum, I asked him to give it to me in exchange for my pick-up. Only for the next few days, of course. So we can talk without being worried that Da Silva and his henchmen are listening to us.», he explained.

«This time I really have to admit you have surprised me positively. Super Matt!», I replied, as soon as I got into the car.

«You know Matt, I find this car very beautiful, I think you should give a little thought to it.», Veronica said, who in the meanwhile sat in the back seat.

«Veronica is right, it might be the right time to get rid of that jalopy.», I added.

«What, are you crazy? Besides the fact that I could never load my surfboards on such a car, and then, except in this exceptional case, you will never see Matt Payne driving a teenybopper car!», he exclaimed, playing the fool as usual.
In the meanwhile we left the airport behind us.

«So Alex, tell us what happened, it's two days we are on tenterhooks…», Matt said.

«Well, all in all I would say that everything was fine, also because now I know with whom I am dealing. Having said that, the situation is much more messed up than we could even remotely imagine.», I replied.

However, I began to be starved. In fact, excluding the subspecies of sandwich I had been fobbed off on the plane, I hadn't eaten since the night before.

«Guys, I'm dying of hunger, how about talking about it while eating a cheeseburger?», I suggested.

«Done deal, neither Veronica nor I we had lunch. In two minutes we'll reach a Inn-N-Out.», Matt said, abruptly changing lane, without using the blinker.

26

Hold on tight

I am free because I am always on the run.
JIMI HENDRIX

**In the meanwhile
in the FBI interrogation room**

«HERE, I did it!», Scott whispered to Bennett, after she managed to snap the lock of the handcuffs keeping her arms immobilized behind her back.

«How did you manage it?», John asked her, astonished.

«With one of my rings, an old gift from my father...», Tina said with a wink.

«Now turn around, John.», she said again.

«Why, may I know what you are going to do?», he asked.

«Take the gun that I keep hidden in my underwear. Is it enough as an explanation, or do you want a drawing?», Scott replied annoyed.

Bennett obeyed and turned his head away.

At that point, trying to avoid movements that could attract attention, Tina undid the button of her trousers, she slid down the zipper and, swaying her hips, lowered them just enough to stick her hand in her black lace panties, which had a special pocket where she had placed the gun, just near her vagina.

It was a Glock 28, a special gun of Austrian manufacturing, famous because, being ceramic, is not detected by most systems of metal detector.

«Done, now you can turn.», Tina said, putting the weapon on the ground.

As soon as he saw it, Bennett opened his eyes wide.

«That weapon is illegal in the United States, how did you get it?», he asked, having immediately recognized the model.

«I think we have something else to think about, or not? Listen John, there's no time to lose, so I would say to act like that: now I'll free you from the handcuffs and this will make them realize immediately that we are trying to escape. Consider that they will take roughly sixty, seventy seconds maximum to get here from the control room.», Tina explained.

«How many men?», Bennett asked.

«They should be in three, anyway don't worry, leave them in my hands.», she replied.

Bennett was surprised, he never would have expected such determination by Scott.

«Leave them in your hands, eh? Okay, I'm ready whenever you want.», he said.

After concentrating for a moment narrowing her eyes, Tina took a deep breath and, with a catlike reaction, she rushed at Bennett, relieving him at once.

«Ok, well done!», he exclaimed rubbing his numb wrists because of the grip of the handcuffs.

They were both standing in the centre of the room. Tina quickly gave a look at her watch.

«Here they come!», she exclaimed.

One, two, three seconds, and they heard the clank of the security door opening.

Bennett drew the gun on the entrance and, with the other hand, jostled Bennett.

«Stay behind, I'll face them!», she shouted.

The door opening, four men catapulted into the room, but they made a serious mistake.

«Stop where you are!», Tina ordered.

The fact of having the barrel of a gun drawn on themselves, completely floored them, they didn't take into consideration the hypothesis of Scott being armed. At that point she was the one running the show. One of them, in an attempt to dissuade her, disobeyed and moved a step forward.

Nothing, not even the time to put his foot on the ground.

Without the slightest hesitation, Scott pulled the trigger, making his head explode into thousand pieces, which splattered on the faces of the other three. The impact of the bullet made that faceless and lifeless body fell backward, forcing his colleagues to jump in order to dodge it.

Just over a minute, and the sweet smell of blood filled the room.

«So, is there someone else who wants to make his end?», Tina asked provocatively, drawing upon herself the bitter looks of the other three men.

«You're just a whore, you know? When we catch you we'll have some fun with you before killing you...», the biggest of the three said cocky, breaking the silence.

Tina looked at him straight in his eyes, cracked a smile and…

Bang! Fired three shots, aiming at genitals.

«Now it will be a little bit difficult for you to have fun.», she said mockingly, addressing contemptuously her target who, lying on the floor, moved jerkily and produced a shrill death rattle, which was smothered by his own blood, which had begun to gush profusely from his mouth.

Time seemed to stand still, suspended. As if someone had pressed the pause button on the remote control.

She's crazy! One of Da Silva's men thought terrified, without being able to take his eyes from his colleague lying on the floor in agony.

«And you, which are your intentions?», she immediately asked, waving the gun barrel. The two men did not dare utter a word and, after giving each other a knowing look, threw down their weapons on the ground and pushed them towards Bennett and Scot with a kick.

«John, throw the handcuffs to them, quickly!», Tina said.

Stunned by the scene he had witnessed, Bennett bent down, picked up the handcuffs with which, until shortly before, he and his colleague were tied, and threw them at the foot of the two unfortunates.

«Pick them up, come on! I will send to hell the first who makes tricks, to keep company with the other two!», she exclaimed, keeping them always in sight.

After forcing them to handcuff themselves next the heater pipe, Tina picked up their weapons, gave one to Bennett and, after searching in their pockets, she also confiscated their phones and badges to enter the control room. In the meanwhile, the smell in the room had become nothing short of loathsome and, as incessant background, you could hear the moans of the man hit in the groin becoming even more insistent.

«You've really bored me!», Tina exclaimed and, turning, fired a shot in his forehead, saving him, in this way, from other long minutes of suffering.

At the sight of that scene, one of the two survivors collapsed on his legs and vomited also his soul, while the other one, petrified, was unable to utter a single syllable.

«Hurry up, let's get out of here!», Bennett said, heading for the exit.

Scott followed him, she turned to cast a last look of warning to the two henchmen of Da Silva and, once out, closed the steel door with vim.

«I absolutely have to get in touch with Jameson, I have to inform him. Anderson is in danger.», Scott said.

«That's all we needed, CIA.», Bennett replied.

«Jameson and Moreau have been working for years at the Dillinger case, and knew perfectly well that among us there was more than a mole playing into the hands of him. We have to find Anderson before them, otherwise things get worse.», Tina explained.

«Okay, but first we have to go into the control room, I need the records of Da Silva's confession.», Bennett said.

«Provided that those four assholes have not destroyed them.», Scott replied.

Inn-N-Out Burger
Sepulveda Boulevard, Los Angeles.
Five minutes later

«Don't touch my chips, you're eating all of them!», I told Matt who, unsatisfied with his two cheeseburgers, kept on stretching his hand in my tray.

«Thus Da Silva and half FBI are a party of Dillinger, they're spies. I feel so bad thinking of all the time he had pontificated about the usefulness of the interceptions, the NSA and the national security. What a sort of false and hypocrite liar!», Veronica exclaimed, after listening my story on the meeting with Jameson and Moreau.

«You don't say! And what is worse is that, if he has had the coldness of killing Nowitzki, his colleague and friend for thirty years, betraying systematically his Country, well, we can expect pretty much everything from him, .», I said, worried.

«You know what? I never liked him. By instinct. But I would never have expected such a thing. He killed his best friend, what a piece of shit!», Matt said, after drinking his Light Coke.

«Listen Alex, how do we have to behave now? Well, I mean, who's going to protect you?», Veronica asked me.

«Jameson and Moreau have guaranteed they are taking care of our security, and I have no reason to doubt it. Of course, we hope to get out of it as soon as possible.», I replied her.

«Oh God, if only I could write an article… we would have Dillinger and Da Silva over a barrel!», Veronica exclaimed.

«And you would win the Pulitzer Prize.», I said, not jokingly.

«Hey, what's so valuable in that bag? You've not dumped it a moment!», Matt asked me.

Actually, I didn't want to risk anything and therefore I brought it into the fast food. I looked around quickly, the situation seemed peaceful.

«Jameson and Moreau gave it to me, I've taken it before at the luggage storage. Actually I haven't opened it yet, I was told it contains what I need to defend myself.», I explained to Matt, holding the bag tight in my arms.

«Come on, let's open it!», he exclaimed.

I was hesitant. I turned to Veronica who in turn looked me in the eyes and nodded. I put the bag next to me, on the chair, so that the table, which was higher, could cover its view; I opened the zip, revealing a rectangular metal box or something like that. The upper part of the box lifted, with only a slight pressure with my hands.

Inside there were a Smartphone, a gun, and something that at first glance looked like a shoulder holster.

Instinctively, I raised my look for a moment to be sure about the absence of prying eyes, then looked at Veronica and Matt, who were also amazed at the sight of that weapon which I took carefully with both hands and watched very closely.

«It's very light, it does not even seem to be iron.», I whispered.

«Read, it's written, it's a Glock. If I am not wrong, they are made of ceramic, in order not to be detected by metal detectors.», Matt said.

«It's true, Matt is right, it seems to me that a few years ago the government forbade its sale, for obvious reasons.», Veronica ascertained.

I put the gun inside the box, and took the phone.

I turned it on

We all three stared at the display.

ENTER CODE TO UNLOCK

Floored, I rummaged in the bag for a moment, but I found nothing.

«So, this code?», Matt asked.

«No idea, Jameson and Moreau have not told me anything!», I replied, while I was trying to get my thoughts in order.

Suddenly, I had an idea.

«Wait, maybe I understood.», I told them, rummaging in my pockets.

I took out the key that Moreau gave me and read again the number on the plastic tag: three hundred sixty-three.

I typed it on the display and pressed enter.

VALID CODE

«Cool!», Veronica exclaimed.

I had not even time to open its menu that immediately the phone began to ring.

INCOMING CALL
UNKNOWN NUMBER

I answered the phone instantly.

«It took you a long time, Mr. Anderson.», it seemed to be the voice of Moreau.

«Moreau?«, I asked.

«Yes, it's me. You and your friends are in danger, Mr. Anderson. Da Silva managed to escape and, in all likelihood, he's now on your tracks.», he said.

«What do mean he escaped? How is it possible to escape FBI?», I asked astounded.

«It doesn't matter. Listen Mr. Anderson, you and your friends have to do exactly what I say. No questions, no objections. Just execute. Understood?», he asked.

«Surely.», I replied right away.

«Good. At the table behind you there are two men of Da Silva, but don't turn. They are two men in their fifties, one of them has a black suit, the other a grey one. They wear old-fashioned ties and short socks: they seem two employees of a shipment office. They are tailing you. Now tell your friends to get up and wait for you in the car; you'll see that one of the two will follow them, while the other will remain seated, without losing sight of you.», Moreau said.

«All right.», I replied promptly.

«Guys, go into the car and wait me there, I'll come straight away.», I told them, who understood immediately.

Indeed, it was just like Moreau said. Thinking of not being noticed, the man in grey suit stood up and, after emptying his tray, followed Matt and Veronica to the exit.

«Albert, done. They went out and the guy with the grey suit followed them.», I confirmed.

«Now look behind the counter where fries are served. Near the clerk there's an escape door, can you see it?», Moreau asked.

«Yes, I see it.», I replied, immediately after seeing it.

«Very good. It's an emergency exit, leading straight to your car. When I say go, you'll have to put the gun away and walk out of that door.», he explained.

«And what about if someone should stop me? This is an area with restricted access only to staf...», I tried to object, being however instantly interrupted.

«I don't care at all. Just do it, Mr. Anderson. Stand up, run to that door and jump on your friends car. Now, go!», Moreau yelled on the other side of the phone.

Without further ado, I grabbed gun and holster, and started walking briskly. In the heat of the moment I hit a guy, he didn't fall for miracle.

«Hey, look where the fuck you are going!», he said, with the unmistakable look of the classic troublemaker perpetually looking for brawl. I looked at him, I apologized motioning with my hand, but without stopping walking.

Having dodged a couple of other person, I found myself at the counter. The guy who was in charge to take chips from the fryer and divide them into portions, immediately noticed me.

«First you must do receipt, Sir.», he said stammering.

He was very young and wore tooth brace.

«FBI, let me pass.», I told him instinctively, approaching his ear.

Then I lifted the wooden counter, crossed the restaurant and walked toward the exit, without any resistance from his side. After pushing the emergency handle, the door swung open and I found myself in front of Veronica and Matt, who were waiting for me next to the car.

«Come on, set in motion, let's go!», I cried, opening the door.

We got off to a flying start.

From the rear-view mirror I saw the guy dressed in black getting straight away in a dark SUV which, what a coincidence, immediately got on our heels.

«What the fuck is happening?», Matt asked nervously.

«Da Silva's men are tailing us, here they are, in the black SUV behind us.», I told them, turning and pointing the car with my index.

The phone began to ring, I answered at once.

«Good, well done. They're behind you, tell your friend not to stop, we'll do the rest.», Moreau said.

«And we, what should we do?», I asked.

«Hold on to your hat.», he replied

«So, what did he say?», Matt asked, becoming more and more nervous.

«To hold on to our hat.», I replied.

«What do you mean to hold on to...», by sheer coincidence, just at that moment the black SUV rammed us.

My head nearly bumped against the windshield.

«So what do we do now?», Veronica asked, holding tight to the back of my seat.

«Moreau said they're going to intervene, I hope they hurry up.», I replied, trying to calm them.

In the meanwhile, the SUV of those two kept on staying close to our tailpipe. After giving another look in the rear-view mirror, Matt further pressed the accelerator pedal.

«Come on Moreau, what the hell are you waiting for?», I exclaimed, as I was still seeing no one.

The black car approached us a few more centimetres. One, two seconds and it rammed us again. For a split second, Matt lost control, ending up in the other lane. But, with a great reflex, he immediately steered the other way, narrowly avoiding a car coming from our opposite direction.

«It's my uncle's car, you motherfuckers!», Matt exclaimed, just after avoiding the obstacle.

«Hey look! They're shooting at us!», Veronica shouted.

I turned and saw the guy dressed in grey putting his head outside the window and drawing the gun on us. Although he was driving, even Matt turned.

«I swear to God if you shoot my uncle's car, I'll kill you!», he shouted. «Down, stay down!», I shouted them.

We lowered all below the level of the windows.

Bang!

Bang!

We heard two shots, we looked at each other.

«I don't think they have hit us.», Veronica whispered, after a few seconds.

I looked up, I looked out of the back window and saw the SUV had been joined by a dark van, from whose windows appeared the barrels of two guns, blasting bullets away.

«Hooray! Here comes the cavalry!», I exclaimed, raising the exultation of both Matt and Veronica.

It seemed to be in the midst of an action movie.

With their shots, Moreau's men riddled the whole side of the SUV, including windows, without, however, being able to stop its mad dash. Veronica and I watched stunned.

«So, what's going on back there?», Matt asked, highly absorbed in driving.

«Just drive!», I said.

«Come on, at least tell me who's winning! Why don't you shoot a nice video with your phone? You can't imagine how many visits on YouTube...», he replied.

«You're not normal, Matt!», I exclaimed, without turning away from the back glass.

«Hey, look!», Veronica exclaimed.

The man at the helm, the one dressed in black, having broken what was left of his window with his elbow, looked out and fired several shots at the van. But he made not even a scratch to it.

«It must be armoured.», Veronica stated.

No time to realize it, and the man of Da Silva was hit by a burst of gunfire, so the black SUV began to skid, with the bloody corpse of that guy dangling in the void.

A matter of seconds.

The other man threw the body of his friend out of the window, taking control of the car.

«Those damned are really hard to die!», Matt exclaimed, using his forearm to wipe the sweat dripping from his forehead.

«I've committed more infractions in the last ten minutes than in my whole life.», he said again.

At that point, another spray of tommy-gun hit fully the left front tire of the SUV which, due to the sudden loss of adhesion with the asphalt, after a half spinout, lifted from the ground and overturned backwards, crushing the cars of the unfortunates who, unaware, were behind.

Few, very few fractions of seconds and the SUV exploded, surrounded by a dense tangle of flames, from which immediately rose a cloud of dark smoke as black as pitch.

«Ahah! I've told you, you would come to a bad end hitting the car of my uncle!», Matt exulted, giving a few hits on the steering wheel.

I looked at Veronica who smiled and made a sort of caress to my hand.

INCOMING CALL
UNKNOWN NUMBER

«Hallo Alex, can you hear me?», Moreau asked, without even giving me time to put the phone to my ear.

«Sure Albert, loud and clear.», I replied.

«Listen to me, now you and your friends go straight to your office in San Pedro, see you there in ten minutes.», he said, ending the phone call right away.

27

Red code appointment

You never win a danger without danger.
PUBLILIO SIRO

FBI Headquarters
Wilshire Boulevard
Los Angeles

«I'm John Bennett, I have to talk to the President.», the FBI Director said on the phone, sitting at the office desk which he had just taken possession, immediately after recovering the file with the video of Da Silva's confession.

«Hallo Director, I put you through to the President.», the secretary replied, after a few moments.

«Hi John, tell me.», Obama began, leaving aside the pleasantries. Since the beginning, the two had immediately established a good feeling.

«Unfortunately I have not good news.», Bennett revealed.

«What is it? What's going on over there?», the President asked straight away.

«Frank Da Silva, the Head of the counter-terrorism division of the National Security Branch, is a traitor and, as we suspected, along with him, also a very large part of FBI top brass: they all support the conspiracy against the State orchestrated by Dillinger. It was precisely Da Silva who killed his colleague, Agent Nowitzki. He confessed it to me, before managing to escape with some of his men.», Bennett explained.

«You have to catch him, and you must do it before this Da Silva can cause more harm. We can not afford this story to become public, America is not ready to bear such a blow and Americans would feel the world collapsing on them, if they knew that a part of our intelligence is plotting against the Nation: this is what Dillinger wants, in order to destabilize the system, and we must make everything to stop him. You have free rein, I count on you, John. Keep me updated.», Obama said.

«I will... ah, one last thing.», Bennett said.

«Yes, tell me.», the President replied.

«I'm sending you an encrypted email with the file of Da Silva's confession, I think you should look at it, it will be useful to understand with whom we are dealing.», Bennett advised.

«Thank you John, I'll watch it instantly. I hope to hear you soon, a hug.», the tenant of the White House ensured.

«See you soon, Mr. President.», Bennett greeted him and, once ended the phone call, he put his hands behind his neck and pressing with his back, reclined the seatback of the black fake leather chair on which he was sitting.

A few moments spent in stretching himself, then he took the remote control on his desk and turned on the television, which was already tuned in to Fox News.

BREAKING NEWS

«... we have just received the images you are watching, and they were taken about ten minutes ago by our crew, who was on a helicopter to shoot another story. It's an incredible chase, which ended with a spectacular crash in which other cars were also involved. Currently this is all, we will update you as soon as we receive more news. »

While he was watching that scene, Bennett took again the phone dialling the number of Scott.

«Hallo Tina, are you watching Fox News?», he asked her straight away.

«Of course I am, I was about to call you. I spoke with Moreau, I'm going to join him and Anderson in San Pedro, see you in two minutes at the exit.», she said.

«I've already lost too much time because of this story, I'm on election campaign, fuck! I already had to postpone a lot of appointments and, as if not enough, tomorrow we have the convention at the Staples Centre.», I told Veronica and Matt, in a fit of rage and despair.

Of course, first of all, I wanted to get back to normality, without me and my friends feeling in danger, but at the same time, I was afraid to frustrate years and years of work.

«Alex, read here, even today Los Angeles Times writes you have clearly the advantage on Spencer, indeed, after the broadcast last night, the gap between you two rose to over eight percent. You earned three points! I would say that, at least from this point of view, you should take it easy, also because, if everything goes as it should, the convention of tomorrow will earn you two other points at least, as you will do the honours.», Veronica said, showing me the poll published by her newspaper.

«I know that, but I can not think about it. What about Los Angeles Times, haven't you gone back to your office?», I asked her.

«Because of everything that happened to us, I wouldn't have had the time even if I wanted to, thus I took a few days off using the most banal excuse of the world: flu. But tomorrow it will be up to me to write an article about your convention.», she replied, while a hint of smile lit her face.

«Tomorrow at Staples Centre it will be a red code appointment because of its importance, and Dillinger and Da Silva will seize upon that great opportunity to contrive something. We'll have to be ready for anything.», Moreau said out of the blue, crossing the threshold of the office.

His words petrified us.

For a moment I had a strange feeling, as if I had already lived that scene, a kind of déjà vu. It didn't happen to me since a long time. After a few moments spent thinking about it, I tried to return to my senses. No, I absolutely could not afford even a single second of distraction.

«Sorry, who are you?», Matt asked polemically, being caught out by the entrance of Moreau who, keeping silent, looked him up and down.

From the way he looked at him, it was clear that he had immediately classified him as a slacker looking dowdy and even indolent. To the point of not giving him the satisfaction of an answer.

«Keep calm, Matt, he's Moreau, that is the person who has saved our lives a while ago. Albert, I introduce you Matt Payne, my friend and responsible for my election campaign, and Veronica Hayes, also friend of mine as well as journalist for Los Angeles Times.», I intervened, introducing them.

Just a few moments, and the entrance door opened again. This time Tina Scott came in, accompanied by a tall and big man, more or less in his sixties.

«Ah, I see you all arrived. If you didn't know, he is John Bennett, Director of FBI.», Scott said.

«At this point I propose to move into the meeting room.», I said, after having welcomed the last two arrived. Along the short walk from one room to another, Veronica and Matt reached Bennett and introduced themselves.

«Mr. Payne, I see you're part of us.», Bennett said, indicating Matt's t-shirt.

«Nice, isn't it? If you want, I have another one in my car, you will look terrific!», he replied, with his proverbial irreverence.

«Forgive him, Mr. Bennett, as you may have already figured out he's got a screw loose, but he's a good guy.», I interjected, being afraid he would de displeased.

«Don't worry about it, Mr. Anderson, I like witty persons. Indeed, you know what? I want that t-shirt!», he replied, bursting into a laughter that infected everyone, except Scott and Moreau who, on the contrary, seemed to be impatient.

As soon as we sat around the table, Bennett and his colleague gave each other a knowing look.

«Okay, bring them in.», FBI Director assented.

«Come in, we are waiting.», Scott said, talking on the phone.

After thirty seconds, eight men came in and, once inside, began to sift every inch of the office. An operation that lasted about ten minutes.

«The building is clean, Sir.», one of them told Bennett, as soon as they had finished.

«Well, you can go out. Please, keep your eyes open. I want to be informed about any suspicious movement.», Bennett ordered, who seemed to be another person compared to when he made that cross joke with Matt.

«So gentlemen, I'm sure you all know the events of the last hours. A moment ago I have informed the President about the incident, and he's following also the development of the situation. Needless to say that everything we're about to say is absolutely top secret and therefore it must not leave this room by no means. If public opinion was aware of the conspiracy in progress, Dillinger would reach his goal, and we won't allow it for no reason in the world, whatever it costs. From this moment on, even though there may be no official status, this has to be considered a joint operation of CIA and FBI, and the presence of Albert Moreau is a concrete demonstration of this understanding. So, that foreword being said, let's assess what can be done. As Mr. Moreau said before, the Republican convention taking place tomorrow at Staples must be considered very risky. Dillinger and Da Silva are ready for anything, and I'm willing to bet they're planning something to take advantage of the huge media limelight of that appointment. Something that we must also take into consideration is the presence of the highest leaders of the Republican Party who, as far as I know, will be there completely. Can you confirm it, Mr. Anderson?», Bennett asked while in the meantime he got up and walked to the blackboard.

«Yes, I confirm it. Unless improbable last-minute cancellations, in addition to Romney, his wife Ann and Paul Ryan, tomorrow there will come the two Bush, Rudy Giuliani, Condoleezza Rice, John McCain, New York Mayor Bloomberg, and it's expected a surprise monologue of Sylvester Stallone.», I said, after giving a quick glance at the schedule.

«In short, considering also you, the declared enemies of Chuck Dillinger will be there in its entirety.», Moreau ascertained laconically, staring at me with his icy gaze.

For a moment I was afraid.

Whatever happens, it will be all over tomorrow. I thought to myself, to pluck up courage.

«That's right. And I believe we'll have to use this opportunity to put an end to this story.», I replied with conviction, in order not to show myself weak and afraid.

«Well, in case we can count on Rambo. Joking aside, I agree with Alex, we must be clever to use the tomorrow appointment to make them reveal themselves. How do you think to act? Do you have a plan?», Veronica asked, speaking to Bennett and Moreau.

«To begin with, considering that it's expected a turnout of about twenty thousand persons, we provided to triple the units of the security service. Sharpshooters, undercover agents, helicopters and even two F-35 flying over the area. Besides this, our computer technicians at the headquarters have already started to work on the creation of a bug whose aim is to deactivate phone networks and data within the range of two kilometres at least. This will allow us to prevent them from communicating with each other, or at least, to complicate their existence. Notwithstanding, however, knowing us, they will be ready to face many of the countermeasures we will adopt, this is clear. Let's say I would like to induce them to underestimate us: after all both Dillinger and Da Silva feel to be teacher's pet, and we have to be good at make them believe in it, leading them, therefore, to make a mistake.», Bennett explained, writing all with the black marker on the board, as if he was giving a simple lesson in front of his students.

«I got an idea.», Matt said, after standing up.

«Please, Mr. Payne, every contribution is welcome, tell us.», Bennett nodded.

«As I understand, we have to do our best to floor them, right? Then, since we are organizing the event, I thought that at the last moment we could upset the order of the speeches. I think that would be a way to upset their plans further.», Matt stated who, soon after, sat down and casted me a glance that I reciprocated immediately making a nod of approval.

«It seems to me an excellent idea, which could give us precious minutes. Very good, Mr. Payne.», FBI Director replied, proceeding to write down the proposal on the blackboard.

«Well done Matt!», Veronica congratulated softly, holding his forearm.

«Mr. Bennett, if I may, I would like to add something.», Moreau said, getting up from the chair too.

«Definitely Albert, come here, take my place.», Bennett replied and, after having passed him the marker as runners do with the witness, sat next to Scott.

«The time at our disposal is short, therefore I'll do my best to make full use of my gift for conciseness. First of all, not to let us caught unprepared, I think we should carefully consider what, at present, seems to be the most insidious wild card, which has a name and a surname, that is Maggie Jones. In my opinion, she might just be the key to lead us to a solution. But let's get to the point. As we have explained to Mr. Anderson, Ms. Jones is missing since eighty-nine, at least on paper. The fact that her body was never found, after the accident in which her parents lost their lives, has led us to track down the trail leading to her aunt and, therefore, to London. Aspect which, moreover, also struck Nowitzki who, incidentally, just after having noticed it, was brutally killed by Da Silva.», Moreau said, making a short break for a sip of water.

«Albert, sorry, I interrupt you only a moment to support your thesis. I assume you mean to speak about Marion Ross, right?», Bennett intervened.

«Precisely, Director. But who is Marion Ross? She's a FBI agent based in London since the end of the eighties, as well as she seems to be the real aunt of Maggie Jones. It so happens that Agent Ross is currently under investigation by FBI itself, because responsible of the office from which leaked the top secret documents that Dillinger then made known to the Guardian journalist, thereby starting off the scandal that we all know as Datagate. This alone would be enough to fuel something more than just a simple suspicious. But there's more, because a few minutes ago Adam Jameson informed me that Marion Ross and her husband Aaron Beck, who's also working for FBI, have disappeared. Can you confirm it, Director?», Moreau asked.

«Yes, I confirm. To be precise they have made lost their traces about forty-eight hours ago. Being under investigation, Ross had her passport confiscated, but it's more than likely that, for an experienced agent like her, it's an easy game obtaining false documents, therefore we immediately passed their mug shots on to all national and international airports. Whatever they have in mind, we'll have to ensure they fail to put it in practice.», Bennett explained.

«I think so too. Indeed, if I can have my say, I have the feeling that Ross and her husband will do everything to be at Staples tomorrow. Another reason to keep our eyes open.», Scott added.

28

Don't say anything

There is a whole lifetime in an hour of love.
HONORÉ DE BALZAC

Marriott South Bay Hotel
Torrance
California

«HOLY shit!», Matt exclaimed in the middle of the hall, making everybody turn.

«Hey, may I know what's wrong with you? I'm fed up to make an ass of myself because of you. And change this stupid t-shirt!», I reacted in a sulk.

«Hey hey, try to calm you down. Rather, do you know who has just written me? Rhonda, the hot chick of last night: she says she's under my house with her friend Charlene Scialfa, a model tall one meter and eighty with two big tits and an ass that, compared to the one of Jennifer Lopez seems like that of my grandmother. And I had to cancel her, can you realize?», he said, putting his phone under my nose in order to read her friend message.

«Listen Matt, I have enough trouble to think about, don't you start now! We'll have to stay here just for tonight, and not for fun, but because at home we would not be safe. One night, Matt. Can you hold back your sexual drives for just one fucking night?», I asked him.

«Problems?», Scott asked, joining us as soon as she finished at the reception.

«No, no problem, we were just having a chat.», I cut her short, feeling ashamed as a thief for the subject of my discussion with Matt.

«Better so. Here, these are the keys of your rooms, we will all stay in the same corridor, on the twelfth floor. For reasons that I don't even have to explain to you, no one must leave the hotel. See you here in exactly two hours to have dinner.», she said, walking then toward Bennett and Moreau to give them the keys.

«You know, looking well at her, Tina Scott makes me horny? Look, Alex, she also has a wonderful ass. In my opinion, behind those bookworm glasses and under that chaste suit, there is a terrific woman, how about it?», he said, keeping on looking constantly at the bottom of Scott.

«I say you are a clinical case, Matt, more than Tiger Woods! Come on, let's go and have a shower in the room, tonight we'll have to work on my speech for tomorrow.», I replied, setting out for Veronica, who was waiting for us sitting on a chair a few steps from us.

«Well, let's consider the glass half full: it seems to be on holidays! In which room are you?», she asked me, shaking her key chain, which bore the number one hundred twenty-nine.

«One hundred thirty, it seems we are neighbours. Do you come with us?», I asked her.

«Yes, let's go, I want to do some press review using the wi-fi.», she said, bending down to collect her bag.

As soon as I walked into my room, I took off my clothes and went straight like a train under the shower, where I stayed for at least twenty minutes to think about what to do.

First of all, I thought that I had to concentrate on the convention that, with or without Dillinger, was an essential appointment not only for the success of my election campaign, but also and especially for future projects.

And I did not want regrets.

Obviously, being concentrated didn't mean to ignore or, even worse, to underestimate the danger, but to try, as far as possible, to divide the two things, at least from the mental point of view.

Difficult, yes, but not impossible.

When my fingertips were completely shrivelled, I turned off the water jet, got out and, after getting dried, I wrapped the towel around my waist.

One, two, three seconds, and someone knocked on the door.

It must be that ballbuster of Matt! I thought.

«May I know what the hell do you wa...», I said opening the door, behind which, however, there wasn't Matt but Veronica, holding her laptop.

«Oh, I'm sorry to have bothered you, don't worry, I'll come back later!», she said blushing, believing I had it in for her.

«No, don't worry, I thought it was Matt!», I promptly replied, inviting her to come in.

«Ah, okay!», she exclaimed, sitting in front of the desk, where she put her laptop immediately.

«I put some clothes on and I'll come! Found something interesting?», I asked loudly from the bathroom, while I put on hastily a pair of underwear, trousers and shirt.

«Yes, they are still talking about you on Huffington Post, come to see!», she replied.

I fixed my hair and went back in the room, sitting next to her.

«Ah, yes? And what do they say?», I asked, looking at the monitor.

«Here it is, read.», she said, after clicking on the link to the article.

The student exceeds the (bad) teacher

According to many experts, what will be held tomorrow in the temple of Lakers – that is Staples Centre in Los Angeles – rather than being the day of Mitt Romney and his deputy candidate Paul Ryan, it will be the coronation of young Alex Anderson. This is not a scoop, you would say. Who can blame you. But then, let`s say it frankly: only a miracle could bring Mitt Romney to the White House. And so why be shocked if the leaders of the Republican Party think to exploit the media limelight of an election campaign already undermined in order to make known

to the general public that, in all likelihood, will
be the horse on which they will bet in four years?
Some might argue wondering why, then, for the
candidacy of the Vice they have not chosen directly
Anderson, rather than bet on Ryan. The reason is
obvious, and it`s much simpler than you can imagine:
don`t tie the image of an alleged winner to that of
a sure loser. Wise decision, in our humble opinion
that, indirectly, gives a minimum of meaning to the
Republican presence in the desperate assault on
Barack Obama. Moreover, our Director has already
dealt with Anderson three days ago, with an
excellent article in which she managed to focus
pointedly his strengths and weaknesses. According to
the latter, it`s impossible not to dwell on the
membership of the young scion to Skull and Bones,
not because the thing itself shocked us, for
heaven`s sake, we`re not born yesterday, but for the
undeniable implications (to say the least) that
involves the membership in what we persist in
defining sect. That said, even in his television
appearance last night, the guy has amply
demonstrated to have genius, and also a lot. In
short, the horse is full-blooded, no doubt about it,
we`ll have to wait and see if he`s free or
domesticated.

«Domesticated... that asshole!», I exclaimed, after
reading it.

«Certainly he was not gentle, but he has given you great
importance. In my opinion you made a good impression, because
now people know this story of Skull and Bones.», Veronica
remarked, trying to make me see the positive side of the article.

Anyway tomorrow I'll go to Staples as protagonist, just
like Kobe Bryant! I thought amused.

«At this point I have come to terms with that and try to
ride the thing, on the other hand I have no options. Listen, how
are you? I'm very sorry to have you involved in this mess.», I
confessed, changing tone suddenly.

In response, she closed the laptop and turned to me.

«You should not feel guilty, Alex. You know what I
think? That, in life, everything has a meaning and that nothing
happens by chance. Evidently it was written somewhere that you
and I should have met in this way, facing together a so

paradoxical situation.», she explained, without looking down, not even for a moment.

«You're probably right. After all, if it is true that we are constantly put to the test in life, its is also true that those who initially appear as problems, with the passage of time, may turn to be real opportunities. Until a few days ago I thought about the innumerable things that have happened to me, and to the few ones of which I was the real maker. Perhaps, what's happening to us in some way helped me to shake me, to make me fully understand that every day could be the good one. Before I had never felt the breath of death on my neck, and I had no idea of the interior big bang it can provoke. It changes your perspective, giving you the strength of not procrastinating, not leaving something untried, not taking yourself too seriously and, above all, giving the correct importance to things. Now I want to make you a confession, Veronica.», I told her.

«Go on, I'm all ears.», she replied, with just a whisper.

«Maybe you'll start to laugh, but I want to tell it to you. Yesterday, with Jameson, we took a long walk on the beach in Aruba, a stunning place, a real feast for my eyes. At a certain point, at sunset, the sky was like on fire, bombed by a burst of colours bouncing on the water. I was so impressed that I stopped my conversation with Adam, I took off my clothes and threw myself into the water. It was wonderful, it seems to be in a painting by Monet. A few meters away there was an Italian couple, who looked and hugged each other issuing a very strong energy, so much that I had to force myself to take my eyes off them and not seem like a peeper. Well, at that very moment, I realized that what I wanted most of all was to have you there with me. Neither Dillinger nor election campaign, the only thing I thought about was you. Well, now I've told you.», I confided her, not feeling, unlike what I thought, the slightest embarrassment.

Veronica tried but could not literally speak. Her blue eyes dampened, and the expression of her face was worth more than thousand words.

Her emotion infected also me.

We seemed two stupid.

We looked each other without being able to untie the knot in the middle of which had remained tangled vowels and consonants. At a certain point, she clenched her fists, stood up straight and took a deep breath.

«Is… is that no one had ever made me feel so important, before.», she managed to say, her voice trembling, choked with emotion.

On my side, still immobilized, I could not help but smile back.

She came up to me.

We kissed.

So, as if we had already made it billions of times during billions of lives. Her flavour transformed emotion into passion in a flash, embarrassment into self-confidence, and fear into audacity.

I gently took her face with both my hands and then, simultaneously, we both opened our eyes. Without dividing us not even for breathing, we got up and walked the few steps that separated us from the bed, on which I laid her down gently, holding one hand behind her head.

In my chest I felt throbbing a strong sensation of heat, a burning and unavoidable desire, I felt it so much that I could also smell its scent.

I felt alive more than ever.

Veronica stopped our kiss and began, button after button, to open my shirt. I was about to ask her if she was sure, but she put a hand on my mouth, interrupting me before I started to speak.

«No, don't say anything.», he whispered.

After removing and launching my shirt somewhere, I slid my hands along her hips.

How beautiful you are! I thought, as I lost myself into her blue eyes.

She wore an orange dress with a pattern of small white aircraft, which fell upon her shapes as if it were a second skin.

I grabbed it by the shoulder pads and took it off. Down, to the feet, dragging my nose all along that soft itinerary.

After exchanging a knowing look, I did the same with her flesh-coloured knickers. I admired her in silence for a few moments, while she undid the buttons of my trousers, which soon suffered the same destiny of my shirt. After unclothing me, Veronica grabbed me by my neck, dragging me with strength on her and then, soon after, turned me face up, putting herself on me, astride.

Instinctively, I touched her breasts, convincing myself immediately that they were made for staying in my hands

In the meanwhile, she began to rub her vagina against my penis and lost control with enchanting «mmm» of pleasure, half-closing her eyes and nibbling at her lower lip, managing to dramatically amplify my great desire.

I grabbed her by her hips, and I too began to sway my pelvis in her opposite direction.

I resisted only few seconds. Ten, fifteen at the most.

Then, with her complicity, I went into her.

I closed my eyes enjoying for a few moments the ecstasy of her secure movements on me. Then, holding her back with one hand and leveraging with the other one, I pulled myself up, being careful not to get out from her. I wasn't satisfied to possess her, I also wanted to kiss and smell her constantly. It was never enough for me. Her skin gave forth a delicate fragrance, lavender or something like that.

I took again her face with my hands, stared into her eyes, and kissed her again. In the meanwhile she kept on swaying on me, taking my head into her arms, until I turned her face up laying myself on her.

«Keep on, please don't stop!», she said, her eyes into mine, clinging her long legs around my pelvis.

I felt the pleasure rising from the point of our union and radiating everywhere, inside every single cell of mine, and then running through my veins with the same strength of a raging river.

«And who stops!», I told her, my voice trembling, because of the immense pleasure.

Temperature had become hot and the more we sweated, the more we were losing control, moving ourselves with force and intensity.

«You are mine, you're mine!», I said, looking into her eyes, keeping on pushing.

«Yes, I'm yours! Go on, go on!», she replied, clutching my hair almost to tearing it.

In the meanwhile I kept on moving inside her.

Strong, stronger and stronger.

Then I felt the arrival of pleasure with the pace of a steamroller, consequently I went out and let myself be overwhelmed screaming, writhing myself and holding Veronica tighter, who shouted her pleasure with me.

Exhausted, we remained tight in our sweaty hug for some sweet minutes. So, in silence, listening each other to our heart beat.

«Hey Alex, may I know why you don't answer the phone? They are waiting for us for dinner!», Matt shouted, knocking on the door of the room.

Veronica and I looked at each other and burst into laughing.

«Damn, it's ten past eight, we must go!», I said.

After giving her a last kiss, I jumped out of the bed.

«Go down, I'm coming!», I shouted to Matt. We both went to the bathroom to tidy ourselves up, we got dressed, and left the room.

«You go down first, I wait two minutes, so they will not see us coming together.», Veronica said wisely.

Even though we had nothing to hide, it did not seem the proper context to show us in public.

Better keep the thing for us.

«Forgive me for being late, but I was exhausted. Actually I have slept more or less five hours in the last two days.», I apologized, as soon as I reached the others at the dinner table.

«Mrs Hayes is still missing, we thought you were together.», Bennett stated.

«No, I haven't seen her, now I try to call her.», I replied, doing my best to seem credible.

For a moment I looked at Matt, who had put a hand over his mouth to hide his sneer. He was about to let out one of his laughers, but I just glared at him and he restrained himself.

«Here I am, sorry, but I was on a conference call with the editorial staff. We were finalizing the last details for the reportage on the convention of tomorrow. Oh, by the way, Alex, Huffington Post still writes about you, look here.», she said, handing me her computer.

«Mr. Anderson, if you don't mind you can read the article after dinner. With all due respect, we have more important things to talk about.», Moreau intervened, sounding calm but clearly annoyed.

«Of course Albert, you are welcome.», I immediately replied, giving back the laptop to Veronica, who turned it off and put in her bag.

29

On the wrong side

*Each of us is a moon: we have a dark side
that we never show to anybody else.*
MARK TWAIN

**Los Angeles Airport
at that moment**

«PLEASE Sirs, your passport, thanks.», the agent asked behind the glass of his box.

Name: **Madlene**
Surname: **Steinharde**
Date of birth: **11/03/1962**
Place of birth: **London – United Kingdom**

Name: **Ted**
Surname: **Singleton**
Date of birth: **06/08/1960**
Place of birth: **Sheffield – United Kingdom**

At the beginning of his shift, the police officer had put on the wall on his right the two new mugshots he had found in the tray of the fax, it were those of Marion Ross and Aaron Beck, both of American nationality but coming from the United Kingdom, and sought after FBI because terrorists.

«Reason of your stay in the US?», the agent asked after leafing through their documents.

«Holidays. We plan to visit Los Angeles and then to hire a car and go to Las Vegas, passing through the Grand Canyon. Even if we suffer from dizziness, my husband and I absolutely

want to get onto the Skywalk. Have you ever been there?»,
Madlene answered.

«For such a long journey you have brought with you only
one hand luggage?», he argued, after reading the boarding
passes.

«Yeah, guess what? A few days ago we decided that we
would leave with the essential and we'd bought everything on
the way. I hope my wife has a little bit of mercy upon my credit
card!», Ted said amused.

«Stupid, I'm making a bad impression because of you!»,
Madlene added, giving a clout to his mate.

After taking a last look at their photographs, the agent
gave the documents back to the couple.

«Enjoy your stay.», he said cutting off and inviting, with
a nod, the next one in the queue.

«Well done, that idiot was not even touched by the
suspect about us.», he whispered, while they walked briskly
towards the exit.

Black van outside Terminal 5.
Waiting for you.

Ok, we're coming.

«It was Da Silva, they are waiting for us at Terminal 5.»,
she said, after putting away her phone.

**Marriott South Bay Hotel
one hour later**

«So we agree that the appointment is at seven in the
morning in the lobby.», Bennett said, getting up. «John, pardon
me.», I interrupted him.

«Tell me, Mr. Anderson.», he replied.

«I guess tonight the hotel will be guarded by someone, can you confirm it?», I asked him, not having seen police agents or cars.

He came up to me.

«Look around, every person you see in the hall is an undercover agent. Tomorrow will be a very important day, have a peaceful sleep, Alex.», he said softly.

While leaving the table, I felt the phone vibrating.

DAD

I showed my phone to Veronica and Matt, they nodded, and I walked away a few paces.

«Hey dad! How are you?», I asked him.

«I'm fine. Tell me about you, rather. Jameson told me everything, I'm very worried.», he said.

«Thank God I'm in good hands. Have you heard what they say about us? I'm referring to our membership in Skull and Bones. I happened to think about it often, in the last days.», I confessed.

«Considering your role, it was inevitable that sooner or later it became public. All Brothers, including myself, expect a lot from you. Alex, I'm sure you'll know how to act in the best way, in the name of our values and our code of honour.», he said self-confident.

As I listened to him, I saw the image of his eyes looking at me through the holes in the jute cap, at the Tomb. For a moment, I was terrified.

«Damn, dad, I will act solely in the interests of my Country and of my people, can you drum it into your heads!», I replied, trying to hold off the volume of my voice.

«Calm down Alex, now you're just nervous and it's understandable. Reasoning about it, you'll understand that we can't change our nature. We can improve ourselves through study, work or love towards our family, but without forgetting who has made sure we became who we are. This does not mean not doing the interests of our Nation, indeed, it means doing it with the support of the best and trusted minds of our Brothers.

Never forget it. Now I have to go, take care of yourself, please.», he explained, not giving me, as usual, the possibility to answer back.

«Okay, I will, say hello to mom.»

Likely he had already hung up the phone a few seconds before. Instead of reassuring me, talking with my father always destabilized me. Perhaps because he never missed an opportunity to call me as to fling the reality under my nose. Evidently, knowing me better than anyone else, he was afraid I could somehow lose the straight and narrow, by forgetting my belonging to Skull and Bones.

At least with myself I had to admit it: journalists were right in writing that, in some ways, my way of acting would always be influenced by the advices of my Brothers. On closer view, however, quite often a business lobby was hiding behind every politician.

Of course, for its history and prestige, it was normal that the thick veil of mystery surrounding Skull and Bones arouse more clamour than a cartel of oil tycoons in Texas. Not surprisingly, Dillinger and the traitors with him had identified in me the enemy to be killed, being his direct expression.

«Worried for tomorrow?», Scott asked me, as she came across while going to the elevator.

«Well, I'd be lying if I said I'm not.», I replied her at first blush.

«It would be strange if you were not. Only four days ago none of us could have imagined anything like this, but here we are. Besides, anyone who decides to serve his Nation, must take into account he can even die to defend it.», she stated, who had suddenly become talkative.

«Sure, but not in this way, without having first had the opportunity to do something tangible. Anyway, apart from that, what really worries me about tomorrow is that at Staples there will be more than twenty thousand people. I hope with all my heart that nothing happens.», I said.

«You see Mr. Anderson, those doing our work always act according to a good rule, the one saying to be prepared for the worst; that is the only way to avoid being overwhelmed by events.», she explained, keeping intact, despite being visibly worn out, her ability not to show any emotion.

«I don't think this is the best way to try to calm me!», I said smiling, trying to relieve the tension. In the meanwhile, the elevator arrived.

«Listen Tina, can I ask you a question?», I said, changing again tone, before she left.

«Yes, of course.», she replied, putting her palm in front of the sensor to keep the door open.

«How did Da Silva manage to escape from FBI Headquarters? I mean, it's a very armoured place, one of the safest in the world and moreover he had just confessed. Honestly I can not come to terms with that.», I asked her.

«All I can say is that he used the authority he still exerts on over most of his men. Now I have to say goodbye, it's quite late. Good night.», she cut short, after getting in and pressing the button number twelve.

«You too.», I barely have time to say, before the door closed.

«I was shocked to see Tina Scott talking to someone on her own volition, I'm serious! What did she say?», Veronica asked me, joining me with Matt.

«Actually nothing special, except for the optimism she oozes from every pore. I don't know, I just can not understand that woman.», I said, while her words and look were still swirling around in my mind.

«I think it's her precise desire to lift barriers with others, evidently it's her way to defend herself or, more simple, her way of being. What is certain is that she really does nothing to be minimally nice.», she said, with a shrug.

«You can say whatever you want but, in my opinion, her ass inspires a great sympathy!», Matt interjected who, thanks to the tiredness, managed to make us laugh out loud.

«On this we had no doubt, is it true Veronica?», I said almost with difficulty because I was still laughing.

«Guys, rather than hold forth on Scott's ass, how about to work a little bit on schedule and speech? The earlier we start and

the earlier we finish, tomorrow we'll have to wake up at dawn.»,
Veronica suggested.

Since the hotel lobby was almost empty, FBI agents aside, we decided to take advantage of it sitting on two swanky Chesterfield sofas at the corner of the bar.

«So Matt, where are we with the work?», I asked.

«Okay. On Facebook the official event of tomorrow exceeded seventy thousand adhesions, while on Twitter the hashtag #conventionla is at the top of the trends since a couple of days, and your profiles are keeping on growing. As for the line up, the official one says that you should speak first, then all the others, up to the monologue of Stallone, which will precede the intervention of Romney and the greetings of his wife Ann.», Matt explained, showing us the printed file received via email directly from the National Committee of the Republican Party.

«We will reverse the order: Romney will open, while I will speak at the end. But we will notify it at the last moment, otherwise it wouldn't make any sense.», I stated, determined to use that card in an attempt to mess up the plans of Dillinger and Da Silva.

«Don't you think that all speakers might not agree?», Veronica asked.

«Maybe, but we will ask Bennett and Moreau to propose it as their initiative taken for security reasons, so no one will have objection. I do not see what else we could do, but to be careful and hope for the best.», I hoped.

After having ordered coffee, we began to work on my speech, on which I had worked in the previous week, before coming back to Washington. All of a sudden, the screen of my phone, which was on the table in front of us, lit up.

I had received the notification of a message on my Twitter account.

Unfortunately you have chosen
to stand on the wrong side.
I'm sorry.

«Maggie!», I exclaimed, showing my phone to Veronica and Matt.

«Answer her, try to keep her on the phone! I'm going to call Bennett.», Veronica exclaimed, standing up and running towards the elevator.

Yes, but what can I tell her now? I thought.

Maggie, are you?

Yes, Alex.

How can you say that
I'm on the wrong side?
I'm defending my Country!

This is what you believe.
I hoped until the last minute
You would change your mind, but now
there is no more time.

Time for what?

To rescue you.

Sorry?

I tried it in all ways,
believe me. I'm sorry.

Maggie, I don't understand.

I'm sorry, Alex.

Enough, she had disconnected.

«Wow, she's completely crazy, rather than little Maggie!», Matt yelled, evidently shocked for what his eyes had just read.

«Do you think it's really her?», I asked him.

«I don't know, brother. Anyway you're dealing with a fucking psychopath, that's for sure!», he said, while Veronica, Bennett and Scott joined us.

«Where's Moreau?», I immediately asked, seeing he was missing.

«I also knocked on his room, but he did not open.», Veronica replied.

«What did she write, Alex?», the director of FBI asked at once.

«Here it is, please read.», I told him, hanging my iPhone at which he looked along with his colleague.

«She sent the message on Twitter, definitely using a encrypted ID address, it would take hours to track her position.», Scott said.

«Tina is right, but just to be certain, I will call our technicians at the Headquarters asking them to track her down as soon as possible. In the meanwhile we can't do anything but wait that the night elapses. Right now there is no safer place than this one.», Bennett tried to reassure and, soon after, phoned the FBI Headquarters.

In the meanwhile, Veronica, Matt and I looked at each other.

At that exact moment, we saw Moreau coming at full speed, and looked strangely out of breath.

He was without a tie and wore his big goggles when he reached us.

«Have you already watched it?», he asked, visibly shocked.

«No, what should we have watched?», Bennett immediately replied.

«Dillinger. Turn on the TV, quickly!», he exclaimed.

30

Assaulting the power

Political power comes from the barrel of the gun.
MAO TSE-TUNG

Matt ran to the counter and grabbed the remote control from the bartender's hands, busy with the final cleaning of the day.

«Hey, how rude, simply ask!», he told Matt in a huff.

«I'm so sorry friend, it's an emergency.», he answered him, dedicated to turn on the TV which was hanging on the wall right in front of us.

We were all impatient to know.

Click, the screen lit up.

BREAKING NEWS

**CHUCK DILLINGER MARCHES OUT,
HIS INTERVENTION IN LIVE STREAMING:
«WE DECLARE WAR TO THIS STATE,
AMERICANS JOIN US. »**

He was not as he had been described or, at least, as I imagined him. In a certain way, his appearance disappointed me. Perhaps because having heard about him so much, besides seeing him as a threat to my existence, had caused me to unconsciously mythologize him, looking at him as a sort of horrible mythological monster, the Medusa of our time.

That moment, in which I saw him for the first time, diluted to the point to seem suspended, fixed, static.

As we were all of us, after all.

Annihilated in front of a damned LCD television worth thousand dollars.

His face was swollen, overdone.

He must have proved a hard trial by some nerve gas breathed in war, or by a fourth-rate plastic surgeon, by drugs and alcohol, or by all these things together. I thought looking at him.

How can a Nation like ours, trust and believe the words of a scum like that? I wondered, still incredulous for what I had in front of my eyes.

Shit, stop thinking, listen to what he's saying! I told myself. Yes, listen to him. That, in a certain sense, meant to give in to him. In the end this was what he wanted to get, no? To catalyse upon himself the attention of everyone. Paradoxical, if we think well about it, he's a bastard son of a bitch who has spent his life betraying systematically the confidence that people put in him.

You're nothing but damned, you'll be punished, for sure you'll be punished! I thought, clenching my fists with rage.

In the meanwhile, other images appeared on television. Besides him, who kept on talking, live connections had been opened with the main US cities: New York, Los Angeles, Chicago, San Francisco. A crowd of dazed people in front of big screens scattered throughout the streets and squares, lying still in their cars looking at the display on the phone or listening to the radio.

Watching those scenes reminded me of September 11. What Dillinger was putting in place seemed to be a mass hypnosis.

Without saying anything, Veronica came up to me, took my hand and held it tightly.

"My dear Americans, the news today is that you are not worth a damn! I apologize since now with moms and dads watching television with their children because of my trivial language, but, today more than ever, frankness is well worth a little bit of vulgarity. What is, then, vulgarity compared to the shit, the real one, they made us swallow for decades leading us also to say thank you for having distributed it? Think about it, meditate on

it. I'm willing to bet that each of you, looking back and making a comparison between what you gave and what you had received, well, you can only come to the conclusion that you've been dramatically screwed! I know, I know, it's so difficult to accept this reality, but now has come the time of the last judgement, in which each of us will have to deal with himself first of all, and decide whether to go on to live a life of fatigue and deprivations or break the chains and rebel against a system based on control and lies. Yes, control. The most ancient and durable instrument with the purpose of preserving power. Nowadays they know everything about you. Where you go, how much you spend, what you eat, what you say. It's a total control! And it is exactly that shit I mentioned at the beginning: mobile phones, computers, social networks, credit cards, all instruments planned with the sole purpose of creating an immense database through which they know everything about everyone. They foisted them to you all, and you have not just accepted them willingly, no, you even got completely hooked on them. Exactly as a drug addict with withdrawal symptoms: he's aware that drugs will kill him in the end, but he can't help sniffing or injecting it into his veins. He can't help it. And then falsehood, whose size is directly proportional to the probability you will believe it. Well then, gentlemen, everything, and I say everything of what government and media are foisting you, is far away from reality. You can take the history of the last century, ball it up and throw it out the window, and you know why? It's all a big, huge, boundless, colossal porky! That's why! Wars, terrorist attacks, economic crises, the fight for freedom. All bullshit. Behind each of those actions there is a goal. No common ideals, no national security, no justice, no democracy. Nothing at all! But only and entirely interests, interests, interests! In short, instead of saying they have made it, we can say with hindsight that the United States have invented history..."

«This Dillinger is a fanatical crazy man...», I remarked in a low voice.

«The problem is something else.», Moreau said, putting himself in front of the TV.

«That is, Albert?», Bennett asked him curiously.

«The guy holding that delirious monologue on television is not Dillinger!», Moreau stated, extremely self-confident.

His words left us dumbstruck.

«Are you sure?», I asked him, incredulous for what I had just heard.

«If I weren't I would have kept silent, Mr. Anderson.», he answered.

«Then, not being Dillinger, who the hell is the psychopath on TV?», Matt asked, evidently shaken.

«Honestly I have no idea. What is certain, though, is that whoever they are, they managed to floor us.», Moreau remarked again.

«Shut your mouth, let me listen!», Veronica uttered.

"... I'm talking to David Cameron, Vladimir Putin, Angela Merkel, Nicolas Sarkozy, Bashar al-Assad, Mahmud Ahmadinejad, Shimon Perez, Hu Jintao, Dilma Rousseff, Julia Gillard, Kim Jong - and, along with them, to all Heads of State and Government who in recent years have been intercepted daily by the National Security Agency: all your phone calls, all your emails, all your private conversations have been recorded, transcribed and used by the US government in order to maintain its leading position in the international arena with the sole purpose of achieving constantly the desired goals of the lobbies financing the system..."

«All this is crazy, he's going to provoke an international crisis, or...», Veronica commented shocked.

«Or a war.», I added, ending her sentence.

"... true unwilling to delegate power like those lurking in the secret society bearing the name of Skull and Bones, which, behind the laughable emblem of a student association, hides the real occult control room where any decision must pass about the decisive choices that the Nation must conclude. They write laws, identify their men, they govern. It's not a coincidence that all the most important places, in the Government, as well as in CIA or

or grandson they want or would have wanted. I can almost hear their comments: 'Look, he speaks well, he's so mannered, and educated! He inspires me confidence.' And then? They vote him, of course. The better informed have already figured out who he is, is it true? But yes, it's easy, we've heard speaking about him since several days. His name is Alex Anderson, and I bet at this time he is in front of the TV, along with his friends of CIA and FBI, they too belonging to Skull and Bones, ready to do anything to defend him. Well, friends, I'm sorry to disappoint you, but it's a waste of time. Peek-a-boo Alex Anderson! Can you see me? Are you shitting yourself, are you? Yep, I can understand. After all, this is not one of those bullshit with which you, your father and your cronies of Skull and Bones were messing around in the Tomb. Here things are getting serious, my dear Alex..."

Strangely enough but his live threat didn't scare me. Probably because, after all, it was not certain a novelty.

In some ways I was used to it.

«Alex, are you feeling fine?», Veronica asked me.

«Of course, why shouldn't I? At least we are getting to the point, isn't it? », I replied, interrupting me right away because I heard my phone ringing.

I went to the table and took it.

MITT ROMNEY

«Hey Mitt!», I told him.

«Hi son, how are you?», he asked.

«Better than you can imagine.», I reassured him.

«I'm glad to know you're in good spirits, good boy. Listen, as agreed with Obama, we just decided to cancel the convention of tomorrow: it would be irresponsible to give such a greedy opportunity to this crazy man, endangering the lives of so many people. They have also assured me that someone is taking care of your personal safety. You'll see that everything will come to an end soon, I promise you.», he explained, fatherly.

«I'm sure about it, Mitt. As for the cancellation of the convention, I can only agree, of course. Let's keep us update, see you soon.», I replied greeting him.

At the end of the phone call, I raised my head and I realized I had all eyes focused on me.

«So it has been cancelled.», Scott ascertained.

«Yes, predictably, given what is happening. We would have been crazy to persist in doing it despite the threats of that psychopath.», I replied, pointing with a nod to the face of Dillinger who was going on with his crazy speech.

"... we would like to tell you that we have just received the news that, in less than twenty minutes, President Obama will report to the Nation about the declarations of... "

A few moments, and Bennett walked away to answer the phone.

«Hallo, who's calling?», he said.

«White House, I pass you through to the President.», a female voice told him. John gulped hard.

«Hey John, how do you plan to act?», Obama asked out of the blue.

«On two frontlines. The first has to do with the protection of Anderson, while the second refers to the work we are doing to catch that criminal. Shortly before he began to speak on TV, one of his men sent several messages to Anderson. If we can locate him, in all likelihood we'll find out where they are hiding. But there's more, Mr. President.», Bennett explained.

«What?», Obama asked.

«Albert Moreau is practically sure that who's talking on television is not Chuck Dillinger.», the FBI Head said.

«I know, I have here in front of me some photos of him dating back to Afghanistan, we have the latest images of him in our hands, and in effect it seems absolutely clear, this is another person. This complicates things further.», he said.

«Whoever he is, we will catch him, be sure Mr. President.», Bennett assured.

«I rely on you, John. Now I'm about to go on television, people need to be reassured, and I will have to try to dampen about the revelations that nutcase made about NSA interceptions, otherwise we risk World War III. I wait for your good news.», the President said, concluding their conversation.

«It was the President. We have to do anything to catch those bastards!», Bennett exclaimed.

«We are all here for this, Director.», Scott replied, almost putting herself at attention.

«That's true. John, if I may, I would suggest to call your computer technicians telling them we need instantly the location of those messages. We have no time to lose. Once we find out from where they have connected, we will have the opportunity to understand how long they will take to arrive here...», Moreau intervened.

«Why, do you think they're coming here?», Veronica asked, visibly worried.

«It seems we were watching the same program, or not?», Albert replied annoyed.

«I do agree. I will immediately arrange to converge here all the men who would be employed tomorrow at Staples, including helicopters. The fool on television and Da Silva will have the welcome they deserve.», Bennett stated.

«Personally I'm looking forward to them coming here, I have to square some accounts with my former colleagues...», Scott interjected, giving the idea she was looking forward to the moment when revenge would be consumed.

«Very good. I'll do the same with my men.», Moreau confirmed who, practically in unison with Bennett, began making phone calls giving orders to his staff members.

31

You must react

The mills of the gods grind late, but they grind very fine.
SESTO EMPIRICO

"... as you have just watched and heard, about thirty minutes ago Chuck Dillinger came out revealing his face to the whole world, with a video message broadcast live streaming in which he cast heavy accusations against the government in office and against those who preceded it but, above all, he revealed that all private conversations of all the Heads of State and Government of the globe had been intercepted by the National Security Agency, on precise mandate of the governments that have succeeded in the last years. Finally, the threat cast live to the representative in Congress for the Republican Party Alex Anderson, accused by Dillinger for his belonging to Skull and Bones. In anticipation of President Obama, who should intervene in less than five minutes, let's watch together this report explaining us that Alex Anderson is..."

On closer look, the lobby of that hotel seemed the perfect setting for the spread of a surreal atmosphere as the one we were living. Throughout Hollywood few, very few directors would have been able to choose a more suitable location than that one.

So wide as to give the impression of being in a square, crossed in the middle by two parallel rows of nut-brown columns about twenty meters high, at the bottom of which was embedded the bar counter, topped by a wall that was a real sparkle of colours. All around, sofas, armchairs, tables and, scattered on each wall, about ten televisions on which, simultaneously, stood the deformed face of the imposter who everybody believed was Chuck Dillinger. Being practically empty, except for us and a dozen of agents, that big room acted as a sounding board for the audio coming out from televisions, amplifying it further and giving it a hint of echo effect, making the sound of those words even more annoying and disquieting than they already were.

«Hey bro', do you want a glass of it? This apple juice is wonderful!», Matt said, trying to distract me.

«No thanks Matt, I don't fancy it now.», I replied, making him understand that I was busy in thinking about what to do. «Quick, hurry up, Obama is about to talk!», Veronica cried, mustering us on front of television.

"Good evening. A few minutes ago we all witnessed the delirious statements of a man who says he's Chuck Dillinger. For those unaware, Dillinger is a traitor to his homeland, who in two thousand and two, in Afghanistan gave sensitive information to the Talebans, allowing them to shoot down two helicopters, killing fifteen of our brave soldiers and injuring hundreds more. What I have just told you is a news so far considered top secret, but I decided to make it public, taking the full responsibility on myself, to let you know what sort of murderer we are dealing with. He accuses me and all the institutional architecture, instrumentally pointing the finger at what it's, however, widely recognized as the greatest democracy in the world. According to him, NSA would intercept, in addition to every American citizen, even all the Heads of State of the earth, in order to allow the government, that is the undersigned, to spy on them in order to better obstruct them. Well, even if it's a lie so great as to make unnecessary any comment, to avoid any misunderstandings I want to state emphatically that no Head of State has never been intercepted neither by NSA nor by any other national security agencies. Strongly I repeat that, the alleged Big Brother which would record conversations, messages and movements of every American citizen, is an invention without any foundation. Not to say unreasonable. Right now we are coordinating with the leaders of our intelligence agencies in order to bring to justice as soon as possible these enemies of the United States of America. In agreement with the Republican candidate, Mitt Romney, we decided to suspend any initiative of all electoral

campaigns, until the situation comes back to normal. Finally, I want to express my personal closeness to Congressman Alex Anderson, who at this time is the object of the persecution carried out by this group of criminals. America is a great Nation, and the Americans are great people, whose general feeling has proven several times to be able to defeat any threat. I'm sure we will do it on this occasion too. That's all. Thanks for your attention, and good night to you and your families."

«Well, he was perfect, nothing to say.», I said, as soon as he had finished.

«Right, and although it's not a nice consideration to do right now, I would say that through this speech he had permanently mortgaged his re-election, .», Veronica remarked.

In the meanwhile Bennett joined us, who had moved away to talk on the phone.

«It was the HQ, I have two news for you. The first one is that the messages Alex had received on his Twitter account were written right here. They sent them by connecting to the wi-fi network of the hotel and using a very simple software that allows you to generate anonymous IP addresses. But there's more.», the FBI Director explained.

«This means they are here.», Matt interjected.

«Someone down at FBI has blabbed we would come here.», I added.

We were all stunned.

Shit, we're trapped! I thought.

«Damn traitors! Da Silva has organized all this, we have to find them before they get us!», Scott exclaimed, pulling out her gun from her shoulder holster.

«Calm down, Tina. The other news I have to give you it's about the madman who claims to be Dillinger. They managed to identify him. His real name is Jason Maddox, an informer close to CIA, an infiltrator in the Russian secret services, about whom we have not had news since two thousand and nine, when he was on a mission in Moscow. Albert, you should know something about him.», Bennett insinuated, evidently upset.

In response, Moreau didn't get perturbed at all.

«Of course I do, and if you want to know why a while ago I didn't say anything, I'll satisfy you right away: the file on Maddox was declassified because we sent him on a mission without the approval by CIA about his role. Formally he did not exist, just like me. For some months he was busy in collecting information about the relationship between Moscow and Teheran, which then would be used to better assess the possibility of an armed intervention as a result of public killings and the threat of atomic that Ahmadinejad was weaving every day. In the beginning his work produced good results but, after some months, through a local informer, we realized he was two-faced and, therefore, we thought the best punishment was to leave him to his destiny into the hands of the Russians. Useless to say that if the history of Maddox became public knowledge, also our attempt of espionage in Russian soil would become public. You'll agree with me that the consequences of a diplomatic crisis with the Russians would be inconvenient to say the least.», Moreau explained.

«The Russians, however, have used him against us.», Bennett objected.

«It may be, although at the moment we don't have any feedback about the alleged involvement of the Russian services in this whole story. Also because, as I know him, I highly doubt that Maddox might have planned a conspiracy of this magnitude on his own.», Moreau pointed out.

«I'm sure about this too, as well as I can't barely believe that a so great segment of FBI may have followed such a person. Rather, I wonder what happened to Dillinger. He's the real author of this criminal plan.», Bennett added.

"... our editorial staff in New York has just announced that a professor at Yale University has been found dead ..."

«Shut up, holy shit, shut up!», I shouted rudely, addressing myself to others, without paying attention at their astonished eyes.

"... his name is Peter Swenson. News keeps on following one another, but it seems now certain that the murder was claimed by Chuck Dillinger..."

«No, no, nooo!», as soon as I heard the news, I was overwhelmed by an immense excruciating pain.

It seemed that my chest had been torn in two by a cleaver. I slumped on the ground and began to cry, as it happened to me when I was a child.

Veronica and Matt ran straight to me, she hugged me on one side, and Matt on the other.

«Alex, please, react!», she pleaded, hugging me stronger.

But I could not stand.

«On the face of his reaction, he must have been a close friend.», Scott whispered to Bennett and Moreau, just shaking their heads.

For a moment I lost completely control, abandoning myself to hysterical tears becoming louder and louder. I sobbed, and in a few seconds my eyes cried all the tears I had not had the strength to cry over the years.

«Why, why, why?», I kept on repeating compulsively.

After letting me to reveal my feelings, Veronica took my face in her hands.

«Alex, look at me! I understand your pain, but you have to react. I firmly believe in you, and even Matt, your best friend, thinks the same thing. You're infinitely stronger than them, and now more than ever it's the time to prove it. We will emerge from this situation and we'll do it together, but to be able to do it we all desperately need you!», she said, wiping with her fingers the tears streaming down my face.

Her words brought back to my mind those that Peter used to say in order to incite me when I was talking about my doubts.

Veronica is right, I can't afford to stay in this mood, I have to get up! I thought.

I gave a push with my hands and got up.

After rubbing my eyes, I caught my breath and tried to calm down.

«Peter Swenson was a very important person to me, my reference point.», I told them.

«Your reaction is perfectly understandable, Mr. Anderson, but now you must be strong. On my side, I promise you that we'll do everything to get back at them.», Moreau replied.

«I agree.», Bennett said, taking the phone out of his jacket and starting a phone call.

«Yes, I'm Bennett. I want you all to surround Marriott South Bay Hotel immediately, apparently those bastards are here.», he ordered, hanging up right after.

«They want war? And we'll give it to them.», he exclaimed, turning to us.

«Tina, gather together all the men in the hotel. We have to search out room by room. I'm tired of playing the role of the mouse.», the FBI Director said also, seeming more determined than ever to immediately put an end to everything.

«That's what I was waiting for!», Scott replied enthusiastically, setting to work immediately.

«Mr. Anderson, please follow me along with your friends.», Moreau said, and took us to the reception office where he opened a cupboard from which he pulled out a black duffel bag.

«Have you ever used one of these before?», he asked us, showing a gun.

«I have, several years ago, during my military service.», I replied.

«What about the one for underwater fishing?», Matt asked innocently.

«Let's move on. What about you, Mrs. Hayes?», Moreau asked.

«No, I never shot in my life.», she said.

«Well, there's always a first time. Take, these are automatic weapons, to shoot simply remove the safety and pull the trigger.», he explained.

After having given one to each of us, he also gave us bulletproof vests.

«Here they are, wear them now, in these situations caution is never enough.», he said.

We wore them straight away, without thinking twice.

I saw my own reflection in a mirror in the nearby, and I froze for a moment. My mind was still clouded, as the windshield of a car when it starts to rain.

With the minutes passing, I felt that my thoughts were becoming lucid again but, not to slip back in the same state of before, I had to force myself not to think about what happened to Peter.

Look at you, you look like Rambo. I thought, smiling bitterly, while I was looking at me wearing a vest and a gun in my hand.

«I hope we don't have to use them.», Veronica sighed, appearing in evident discomfort.

«Hey brother, I want to tell you something.», Matt said, putting his arm around my waist.

«Sure Matt, tell me.», I replied, reciprocating his embrace.

«You know me, and you know it is difficult for me to do certain speeches, but I would feel like a shit if I shouldn't tell you anything and, unfortunately, something should happen. I think I would never forgive me for the rest of my days. You know Alex, now we are almost forty, we practically grew up together and, well, I know it's difficult to put up with my character, think that sometimes I can also barely put up with myself! In short, I also know that too many times you made a bad impression because of me...», Matt confided, with tears in his eyes.

«Listen Matt, it's okay, there's no need for you...», I interrupted him.

«No, instead I absolutely need it, let me finish! Yes, because any other person in your place and in your position, would have taken just a moment to get rid of me. But you've always defended me and you've always been close to me, even entrusting me important responsibilities, not caring of people telling you "that Matt is an idiot, get rid of him, you can not work with a fellow like that!". I always knew these things, you know? Well, what I want to tell you before I start crying is that you are much more than a brother to me. I care for you!», he exclaimed in one go, before bursting into tears.

I tried to restrain myself, but without success.

So it was that I also burst into tears, this time for the great emotion triggered by the words of my best friend.

We looked like two stupid.

«I care for you too!», it was the only thing I managed to say among all my sobs.

«But now let's go there and give those assholes hell, because the big-breasted model is waiting for me at home!», he said, trying to dissimulate because, being so proud, he had always banned hearts and flowers, playing the role of the hard-ass. Veronica ran up to us, hugging both.

«I love you both, I thank God for letting us meet!», she said, letting go a liberating weeping.

We were all three in a tight embrace that, on that moment, was the most beautiful and intense emotion I remembered. Able to fade away, if only for a few moments, the hell awaiting us once we got out that room.

With the corner of my eye, I saw that even Moreau, by watching us, was moved to the point to take off his glasses and pass a handkerchief over his moistened eyes. Yes, the unflappable Moreau, who would have thought it. Not to make him uncomfortable, I turned immediately and pretended not to have seen him, keeping on enjoying the unforgettable and apparently endless embrace of the people at that time dearest to me.

32

Jason Maddox

Those whom God wishes to destroy, first drives them crazy.
EURIPIDES

Open your eyes, open your mind
proud like a god don't pretend to be blind
trapped in yourself, break out instead
beat the machine that works in your head!

THE sudden and deafening sound of Guano Apes electric guitar, made us jump. It came from the lobby. We looked at ourselves in the eyes.

«It must be him, we have to go!», I said, heading for the door.

"Open your eyes, open your mind... Alex, do you know why I chose this song? Now I explain it to you. You know when it happens to hear a song and you think 'shit, it seems written just for that person!', So here I think that Open your eyes suits you to a T. Have you already figured out the reason? Of course you have, after all you are too smart not to understand. Oh, what a fool I am! I almost forgot to tell you that I'm all yours this time. Yes, no live, I'm broadcasting closed-circuit, exclusively for you and your friends. Happy about that?"

The ugly face of Maddox was on all televisions in the lobby. During his delirious speech, Bennett and Moreau looked at me pointing with a nod to the cameras placed in each corner of the ceiling.

"Don't worry, I see you too. Indeed, telling you the truth, controlling the cameras with this joystick, I can watch every movement of yours. I enjoy it a lot, this thing! It's so cool, isn't it? About finding, I know that Bennett has sent some of his henchmen to seek us: I'm so afraid! Look, I'm so scared that I have the creeps two centimetres high. So Alex, we're finally getting to the heart of the matter, how about it? Personally I believe we should handle it as gentlemen, as in the old days. Clear and precise rules. In this regard, I took the freedom to write down a draft of rules. That's just a pro forma. It consists of only two articles. The first says that we're coming there in a while, and the second that we'll kill you all. Well, at first glance it seems to me it's watertight, do you think it might be good?"

«I think you should take here your broken ass, so I'll burst it for sure. Ugly piece of fucking dry shit!», Matt exclaimed aloud, addressing to the television.

"Piece of fucking dry shit, I like it, really. That said so, just out of curiosity, I would like to know who the fuck has authorized you to talk to me. I don't talk with employees, asshole!"

«Then come here! Come here if you dare, shit!», Matt answered back, almost with froth at the mouth.

«That's enough, Matt! Don't stoop so low as to his own level.», I told him, holding him by the arm.

«Rather, since you're such a bragger, you could explain us why you need to hide yourself behind the name of someone else. Bur perhaps, thinking well about it, you're just a double. Indeed, what did De Niro say? You're nothing but a lot of talk and a badge. Well, consider that you don't even have the badge, my dear Jason Maddox!», I exclaimed.

Bang.

Stricken.

For a few moments he dried up.

What I told him unnerved him to the point that his facial muscles twitched, emerging from that flaccid artificial puffiness which had turned his face into a kind of deformed mask.

Bringing his index to the nose, Bennett invited me to stay in silence, waiting for his reaction.

On his side, after a gesture of anger, Maddox went forward with his trunk, bringing his face closer to the camera that was filming.

"Alex, Alex, Alex... to be honest, I'm a little bit sorry for you, you know? But after all, no one to blame but oneself, isn't it? In your little head you deceive yourself to have made who knows what a discover, is it true? The problem is that you stopped at the form. Yes. Think well, basically what's a name? Form. However, our actions are substance. This consideration is such a commonplace that, with a little bit of commitment, could be understood even by an hydrocephalus like your friend. Then, it does not take much to understand that Chuck Dillinger is not only a name or a person, no, he's much more, he's an ideal to be implemented, a dream to chase."

We all looked each other in the eyes, evidently we all thought the same thing.

«Dillinger is dead, isn't he, Mr. Maddox?», Moreau asked point blank.

"Oh, Albert Moreau, what a honour! It was a real pleasure to tell Russian and Iranian friends about your deeds! As for Dillinger, he's far from dead, on the contrary, today it could be me and tomorrow someone else, this is just a detail. His battle and all that he represents, will be carried on by an increasing number of people and, by changing the United States, the whole world will change, disrupting and eradicating the current order of which you, my dear Alex Anderson, are the worthy heir ."

«You're just fooling yourselves. Give yourselves up, you can still save your lives.», Moreau replied, without getting perturbed even in front of allusions concerning himself.

«Give ourselves up? Come on Albert, don't offend your intelligence!», Da Silva exclaimed, coming into the lobby with

Richardson, Ortega, Rice and twenty other men, all with guns in their hands.

In a flash, the agents of CIA and FBI in the room pointed their weapons against them.

«However Moreau is right, the building is completely surrounded. You have no way out, Frank.», Bennett threatened.

«John, what do you think to do, huh? Do you really believe you're able to stop us? You're a poor fool! We're the real FBI, not you! I've worked for more than thirty years believing to defend my Nation, but nothing was true, nothing at all!», Da Silva shouted, seeming possessed.

«How can you say it was not true, Frank?», Bennett replied back.

«What the fuck John, do you really believe you had become the FBI Director thanks only to your merits? No way! I have the respect of the men, I have always worked on the most difficult cases, I risked my life, not you! Easy, isn't it? You've always kept your ass safe, you've licked the ass of Bushes, and you took what was mine. Do you believed to have a lucky escape? No fucking way, John!», Da Silva shouted proving that, by now, he had completely lost his reason.

«Now everything is clear, is it true Frank? You have not embraced the cause of Dillinger for ideals, no sir, you're eaten by bitterness and envy for not having fulfilled your ambitions. What a sadness. Do you know what amazes me most in this whole story? That, despite the fact you had not qualms about killing in cold blood your most close colleague, some men let you subjugate them morally to the point of following you in this crazy plan! Tell me guys, what has he promised in order to convince you, eh?», Bennett provoked, making Da Silva hit the roof, and did not hesitate even a moment to pull out his gun from his coat, pointing it against his former colleague.

«I kill you John, I swear to God!», he screamed with all the anger in his body, while his index nervously stroked the trigger of his gun.

Everyone from both sides were ready to open fire. I looked at Veronica and Matt, and I saw the fear carved in their eyes.

No pin drop was heard, we were surrounded in a strange silence, which brought an unusual smell of burning.

Suddenly, a hiss.

At first it was subtle, almost imperceptible.

In just a second, it increased until it became a devastating roar.

Boom!

The blast threw all of us on the ground on the shards of shattered glasses. My instinct made me raise my head straight away looking for Veronica and Matt.

They were few centimetres from me and, at first glance, they seemed to be fine.

Thank God! I thought.

I narrowed my eyes for a moment, thinking it was enough to put me back on my feet.

«Help! Alex, Alex!», It was Veronica's voice. I opened my eyes wide.

Maddox, had caught her.

He gripped her neck with his left arm and, with his right hand, pushed hard the barrel of the gun against her temple. He dragged her back a few steps, just enough to reach Da Silva and his men.

In the meanwhile we all stood up.

That scene set fire in my guts, powered by a mixture of anger and terror. Anger and terror.

Now I kill him. I thought.

I drew my gun on him.

At that precise moment, on the chest of Maddox, appeared an indefinite number of red lights that, at first sight, resembled those of laser keychain.

«Make just one move and you're dead, Maddox! Let her go!», Bennett ordered.

I turned back for a moment, and I realized that the men of special forces had came in. They were completely dressed in black and with tommy gun in their arms from which came out beams of red light illuminating the chest of the psychopath who was holding Veronica as hostage. Out of the blue, I began to feel the beat of my heart

Thump-thump, thump-thump, thump-thump.

Louder and louder.

I swallowed.

Maddox looked down and watched the red lights on his old black leather jacket.

Da Silva's forehead was furrowed with dozens of sweat drops.

On the faces of Richardson, Ortega and Rice, you could see the awareness of having committed the biggest mistake of their lives. They knew that, in all likelihood, they would have died at any moment.

Maddox pushed the greased steel of his gun with even more violence against Veronica's temple, who was literally speechless.

«Hurt her and I swear to God I'll kill you!», I cried, keeping on drawing my weapon on him.

«It will be better that you and your friends calm down. You see, before reaching you I decided to make you a little joke. I love playing. Let's say that under my jacket I wore a nice vest of nitro-glycerine. Here, as you certainly know, if you shoot me you would kill also this nice titbit. Alex, I'm sure you will never forgive yourself, am I right? After all it's understandable. You know, before I was fixing the cameras and, by chance, I ended up on the images of you two in the room. You were so sweet, really! I'm sure your heart will never hold up such a blow. To lose the woman with whom you feel in love just after having found her. Terrible. If then we consider that you just lost one of your best friends, well, it's easy to understand your mood is not exactly the best. By the way, that Peter really loved you, you know? Think that he preferred to die rather than to answer a few simple questions about you. What a pity! Well, well, well, you may decide to open fire and kill me, knowing that it would mean kill Ms. Hayes too, or you may give Alex Anderson to us. Now, it's up to you.», Maddox said who, probably because of a nervous tic or the cocaine he had just sniffed, began to move his head jerkily, unable to stop it.

«You're bluffing.», Moreau replied icily.

«Well, if you are so sure about it, why don't you open fire and put an end to it?», Maddox replied back immediately.

Bennett and Moreau looked at each other searching in the eyes of one another the confirmation of what to do.

Risk it all or negotiate to the end?

«No, stop, don't shoot!», I intervened, throwing the gun on the ground and raising my arms in resignation.

«If you want just me, here I am, take me, but first let her go!», I said, stepping slowly toward them.

I turned looking for the eyes of Bennett and Moreau and then, in quick succession, even those of Da Silva and Maddox. I wanted to show them I was not afraid.

Then I looked at Veronica.

«I love you.», I told her, fearing it would be the last opportunity to say so.

«I love you too. Please, don't do it, go back, Alex!», she implored me, bursting into tears.

«Lower your weapons!», Bennett ordered who, at that point, could not help but play along with me.

The red lights went off immediately.

Still one, two, three steps.

Albeit slowly, I walked over them.

«Good boy Anderson, well done!», Maddox exclaimed, then starting a laugh full of hysteria.
«Catch him!», Da Silva ordered.

Ortega and Richardson immediately grabbed me by the arms and dragged me farther with strength.

«Yes, now we've got it!», Maddox said, keeping on, however, drawing his gun on Veronica.

«I've abided by the rules, now let her go!», I screamed.

«Ah, you want me to let her go, have I understood correctly? Okay, I satisfy you right away!», he said.

After that, he pulled the trigger.

Bang!

«Nooo! Veronica!», I yelled and shouted, in despair.

Thousands of seconds.

Veronica fell to the floor.

I felt myself dying inside.

Come on, go ahead, shoot me, torture me, in any case you would do less harm. I thought, with my head more and more muffled.

Then, along with Veronica, also Maddox fell on his knees who, before touching the ground, threw up a litre of blood at least.

Matt appeared behind him, holding his gun still steaming.

He winked at me.

So then Veronica… I did not even dare to think of it.

Thousands of seconds.

The little red lights appeared again on the chest of Da Silva and each of his men.

Just one move and they would die.

They were aware of it.

Ortega and Richardson let me go. I immediately dashed over to Veronica. My God, so much blood, no, fuck! I thought, seeing her lying in that pool of warm and tacky liquid.

I took her head in my hands, and began nervously to untangle her hair which had became one thing with the blood that, in the meanwhile, had already begun to coagulate.

The temple, I must see her temple! I thought.

In the meanwhile, with my hands shaking, I kept on moving strands of her hair soaked with blood, trying to understand if that son of a bitch had hit her or not.

My God, make sure this blood is not hers!

I prayed.

33

The showdown

I knew all eyes were focused on me, but it was as if just Veronica and I existed. Matt bent down and just looked at me, without saying a word. She did not move and I began to fear the worst.

I burst into tears.

By instinct, I started to rub even stronger, helping me with my shirtsleeve. Some tears of mine fell on Veronica's lips, who kept on being still.

A matter of moments.

She was lying there, in my arms, fragile and defenceless. The more seconds passed, the more I felt to become invisible. If you go, I will disappear too. I thought, staring at her.

I breathed deeply, with the illusion it could serve to quench my crying fits. Matt put a hand on my shoulder to encourage me.

All of a sudden, Veronica's eyes opened wide.

I smiled at her.

She did the same.

God, thank you! I thought.

With a jerk, Matt got up and walked to the dead body of Maddox, who was less than a meter further. He kicked him in his face, spurting blood towards Da Silva.

«That's because you tormented my brother and made me miss the appointment with my friends, asshole!», he inveighed, leaving everyone speechless.

Then, with one foot, moved one side of his leather jacket, under which there was no nitro-glycerine charge.

«Thank you.», Veronica whispered to me.

«Oh no, I have to thank you.», I replied, caressing her face.

«Veronica, how are you feeling?», Scott asked, bending down next to me.

«Just a little dazed.», she said, trying to get up.

«No, stay down, don't make efforts. You cheated death.», Scott said, caressing her forehead.

«Tina is right, if it had not been for Matt...», I added, without ending the sentence.

A matter of moments.

Suddenly I felt my blood chilled.

«Get up, come on!», Scott exclaimed, drawing the gun on my forehead.

I could not say a word, I was petrified.

«Now you do what I say. Throw your weapons immediately, or I'll blown his brain!», she threatened.

«Tina, what the hell are you doing, are you crazy?», Bennett asked, who could not believe what he was seeing.

In the meanwhile Marion Ross and her husband Aaron Beck made their entrance in the hall, showing up from the corridor leading to the elevators.

«I said to throw your weapons, otherwise I kill him!», she repeated, pushing the gun barrel against my neck, just below my chin.

«Do as she says, throw your weapons!», Bennett ordered.

«Tina, however now try to reason, let him go.», the FBI Head said.

«Shut up!», Da Silva shouted, shooting him in his abdomen. Bennett slumped to the ground.

«I told you I would kill you!», Da Silva yelled, sweaty wet.

Along with other agents, Moreau immediately tried to help him, but right away Da Silva threatened him drawing his weapon on him.

«Leave him alone, if you don't want to meet the same end!», he shouted. He seemed possessed.

«Back, go back off!», Ortega intimated to Veronica and Matt, drawing a tommy gun on them.

«Tina, what happens?», I asked, with the vocal cords choked by the iron of her gun.

«I warned you, Alex, it was you to force me to go that far!», she replied.

Instinctively I turned my eyes at her left forearm.

No, I could not believe it. I did not want to believe it.

«Maggie.», I said.

«Bravo, finally you got there.», Marion Ross intervened.

I gave a glance at Veronica and Matt, who looked at me aghast.

«Yes, it's me. I'm sorry Alex, but I can not respect our oath.», she replied.

Memories began to overlap, swirling around in my head like a thousand busy bees.

«Why are you doing this to me, Maggie? I want to know, you owe it to me!», I yelled in despair, with all my strength.

«If that's what you want… After all it's right for you to know.», she softened without, however, ease the pressure of her gun against my skin.

«Unlike what was given to know, my father Frank was not a mere employee, but a CIA agent infiltrated into KGB, under the name of Valeri Zykov. His task was to recruit men of Russian secret services in order to acquire top secret information. We were still during the Cold War and, in the late eighties, President Reagan sped up by using in the field a series of actions covered by state secret aimed at promoting the demise of communism. Those were mostly espionage activities, which were put in place to create a dense network of flaws in the special services of the Soviet Union. Let's say that the principle by which the leaders of our intelligence were inspired, was that of a virus attacking the immune system of an organism to lower its defences, and then hit. Each of those actions was carried out to open a gap in what was considered the mother of all battles, that is Operation Charlie.», Maggie explained.

«Never heard about it before. What was this Operation Charlie?», I asked her.

«Your friends Jameson and Moreau should know it very well, is it true Albert?», Ross intervened provocatively.

«I don't understand which is the link and, in any case, there is no justification for the treachery you have committed!», Moreau accused, pointing one finger towards Maggie and Da Silva.

«Treachery? This is just your opinion. But let's go on. Operation Charlie was nothing but the initiative through which the Berlin Wall came down. How? Easy, through a meticulous work of persuading important men of KGB on one hand, and almost all the government of DDR on the other. Reading history books, have you ever wondered why such a rapid succession of events? Think about it. First Hungary, which in late August abolished restrictions on the border with Austria and then, after a few weeks, came the resignation of Honecker, that is the most fervent supporter of the Wall. After a few days, the new government in office became involved in an escalation in some ways even farcical. First they announced they would grant the permission to travel from east to west and then, once unleashed chaos, came the sudden and unexpected announcement by which the Minister Schabowski, de facto, sanctioned the fall of the Wall. So, do you still believe the fairy tale you have been told in history books? What happened in those frantic days was the winning epilogue of Operation Charlie and the beginning of the end of communism and, consequently, of the Cold War. Well, despite the fact my father having been one of the absolute protagonist of what was then a victory of historic proportions, just some allegations on his behalf by a KGB agent, a Evgeny Morozov, were enough so that the heads of CIA considered him as a dirty traitor, believing that he could prejudice the success of the whole operation. This is far from the truth! My father would never have betrayed the ideals of his Nation!», Maggie exclaimed forcefully, bursting into hysterical tears.

«But what have I to do in this whole story?», I asked after having listened to her. In response, she tightened the grip even more.

«You have to do with it because you're the direct expression of the clique who preferred to believe the infamies of Morozov, which were an obvious attempt of counter-espionage, rather than the good faith of an American as Frank Jones. When in August eight of nineteen eighty-nine he and his wife lost their lives, it was not an accident, but a state execution in full rule, carried out by our intelligence services with the approval of the then newly elected President Bush, who was also among the founders of Skull and Bones, just like you, your grandfather and your father. Amidst all this rottenness, the only act of pity consisted in sparing the life of little Maggie, who was entrusted to me and Aaron when the FBI leaders knew that for years we tried to adopt a child, because we could not have our own. We were trustworthy, and moreover based in London and, therefore, quite far away from Los Angeles and from any detail that could somehow awaken the memory of Maggie who was so young, but not so much to let the passing of time remove completely her memories. Indeed, the more time passed, and more details re-emerged. So, very soon, nightmares turned into doubts, and doubts into certainties. Aaron and I, loving her more than anything else in the world, we could just tell her the truth and help her to get justice.», Marion told.

«Do you call justice persecuting and killing one of your childhood friend? You should be ashamed!», Matt intervened furiously, railing at Maggie.

«Shut up, Matt!», she replied.

«You don't have the slightest idea of what I went through. None of you have it!», she added, giving the impression to lose her reason at any moment.

I have to make her speak, it's the only way to take time. Veronica thought.

«I don't understand what's the role of Dillinger, in this whole story.», she stated, turning to Maggie, who looked at her, keeping in silence for a few moments.

«Chuck Dillinger was only the symbol, the icon we needed to fight our battle. Actually he has never taken part in it, for the simple fact he died in Afghanistan a few months after Operation Anaconda, at the hands of Talebans, because they did not tolerate his inordinate ambition and his pitch invasions. They used him and then killed him. We needed a name to which attribute the revelations about the abuses carried out by NSA and American government, so we thought of him even though, actually, the ones who sent those documents to the Guardian were my parents and I. In a certain sense, he became our avatar. Then, thanks to the collaboration of brave men such Frank Da Silva and Jason Maddox, we were able to find way into the heart of several segments of FBI and CIA, being tired of serving a State whose foundations are on a rotten and corrupt system hiding itself behind the puppet of the American dream whose strings, actually, are pulled by people like Anderson and Bush who, over the years, have almost monopolized the defence sector and the intelligence services, reducing them to the role of mere executors of the dirty work needed to achieve their expansionist and despotic goals.», Maggie replied.

«You're wrong, Maggie, things are not in this way!», I tried to argue, but I was abruptly interrupted. «Don't force me to kill you!», she replied.

«Do you love him, don't you?», Maggie asked, turning again her gaze to Veronica who, even striving, could not hold back her tears.

«Yes, I love him.», she said, sobbing.

Maggie pushed her gun even stronger. I screamed from pain.

«Kill him Maggie, what are you waiting for!», Da Silva encouraged her.

«I'm sorry, Alex!», she whispered. I closed my eyes, I don't know if by instinct or for fear.

«Now! Open fire!», someone shouted, probably Moreau, judging from the voice. The glass ceiling, already damaged by the explosion of a moment before, was shattered by the boots of dozens of soldiers who came down on us from the top.

Just a moment, and the hell flames burnt up.

The bullets gusts were so dense as to seem a fierce hailstorm in late summer, able to pierce the car body or the house roof.

My ears heard screams coming from all directions, and my eyes saw bodies dying and falling to the ground, from both sides.

It was a massacre.

However, Maggie did not slacken off.

I lost sigh of Veronica and Matt.

Despite I was trapped in that grip, I managed to turn my neck, but I didn't see them.

For God's sake, no! I have to find them! I thought.

I tried to free myself from the murderous and treacherous embrace of Maggie grabbing her gun.
So, point blank, out of the blue.

She fired a shot.

Bang!

I began to hear hiss in my ears.

I looked at my hand, it was full of blood.

Then, darkness. Total darkness.

34

It's hard to say goodbye

I fell, like a dead body falls.
Dante Alighieri

ALEX, when was the last time you did something for the first time? I wondered, when I realized that I was about to die. However, life is really mocking, not to say bitchy.

Well, I mean, I could understand if to pull the trigger was that infamous Da Silva or, at most, one of his henchmen, but not you.

Holy God, in all my thirty-seven years, not a single moment has passed without thinking about you. Would you believe it!

While watching a sunset, when looking at seagulls challenging the wind, every time I read the last page of a book: I often wondered about it, almost always. Where little Maggie could be. I'd be really curious to know what was going through your mind, at that moment.

Death.

It is not absolutely as I thought.

In some ways I was more scared of the initiation rite down at the Tomb. But the point is not even this. I'm about to die, who the fuck cares about fear! I still have to get used to the idea. No, I was referring to the stereotypes we were fed in many different ways, like those telling you you'll see a white light, the doors of Heaven, and so on.

All bullshit, I can tell you.

Do you want to know what I see right now?

People. Three or four guys pushing my stretcher at full speed toward the ambulance.

Wait a moment, among them I can distinguish the faces of Veronica and Matt.

Their lips are moving, it seems they are trying to tell me something, but I can't hear anything. I'm glad you two are taking me along the short path of this last journey of mine!

Being killed by the woman you've always belied to love, under the eyes of the woman you really love, just after a few hours you've declared your love for her. I'll be honest: I would not be able to imagine such an end. Never, not even after drinking a whole case of Italian chardonnay.

C'est la vie.

If I told you I'm not sorry and I have no regrets, well, I'd be telling you a colossal lie. For, then, how is it possible to believe in common phrases, mixed with kilos and kilos of sticky cheap rhetoric, of those who say to have no regrets? You must be insane to believe in these craps!

We all have regrets.

At thirty-seven or at ninety.

Then, we carry around with us some of them throughout our lives, as a burden which we persist in not wanting to throw away, despite being bothered by its weight. For example, I'm thinking about lots of them, now more than ever.

I'm thinking about all the sunsets I missed just to sit in front of the telly; the night when I could have fucked Sofia McNamara, the prettiest girl of Yale, and I did not do it because I was thinking about Maggie; all the times I could have told my loved ones that I loved them, but I held back; the situations to which I preferred to adapt, instead of finding the courage to risk; time and energy I gave to people who did not deserve it at all; the days when I gave up to devote myself even a minute to something that would make me feel good; issues I put on ice, even if I had plenty of time to resolve them; when I did not give heed to Matt who wanted to convince me to invest ten thousand US dollars to open a dating website; the importance I gave to people who felt envy towards me, being upset for their shitty critics.

So, just to name a few of them.

Obviously, what bothers the most are the regrets for what might have been and instead neither has been nor will be.

Veronica.

Would we get married?

Would I be a good father?

My Veronica, how I wish you could hear me.

Even just for one last handful of seconds.

I would use them to tell you that if I had to invent you, I would have imagined you exactly as you are. I'm looking at you, you know? While we thought about the year in which that song came out on the plane back from Washington, with our hands dirty with sauce at Fish Market, or when you got moved just before we made love.

I told you I would have liked to be in Aruba with you. Gee whiz, this is true. If I think about that sunset, I immediately visualize your eyes and your beautiful smile.

You were there with me even if you weren't yet, compared to all the others who were really there with me.

Here it is, you're the answer to the question I made at the beginning: the last time I did something for the first time was to truly love. To love you.

It's hard to say goodbye.

Better to say see you soon.

I already know that our souls will meet again, without even the need to seek each other.

35

Epilogue

Life is a thrill flying away,
it's a balance over the madness.
VASCO ROSSI

FUCK, it's true there's the white light!
I was literally dazzled.

«The dilation of pupils is decreasing.», a female voice exclaimed.

«Hey you, can you hear me?», a woman asked snapping her fingers and making funny gestures right under my nose.

Have I already been born again? I wondered.

Negative.

Turning my eyes with difficulty, I concluded I was not a baby and that my body was that one of always. I felt completely wrapped by a tingling, identical to the one that occurs to your legs when you stay still for long time in the wrong position. Thus, I thought to make it cease by clenching my fists and closing my toes.

«He moves, now you can let her in!», that woman shouted.

The door swung open.

The first person to enter was Veronica, who ran to me with tears streaking her face, but she was also enlightened by one of her unmistakable smiles.

The emotion did not allow her to speak, just as in the hotel room. She threw her arms around my shoulders and dropped her head on my chest

«It was too hard to say goodbye.», I whispered, with a faint voice.

«What?», she asked me, caressing my face.

I took a breath. My throat was hurting a lot.

«I told you it was too hard to say goodbye. In fact I could not!», I said, trying to raise the tone of my voice.

«Thankfully, thankfully…», Veronica replied, unable to hold even a tear.

«I thought I was dead, and lose you was my biggest regret.», I told her.

«Instead, we are together. I love you!», she exclaimed.

«I love you!», I replied.

In the meanwhile, the same woman came back and inserted a needle into the tube of my drip.

My sight clouded suddenly, and their voices became confused.

«Miss, I'm sorry but now I have to ask you to go out. Mr. Anderson just woke up: we must make a check-up and he must rest for another few hours. Because of the wound, he lost a lot of blood, and the operation has been tough. He will take some time to recover.», she explained, turning to Veronica.

«Okay, but here outside there are some friends waiting to greet him, when can they come in ?», she asked.

«Let's do in this way. It's almost lunch time, go and eat something and then come back to the waiting room. I'll call you as soon as he awakens, okay?», the nurse suggested.

About three hours later

«He's opening his eyes!», I recognized it right away, it was Matt's voice. I woke up and, around my bed, besides him and Veronica, there were also Jameson and Moreau.

I was dazed.

«What happened?», I asked them.

«Here it is, brother, read it, you're on all front pages!», Matt said, handing me the Los Angeles Times.

Night of terror in Los Angeles,
terrorist attack vanquished.
Dillinger killed by special forces.
Obama: "Victory of good against evil"

The starry sky above Los Angeles was lit by the
explosions that have taken place during the savage
gunfight between the special forces of CIA and FBI
and the followers of Chuck Dillinger in a hotel in
Redondo. American institutions, after been publicly
threatened through a video message that was quickly
shown in the whole world, the former CIA agent, who
has dominated the headlines for making known top
secret documents, relating to the activity of the
National Security Agency thereby starting Datagate,
attempted to implement his crazy plan, laying siege,
along with his command, at the hotel where Alex
Anderson was under protection, the young congressman
pointed by Dillinger himself as the emblem of the
system he intended to subvert. An attempted coup in
full rule, foiled in a few hours thanks to the
excellent work of the American intelligence and the
direct effort of FBI Director, John Bennett,
seriously injured during the violent gunfight in
which the head of the counter-terrorism division of
National Security Division, Frank Da Silva, and
agents Ortega, Richardson, Rice and Scott tragically
lost their lives. President Obama, who has followed
step by step the operation from his office in the
White House, during the night has held a second
speech to the nation, in which he expressed «immense
sorrow for the loss of brave servants of the State»,
thanking them «in the name of all Americans for
having sacrificed their lives in defence of supreme
and inalienable values of freedom and democracy».
The President, then, reflected on what he did not
hesitate to describe as «an attack on democracy,
orchestrated by a traitor with the sole aim of
discrediting United States in the eyes of the world,
trying to undermine the stability of the
relationships with our international partners
through the disclosure of documents and revelations
totally false». Finally, Obama, after dedicating a
thought to the families of the fallen, concluded his
short speech by saying that last night there has
been «another victory of good against evil».

«I can't believe, not only Da Silva and Maggie were shown as heroes, but they also hid the true story of Dillinger. But perhaps this was inevitable, isn't it?», I asked as soon as I finished reading the article.

«That's true, Alex. We are facing one of those cases in which the truth would be infinitely more harmful than a lie. The events happening inside that hotel will be covered by state secret, forever.», Jameson answered.

«So Maggie is dead.», I said.

«Yes, shot in the head just when she tried to kill you. Thank God, trying to wiggle out, you managed to avoid her bullet to hit you right in the neck. You have been lucky.», Moreau explained, astonishing me for his informal manner.

«Yes, I've been lucky.», I said, holding tight the hands of Veronica and Matt, who were sitting on both sides of my bed.

Two months later
Manhattan Beach
five PM

«You'll see you will enjoy it immensely, make sure the harness is well tied, relax and enjoy the landscape. Are you ready?», Matt asked, putting his hand on the knob of the throttle lever of his motorboat.

Veronica smiled at me and nodded.

«Ready, go!», I shouted to Matt, who did not lose even a second and departed immediately at great speed.

We looked up and saw the parachute swelling above us. Gradually we began to gain altitude.

Five, ten, twenty, thirty meters.

«Hey guys, how's it going up there?», Matt shouted loudly, greeting us with his hand.

«Wonderfully!», Veronica replied.

We were witnessing a truly sensational panorama. We were there, suspended in the air, in the middle of a sky that gradually was tingeing with bright red, and facing the sun which stood out exactly in the centre of the horizon line, passing it slowly.

Seen from there, it seemed it was afraid to go into the water. Besides the roar of Matt's boat, that the distance has turned into a kind of a buzz almost imperceptible, the only sound we could hear was the wind blowing.

«Matt was right, parasailing at this hour is really exceptional!», I said.

«It's true! May I ask you a question?», Veronica replied.

«Of course!»

«Do you remember when was the last time you did something for the first time?», she asked me.

Thump-thump, thump-thump.

My heart began to beat wildly.

I looked at her, losing myself as always in those eyes smiling at me.

«Yes, this one!», and I kissed her.

Thanks

To Irene, for her infinite patience and more or less for another zillion of reasons, and to Vittoria for having given a meaning to my existence.

To my father Gregorio, if writing is my passion is mostly thanks to him.

To all the people around me who have supported me, gave me ideas and, above all, never stopped believing in me. Unconditionally.

To Guido Giraudo, Carlo Cattaneo and Antonino Caffo, notwithstanding.

To Miriam Mazza, for her fundamental contribution.

To Alessandro De Giorgi, CEO of Youcanprint who, from the first moment, married this project, allowing you to find *The Predestined* in a great number of bookshops.

To the lady I met on that train to Zurich.

To you, having just finished reading it.
I hope this journey enjoyed you, thrilled and excited you and, why not, perhaps made you reflect.
If it were so, I would have already won.
In the meanwhile, I thank you all … until next time!